I0594168

THE POET'S EYE

LAURA VANARENDONK BAUGH

ÆCLIPSE PRESS

Copyright 2025 by Laura VanArendonk Baugh

All rights reserved. No part of this publication may be reproduced, distributed, or transmitted in any form or by any means, including photocopying, recording, or other electronic or mechanical methods, without the prior written permission of the publisher, except as permitted by U.S. copyright law. Not to be used for training generative software. For permission requests, contact the publisher.

The story, all names, characters, and incidents portrayed in this production are fictitious. No identification with actual persons (living or deceased), places, buildings, and products is intended or should be inferred.

Cover by Damonza

All words and images were created by human professionals, and no generative AI was used in the production of this book.

ISBNs:
Audio - 978-1-63165-045-1
Ebook - 978-1-63165-051-2
Paperback - 978-1-63165-050-5
Hardback - 978-1-63165-052-9
Special Edition Paperback - 978-1-63165-044-4
Special Edition Hardback - 978-1-63165-043-7

THE POET'S EYE

THE EYES OF MANDORAL
BOOK 1

LAURA VANARENDONK BAUGH

JUST
ANOTHER JOB

SAYINIA

CHAPTER 1

GALEN STEPPED TO THE side, making room as Lisveth leaned over the table. "We did everything we were supposed to," she growled. "We held up our end of the deal. We got rid of the gang and put a stop to the protection payments."

The baker across the table could match her for anger. "My glass window was shattered, and my oven is broken!"

"The oven wall's not broken. It's just the door, which can be repaired. And that was not our fault. That was not even, strictly speaking, caused by the gang we were supposed to run off. That happened because someone got in the way while trying to watch, like we were a puppet show in a square."

"But my window! Real glass!"

"And your son wasn't injured when he put himself into the middle of a fight, because Galen here used a rolling pin on the miscreant who was about to heave a table over on him. It's unfortunate that the miscreant in question was beside your front window, but I think we all agree the glass is a better sacrifice than your boy, foolhardy though he is. Again, we did everything you asked—more, with the babysitting—and we expect you to keep your word. That's the full amount we agreed upon."

"I'm not paying that," the man said firmly. "I can't pay that, not with what I'll have to repair."

Galen touched Lisveth's shoulder. "Let's talk a moment." He looked at the consternated baker. "Will you give us a bit?"

The baker flapped his hands to shoo them away, probably happy to see them take a moment, or an hour, or simply to leave entirely.

Galen moved to the front of the shop, gesturing for Lisveth to follow. She did, stiffly. He lowered his voice. "He probably can't pay the full amount and pay for repairs, both. That makes sense. Glass is expensive."

"Lots of bakeries don't have glass windows," Lisveth said firmly, "and we didn't break his oven door."

"No, we didn't. But we did agree to help this man and his family, and taking more than he can afford to give is not helping. Even if," he added quickly, "even if he promised it beforehand, when he thought he had it."

"It was his own son who caused the damage," Lisveth protested stubbornly.

"It was."

"By climbing through a window when he'd been told to keep away entirely."

"That's so."

"And we not only schooled some poorly behaved brutes, but you nearly got your arm broken when you suddenly had to work around a child."

"All of that is true."

"And you want us to have done all of that for less than promised."

Galen sighed. "Want? No. But there's only so much water that can be squeezed from a stone. And I wouldn't feel right leaving this man in worse condition than when he hired us, even if it's not our fault."

Lisveth blew out her breath in an irritated little puff and crossed her arms. Galen relaxed; she was acquiescing. "I don't like it," she said. "But I wouldn't feel right, either."

The baker ruined it by calling to them. "I'm not paying that much after my oven's broken. And if you keep insisting, I'll tell you to get out."

Lisveth turned on him. "Get out? Or what? Or you'll walk two towns over to fetch the sheriff? The same sheriff who couldn't handle the riffraff you needed us to get rid of?"

He scowled, lacking an effective answer to that.

Galen stepped back and scuffed his foot, drawing Lisveth's attention back to him. "Let it go. We'll take half."

"What's that?" the baker called.

"We'll take half," Lisveth snapped. "And you can thank my soft touch of a partner for it."

The baker jerked his head in a nod. "I'll agree to that. I'll get it for you." He rose and went into the back living quarters.

Lisveth blew out her breath again.

Something moved beside Galen, and he jumped in place, bringing a blocking hand up. But it was a child looking in the broken window. The head dropped out of sight, and a moment later a little girl ran into the shop. "I'm sorry about the oven," she said without preamble. "I'm sorry you won't get paid."

"We'll be paid," Galen corrected her gently. "Just not as much."

Lisveth sat against the wall, resting her arms across her upright knees. The little girl turned to her. "If my papa can't give you all the money, I can help," she said earnestly. "Do you want my bracelet?"

"I don't want your bracelet," Lisveth said wearily, without looking. "You can keep it, thanks."

The little girl drew the bracelet from her skirt pocket. It was a braided leather band, set with a dozen tiny round bells which rang as it came free of the fabric. Lisveth twitched. The girl extended the belled band. "It was a present from my Uncle Vann, but you can take it. He said it's from the Vernal temple. In the city!" She pushed the bracelet toward Lisveth's face.

Lisveth's hand slapped the extended bracelet away. It fell jangling to the floor, and the girl drew back, mouth agape with dismay.

Galen dropped to one knee and gathered up the leather band. It rang in silvery tones as he reached for the girl's wrist. "Let me tie this in place."

"I've got it," Lisveth said quickly. "Here." She held out her hand, and after a second of hesitation, Galen set the bracelet on her palm.

Lisveth regarded the bracelet a moment, and then she lifted the little girl's wrist. "Let me put this on you. It's one thing to carry it in your pocket, but it's meant to be worn."

"I'm not supposed to lose it," the girl contributed.

"It's something dear to you, isn't it?" Galen asked. "That was thoughtful of you to offer it. But we couldn't take your gift from your uncle. You keep it, and we'll make do." He watched Lisveth finish the knot. "Now, can you make it ring?"

She shook her hand, and the bells gave out a shimmering chime. Lisveth closed her eyes.

"That's it!" Galen cheered. "Now, go on and ring it outside. I think your mama said she didn't want you in the shop, what with all the damage."

The girl nodded and dutifully left by the same door.

Galen looked at Lisveth.

Lisveth looked at the floor. "Sorry. I just—I'm frustrated."

"Not with her."

"Not with her," Lisveth agreed bitterly. She propped her face in her hands, covering her eyes, and then she sat back. "We're down to almost nothing."

The baker returned at that moment. "Here." He counted out a dozen coins onto the crooked table. "That makes ten taler."

"Thanks," said Lisveth dryly, standing.

"Thanks," repeated Galen. He crossed to sweep the coins into his palm.

The baker's expression softened. "I'm sorry. I wish—but I really don't have the money."

"I understand."

Galen gave the coins to Lisveth as they walked out, and she dropped them into her moneybag. "Now that's almost nothing, plus ten taler," she said. "Still pretty lean. And I need my knife repaired."

Galen sighed. "Two towns over, besides the ineffective sheriff, there's a ring for matched fights. I heard some talk in the public room. I'll put my name in, and we'll pick up a little that way."

Lisveth looked up at him, pushing her blonde hair back. "Are you sure?"

"It looks like I'll have to be." Galen didn't enjoy matched fights, but at least he had a fallback he could live with. It had been nearly a year since he'd had to enter one, and he should be glad of that, at least.

Lisveth's tone lightened a little. "No one there knows us, so I can arrange for a cut of the odds on you. That should help."

"So long as you don't also bet against me yourself."

"I would never."

They walked on, toward the second town over, toward the arena and the ineffective sheriff.

Galen peered through the slats of the wooden gate, trying to see to the far side of the arena. Outside, chants and foot-stamps rose from the crowd that ringed the fence and filled the raised benches. They were impatient.

In the center of the little ring, a short, balding man tried to speak over the crowd, explaining the books were still open for last-minute bets. The crowd was not interested in him or his last-minute bets, and they shouted for the fight.

The balding man gave in and flung one arm toward the far gate. "Nebre the Bull!" he declared.

"Any ring name in the world he could pick, and that's what he comes up with," Lisveth muttered beside Galen. "No wonder he has to punch things for a living." She ran her fingers over the wraps on Galen's hands, though he'd checked them twice already.

The far gate burst open. Two buxom girls pranced out and struck provocative poses on either side of the gate. They flung handfuls of flower petals into the air, smiling as if they were paid by the tooth. Between them stepped a broad man, stripped to the waist and gleaming with oil.

The crowd roared. The girls leaned close on either side and kissed him, one on his mouth and the other sucking an earlobe.

Nebre slapped their cocked hips and waved to the cheering spectators.

"What a disgusting beast." Lisveth sounded simultaneously disdainful and bored. "Do me a favor and butcher him neatly, all right?"

Galen wished he could promise to oblige her.

At his silence, she gave him a concerned glance. "You okay? Don't let him get to you. Remember, the whole point of the entrance is to impress the crowd and intimidate the opponent. Yours will do the same to him."

It wasn't the girls and flower petals that worried Galen, but he nodded once.

"Besides, crowds love an underdog." She shrugged. "Except when he beats their local hero. It's a gamble."

Galen glared at her, but any retort was prevented by the balding man's shout. "And your challenger, the Hungry Farmer!"

He turned to gape at Lisveth. "That's what you called me?"

"We're low on coin, and nothing sells like honesty—slightly twisted." Lisveth gave him a punch on the arm. "Go on, farm boy." She turned and pushed the gate open.

Twin fountains of fire roared up from the ground on either side, flames licking out into the arena and coiling into the air. The crowd gasped and shifted. Galen took a deep breath, exhaled for a slow count of five, and ran forward. As he reached the fire he bounced and tucked into a forward roll that carried him between the flaming fountains and through the fiery curtain.

The flames were hot against his skin, but there was no pain. Lisveth had explained that, with illusions, the mind provided its own pain—that burns were preceded by intense heat, so at the sensation of intense heat the body expected to be burned. But if one truly disbelieved, one felt no pain. It had taken hours of practice and conviction, but now he could move about the illusory fire nearly as smoothly as Lisveth herself.

He burst from the flames and uncoiled, landing on the packed dirt before the fiery backdrop. He wobbled slightly more than he'd wanted, but the spectators hadn't noticed or didn't care. They roared and shouted and clapped, stamping their feet on the wooden risers, and for the first time Galen considered that maybe they would like him and want him to win.

He looked across the arena to where Nebre's two girls shrank from the fire, eyes wide, and Nebre himself looked startled. Lisveth had been right; Galen's entrance had stunned him and given him doubts.

Doubts could be exploited. Doubts offered the toehold Galen needed. And now the crowd who had cheered the big man was cheering the unknown.

But winning the crowd availed him nothing. He needed to win the fight.

The balding man raised both arms, said something none of them heard over the shouting, and dropped his hands.

Nebre charged, apparently planning to regain the initiative. Galen watched him come. It was a longer distance than in the attacks the temple brothers had taught, but the principles were identical.

As Nebre closed, swinging one over-sized fist, Galen shifted his rear foot and simply fell backward a few inches, catching himself. The fist shot uselessly into empty air where Galen's skull had been, and he brought up his forearm to strike it, perfectly catching the inner wrist with his wrapped knuckles. That could not have gone better—if only Brother Toller had been able to see it.

Nebre recoiled, and Galen stepped in with an attack of his own. He caught Nebre squarely in the face, which surprised him; he had expected Nebre to dodge or block. But the blow didn't seem to affect Nebre as much as such a hit would have stunned Galen. The big man blinked and came at Galen again.

The crowd was making a great deal of noise, but Galen couldn't hear whether they were cheering for him or for Nebre. Nor did he have attention to spare for the spectators.

Nebre was oiled to reduce the risk of a grappling hold. Galen instead relied on short, hard punches to the torso, targeting diaphragm and kidneys as they circled and twisted. Nebre grunted and struck back, but Galen was able to strike aside or blunt most of the blows. The few were enough, though; Nebre hit hard.

Nebre began to wheeze. There was a roaring in Galen's ears, but he wasn't sure if it was the blood pounding through him or the crowd shouting encouragement. Nebre had struck his head a couple of times, and details were blurring.

Then Nebre left his arm a bit too high, and Galen dropped and bull-rushed him, punching up solidly with his shoulder as he wrapped his arms about Nebre's torso. Nebre stumbled backward, trying to keep his feet beneath him, and hammered at Galen's back. But Galen squeezed against the oiled skin and lifted Nebre slightly, just enough that he missed a step and stumbled down.

Galen flung his arms wide and leapt away before Nebre could trip or pull him down with him. He stood ready, fists balled, but Nebre rolled, his oiled shoulders picking up dirt. Shoulders to the ground—that was one of the possible defeats.

Before Nebre could regain his feet, the short balding man threw his arms in the air and called an end. He pointed at Galen, and the crowd shouted and stamped and cheered.

Galen panted for air as the short man slapped him on the back. It stung, even after the harder blows. He extended a hand to Nebre, who shook it with only a hint of grudge, and turned back to his own gate.

"Wave at them!" hissed Lisveth, pointing at the stands. "Smile! Wave!"

Obediently Galen waved, and they responded appreciatively. He reached the gate, and Lisveth handed him a shirt. "That went well. You feel okay? Anything particularly bad?"

He shook his head, pointing to a seeping cut above his eyebrow. "Just this, I think. I'll be sore tomorrow, but nothing unusual."

"We'll pick up some more willow bark tonight. We're a bit low for this kind of thing." She grinned. "He sure didn't like you flipping through that fire. That threw him off his stride right at the start. I told you it'd be a good idea."

Galen pulled the loose shirt over his head and caught his breath. "Okay, my ribs are going to be sore, too."

"But we're going to be flush again. The last week was too near to nothing. Well done, farm boy." She reached for his wrist and began unwrapping.

The organizer came in through the door, smiling. "Well done, Galen! Here's your winner's purse."

"And our two percent?" prompted Lisveth.

"Yes, of course. You can pick that up tonight, after the bets are all settled. That was probably our last time to run such long odds on you, but we'll have come out nicely." He looked pleased.

Lisveth looked pleased as well. Galen dropped his old amulet over his head and let it fall beneath his shirt.

Another man called from the door. "Hello? May I come in?" He ducked inside without waiting for a proper answer. "My name is Andrew Lawson. I saw your work in the arena just now, and I was most impressed."

Galen's face grew hot as always under a compliment. "Thanks. I just, you know, wanted to keep it straightforward."

But Andrew was looking at Lisveth. "It was you, wasn't it? With all the fire?"

Lisveth nodded. "Yes, it was."

"I thought so. I came to watch today because I heard that when you're not running long odds on local fights the two of you will, well, take on quiet jobs."

Lisveth cocked her head. "We've been known to freelance, but it depends on the job."

"I hope you'll feel comfortable considering this one. Would you two care to join me? I'm going to the Mare's Head for a poultry pie, and I'd be glad to treat each of you to another."

Galen and Lisveth exchanged only the briefest of glances. It was, after all, a free meal. Lisveth nodded. "We'd be glad to, thanks."

CHAPTER 2

THE MARE'S HEAD SERVED a tasty pie, steaming and surprisingly full of vegetables and poultry. The pastry was a bit dry, but it wasn't worth complaint. They took a table in the open air eating space, where the sun from the street could warm their backs.

Andrew worked steadily at his pie, hardly looking up, and Galen and Lisveth saw no reason to interrupt him. They ate their own meals, savoring the meaty gravy, until Andrew paused between bites. "I suppose you'll want to know why I asked you to join me."

"In your own time." Lisveth spooned another bite into her mouth.

Galen spoke with his mouth full. "You're not just hospitable?" He smiled apologetically, still chewing.

"I like to think that I am, but that is not what brings us here together." Andrew set down his spoon and stared at his plate. "I want you to help my daughter. And to do that, I have to ask you not to think ill of her."

Lisveth kept eating. "We can hardly think ill of someone we haven't met."

Galen nodded agreement, still chewing.

"You might think differently when you hear what I have to say."

Lisveth shrugged. "Did your daughter fall into the family way? Steal something? Run off with the wrong sort? Hardly an original offense, even if it feels that way."

"She did run off with the wrong sort," he said. "Road bandits."

Galen scooped together a few vegetables. "We know something of road bandits. We've even earned bounties on a couple of them." Which was true, although the bandits had been no one of consequence and the bounties had amounted to a pitiful forty taler all together.

"Really? But I wouldn't want you to bring in my daughter for a bounty—not that I think she has one," he added. "But I would pay more for her safe return, in any case. She's gone along with the Fire Brigand."

Lisveth stopped chewing. "What?"

"Surely you've heard of the Fire Brigand? She robs caravans, burning them unless they pay her a weighty tribute."

"Oh, of course I've heard of her," Lisveth said dryly. "It's only that I thought no one else had, not for the last couple of years. Hasn't she closed up shop, so to speak?"

He shook his head. "I suppose she had, but a few months ago, she reappeared. She and her gang are—"

"Her *gang?*" Lisveth hastily put another bite in her mouth. "I thought she worked alone."

"Oh, no, she's collected a small horde, now including my daughter. They fired out a spice caravan over near the Sung Mountains. She killed three people in the attack and burned another to extort the money chest from the caravan master." His mouth flattened into a grim line. "I don't want my girl involved in killing or torturing. And I don't want any of them turning on her. I want you to bring her back home."

Galen looked at Lisveth, who was still in her chair. He wondered if she had ever really heard it before, when people talked of the destruction wrought by the Fire Brigand. It probably never really struck her.

But all she said aloud was, "Galen and I know something about runaways. It might help us to have an idea about why she left in the first place."

Andrew chewed the inside of his cheek. "I just want her back."

Lisveth looked at him. "Finding her will be difficult, but the harder bit will be convincing her to come back with us. I'm not keen on abducting her and trying to drag her back across foothills and plains and Fortuna-knows-what. I can't think it will make her happier to reach home, and it's too dangerous for us. And it won't help you much if we're arrested for girl-stealing and she's on her own again, now with more motivation to hide."

Andrew looked at his mostly-eaten pie. "We had an argument. A row over a boy, which sounds all too common and stupid when I tell it to you now. But it's true. We fought over a boy, and I told him he wasn't to speak to her again or I'd break both his arms, and when he took heed of that, she got angry and ran off."

"That's a considerable threat to make. Did you mean it?"

"I did. I gave him a little bend of his shoulder to emphasize my point."

Lisveth whistled. "I don't suppose that could have had anything to do with her departure?"

Andrew's jaw set. "I'm not going to feel sorry about it, if that's what you mean. I knew him for what he was, and since then, he left the baker's daughter bloodied and pregnant. I wasn't going to see that happen to Andrea."

"Well, that makes some sense," Lisveth said, more steadily. "We'd need to know a bit more about her: her looks, where you think we might find her, why she might have gone in with the Fire Brigand in particular."

Galen glanced at her, suspicious at this last phrase, and now he recognized the set of her jaw. Yes, she might care about the missing daughter—she had, after all, taken pity on another hapless runaway once—but she was definitely interested in the Fire Brigand. Galen thought her pride was piqued.

"She wanted to hurt me," Andrew answered with grim honesty. "My father was our town's deputy and I've done some similar work; she knew joining the lawless would wound me."

"Why the Fire Brigand?"

"The most lawless, of course. I imagine hers is the most hated name on the High Road about now."

Lisveth's jaw clenched, and Galen knew he'd been right. Her pride had been touched. She didn't mind the despicable reputation, for she had built that herself—but she minded greatly that it was benefiting someone who had simply stolen it.

"Can you describe her to us?" Galen put in.

"Andrea, after me. Andrea Lawson. She's got nutmeg-brown hair down to her waist, if she hasn't cut it, and her nose is a bit...prominent. Doesn't do a thing to hurt her looks, though. I do have a sketch of her done a couple of years ago."

"That will help." Galen realized they had been talking as if they'd agreed to take his commission, though he and Lisveth hadn't spoken yet. But if Lisveth had the bit in her teeth over this Fire Brigand news, there was probably little point in discussing it. They'd go, and they'd find this new Fire Brigand, and they'd probably even happen to pick up the daughter on the way.

Lisveth wasn't quite ready to hit the road, however. She nodded and set her forearms on the table, leaning forward. "And how would you like to arrange payment?"

CHAPTER 3

THE FOOTLANDS WERE NOTICEABLY more challenging than the plains, even using the High Road. Galen and Lisveth were less interested in the rising terrain, however, and more interested in the remoteness from the capital. The bandits were more plentiful this far east.

Galen mused on the linguistic irony of the footlands being so far from the Heel while Lisveth bartered with an inn's landlord, finally splurging a bit of Lawson's coin on padded beds and warm quilts.

They had walked hard to get here, covering long miles each day for eight days and more than once sleeping away from the road and in the open air, back-to-back within their shared cloaks. They'd had a few soft nights, paid for by another quick job at a wedding party. There was, as Lisveth said, little harm in completing one task while en route to another, and a day or three was unlikely to be key in finding the bandits. But they had traveled quickly and with purpose, though neither of them had mentioned the hurry. Galen thought again and again of Andrea Lawson, run away to spite her cautious father and caught instead in another danger.

He might have been the same, caught up with bandits when he had nowhere else to go. Well, he had been, actually—though his circumstances had been different from the start. He had been protecting his family, not the other way around.

Galen slid onto a bench in the public room, keeping a space beside him for Lisveth. At the end of the table, several locals drank and bickered over gossip.

"That's a bucket of hogwash," protested someone.

"Nope, it's truth." The speaker took another drink. "I heard there was another raid. That's several now, all demons. No ground taken—they're just probing our defenses."

"What if that's true? If the demons really are moving?"

It was like a favorite ghost story. No one quite believed it, that was plain to see, but it was a fun tale to frighten themselves as they pretended to believe.

Galen knew only some of the stories; the temple brothers had focused more on the Heel's own tumultuous history. "Could they?" he asked the locals, playing along. "Why haven't they come before now?"

"Don't let them scare you," an older man beside him murmured, nodding sagely. "They just like to work themselves into a lather. Demons can't come over the mountains, even if they wanted."

"Why is that?" Lisveth asked, arriving at the bench with two cups of ale. "If that were really so, it seems we could have saved ourselves several generations of worry."

"Oh, it's always worth the worry, just in case," he answered with a smile. "But the demons cannot cross the mountains. The magicians of old laid powerful charms on the whole of the Sung

Range, when the wars were ended, and since that time no demon has been able to cross over to Sayinia." He took a drink with a nod of satisfaction. "As it should be."

"Charms on the mountains?" A young man at the next table leaned nearer, a curious look on his face. "What sort of charms?"

"How should I know?" The speaker seemed mildly annoyed at having his tidy explanation questioned. "I'm no magician, and even I was hardly around centuries ago when the spells were made. But here we are, and here they aren't, and that's evidence enough. Bloodthirsty lot would have stripped us bare if there wasn't something holding them back."

The young man frowned. "I suppose something must be holding them back, after all."

He was a little older than Lisveth, herself a couple of years up on Galen, and he was the kind of handsome that drew eyes from across a room: high cheekbones, strong, lean features, abundant waving hair. His only flaw was the color of that luxuriant hair, a dark red. That caught Galen's attention.

The older man had noticed it too. "Now you look at that," he commented, gesturing to each of them. "Two red-hairs together. Are you related at all?"

They shook their heads, glancing at each other and then back to him.

"Huh. Not many reds, though people don't react so strong to a red child nowadays. Still, most of those with red hair will darken it. You're brave to wear yours." He winked at Galen and nodded toward Lisveth. "Though it doesn't seem to be hurting your chances."

Lisveth exhaled with a subtle exasperated note.

"We're not together," Galen corrected. "That is, we're traveling together, but we aren't—we aren't a couple. Er, you say people used to think even worse of red-haired children?" He'd never guessed there might be a cause behind the curse, other than the general disdain for the color.

The man squinted at him. "Bless you, boy, aren't you one yourself? Didn't anyone ever say anything about it?"

"Well, yes," Galen admitted. "But I had brothers and cousins, and to be honest, I think my hair color had little to do with what they called me." It had become easier to joke about his family, and joking about them was easier than thinking of them.

The man laughed. "Boys of any color can be a handful, I'll grant you that. But there's a foothill superstition that red children have demon blood. Some said the women dally with demons, others say the demons force the women in the night—but the children aren't thought to be all human." He gestured again to the two of them. "You go around together, you're going to draw some looks."

They glanced at each other again. "We don't even know one another," said the newcomer. "I'm just traveling alone."

"I'm not from the foothills," Galen added. "I'm from the Heel."

"Long way from home," the man said. "Maybe feelings never ran so strong there, being so far from the mountains. But it wouldn't do you any harm to wear a hat and keep a smile on your face if you're thinking of going to any of the smaller towns or villages. They're not so sophisticated as us in the trade cities. A lot of people remember they don't like reds without remembering why."

Galen glanced at the other man, who was fingering his own dark red hair over his ear. He'd never thought about why red was a curse or an insult, and it was odd to hear an explanation, like hearing why water was wet. Galen shrugged. "Can't help how I'm born." He tried to make his tone flippant.

"I'd have to ask my mother," offered the other, "but I'm pretty certain I'm not half-demon." He smiled and leaned to extend a hand to Galen. "My name's Kayvin."

"Galen." He shook the hand. "Nice to meet you."

"It is indeed." Lisveth took Kayvin's hand as soon as Galen released it. "I'm Lisveth. It sounds like you're a traveler, too?"

Galen felt a twinge of something like jealousy. It was wholly out of place—hadn't he only just said that he and Lisveth weren't a couple?—but she was leaning over the table so eagerly, and Kayvin had that easy attractiveness even with his red hair, which Galen knew he could never master even without it.

Kayvin nodded. "Just thought I'd get about a bit, see what the world's like away from home. If something catches my eye, I'll stop for a while."

"Careful," Lisveth warned, "that's how I got started, and now I'm practically a mercenary. Or at least I'm running errands, which is as much work and road dust without the reputation or spoils."

"Have you been traveling much, then?"

"Some years."

"And you've been a mercenary? Is that common?"

"Not common, no. Most of the lords don't bother with a standing army now; there aren't many squabbles and when there are, they just conscript some farmers, send them at each other with hoes and pitchforks, and then call it all off when harvest time comes and everyone's needed back home." She chuckled. "Not much money in it, though. Better to find something else."

"But what about the demons?"

She shrugged. "For all that these friendly folks keep saying they're coming, I haven't seen any. It will take more than the word of some pub slugs to convince me—and certainly none of the lords are going to waste money or their field time on rumors."

He nodded. "Makes sense."

"Why do you ask? You weren't thinking of looking for soldiering work, were you?"

"Oh, no. Just curious." Kayvin grinned. "I've heard of women fighters, and I thought maybe I'd met one."

She snorted. "I like to fight with my brain. I'll leave the shield-bashing to the meat-heads." She reached to ruffle Galen's hair.

He jerked away. "I'm going upstairs."

Lisveth looked after him, seemingly surprised. "All right, then."

Galen avoided Kayvin's eyes, just in case there was triumph there, but the other didn't seem to be looking at him. Galen picked up his cup, still half full, and took the rest in a single long pull before thumping the cup back on the table.

That had been more than childish, he reflected as he climbed the stairs to the half-floor above, but he hadn't been able to stop himself. More, it was over nothing, as he and Lisveth were friends and traveling partners only and nothing more.

But even if he thought of Lisveth as his sister, he told himself, he wouldn't want his sister taking up with a stranger who was admittedly drifting without purpose or profit. His irritation was well-founded.

Music drew his attention, and after a moment of sulky resistance he peered out through the cracked door, staying low so he wouldn't be seen. Kayvin was cranking a turning lute as the room watched approvingly. Then he began to sing, and his voice was as good as his looks, rich and sweeping and inviting the room to drift along with him. The watchers joined in the repeated lines—Galen could not see over the edge to where Lisveth sat—and clapped as he cranked a finale and then passed the instrument back to someone. A man handed him a drink.

Of course he sang, too. Galen closed the door softly. There was nothing to be jealous of, and he felt beyond foolish.

He sat on the bed and began to clean and oil his sword. It hardly needed it, but the task occupied his hands and mind.

Lisveth came up a few minutes later. "What was that about? Your nerves up, with all that talk about red hair?" She dropped down on her bed and toed off a boot.

And of course, her notice of how childish it was made Galen's anger at himself flare anew. He opted to play ignorant. "What was what all about?"

She eyed him skeptically. "All right, then, we won't talk about it."

"I just didn't think he had any right to know your business." Oh, fair night, he was making it worse.

Lisveth kicked off the other boot and looked at him with faint incredulity. "Are you..." She seemed unable to form the word.

"It's not like that!" he snapped. "I wouldn't want my sister taking up with some drifting stranger, either!"

She blinked at him and then seemed to grasp some concept. "Oh! Did you think I was chatting him?" She laughed. "Wheel and wicker, no! Didn't it occur to you that a drifter like him is exactly the sort who might fall in eventually with a well-funded bandit?"

Galen stared at her. It hadn't.

"He's the kind who's used to getting by on his charm, and it's going to pinch him when he can't keep it up and his purse runs thin. And then he's going to look for easy money."

"Oh," Galen managed. "That's good thinking."

"Of course it is." She laughed. "Silly farm boy. He's not even my type."

Red. The word came unbidden to Galen's mind, and he pushed it angrily away. This was entirely inappropriate, and anyway by now he suspected Lisveth wasn't interested in men. Not that she seemed to be interested in women, either; she just didn't seem to be interested.

Regardless, she certainly didn't care when he chatted with the serving girls or joked with the women who came in to drink in the evenings with the laborers. He should afford her the same courtesy. "Sorry," he said. "For—I don't know. For thinking anything. Which I wasn't."

She laughed. "Neither of us was thinking anything. And we like it that way. Let's go right on thinking nothing." She flopped backward onto the mattress, raising a small cloud of dust.

Galen put his newly oiled sword away and stood. "I'll be back. Privy." And it would give the air a few moments to clear, and maybe he could forget what he'd said.

He went downstairs and out the rear of the inn, where there was an outhouse a bit too small to service the sizable public room. Heading back, Galen looked up and saw the red-haired young man—Kayvin, he'd said—standing at the base of the stairs, ignoring the fading conversation in the public room, staring up at the second floor. Staring at the door to their room.

Staring after Lisveth.

Galen cleared his throat as he came into the corridor, and Kayvin casually shifted his weight without looking back at Galen. But he gave Galen a pleasant nod as he passed. "Good evening."

Galen jerked his head in response. "Evening."

He went up the stairs, feeling stupid.

CHAPTER 4

LISVETH PICKED OUT THE caravan—she argued, quite reasonably, that she had the better eye for what goods would be most attractive to steal and which guards the easiest to negate—while Galen visited the market, buying rations and replacements for bits of gear worn beyond repair.

When they met again, Lisveth took the half of a pear Galen offered and nodded toward a staging ground full of activity. "That one."

"You sound pretty confident."

"If I were choosing a target, there'd be no other consideration. The best cargo by far, and half the guards are raw rookies, probably brought in because of the bandit threat but still lacking experience or brains. It's so obvious, I'd suspect a trap, except I've managed to catch a few of the overseer's conversations and I don't think he could manage a trap. He may have enough to manage keeping his own feet both pointed in the same direction."

Galen frowned. "If he's so incompetent, how'd he make that position?"

She made a face. "The owner's grandson."

"You really have been listening."

"Quite a few of his more experienced guards aren't happy with him. They think he's putting them at unnecessary risk." She smiled a little cat smile. "And he is."

They followed the caravan out of town, staying about a half-mile behind. It was a slow pace for two people traveling simply, but they stayed far enough back that no one seemed to notice their contrived delays and distractions. A group on horseback passed them and then the caravan, and then a man with a laden mule outdistanced them as Lisveth bent to fuss with a lace on her boot.

Galen had suggested joining the caravan itself under the premise of seeking protection from the bandits, which would have alleviated the burden of staying close enough to observe but not so close they were observed. But Lisveth preferred freedom of movement. "And if someone does drop a fireball on a wagon, real fire," she said, "wouldn't you rather not be in it?"

Sometimes Galen found it difficult to argue with her logic.

At night, they camped within hearing of the caravan, keeping their own fire and voices low. On the fourth night, they were apparently no longer low enough, and two guards came over the hill and approached them in the twilight.

"Heads up," Galen said quietly, crouching over the fire with a pan.

"They probably smelled that bacon," said Lisveth. "Keep cooking while I talk to them. It'll look less suspicious, and besides, I'm starving."

It was a man and a woman who approached, weapons slung loosely at their sides but within easy reach. "Good evening," the woman called. "Got a moment to talk?"

It was a pleasant and innocuous opening. Galen shook the bacon in the pan.

"Certainly," called Lisveth. "Not much supper to share, but you're welcome to a bite if you like, too."

"That won't be necessary," said the man, not too gruffly, "but thanks for the offer. We have our own supper with the caravan." He raised an eyebrow. "As I'm sure you know."

"Well, I guessed as much," answered Lisveth, "but I was only trying to be friendly."

Galen felt their eyes passing over him, gauging his build, the sword at his side, the crouch of his legs. He rocked back and sat solidly on the ground, trusting to Lisveth's silver tongue. If it somehow came to a fight, she'd be quicker with her magic than he could get across the fire, anyway.

"Talking of being friendly," said the woman, "we note you've been trailing us the last couple of days. Not walking with us, but staying close."

Lisveth's mouth firmed into a sulk. "The Octovirate's roads are for the use of all. We're heading south, same as you. Nothing to say we can't cover the same road."

"You don't have wagons to handle or gear to manage," the man pointed out. "You look reasonably healthy. You should be making better time."

Lisveth looked faintly flustered and she glanced at Galen. "We—we wanted to be near someone. In sight or hearing. Not everyone can afford to pay for guards, you know, and well, we couldn't afford to join the caravan, right? But we don't want to walk alone in bandit country. Felix is okay with that sword, but there's just the two of us, you know?"

Felix? Galen resisted the urge to roll his eyes.

The woman seemed to consider this. The man frowned. "So you're hoping to use our protection without paying for it?"

"We're not hurting you! We're not in your way. We're on the high road, same as you are." Lisveth's lower lip jutted slightly, and the other woman nearly rolled her eyes in irritation.

Galen had to look down at the bacon to keep from smiling. It was starting to burn, so he set the little pan aside.

"There's no one saying you shouldn't be using the road," the man amended, sounding more exasperated now than suspicious. "It's just that, well, there are bandits, and with you shadowing us so, some people are wondering if you aren't...connected in some way."

"What?" Lisveth didn't seem to understand him.

He looked a bit pained. "You know, scouts or something. Watching. For the bandits." He turned abruptly to look at Galen. "You aren't saying much."

"Not much to say," Galen answered. "Just, I don't think I could take a whole set of guards by myself."

The man huffed with frustration. "I didn't mean you could do it yourself. Not like the two of you could present much of a threat, I'll grant you that. But if you were working with someone, scouting for them..."

Lisveth gave him a dubious look. "And somehow we'd signal them that you were coming? From behind you?"

"Well..."

A whisper of sound came from the direction of the caravan, and then there was a hollow roar like a bonfire. Together they swung and stretched on their toes, trying to see over the rise between them and the wagons. Light blossomed on the horizon, but it was in the wrong direction to be the fading sun.

"Fire!" gasped the woman.

"Fireball," confirmed Lisveth softly to Galen. It had started.

The two guards sprinted for the caravan. Galen had to admire their dedication, though it was unlikely they'd reach it in time to do much—nor find much to do once there, either. The Fire Brigand, the new one, was probably safely hidden behind rocks or other cover, watching her targets burn. She and her accomplices wouldn't come out until guards and travelers were thoroughly disorganized and fleeing.

So he wasn't exactly sure what he and Lisveth were doing running in the same direction.

She seemed to anticipate his question. "Judging from the whistle and angle of ignition, I'm guessing she's to the southwest. You go around and see if her flunkies are flanking—but don't get among them. We're not here to fight anyone. Just find where they are."

"Without being mistaken for a bandit myself and cut up by the guards."

"Right."

CHAPTER 5

THE BANDITS WERE CHARGING from the north, opposite where Lisveth estimated the new Fire Brigand to be and right where she had sent Galen. He took a scant moment to appreciate her grasp of their tactics as he drew his sword and scanned for a way to intervene without putting himself among a dozen hostile bandits.

No, not intervene. Lisveth had been very specific that they were not hired to protect the caravan, but to find the missing daughter Andrea. The caravan was its own concern; Galen was looking for the bandits and the girl described.

This did not stop him from hamstringing a lone bandit about to skewer a caravan guard. He ran on down the line of wagons, weaving through alarmed livestock and fleeing caravan passengers.

The bandits were concentrated near the center of the line, where a knot of guards clustered against a wagon. Probably a cargo of the most valuable goods, or the guards' payroll, or some other prime target. Galen hesitated and tried to peer through the chaos for a particular face.

A whistling sound came overhead and Galen registered it dimly. Then memory returned with an urgent rush: *This one is real. Real fire.* He ducked and spun toward the warning sound, and he heard the screams of a little bunch of travelers watching their deaths fall upon them.

The incoming fireball sizzled toward them as a woman drew two children behind her pitiful shield of a body, and then it flashed and whiffed out, leaving a sharp crack of collapsing air and a wave of heat and smoke.

Galen whirled and found Lisveth in the twilight. She stumbled and nearly fell, her eyes rolling, but caught herself. She was best at illusions, but she had control of real fire when she wished, though it took more effort.

The woman seized the two children and dragged them away with her. Bandits jeered and tore into the cargo. Galen snatched up a third straggling child, who screamed and kicked. He spun in place, watching for incoming danger and counting bandits, and then ran after the escaping family. "Take this one!"

The woman glanced back, eyes wide and frightened of Galen. "He's not mine."

Galen pushed the crying child ahead of him. "I can't keep a child and fight."

She nodded and gestured the child toward her, still watching Galen suspiciously. Of course she wouldn't know him from a bandit.

Lisveth ran toward him. "Galen?"

"A dozen or so," he said, pointing, "and at least two-thirds of them are pulling apart the cargo."

Lisveth waved Galen toward her. "Let them distract themselves."

The bandit Galen had cut was calling for help. Galen turned and followed Lisveth into the dark.

"I couldn't find her," Lisveth muttered, embarrassed. "She fired and ran. She's still out here somewhere."

She wasn't talking about Andrea Lawson. "And we're going to run around in the half-dark until we find her?"

"Or until she lights up and we can spot it," Lisveth answered. "You got a better idea?"

He didn't.

A whistle sounded to their left, and Lisveth whirled. "There!"

Galen traced the flaming globe's track backward and selected a clump of bushes as its likely point of origin. "I'll take the left," he said.

Lisveth caught his arm. "Hold on."

He followed her eyes and saw that while some bandits were still skirmishing with a few remaining guards, others were already settling down, pulling the cooking suppers from the pots and making themselves comfortable where their victims had been an hour before.

He nodded. They didn't have to go looking for the sorceress; they could join her at dinner. He and Lisveth squatted and let the deepening twilight cover them.

The bandits rummaged through the cargo, arguing over choice pieces or rejoicing at a special find, and gradually grouped about the central cook fire, sharing out the guards' meal. Galen glanced at Lisveth, who nodded readiness.

A line on the ground glowed, a series of sparks sprang among blades of grass, and then fire roared up in a roiling wall of yellow and orange flame. The bandits leapt back, bunching together and spinning to follow as the wall rose about them, entrapping them with a hedge of flame.

Swords appeared. "Show yourself!"

The ring of fire faded but for a few lingering burns to offer additional light. "Hold it, hold it, wait up," Lisveth said, hands held high to show a lack of weapons. "We're just here to talk. Wanted to let you know we were here."

"I'm not interested in what you have to say." A woman glared haughtily at them. Her hair was black, with a few bright streaks of red cutting jaggedly through it. Both colors were plainly artificial, and the effect was striking but not quite flattering.

"Well, we're not here to talk to you, so I suppose that all works out nicely," Lisveth replied in airy dismissal. She made a show of looking up and down the faces now closing in a half-circle about them. "Is everyone here? Anyone missing? We're looking to deliver a message."

The woman with streaky hair was not to be put off so easily. "Wait a minute! Do you know who I am?"

"Now how exactly should I know that?" Lisveth looked exasperated. She glanced at Galen. "You ever seen her before?"

"Nope." Galen crossed his arms over his chest. Compromising his sword hand displayed a lack of concern for any threat the others offered and made them less jumpy about him. It simultaneously offered both peace and insult, a negotiation tactic he was learning from Lisveth.

It seemed to be working in both approaches. Most of the group had released their various weapons, and their leader was growing impatient and irate. "You don't have to have seen me!"

Galen shrugged. "Glad that's settled, then." He turned and looked around at the others.

"I just leveled a caravan!" snapped the woman. "I just killed a dozen professional fighters! Don't you know who I am?"

"Calm down, Ember," said a dark-haired man with premature grey at his temples. "They weren't here, probably, and anyway we don't want to tell them so much."

Lisveth turned an incredulous and faintly disgusted gaze upon the woman. "Ember?" she repeated.

The woman's mouth twisted into a sardonic smile. "Maybe the name offers you a clue, now?"

"Are you serious? Ember?" Lisveth shook her head. "You weren't born with that name any more than with that hair. Which did you first dye it patchwork to match, your new name or your new hobby?"

Galen guessed Lisveth was buying him time, and he tore his eyes from the conflict to scan the rest of the group. There, a brown-haired girl with a nose slightly too large for her face. He took a few casual steps in her direction. "Is your name Andrea?"

Andrea froze, and her face worked through a short series of expressions before settling on outrage. "Did my parents send you? Did you come to drag me home again?" Her mouth twisted. "Because that's not going to happen."

Galen raised his hands. "I'm not dragging anyone anywhere."

"That's one thing certain," snapped Ember. "Andrea's not going anywhere. She's with me, now, and she stays with me. One of my gang. Under my protection."

"She doesn't need *protection*." Lisveth's voice dripped contempt. "She left home because she wanted to manage her own affairs, and here you are, telling her what she can't do."

Andrea turned her eyes to Lisveth, blinked, and then looked at the Fire Brigand.

"Anyway, you're wrong." Lisveth focused on Andrea, ignoring Ember, whose widening eyes indicated she wasn't accustomed to this kind of cavalier dismissal. "As my friend said, we aren't going to drag anyone to anywhere. That's not what we do, and you look like the type who likes to make her own decisions. We're just here to deliver a message, like we said."

Andrea's expression was guarded, but her curiosity was piqued. "What kind of message?"

"Just this," said Lisveth. "Your dad's a horse's arse."

Andrea, ready to be defensive, was caught off guard. "What?"

"He's an arse. He got angry and protective and he flubbed it all, mishandled the whole thing. He shouldn't have shouted at you, even if he was scared. And he's really sorry, and someday he hopes you'll find it in you to forgive him, wherever you are." Lisveth delivered this flatly, as if she'd memorized a speech of little interest, but she recited clearly and slowly enough that Andrea could take it in.

It took her by surprise, and her defiant protest faded unspoken. Still, she was suspicious. "That's it?"

Lisveth shrugged. "That's the important part. There was something else... Nope, not coming to mind. I kind of didn't listen to the last bit as closely." She grinned and picked at her ear with her little finger.

Andrea frowned. "Was it about coming home?"

Lisveth frowned back in concentration. "Maybe something about a baker? Can't say for certain."

"The baker's daughter, maybe?" Andrea supplied. "Kerra? He liked Kerra, too—not my da, I didn't mean that."

"What is all this?" demanded Ember. "What has any of this to do with us?"

Andrea turned on her. "It's something to me!" She turned back to Lisveth. "The baker's daughter? Is that it?"

Lisveth nodded. "Yeah, about her. Did you know her?"

"Do not cross me!" snapped Ember. Lisveth's baiting had angered her, but Andrea's insolence before the others had been the final straw. "I'm the leader here, and—"

"And you'll decide what matters to Andrea?" finished Lisveth. "Guess that makes you a horse's arse, too. At least her father had the sense to be sorry about it."

She was attempting to draw Ember's fury from defenseless Andrea, Galen realized, like a rod draws lightning from a barn of dry timbers. It worked. Ember raised her hands with an inarticulate cry and the group, recognizing the gesture, scattered backward.

Galen ducked low as heat flared over him. Lisveth was moving, circling Ember; when fire was a projectile, she'd explained, it was just as difficult to hit a moving target as with a rock. And splitting Lisveth and Galen so the bandit couldn't strike them both at once was a good idea.

Galen looked around for Andrea, but she was stumbling away with the others taking shelter behind rocks and trees. It seemed they did not trust their leader's aim or temperance. Galen started after them, calling Andrea's name, but when he slid into a natural dip where three bandits were crouching, none of them were Andrea. A man started at him, scowling and reaching for a knife, and Galen jerked backward and slid back down the hill. They did not follow.

Lisveth was working magic, gesturing from side to side as she slapped away Ember's repeated bursts of fire. For a moment Galen wondered what was wrong, why there was so little of it, and then he realized that he was accustomed to Lisveth's overly ornate and showy fountains of illusory fire. As with fists, real combat was different.

Ember called fire between her cupped palms, and Lisveth snatched it out of existence with a crackle of air. Ember stared at her empty hands, but Galen saw Lisveth waver with exertion.

"You're a thief," Lisveth growled, "but not a very smart one. You should check to see who owns things before you take them." She bared her teeth in a skull's smile. "Like names."

The hint had its desired effect. Ember hesitated, her eyes wide, as she wondered whether Lisveth lied.

"I didn't put that reputation down so just any street trash could pick it up." Lisveth glared, hands ready to deflect the next bolt of fire.

Galen began to edge around them, watching for an opening. Lisveth was talking for time, stalling to recover from the magical effort.

"You can't be," Ember breathed, more in angry denial than in disbelief.

Lisveth grinned savagely. "But I am."

The Lost Farm Boy

SAYINIA

CHAPTER 6

Three Years Before

"Hey, fumblelump, you up there?"

His pillow was damp, betraying the tears he'd smothered, so Galen hurriedly shoved it into the narrow gap between bed and wall. "Yeah, what?"

"You up there?" David's voice was muffled by the other shouting downstairs.

Galen rubbed his eyes, just in case David came up. He dared not be caught crying, not as a man of nearly twenty. At least it was too dark to show red eyes. "I'm in bed already!"

"Did you put up the geese?"

Some predator had picked off a laying goose last week, so they were keeping the flock penned at night. "Yes."

Footsteps slapped up the stair-ladder, and David pushed open the door. "Did you put up the geese?"

"Yes, I said." Galen checked his tone just short of frustration.

"Say it louder, bumbleclot. There's a lot of noise down there."
David pried off a boot with the other foot.

Galen didn't say anything.

"I think Uncle Idorn might kill Uncle Parn." David said it with
too much casualness as he pulled off his shirt and rolled onto the
bed they shared.

Galen didn't argue; he believed his brother.

David lay on his back, arms behind his head. "Not tonight. But
soon."

Galen licked his lips. "What if..." He couldn't finish the question.

David's voice was thoughtful. "If that happens, I might have a
chance to inherit over the cousins. Da was the eldest, so his line
should have precedence, right?"

Galen turned to the wall, arms crossed. "Dunno."

"Wouldn't matter to you much anyway, I guess." David pulled at
the blanket and scrunched his pillow beneath his head.

Galen did not sleep, even after David's soft snores began. He
stared into the darkness and listened to the men and women still
shouting downstairs.

It was such a stupid thing to argue over. They fought over
everything already, and it wasn't as if they used the amulet,
anyway, as they faced few threats on the farm. Even when they
turned back the occasional bandit party, they hardly needed a
magical amulet. It wasn't worth even a garden-variety argument,
much less the increasingly loud debates.

They should just give it back to the temple. Except that would
mean admitting they'd stolen it in the first place.

There was a scrape of furniture and then a heavy crash
downstairs, and a woman cried in protest. Then the fight subsided
again to harsh voices. Galen retrieved his pillow from the gap and
pulled it over his head.

It was just a silly amulet of protection. Only it wasn't doing much protecting, because in the two years since they had brought it home, things had gotten steadily worse in the house.

Galen tightened his fingers into the pillow. How could David sleep through this?

The voices downstairs settled into grumbles and murmurs, and Galen took a full breath for what he realized was the first time in a long while. He had been unknowingly waiting for something worse. David was right, and someone was going to die.

Galen squeezed his eyes shut. If they wouldn't give it back to the temple—and they wouldn't—they should just throw the thing away.

The idea caught in his mind. What if he did just that? He might toss it into the ravine at the rear of the sheep range. No one would find it in such a lonely place.

His mouth twisted. When they discovered it missing, they might leap straight to conclusions and murder, accusing one another. And if Galen stepped in to say that it wasn't one of his uncles who had taken it, they'd string his teeth on a wreath and then send him down into the ravine to find it.

Someone stomped up the stairs, and then the narrow house fell mostly silent.

"Now the fourth proficiency," called Master Caine. "Ready."

Galen brushed his red hair from his eyes and took a ready position, sighting along the lines of youths. At Master Caine's instruction, they flowed through a series of movements, each a rhythmic simulation of blocking a strike, turning a weapon, or deflecting and evading an opponent's attack. This was one of his favorite times of a temple day, strangely soothing despite the subject.

Generations ago, when waves of pirates and brigands had crashed regularly against Sayinia, the Senate had mandated combat training for every able-bodied person under fifty, and forts and temples across the land drilled dozens every day. Since the river's shift, however, the capital was better protected and didn't need the diligence of peasants. Reduced river trade had made the Heel itself a less attractive target, and most raiders had moved on to richer prey. Only a few temples kept up the training, no longer mandatory, and Galen knew of only one fort remaining.

They finished the final movement, a rotation to disarm and lock the elbow, and then turned in unison to face Master Caine. He nodded approval and gestured them to the end of the temple yard and the gate to the gardens.

Galen lived for the days at the temple. In the cool mornings they practiced the fighting forms, and sometimes the masters would allow them to spar. Then they tended the temple's beans and vegetables before going inside to eat their lunch from the same plots. The afternoons were filled with other lessons, reading and history and arithmetic and stories from beyond the Heel.

Some of the family thought Galen should be spending those three days of seven in more farm work; there was never a shortage of goats to be milked or fences to be mended. But one time Galen had calculated winter fodder in bales at interest was a better investment than buying bags at cash down, finding the error in Uncle Parn's figures, and so a triumphant Uncle Idorn had declared Galen could keep attending as long as he didn't slack the other four days. Galen didn't.

A green bean struck his shoulder, and Galen was startled out of his thoughts.

"Pay attention." Jonas dropped a handful of beans into his basket. "You're pretty distracted."

"What?"

"Exactly. And you just weed-pulled a rutabaga. You might want to stick it back in the ground before Brother Toller notices."

Galen looked down at the plant in his hand. "I never remember these leaves." He replaced the undeveloped root and tamped the ground around it. "I'm just tired. Didn't sleep much."

Jonas eyed him. "Doing anything interesting?"

Galen shook his head. He didn't talk about it. Family business was family business, as his uncles would say, and it might come up somehow that they were fighting over *something* as well. And Galen would never risk bringing up the amulet here, not at the temple from which his father and uncles had stolen it.

Jonas grinned. "I know better. I know Brother Athgar has been giving you extra lessons in the morning."

"That's just once a week," Galen said quickly. "I come in early. Don't—don't say anything."

Jonas shrugged. "I don't know that anyone's jealous, if that's what you mean. No reason to do extra work for no reason."

Most of the temple students did just enough of the fighting forms to meet obligations and attend the more academic lessons in the afternoon, without particular interest in outdated lessons whose techniques did not help in the fields. Galen, though, treasured the predictable control of the forms and the extra hour away from his tense farmhouse, and he would never have admitted it aloud, but he was glad and proud to have been recognized and invited for additional instruction. It wasn't the other students' jealousy he feared if word got out he was at the temple more than necessary.

Brother Toller called them in for lunch, and as Galen passed he gave him a smile. "Rutabaga leaves have a bluish tint to them," he said softly, and Galen's ears grew warm. For all his amiable expressions, Brother Toller missed little. The monk jerked his head toward the eating hall. "Go on and review what they taste like, too."

It was also Brother Toller's turn for the history lesson. Today's was an old lesson, repeated for the newer students in their first year. "With so many invaders pressing through to the capital, the Senate sent sorcerers and magicians to aid the outer regions' defense. They wove fantastic magics about the land and lent strength to our warriors, and the pirates were turned back at the Battle of Oku, at great cost."

Galen wrapped his arms about his knees, drawing them close to his chest. Beside him Jonas shifted and leaned back on his hands, cross-legged on the floor.

"After Oku, the sorcerers bestowed additional power upon each outpost, to prepare it for the next assault. This took the form of gifts, one to each temple and fortress. Enchanted weapons for fighting, some were, and others long-seeing glasses to spy the enemy's approach. All things of myth and legend. Our own temple had one of the most powerful, an amulet that protected the wearer from harm."

Galen looked at the floor between his feet.

"But when the river moved, the magicians were recalled, and they took most of their gifts with them. Few remained, and many of those have since been lost. Our own amulet was stolen only a few years ago, taken by brigands who killed two of our brother monks."

Jonas coughed, and Galen jumped and looked at him. But Jonas only wiped his nose on the back of his hand.

"Fortunately, we have less need of the sorcerers' gifts now. The Senate takes so little notice of us these days that it is even safe to openly complain we are neglected." Brother Toller smiled and tapped the side of his nose conspiratorially. "And with the prize of the capital no longer within reach, there was no reason to fight. The great pirate fleets left as well, leaving only the common bandits you know today."

"What about Fort Hope?" asked a younger girl. "Are there still soldiers there?"

Galen ignored the rest, as Brother Toller's words were echoing in his mind. *With the prize no longer within reach, there was no reason to fight.* Galen had been right; stealing the amulet was the only way.

The rest of the lessons passed in a haze, and the road home blurred in Galen's unfocused vision. With the prize gone... He had to take it. He could hide it, maybe, or maybe even return it to the temple. They surely wouldn't steal it a second time.

What if—what if they did, and more died? Two monks had been killed the last time, and Galen's own father. If he gave it back to the temple, would anyone else be hurt?

Well, Galen would be. If the amulet turned up at the temple, Uncle Parn and Uncle Idorn would surely guess how it had gotten there. Maybe Galen could stay at the temple for a while, too.

A goat bleated at him, and Galen realized he was nearly home. He jogged forward and turned the stray back to the little bunch his cousin Locke was swearing at. "Thanks," Locke said before he caught himself. Quickly he added, "Stupid goats are as scatterbrained as you. Give me a hand, now you're done wasting your day in stories and dancing."

Galen did, saying nothing. They shooed the goats into a pen and Locke tied the gate shut, adding extra ties at top and bottom. "This needs fixing," he pointed out unnecessarily. "Maybe you could do some work tomorrow, like the rest of us did today."

Galen wanted to ask what Locke had done all day if the gate was still loose, but he didn't. Locke had only a year on Galen's nineteen, but he had his father's temper and quick fists.

Aunt Lartha stood outside the kitchen, her hands pressed to the side of her head. Locke cut in front of Galen and started toward her, but not before Galen saw the worried hurt on his face. Idorn and Parn were at it again, not even waiting for supper this time.

"Carry the wood," Locke called back over his shoulder, and Galen's stomach fell. He wanted to flee to the barn, to hide among the cows and barn cats until this subsided, coming in too late for the fight and with buckets of fresh milk to his credit. But he went to the woodpile—maybe he could come again after and split wood until the current round died down—and gathered an armload to carry into the kitchen.

The angry voices carried well outside the stone walls, and Galen shoved the door back with a shoulder. Aunt Beni stood to one side, alternately pleading with both men to stop and turning hotly on Idorn at her husband's shoulder. At the table, Galen's mother stood chopping vegetables, her head down, her knife working briskly and regularly.

"You think I'll let you keep it?" Uncle Parn leaned over the wide table, gesturing, his shadow falling over the vegetables. The knife made steady little *ploks* against the cutting board. "Like you're some sort of captain or magician, running off pirates or demons instead of bandits?"

"I keep our food on our own table and our produce in our own markets," snapped Idorn. "I keep us fed and safe in our beds at night. You didn't complain when the bandits dropped the Uphill wool they stole with our own as they ran, did you?" He sneered. "What is it you're afraid of, that you need protecting from?"

"And so I should let you have the thing? Wear it to protect yourself from hill bandits and ditch-robbers? While maybe you'll just take a chance and kill me too, same as Ablo?"

Galen froze, the firewood hesitating over its box, his breath caught in his chest. Uncle Idorn had killed his father?

Idorn curled his lip in disgust. "I'd have less reason if you weren't always snapping at my heels about the thing. You're as greedy as he was."

The sound of the knife against the cutting board continued unbroken, a steady rhythm of chopping. Galen's mother had not looked up, had not so much as flinched.

Locke pushed open the door, shoving into Galen. "Get on, you're in the way. Da, there's a man here says the red cow got into his peas and tramped all the young plants. Wants payment to plant new."

"Curse that red thing," snarled Idorn, "and all red things like her." He started toward the door, and Galen and Locke slid out of his way.

Galen dropped the armload of wood into the box, and Parn looked at him sharply. Galen didn't raise his head, busying himself with pulling a few crooked pieces into alignment so the wood settled properly. The steady *plok* of the knife through the vegetables continued.

Galen went out again and, head down, walked to the far end of the yard, circling to the far side of the feed barn and dropping behind the last of the winter hay. Hidden from sight, he let it finally settle, finally become real.

Uncle Idorn had killed his father. And his mother had known.

They had told David and Galen and the others that the monks had pursued them, that Ablo had been killed in the fight. But Galen could guess now how it had happened, how Ablo had claimed the amulet as the eldest and the fighting had begun. Had they betrayed him, turning on him in the fight with the monks? Had the monks even come after them at all, or had they been killed in the temple robbery and not as they pursued the thieves? Was Idorn's act one of blind fury and hot greed, or had Idorn and Parn conspired to seize Ablo's birthright as well as the amulet?

And his mother had known. And she sat quiet and still, preparing food for his murderers as they argued over the spoils of his death.

Galen's breath wheezed in his throat, and the tears he almost wanted wouldn't come, burning instead in his chest. He clenched his fists until his knuckles hurt and his palms bled. He wanted them all to pay—Uncle Idorn, and Uncle Parn, and his mother, and Aunt Beni and Aunt Lartha, all who had known and who continued this—

But deeper, deeper, the fury faded to a soundless ache, a rift that could not be plumbed, a sorrow for his family and their danger to themselves. They had not been like this when he was a child, not this bad. They needed something to fight over, and that was the amulet.

He had to take it. The stupid amulet, an amulet of so-called protection—he had to steal it to protect what was left of his family. And he couldn't merely hide it, couldn't take it to the temple where they would find it again. He had to get it away from them.

He would do it tonight.

CHAPTER 7

HE COULDN'T TAKE MUCH. There was no chance to pack before David and he went to bed, and once he'd crept downstairs and risked a candle, wick trimmed cautiously short, he couldn't rummage too much for supplies or risk awakening someone. Galen found bread, hard cheese, and some dried jerky forgotten on the back of a shelf. It would have to do.

He saved the amulet for last. If caught in the kitchen, he could blame midnight hunger pangs, but no excuse would save him if the amulet were found in his hand.

He put out the candle and stood for a moment in the dark, letting his eyes adjust. This was the point of no return. He set his boots beside the door along with his knapsack, and he crept in stocking feet back up the steep stairs, keeping close to the wall where the squeaks were fewest.

The amulet was the most dangerous, but almost the easiest part. Neither Idorn nor Parn would let it remain in the other's reach, so it was kept in a coffer on the tiny landing—unlocked, since neither would trust the other with the key. Galen knew the steps by heart. He stretched out a hand to touch the door frame to the room he shared with David and their cousins, and then he advanced to the squat, heavy coffer just beyond.

Maybe his da had done something like this. Maybe he had taken it to stop fighting, to save lives. Maybe he had never meant to hoard it, and maybe he'd gotten between Parn and Idorn as they were arguing over it. Maybe.

Galen shoved down the bitterness and hurt and wrapped his fingers about the cool object inside. He withdrew it, gathering its light chain so it wouldn't drag or rattle, and eased the coffer lid down again. Surely his uncles did not check it each morning? They might notice Galen's absence before the amulet's, and they might think him at the temple or something. Anything to buy him a bit more time.

It was the first time he'd touched the thing. Despite the urgency of the moment, he hesitated, trying to sense a magical tingle or something. But he didn't know what to look for, and if there was anything unusual about the amulet, he couldn't note it. He dropped it over his neck and slid the amulet beneath his shirt.

"Who's there?" called a rough voice. Galen froze. A bed frame creaked, and Uncle Idorn called again. "Who is it?"

"It's just me," Galen forced, and his voice sounded thin. "I just—taking a leak."

There was a short grumble that faded away, and the bed creaked again. Then silence.

Galen drew a shaky breath and eased down the stairs. No turning back now. He took his heavy cloak even though the spring night was warm; the seasons would turn no matter where he was. He pulled on his boots, settled the sack over his shoulder and across his chest, and ran through the half-moonlight until he had put two hills between him and his sleeping uncles.

Galen cradled the amulet. He hated the thing—hated it with all the hatred he had never allowed himself to feel for his uncles, his cousins, his older brother, with the hatred he had not known he should have felt for even his mother, who had known and had done nothing.

Selfish fools, all of them. Selfish, hateful fools. Yet his eyes burned for the loss of them.

And now he had taken it away, had saved them though they did not deserve his help. He was a homeless road boy now. He had seen such men before, traveling the roads in search of farm work, spending a week here and two weeks there and taking payment in small coin or even in food and bedding.

If only he had simply thrown the thing in the ravine, as he had considered. But they would have known it was him, no matter how he had denied it, and then he would have paid dearly.

The amulet's eye flashed in the light. It was a beautiful thing, whatever he thought of it and whatever it had done to his family. The eye was a brilliant blue, iridescent in both sunlight and firelight, with flashes of all colors as it moved. The pupil was a long vertical slit, as if it came from a cat, but the eye was as large as a horse's.

He'd heard once in a lecture that horses had the largest eyes of any animals. Even larger animals, such as the great pulling oxen or the dragons that had once existed, did not have larger eyes than horses. But no horse ever looked upon the world with a vertical slit like that in a cat's eye.

All around the eye were coils of wire and twists of metal, the workings of a mad jeweler. Galen was not sure if the twists and coils served a magical purpose, directing power or some other arcane working, or if they were just a display of the device's richness and rarity, absorbing so many hours of the maker's craft. Or perhaps this had been all the rage in jewelry styles centuries ago when the thing was made.

Regardless, it was not something that could be carried openly. It would identify him immediately if recognized, and make him a laughingstock if not. He tucked it again inside his shirt and this time ran the chain through the laces, out and then in, to keep it secure and hidden if he bent over or moved too much.

Someone in the capital would know what it was. Maybe he could give it to another temple there, where they could keep it safe. Or maybe...maybe he could keep it himself, use its power to protect himself as he made his way alone on the roads. Was that stealing? Was it stealing to keep what someone else had stolen? But he had stolen it from his uncles, or at least that's what they would call it—but he had stolen it for good reason, to keep them from harm, no matter how little they deserved protection.

Because if they did not kill one another, his mother would be safe. She had known, but in truth, where could she have gone? Maybe she had no choice, either.

...Had David known? Had Galen been the only one ignorant of the truth? Had they all been living with the knowledge of murder, but for him?

He shook his head. No matter. The thing was the size of his palm, including the metalwork about the eye, and it had to be hidden. He could decide later what to do with it. But he could not donate it to a temple in the capital until he had reached the capital, so it was his at least for a time.

It was time to start walking.

CHAPTER 8

HIS MEAGER RATIONS LASTED two days.

He had never traveled so quickly, pushing himself to a jog again whenever he'd caught his breath from a fast walk, and his muscles were aching. He was accustomed to farm work and the fluid movements of the temple's training, and though he was in good condition, this was a different kind of challenge.

When his food ran out, he paused for drink at the streams he passed, but he did not stop to fish or hunt fruit. There would be little left on the bushes and trees anyway, stripped by the animals over the winter, and he could not stop imagining Parn and Idorn and Locke and the others behind him, pushing as fast as he did.

He did not stop at any of the houses where he might have asked for a meal in exchange for some chores. He wanted no one to be able to report him to his uncles. Let them wonder if he had come this way or another.

By the fourth day, his stomach was growling and cramping, and he guiltily plucked a shriveled pear from the rear of a passing wagon. He had reached the high road at last, where traffic was more common and strange faces less noteworthy, and for the first time he let himself slow and match the resigned, efficient strides of the walking traveler.

He had been this far once before, when his father had taken a particularly fine crop of squash to compete in the greater market of Abbay and Galen had ridden with him. That was six years ago, and he doubted he remembered enough to find his way. But his father hadn't known the city, either, and surely such a place would be used to people asking directions.

If only he knew where he wanted to go.

The pear wasn't much, and his stomach continued to growl. He took a drink from his refilled bota—at least water was plentiful in the spring—and pretended it would help. Voices chattered behind him, growing louder, and he realized his pace had fallen to a trudge. The sudden awareness stripped him of his mindless navigation and he stumbled in a rut. His ankle rolled, and he staggered to the side.

"Steady!" called a man's voice. "You all right there, son?"

Galen straightened and nodded. "Think so, thank you. Just rolled it."

A dozen people were coming up behind him, most bearing packs and leading a single donkey cart piled high. "You'll want to watch your step," the man at the front said. "This is a lousy place to lose an ankle, and our cart's too full to load you." He smiled.

Galen shifted his slim pack and fell into step alongside him. "Lost thought of what I was doing, I guess. Even just the walking."

His stomach growled again, loud and humiliating. Galen hurriedly crossed his arms over it, trying to press it into silence.

The man magnanimously ignored it. "Going into Abbay, or somewhere beyond?"

"Just to Abbay." He needed to get further, put more miles between himself and his uncles, but he wouldn't last on the road without fresh supplies.

"Same as we, then. And what's your business there?"

"I guess I'll look for work." He hadn't really thought so far, yet, in part because it was too daunting a thought. But he was strong and unafraid of work, and he had both farm skills and his learning from the temple. Surely he would find something.

The man nodded, his face impassive. "I see. Lots of young folk go into the city for work."

Galen wasn't sure what he meant by that. He was debating whether to ask when his stomach rumbled again, as loudly as before.

This time the man laughed. "Can't hide a gut, can you? Don't fret, son, you're not the first caught hungry on a road. You're in good shape, clothes whole and fitting, if a bit dirty, so you haven't been out long. What's the story?"

"What?"

"Why are you out on your own to Abbay? Did your father remarry, and she doesn't like you in the house?"

Galen hugged his arms to his torso. "Something near enough to that."

"Well, don't you mind. We're on to Abbay ourselves, as I've said, and we have enough to share a supper tonight. We're going to meet up for a proper caravan before heading east. Safer on the roads that way."

"Safer?"

"Bless you, son, you'll want to know something about the road before you try to live on it. Bandits, and they're thick in the east. The ordinary sort are bad enough, but no one wants to meet a robber-mage alone."

"Robber-mages?" His curiosity outweighed his hunger.

"I daresay you don't have many of those where you're farming, that's so. There's a sorceress who uses fire. She'll appear on the road and demand you stand and deliver, and if you don't pay up she blasts your wagons and gear and burns it all." The man shook his head. "So there's something to avoid."

Galen blinked, trying to imagine it. "We have robbers and bandits, but nothing like that." That was something out of the temple stories, something from time long past. All such magicians had left the Heel long ago, the brothers had said. Was this a rogue magician from the Capital? "Um, and thank you, for the offer of supper. Thank you very much."

"You're welcome. I had a step-mother, too. Just chew your tongue until we stop for the evening."

It seemed evening would never come, but at last it did, and Galen offered to help with the donkey while the group prepared supper. It was a simple meal, bread and dried meat and pickled vegetables all warmed over, but it smelled heavenly as it hung above a fire, and Galen's mouth watered even as he brushed dried sweat off the donkey's harness.

He tried not to embarrass himself with his eagerness, but the man—Nathan, he was called—gave him a second helping before he'd even finished the first, and Galen didn't have the pride to refuse.

"A song before sleep," a woman declared, moving the pot aside. It came to rest beside Galen, and she gave him a significant look as she said in a lower voice, "Go ahead and scrape the pot. Saves on the cleaning."

Galen took his remaining slice of bread to the contoured interior, scraping the remaining vegetables and swallowing them. He was full now, but who was to say when he would be again?

"Maria," Nathan called. "Lead us in a song, if you would, to lighten the road and calm us for sleep."

"Happy to," she said, and she put on an expression of considering. "What kind of road did we have today? Was it a tinker's road, or a bard's?"

"A bard's road!" called one of the younger boys. "And full of dragons!"

Maria laughed. "I don't know that we saw any dragons today," she said. "Or maybe your eyes are just better than mine. But a bard song it will be."

The group faced the fire and sang, and though Galen didn't know the song, he quickly found himself caught up in the rollicking melody and lyrics of a bard's adventures on the road. Bards were a thing of fable, like the powerful magicians of old, and it was fun to hear the song's story unfold.

And then the cook fire burst upward and outward, a fountain of flame, and they all screamed and recoiled. Heat seared Galen's face as he scrabbled back.

"Stop! Stop!" Nathan cried, spinning and calling into the dark. "We'll give you what you want! Don't hurt us, don't destroy what we have!"

The fire steadied and lowered, and a tall, slim shadow formed at the edge of its light. "What will you give me?"

Nathan held up his hands. "One moment. We have some money set aside. I'll get it for you."

Galen stayed where he was, but his thoughts were not still. The sorceress stood a half dozen paces from him, cloaked in dark red, and she was looking at Nathan. Galen might be able to rush her off her feet, and he had the magic of the amulet to protect him.

And then she turned and looked at Galen, flickering firelight reflecting in her eyes beneath the shadowing hood, and his resolve weakened. The leaping fire had been hot against his flesh, and the amulet had never been tested. He had only the brothers' word at the temple, and who of them had tried it?

Nathan went to her, hasty and hesitant, and proffered a small, heavy bag which clinked as it moved. "Please accept this tribute and let us continue on our journey."

She weighed the bag in her hand, looked inside, and nodded once. Nathan breathed out, visibly relieved. The sorceress turned away, tall and terrible, and walked into the night.

The fire settled into its normal cheery crackle, and Nathan sat abruptly, his breath wheezing out of him in a long whistle. "Well. That worked even better than I'd hoped."

Galen glanced at the others returning slowly to the now-friendly fire, and he came forward to resume his place. "That's the sorceress you mentioned."

"The bandits are usually further east, and we didn't expect trouble so near Abbay. Even in the east, we've managed to avoid them most of the time, but there's always that chance. Tonight we weren't so lucky."

"Not so," said Maria. "We're all here, and we lost only what we'd planned. We are very fortunate."

"True, true." Nathan bobbed his head. "We should offer an extra candle when we reach Abbay."

Galen's muscles prickled with unspent energy, and he looked at the ground between his feet. Should he have tried to stop her? These people had been kind to him; shouldn't he have tried to protect them?

"At least here," Nathan was saying, "the bandits aren't in Senate uniform. Let's be grateful and get our sleep."

The city of Abbay rose high over the rolling horizon, with mud-colored walls and glimpses of taller buildings peeking above. The traveling group made for the west gate as the most conveniently near. Galen tried to imagine so many people living so closely together. Where did they drink? Without fields, what did they do with their waste? Where did they put their animals?

The road grew more crowded as they neared the gate, choking to a slow crawl. Galen had not realized the gates would be guarded. Were there still troubles here, like the old battles? But it did not seem so serious, as he watched. Armed men waved a few travelers through, probably regulars known by sight, but halted most to question briefly. Galen's stomach tightened as he realized that he looked like a vagabond and had no evidence of business in the city. He would likely be turned away.

A guard waved, and their little group halted behind another wagon. They would be questioned next, and Galen would be plucked out.

Maria stepped near to him and took hold of his shirt with sudden disapproval. "What is this? Is this how you think you'll present yourself in town? This isn't one of those country villages where the streets are paved with manure and the people wash up once a year."

Galen started to protest, humiliated and afraid she would draw the guards' attention to him even sooner. They were approaching now, and Nathan was turning to meet them.

"Don't argue with me!" she snapped, cutting him off. "I'm tired of your excuses. It's no wonder she dropped you, the way you keep yourself and the way you slack off at everything. Pretty girl like that, she could have any boy on the road, and she gave you more chances than you deserve. Of course she left you for Zekery Needle, when he's put together smartly and earning proper money beside. You'll never have such a girl again, feathers-for-brains, and you've lost her."

Galen gaped at her.

"And you'll never make me a proper grandmother, the way this is going. Maybe some bastard brat at some cheap inn that I'll never know and never see, and that's no credit to your father and me. Maybe I should be talking to Zekery Needle, you think? I'll bet he'll have a proper family in short time!"

The rest of the group was looking awkwardly away, as were the other travelers waiting near them. The guards glanced briefly from Nathan to Galen and Maria, and then back to Nathan's inventory log.

"Don't you even try to explain! There's nothing you can say that can make this up to me. I was going to have a lovely daughter-in-law and lots of chubby sweet babies, and you had to screw it all up, just like you fumble over every single thing you touch! It's a good thing we're stopping at Abbay, because you make me ashamed to show my face at home!"

A guard returned Nathan's records. "Have a good day, and maybe tell her to go a bit easy on him." He smiled and gestured into the city, and Galen blinked and shuffled after Nathan, bowing his head under Maria's scolding.

When they were safely out of the guards' notice, Maria laughed and hugged Galen to her. "I would have warned you first, but I hadn't thought to do anything until I saw you ready to bolt like a skittish pony."

"Thank you," Galen told her, his face hot. He wondered how badly he had flushed under her scolding. "I'm sorry I didn't catch on at first."

"That's all right. You being all embarrassed and ashamed made it look more real. Even got color into your cheeks and ears." She laughed and tweaked his ear.

Well, that answered his question. He'd always flushed easily, and he'd always hated it. *Red on red*, his family had said, laughing, and of course the angrier or more embarrassed he been over it, the redder he'd grown.

Nathan stepped to his other side. "You have an idea of where you're going?"

The question might have been a simple offer of directions in the unfamiliar city, if Galen wished to hear it that way. But he answered, "I thought I might find guard work with a caravan. I have a little training, and now that I know about the bandits..." He trailed off. "I'm sorry, that sounds—I should have tried to do something, when she was there, but I..."

"What, yourself as one man against the Fire Brigand?" Maria shook her head sternly. "Good intentions are one thing, boy, but stupid is another. You might go up against her when it's a company of you and maybe a sorcerer or two alongside, but not on your own. We wouldn't have thanked you for turning robbery into murder, and having your death on our heads wouldn't have improved much."

Galen gave her a weak smile. "Thanks. I felt much the same at the time."

Nathan took his hand and dropped a few coins into it. "It's not much, but even caravan guards need to eat, and you'll need to look competent and fed if you want to impress the master. No, don't argue, or I'll set Maria on you again." He grinned.

Galen's throat felt tight. "You have been so kind to me, and there was no reason."

"That is a reason itself." Maria ruffled his hair. "Now get off and find yourself a job, feathers-for-brains. Good luck."

CHAPTER 9

THE STAGING GROUND WAS crowded and busy with people, mostly bumping into or shouting at one another. A few men stood to one side, however, more bored than busy and visibly armed, and Galen guessed these were the guards.

"Hello?" He started toward the men and gave a little self-conscious wave. "Hi? Um, I'm looking for the caravan master?"

They looked at him with cool eyes, and he wondered if they'd guessed why he'd come, and if they'd resent him seeking a job they already held. "That'd be Jerrock Highgate, that way," one said after a minute, jerking his thumb toward what Galen saw now might be a sort of enclosed office.

Galen thanked him and started for the open door. There was a steady stream of people in and out, but he slipped among them and, hat in hand, edged along the wall. Men and women argued over a long counter, and Galen watched a moment to get the lay of the land.

One man stood to the side, frowning over papers but not engaging with the stream like the others behind the counter. He frequently exchanged his papers for a new set or answered a question from one of the men and women Galen guessed were clerks, but for the most part he worked alone. Galen supposed this made him an owner or supervisor or the caravan master, and he slid along the wall to try to listen over the din.

After a few minutes, his opportunity came. "Master Jerrock," a woman with ink-stained fingers called, working behind the counter toward him, "Fenniston wants—"

"Can't do it," Highgate answered tersely. "Fenniston wants three guards assigned around all his wagons, I know, and I haven't the men to promise that. Either he gives up his pretense of being royalty, or he pays enough I can hire additional guards. And with the roads the way they are this year, guards aren't cheap."

Galen pushed forward. "Excuse me, sir? I think I can help. I came to offer work as a guard for you, sir."

Highgate's eyes shifted to him, and he looked faintly annoyed. "Go back home, boy," he said. "Your mother's probably putting your lunch on the table."

"I'm trained!" Galen burst, his ears growing hot. "I can handle a fight. And you can make back my cost with the extra headcount." He swallowed, and added, as much to himself as to Highgate, "I won't run."

"You will when you get an eyeful of a band of bandits or a sorceress."

"The Fire Brigand? I've seen her already." Galen straightened. "Coming into town, last night. She robbed our caravan and our leader paid tribute."

That caught Highgate's attention. "So you've seen her?" He quirked his mouth. "Did you fight her as bravely then as you pledge to do now?"

"No," Galen said, a bit reluctantly. "I was only one man, and she had a pillar of fire right beside me. Women and children would have been hurt if she'd been provoked. It would have been different if I'd had armed fighters with me."

"Hm." Highgate made a show of looking Galen from red hair to dusty boots. "And what were you armed with?"

He was flushing again, and there was nothing to do about it. "I didn't have a weapon, sir. But I can fight with my hands well enough if need be."

"You would be a guard without so much as a weapon?" Highgate shook his head. "Go on and—"

"Let me try!" The outburst startled Galen as much as the caravan master, but he pressed on in the other's stunned silence. "Lend me a sword or axe, and take it from my wages." He swallowed. "I'm not asking favors, sir. I'll be worth it. Give me a chance."

The clerk looked at him with disinterested eyes, waiting for his petition to be done so she could have Highgate back for her own work. The caravan master looked over Galen again, seeming to evaluate his shoulders and arms, and then asked, "You've actually trained with a sword?"

"Yes, sir. I was a temple student."

"Heh. There's temples and then there's temples." But at least now he was asking questions. "And an axe?"

"I haven't drilled with an axe," Galen confessed. "But I can split wood, and I wouldn't shrink from splitting heads or chopping limbs if necessary."

Highgate snorted again, but this time he nodded afterward. "Fregal! Sign this red-headed turnip as a guard, and get him some sort of sword against his wages. He'll need a dozen runs or so to earn it out, so he won't be too much a loss to us, and at least he'll be an extra set of hands. And he can help with the animals too, unless my eyes greatly deceive me. What's your name, boy?"

"Galen Heelsbottom." He was so pleased at his success that he answered honestly, without thinking.

"Jerrock Highgate," said the caravan master, extending his hand. "Go with Fregal, and he'll find a sword that fits you."

At the far side of the yard, some of the guards had shed their weapons and outer layers and were wrestling or boxing, cheering and betting on one another. Galen followed Fregal behind them to a locked armory, and the third candidate fit his hand and style with a proper balance. Fregal tagged and replaced it; Galen wouldn't receive it until the caravan was departing, to prevent both new guard and sword disappearing into the Abbay crowd.

Then Fregal pushed a contract and a writing pen toward Galen. "Sign here," he indicated.

The dates on the contract indicated the caravan wouldn't be leaving for two days. Galen hesitated, suspecting the answer but needing to ask anyway. "What about meals before we leave?"

"What? You eat with the caravan, when you're working."

"I, um, I don't suppose you need guards here while things are coming in, do you?"

Fregal sighed and pulled the contract back, making an addendum. "Sign here, too," he said, "for an advance. You'll have to earn it out too, but this will feed you for now and between runs. Don't lose it." He opened a purse at his waist and counted out fifteen coins.

They were taler, heavy silver coins he had seen only a few times at home. He tried not to gape at them. "Thank you."

Fregal was unimpressed with his gratitude and ushered him out of the armory, locking the door again behind them before returning to the bustling office. Galen put the coins safely away in his bag before starting into the yard.

"Hold a moment, Galen Heelsbottom," said a voice.

Galen turned to see a squat man he did not recognize. He'd apparently been waiting beside the armory door. "Yes?" Who here should know him?

The man nodded. "No mistaking that hair and that name," he said with satisfaction. "You're now in custody, by authority of the Abbay sheriff, and me as deputy."

Galen blinked. "What?"

Another man Galen hadn't noticed stepped up behind him, where he could easily block an attempt to bolt. "Word came in just this morning, so it's fresh in my mind," the deputy said. "Galen Heelsbottom, red hair. Ran away from home, his family wants him back." He nodded again. "There's a reward on you."

A hand fell heavily on Galen's shoulder, and he jerked away. "No! Please, don't. I can't go back."

"That's not very sweet to say of your own flesh and blood."

The man behind him moved again, catching Galen's arms and locking them behind his back. Galen twisted but was held fast. "Please, don't send me back!"

The squat deputy sniffed a laugh. "What's the matter, boy? Did you maybe rock the wrong man's daughter? Don't want to face marrying her now she's in trouble?"

They hadn't labeled him a thief. No, of course they couldn't; they couldn't say what he'd taken without admitting their own theft of the amulet. "I didn't do anything wrong."

"I never said you did, boy. Just said there was a reward on you." He scratched his chin. "Not much of one, though. They don't seem to miss you so strong as that, maybe not as much as you want to stay here. And by the time I feed you and someone else to march you back, and give the sheriff his own share, it'll be little enough." He looked at Galen and smiled significantly. "Which means, if you can beat their price, you can walk away from here."

Galen nodded immediately. "How much?"

"Twenty taler."

"No!" His family had never had so much coin. "They couldn't."

"No? Then bring him along," he said to the man holding Galen's arms. "We'll start to the—"

"Wait! I have fifteen." He'd have to go hungry until the caravan left, and then between runs until he'd paid off the sword and was earning coin again, but there was nothing else to be done. "You can have that." He jerked his chin toward his bag. "It's in there."

"That leaves five taler."

"I don't have any more!"

The deputy shrugged. "I keep the fifteen and you go back to your family, or you find another five and stay here."

Galen looked around, ready to beg for help, pledge years of service to Highgate if necessary, but there was no one but the watching guards, who had broken from their gambling for the fresh amusement of his arrest. "Wait—let me fight one of them."

"What?"

He was trained to fight, and he had the amulet to protect him from harm. "Bet on me. You'll make your money."

The deputy snorted. "Careful, boy, I'm like to take you up on it and set you to be pummeled."

"I'm in earnest. Go and make a match, and bet on me."

The man frowned and then spoke to the man holding Galen. "Keep him here."

He went to the watching guards and spoke, nodding back toward Galen and speaking with a mocking smile. Most of the guards laughed or snorted and then shook their heads, plainly considering it more abuse than sport. One at last agreed, and he stepped into the clear area they'd been using for a ring.

The squat man turned and beckoned Galen to join them. The second man let him go, and Galen started forward, the man following to keep him honest.

The guard looked big. Galen hoped the amulet was as good as it was supposed to be.

"Fight to the fall, count of five," the deputy said. "I'm riding three to one on you. Don't let me down."

The man's disappointment would be the least of Galen's worries if he failed. He nodded, swallowing through his tight throat, and shrugged out of his jacket. He left his shirt on, concealing the vital amulet.

How would it protect him from a punch? Would it blunt it like armor, or would it give him strength to resist it?

Galen faced the guard and gave him a nervous smile. "Hi," he said.

"Hello," said his opponent in a genial tone. "Welcome to Abbay." And then he swung.

Galen only just evaded it, falling back and deflecting with his left hand as the temple drills had taught. His forearm caught the guard's, and he moved in to strike with his right. But the guard was ready for him and stepped close with an uppercut. His fist skimmed up Galen's chest and into his jaw.

Galen stopped, stunned by the heavy punch and additionally by the fact that he'd felt it so very clearly. Shouldn't the amulet—

The man was hitting him again, and Galen wasn't ready. He retreated, raising his hands to defend himself and trying to strike away the punches as rapidly as they came. He could hear voices calling indistinct encouragement. And then the wall was close behind him, and he was trapped.

He ducked his head, hands high to protect it, and almost missed the sideways blow that came at him. But it was a feint, meant to distract him from the heavy fist coming into his diaphragm. He grunted and faltered and tried to shield his abdomen.

He'd meant to bring up his leg only as a block to shield his gut. Even in the field scraps between farm boys at home, basic rules were observed. But the guard was moving in close to pin him against the wall, and Galen's knee caught him between the legs.

In the guard's second of shocked hesitation, Galen slithered out from the wall, turning back and raising his hands. "Sorry! I—"

The fist shot between his exposed palms and caught him solidly in the face. Galen reeled back and another slammed into his jaw. Belatedly he tried to form a defense, but he was faltering now and couldn't keep up with the rapid punches. Desperately he hunched and drove into his opponent, hoping to knock the guard off balance at least, but he was slow and the guard got an arm beneath his chin. Pinned and choking, Galen could do nothing to escape the succession of gut and head punches which pounded into him.

They tore the guard off him with shouts to stop, though he landed a final rounding blow to Galen's cheek. Galen dropped, the world wavering around him, and a chorus of angry voices swirled about him like hornets.

After a moment he realized his face was pressed into the ground and his buttocks were somewhere above him. He tried to move, but one arm was pinned beneath him, tying him down. Where were the rest of his limbs? He tasted dirt.

"Hey, you in there?" A female voice spoke to him, and a few hands grasped his shoulders and arms, rolling him to one side and then upright. It hurt, and he groaned, and someone laughed from a few paces away. He squinted up to see another guard regarding him critically.

"He's awake, anyway," the new guard said. "Strictly speaking. Boy, you are the stupidest cockerel ever to strut, you know that?"

"Ow," whispered Galen.

"You really shouldn't have kicked him dirty."

"Didn't mean to."

"Actually, I saw enough to believe that." The man sighed. "You want him now, sister?"

"Help me get him on his feet, and I'll take him from there."

"Arms over shoulders, and...up!"

Galen's legs held him, but he didn't trust them. The guard clapped him on the shoulder. "See you in a couple of days, cockerel."

Where were the squat deputy and his assistant? Galen didn't see them, but already he was facing the street and limping alongside a blonde woman who took much of his weight on her shoulder. He didn't recognize her, so he kept silent.

She guided him toward a bench outside a tavern, putting him down on an empty end. The bench's other occupants stared as she bent to brush dust from his swelling face. "Well," she said, "you're a mess and a half. Sit still, and I'll be back with a rag and a beer."

She returned in less than a minute and dabbed away what must have been blood over his eye, none too gently. "This will mend clean enough, no stitches. Lucky."

He tried to speak and found there was blood mixed with the dirt in his mouth. "Are you one of the sheriff's?"

She laughed. "Oh, no. If you're thinking of Deputy Alfen, he's got his twenty taler and gone. You're in the clear, and I hope it was worth it to you."

He worked dirt from his mouth. "But I lost."

"Oh, that you did, no question." She sounded amused. "I paid Alfen the remainder. He was kicking things and swearing and furious you'd talked him into it. You'd lost him the money he'd bet on you."

Speech was coming more easily now. "You? Why did you pay him?"

Her mouth twisted into a wry smile. "I'd like to look off into the distance and say mysteriously there's a place I can't go back to, either—but the truth is, I like to see that deputies of his kind remain open to that sort of negotiation, and I couldn't let you sour him on the concept."

Galen only half followed this as she put the beer into his hand. He took a drink, and it stung his lips and mouth.

"Were you that desperate not to be caught?" she asked. "What made you offer to fight, anyway?"

Galen sipped more beer. "I thought I could win."

She laughed before she could stop herself. "That first punch, you stood there like a cow surprised to see the butcher."

The amulet had failed him. It had not protected him from harm, not in the least. And his faith in it had brought him to near disaster.

"You are stupid," she said gently, and she raised a finger to flick him in an uninjured part of his forehead. "Take care of yourself." She started away and then paused. "The beer's paid," she said. "Savor it, as I suspect it'll be your last for a while." And then she walked away.

CHAPTER 10

GALEN STAYED ON THE bench the rest of the day. A barman retrieved the empty mug from the seat beside him and gave him a frowning look, but no one spoke to him. The strange young woman had left his jacket and bag beside him, and he worked the jacket on with a slow care that did little to spare his battered torso.

When the last of the tavern's customers went out into the dark and he heard the scraping thump of the door being barred from within, Galen slumped further onto the bench and tried to curl his protesting muscles against the cooling air. He did not worry about getting out of sight; he had nothing left to rob.

He slept poorly, alternately shivering and wincing against the pain it brought. He woke before the dawn was more than a grey hint, and he urinated against the tavern wall, as there were few to see and the thought of moving to find an alley was too daunting.

The street began to fill with morning laborers and vendors, and when the barman unbarred and opened the door and gave Galen a stern look that spoke clearly that he'd better not find him when he returned, Galen eased to his feet.

All of him was stiff and sore, and his face felt enormous and tender. He was so very thirsty. He remembered the sound of a fountain near the caravan staging ground, which was likely just around the corner. He knew the young woman hadn't brought him far.

He limped gingerly down the street, each step slow and aching. A driver shouted at him when he didn't move quickly enough out of a wagon's path, forcing the horses to check their pace. Galen wondered briefly whether Nathan and Maria's group was nearby, and whether the humiliation of their finding him would be worth the care and food they would undoubtedly give him, though he had taken so much already.

But he had no way of knowing where in the city they were, and Abbay was so huge and so loud. The hawking of vendors and morning greetings across the streets battered at his ears and aching head. He reached the far wall and followed it toward the staging ground.

There was a fountain, he saw gratefully, at the far end of the plaza. It was a simple pipe draining into a basin for stock, and after he'd limped toward it he cupped his hands beneath the pipe, pretending it would be cleaner than the pooled water below. He drank long, ignoring the stale taste, replenishing what was lost to the sweat and blood and swelling. When at last he was no longer thirsty, he drank a little more anyway, hoping to fill his stomach. There would be nothing else to put in it.

He sat behind the fountain, tucking his legs out of the way so horses could stop to drink as intended. He had to pull his knees to his chest with his bruised hands, as his abdomen wasn't up to the task yet. He leaned back against the wall and closed his eyes, listening to the growing bustle around him. Abbay was so loud when the city awoke...

He wasn't sure how long he had been there, half-asleep, when someone spoke to him. "Fair night, little cockerel, did you sleep here all night?"

Galen started and squinted up at the guard. "I—uh, no." He licked his split lips. "I stayed in front of the pub. Bench there."

The guard stared at him a moment, probably trying to decide if Galen was joking. "Serious, now, didn't you get in out of the dark?"

Galen shook his head, slowly so that it wouldn't hurt. "Nowhere to go."

The guard made an exasperated noise. "Fair night, boy. You're properly signed with Master Highgate, aren't you?"

"I am."

The guard put out a hand. "Then on your feet. Can't have you embarrassing us by lying about the staging ground. You'll scare off the customers like that." He pulled Galen to his feet, ignoring his wince. "I'm San, and I suppose I'm captain of a sort. Not my proper rank or anything, but I call marching orders for Highgate. However did you come here, little cockerel?"

Galen kept it short. "Need work."

"I can see that." San shook his head. "But if that's how you plan to defend Master Highgate's wagons, you—"

"No!" Galen blurted. "No, I can do better. I'm properly trained with a sword, I am. I just—yesterday—it was different." He kept his eyes on San's, trying to straighten and hold himself like he imagined a soldier rather than as the sore, hungry vagrant he was.

San made a tiny sound that certainly was not a laugh. "What say you come along and tell me about your training over some boiled oats? I've got a breakfast waiting for me, and I'm willing to wager they can scrape up an additional bowl."

Galen started to speak and then caught himself. He glanced down. "Yesterday... That was the last of my money."

"Yeah, I supposed as much when you made a deal to fight a bigger man for coin. Don't worry, oats are still cheap. You can pay me back with a story good enough to explain why you made such a bet and then stood like a sheep the first time he hit you."

Galen followed him through the street, thinking. He couldn't tell him the truth, of course—or could he? If the amulet didn't work, there was nothing to conceal, nothing to hide. It was supposed to protect the wearer from harm, and Galen had ample evidence over much of his body that it had done nothing of the sort.

They entered a little booth attached to the side of a bakery, looking like a builder's afterthought. San took a seat on a rough bench along one wall of the booth, gesturing for another patron to make room for Galen to sit beside him. "Oy, Harris! Two more!"

Galen looked around. Some customers were already eating from wooden or earthenware bowls, using chunky wooden spoons or their fingers. They seemed to be a mix of men and women, vendors and laborers and others who needed a quick or cheap meal in the morning. A half dozen seemed to know San well and were dressed similarly, even to the weapons at the hip. "Say," one said through a mouthful of meal, "ain't you the kid what got slapped around by Ned yester-midday?"

Galen's ears started growing warm. "If his name was Ned, then yes, I suppose I am."

"Go on! And you're still here? You have to tell us now what possessed you. I wouldn't throw down with Ned unless the girl was really, really pretty." He snorted a laugh.

A man in a smeared apron brought out two more bowls, and San traded him a couple of copper bits. "Thanks, Harris. And that's right, little cockerel, you've got to sing for your supper—or breakfast, as the case may be. Why did you come and tangle with Ned? What did Deputy Alfen have to pay on you?"

Galen accepted a bowl—stoneware, warm with the hot oatmeal inside—and said, "My family has a reward on me, he says. I left home a se'nnight ago, and I guess they want me back."

"But you don't want to go back." San scooped steaming meal into his mouth.

"They want me because it's planting time," Galen said, "and there's never quite enough hands to get all the work done. But now there's one less mouth to feed, too, so it should balance out, more or less."

"And you got tired of the work?" a woman in worn boots asked. She wore a short sword and two knives at her waist, and he could see the grip of a third protruding from her boot.

The question sounded friendly, but Galen wondered if there was more meaning behind it. Was the guard guessing whether he would shirk on the road with the caravan? Was this a test to determine if they would accept or despise him?

"My da died a couple of years ago," he said. "My uncles fight a lot. It's not a big house." He hoped that would be enough.

It was. She made a face. "See, that's what I was talking about the other day. You put too many people in a house, things go sour. Out on the road, you get to chafing about someone, you walk on the other side of the wagon and then you sleep up the line a bit, and things sort out. Packing folks into a house, it's just asking for trouble."

"So you gambled on beating Ned to buy your way off of Alfen," said the first guard. "But you didn't exactly look like you were ready for it. Don't you have fisticuffs out in the Heel, or are you country folk too busy poking the goats?"

"Hey," cautioned the woman, but the rest of them looked at Galen expectantly.

For a moment he wanted to tell them about the amulet, and about how he had been stupid enough to trust it, but... He ate some oatmeal to buy himself time, and then he said, eyes on his bowl, "I let myself get distracted."

"Oh? Were you eying that girl who came by to watch? The one who carried you out after?" He snorted. "Not a bad ploy I guess, if it worked, but there's easier ways to get laid."

"Hey!" This time the woman guard flicked a bit of oatmeal at the speaker. He grumbled and brushed it off, but he avoided looking at her.

"I didn't see her," Galen said. "Not until after." He hesitated, but they were all looking at him, waiting. He swallowed and decided on a half-truth. "I'd picked up a sort of charm. It was supposed to help me win a fight. It wasn't worth much, after all."

They laughed, loud and good-natured. "A charm? Fair night, boy, you really are from the Heel, aren't you?"

"Go lightly, Mackle, there's magic-sellers everywhere. There's probably such a charm for sale not two minutes' walk from here."

"Yes, but the only buyers are from out of town." The man called Mackle grinned, showing two broken teeth. "Mages and sorcerers tend to stay near the capital, where they can get paid more prettily. No reason for anyone with real magic to go out to the Heel."

"Yeah, well, I know that now." Galen gave them a chagrined smile. It was an easy story to swallow, the country bumpkin swindled in town, and no one asked further questions.

"But you can fight, when you're not hoping for a magical charm to save you?" The woman raised her eyebrows. "Or did you buy a charm for that, too?"

"No, I was trained with a sword," Galen said. He didn't mention the hand combat, not after his last demonstration. "In one of the temples out west."

"Really? One of the old schools?" Mackle nodded approvingly.

Galen decided to try a question of his own. "The people I met on the road, they said that bandits are a real problem to the east. Is that true?"

"True enough that Highgate's hired a whole company of guards," San answered. "He's not in for charity. He hires us because we're needed."

"What kind of bandits are they? We used to have the pirates and the great raids out in the Heel, but now it's just hill bandits. But they're bad enough; we lost a whole year of lambs and too many ewes to them once."

"I doubt it's anything like your hill bandits," said the man who'd had the oatmeal thrown at him. "These folk aren't after sheep, they want mercantile goods. They're properly armed, and not with pitchforks."

Galen frowned. "The hill bandits have swords and bows."

"You wait until you meet some real bandits out in the east with us. Swords, bows, axes, some sort of spear they call something I can't remember. And that's not counting the magicians."

I thought all the magicians were in the capital, Galen thought, but he kept it to himself.

"Oy, Perr, don't forget to tell him about the demons," laughed someone else. "If you're really trying to scare him off."

"That's right," said Perr, widening his eyes for dramatic effect. "Demons from over the mountains. They work strange magics and they can suck your soul right out any hole in your body, your eye or your mouth or your arse or any wound it pleases one to give you."

They all laughed, and now Galen joined them. "You'll have to work up a better story, sorry. I know they're not demons, not really. They're creatures of flesh and blood, just flesh and blood and something else, so they can do more and greater magic than we can."

Perr howled and slapped his leg. "Look at him! Thinking the Selks are real! Fair night, farm boy, no wonder you lost your money on charms."

Perr laughed alone, and for a moment none of the other guards spoke.

At last San, with a suppressed smile, said, "The joke's on you, Perr. What the little cockerel says is right. The Selks are real enough." He nodded approvingly toward Galen. "This country clod had some lessons between the sheep and the corn."

Perr looked around at them suspiciously. "You're just saying that to make me look a fool."

"That'd be a waste of effort, seeing as you do it yourself without help," said the woman. "Selks are in history books as well as tales."

"You never read a history book."

"Nope, but I bodyguarded a man who wrote one. Kept him safe while he went around and wrote up new things. I heard more than I ever cared to about the old wars."

Perr set his jaw. "Prove it. What were the Selks in the old wars?"

The woman nodded toward Galen. "Let's ask the clod."

The eyes turned to Galen again, and he cleared his throat self-consciously. "Uh, the Selks live beyond the Sung Range, in Mandoral. They can work great magic, but they are mortal and corporeal, though they're often called demons in tales."

Perr snorted. "You've said nothing that wasn't said already."

"In the old wars, Sayinia and Mandoral fought, and they were driven back beyond the mountains, where they have remained.

And..." Galen hesitated. The brothers had emphasized this last bit was the oldest of lore and the most suspect.

"Well, go on," prompted San.

"This is only legend," Galen hedged, "but the oldest stories say the Selks were once our allies against a common enemy."

The woman grinned. "Now that I don't believe." She scraped the last of her oatmeal from the bowl. "I can't think of much worse to fight than something more magical than a magician, and I can't imagine the Selks helping us. More likely they'd just take it all."

Galen shrugged. "I said it was just a story."

"Since you're not just a clod," said Mackle, "you got a name, boy?"

"Galen." This time he left off the latter part.

No one pressed for it. "Good to meet you, Galen," said Mackle, extending a hand. "Hope you'll have my back when we meet trouble."

CHAPTER 11

CARAVAN GUARD WORK WAS much less about fighting bandits, Galen realized, and much more about herding—mostly the people, but also even the actual little bunch of goats one of the caravan clients was taking with them. That was relatively simple, to Galen's farming mind; he helped the woman pick out a couple of influential goats and tethered them to the rear of a wagon, and then she had a long, thin reed to guide the others if they were distracted from following.

Herding the clients themselves was another matter. Galen was a farm boy, unused to crowds, and even market days had not prepared him for the sheer volume of bickering and jockeying for position in the line and insistence upon details, many of which couldn't possibly have mattered but for emphasizing the petitioner's own importance.

Galen hurried from place to place, fetching and carrying and agreeing to walk beside a particular merchant's goods. He was explaining to another that he'd already agreed to a place when

San's voice interrupted him with a stern, "You'll walk where I tell you, little cockerel, and nowhere else."

Galen glanced over his shoulder. "Right, sir. I only—"

"Get over there and help Mackle sort that potter, or nothing will arrive intact, the way he's stacking those crates."

Galen left the merchant to San and went to tuck crates more securely into the wagon's bed.

A few minutes later, San paused beside the wagon and beckoned to Galen. "Everyone's going to want something," he said quietly. "You can't please them all. If it isn't something you can grant yourself, like fetching or lifting for a moment, refer them to Master Highgate or myself. Don't make promises you can't keep, like guarding a particular wagon. We're all in this together."

"Yes, sir."

"And stop talking like a capital cadet. We're a caravan, for Fortuna's sake."

"Yes, sir." Galen grinned.

San laughed. "You'll be okay, little cockerel."

They pulled into formation and started out about midday, which was later than Master Highgate had wanted but about what he had predicted. They wound toward the nearest gate, caravan clients shouting at the other traffic that occasionally split the line and the other drivers and peddlers and vendors shouting back. Galen marked several new insults he hadn't heard back in the Heel and stored them away in case of future need.

Once they passed through the gates and struck the road, stone-paved this near the city, the wagons and walkers spread into a comfortable line, and Galen kept an easy pace in the position San had assigned him. He fell into conversation with the potter—an easily distracted man in his forties who had dubious tales of sculpting nude twin sisters from life for a nobleman's private collection, but who was generous with his dried fruit—and the rented sword rode easily on his hip as if it always had. The swelling in his face was easing and his bruises ached less with movement, and that night, he watched for just a couple of hours; the number of guards meant they had short watches, with occasional nights off.

I should thank Uncle Idorn, he thought. *And Uncle Parn. Without them, I never would have come here.*

He pushed the thought away guiltily. He had friends now, he thought, and even Ned had greeted him with a wry smile when they'd finally met again. But as much as he was enjoying his journey with the caravan, he had left his mother with them all. What if Parn and Idorn had turned on her once they realized the amulet was missing and her son had taken it? Would David and Locke have fought by now as well?

But his mother had *known.* She had known they had killed her husband, and she had done nothing.

Yet, what could she have done? Even Galen had simply fled. What more could she have done?

He shook his head. He had left it all behind, and there was no point to turning over old soil. What was done was done and could not be undone.

It was the fifth night, and Galen had no watch duty. He curled into his blanket, anxious for its insulation against the cool spring air, and dutifully left his sword within reach. He kept it scabbarded; mist or dew would rust it, and scraping it clean was a chore he didn't need.

He rolled beneath a wagon, pleased with his shelter from the condensing mist. It had not-quite-rained much of the afternoon and evening, and they were all wrapping themselves against the damp. Beside him Ned claimed another sheltered spot. He had forgiven Galen his knee, it seemed, and Galen suspected San had taken the guard aside and explained its lack of intent. Galen would never bring it up, however. Never.

He was thoroughly asleep when the attack came.

He awoke to people screaming and shouting for aid. Galen jerked upright and struck his head on the underside of the wagon. Cursing, he untwined his arm from the twisted blanket and felt for his sword.

A whistling hiss was the sole warning, a sound he remembered only afterward. Then a bright ball of flame dropped out of the sky and landed on another wagon he hadn't realized was so near beside them. It caught immediately, wood cracking and popping with the intense heat.

Horses screamed and the mules brayed, jerking at their tethers. Several goats ran past Galen as he crawled from beneath the wagon, one knocking into him and catching a horn on his arm. He pushed it away and it ran bleating after the others.

A woman was calling and gesturing for her children to hide in the wagon, and they were already crying as they climbed toward her. Galen wasn't sure if the wagon was any safer than in the open. He gripped his sword and turned, but there was no one to fight.

Another ball of flame dropped, this time striking just beside the tethered horses. They reared and threw themselves against their halters, and several of the ropes gave beneath the strength of their terror. Galen pressed himself close to the wagon as they bolted past him and into the darkness.

San was shouting somewhere near the head of the line. The edge of the road was burning, and smoke burned Galen's nose. The ground was wet, he recalled. *That must be some fire.*

He dashed from between the wagons and directly into the path of the next falling sphere of fire.

He froze like a rabbit, unable to decide which way to run, and it drenched him in a wave of searing heat. Flame dazzled his eyes and he wanted to scream in pure terror. But then the fire splattered across the ground, scattering little islands of flame, and he was still standing.

He pressed a hand to his face, testing the consistency of his flesh, but he was unscathed. His clothes, too, were unburned. He felt his jaw hanging stupidly. How?

"Galen!" San's voice was raw. "Get to the back and get the children together! Ned, Mackle, watch and find where they're coming from. If she can reach us with a flame, we can reach her with an arrow. Lina, get everyone against the center wagons. She won't want to roast the best goods if she can help it."

But the terrified merchants and travelers wanted only to escape. They paid the guards to defend their goods and lives, but depending on them looked less and less promising as fire rained from the night sky. The Fire Brigand did not want people, she wanted treasure, and they were inclined now to leave it to her.

The next explosion shattered their fragile control, and men, women, and children broke apart and ran for the scrubby growth at the side of the road. Some of the guards ran with them, though whether to protect them or flee with them Galen couldn't guess.

He came around the corner and stopped short. A body lay face-down before him, blackened beneath dancing flame. He stared, unable to breathe.

San's voice rose again, and it shook Galen from his trance. "Get cover!"

The wagon beside Galen seemed to explode into flame, and the heat struck him like a hammer blow. Galen gulped and ran into the dark, stumbling over the uneven ground and going forward onto his outstretched hand. He landed hard.

"Galen!" San's voice shouted. "Come back!"

Galen scrabbled forward, away from the voice, away from the burning and the screaming.

Galen crawled away through the scrub, panting and wheezing and trying to muffle the little sobs of terror that broke from him. When he could no longer see the wagons, he clawed to his feet and ran, stooped over and stumbling. He had no destination except away from the road.

She had destroyed them. She had rained fire and death upon them, and she had destroyed them.

Who had it been on the ground? He couldn't recall details of the face or clothing, only the stark fact of *burned to death*. Was it one of the merchants? A guard?

But Galen had not burned. Miraculously, the fire had rolled over him, bathing him in its heat but without harm. How was that possible?

He tripped and fell, sliding down a short slope he'd missed in the dark. He lay on his side, panting, and saw that the slope deepened into a little gully about a dozen paces further on.

She would never see him in there. He rolled upright and scrabbled toward it.

The night was cold, away from the fires. Galen drew his knees to his chest and shivered, still clutching his sword's grip as if someone would burst upon at him at any moment. But no one else came.

Gradually his fingers began to numb, and he set down the sword where he could reach it at need. He had his blade and flint with him, but he dared not risk flame, lest he draw her attention. What if... Would fire call to her, an element to its mistress? Could she feel it from afar? He knew almost nothing of magic. The brothers at the temple had told stories of it, but no one was left to teach practicalities. Galen knew only legends, and he had certainly never experienced it except for the conjured flames.

Except—the flames had not harmed him. Somehow, he had been preserved.

With slow wonder, he drew the amulet from beneath his un-singed shirt. Could it be? Could it be that the amulet preserved, not from all harm, but from dangerous magic?

That would make sense. It was a gift from magicians, who wielded magic against one another. It could not have helped him against the guard Ned, who had offered purely physical threat. But the fire, the magical conjured fire, had rolled over him like a wave and left him unburned.

If this were true, then the sorceress could not harm him. He stared at it, his mind working at the realization. And if she could not harm him, he could be the one to bring her down. He could avenge the caravan's fallen and win honor for himself. And he needed honor; he had fled, had run like a terrified rabbit, had not even thought of what he was doing. He couldn't return to San as he was now, without any explanation but his cowardice. But if he returned with the captive Fire Brigand, it would be different.

And surely there was a bounty for the Fire Brigand? He could gain wealth and renown, and he could make San proud of him.

He squeezed his fingers about the amulet until the twisted wires pressed grooves into his skin. How foolish of his uncles to argue over the thing when it was of no use to them, could never be of use to them. The Heel had not faced magical danger in generations. But now Galen, son of the Heel, could use it once more to make the world safer.

He replaced his sword. He got to his feet, bracing himself against the slope, and sniffed the air. He could not smell the smoke of the burning wagons; he must be below the prevailing wind. He listened, and he heard nothing. But now he knew he could move without fear, and he stood straight and began to climb out of the gully.

CHAPTER 12

HE FOUND HER TWO miles away. She was easy to locate, once he was looking, by her campfire. It was foolishly confident of her, but of course she expected no pursuit. And if anyone did come after her, she probably expected she would incinerate them.

She would be surprised.

Galen approached from above, looking down from the ravine wall that formed a windbreak for her and her fire. He had smelled smoke for the past mile, and as he watched, she fanned the branches and muttered at them, struggling to keep the damp wood alight. For a moment he thought he must have found the wrong person—surely the Fire Brigand wouldn't be bothered by damp wood—but no, she was wrapped in the same hooded cloak of dark red she'd worn when she'd taken Nathan's money. She must have exhausted herself in the attack, spent all her magic in destruction and left nothing for her own needs. So much the better.

Galen drew his sword. He observed for a moment as she coaxed another thin branch to life, sending more underlit smoke into the air. She was so evil, she had done so much harm, and yet it felt wrong to simply drop upon her from behind and above. But it would be folly to give a sorceress any advantage when he might have surprise. She had given no warning to her victims this night. He flexed his fingers upon the sword's grip and edged forward.

The brittle edge crunched beneath his weight and crumbled, dropping him down the windbreak wall. He pushed the sword away from him, lest he roll onto it, and tried to stop himself. He hit the base hard and skidded across dirt and scree. Almost before he had come to a halt, he blinked the stone dust from his eyes and looked around. Where was she? What was she doing?

She crouched across the fire where she had fled, presumably staring at him from beneath the dew-spotted shadowing hood. Her half-open mouth and one cheek were partially lit. She had raised her hands defensively, though he saw no weapon nor any flame other than the smoking pile between them. "Who are you?" she demanded, her voice strong but laced with alarm.

The voice was vaguely familiar. Could the sorceress have concealed herself within the caravan, to attack at her convenience?

"Murderer!" he snarled. Where was his sword? He did not dare to look away from her to search for it.

The hood shifted as she lifted her chin. She was shorter than he remembered from her first attack. "Murderer?" she repeated, and the fear was gone. "What are you—"

"You attacked us and you killed—"

"Wait a moment." She straightened and pointed at him, apparently unconcerned with his wrath and threat. "I know you, I think. Aren't you the one who... Yes, you gambled on a fight to pay off Deputy Alfen. Got your arse kicked halfway up your spine. What are you doing here?"

He stared at her, startled out of his rage, and then he recognized the curve of her cheek. "You. The one who paid the rest."

She nodded, pushing back the hood. "I am. And with all respect, it's sad gratitude to call me a murderer and leap at me in the night. A girl could take that poorly."

He opened his mouth and stopped, confused. "But—I thought—I came here because... Fair night, I thought you were the Fire Brigand."

Her mouth quirked into a mocking smile. "Well, that was stupid of you."

"No! That is, I know she's nearby. She just—she just destroyed a caravan. Half of it's afire, the rest is scattered. I don't know how many got away or how many she killed. I only just escaped. And she can't have gone far..." His voice faltered as he realized that she was listening without horror, without rushing to put out the smoking campfire that might draw an attack.

As he fell silent, her smile broadened. "And what did you think to do when you found her?"

Whatever humiliated gratitude he might have felt for her aid in Abbay vanished in his returning fury. "I'll avenge all of them! And I'll take your head to Abbay and give it to the deputy, and no one else will be troubled by you again!"

She cupped her hand, and little fingers of flame formed to dance in her palm. "Will you?"

He clenched his fists. "You cannot harm me."

Her expression flickered, and fresh alarm showed through the crack in her smile. "What?"

"You didn't expect to hear that, did you? But I'm invulnerable to your attack. I wear an amulet that protects me from all magical harm, which is how I survived your flames on the road below. I stood right in the center of your ball of fire, and it passed over me without so much as smoking my jacket. Your magic cannot touch me, and I—"

He stopped, because she had started to snicker. She looked down and away, covering her mouth, but her amusement grew until she was laughing openly, rocking with merriment and utterly heedless of his confused anger.

"What?" he demanded. He realized belatedly he should take advantage of her distraction to search for his sword, and he risked a glance away.

"An amulet?" she managed.

"It is one of the old—" He probably shouldn't tell her its provenance. "Yes, an amulet to protect me from magical harm."

"Oh, you foolish, foolish boy. I shouldn't, I really shouldn't, but I just have to see the look on your stupid face." She gasped for air and tried to sober herself enough to speak. "Your amulet, whatever you paid for it, didn't do anything to save you."

He looked back at her.

"The fire—that fire wasn't real. It's illusion."

He stared at her. "Don't lie to me, sorceress. I stood in the midst of your carnage. I saw the destruction you wrought."

She formed a ball of flame in her palm and passed her other hand through it. "See? No burns. It's not real fire."

"Well, of course it doesn't burn you. You're a sorceress. But I felt its heat, and I saw it burning—"

"Yes, you can see it, and yes, you can even feel it, because I am very, very good at illusions." She snorted. "Illusions. Not fire."

"You murderer! How many did you kill tonight, and you won't even acknowledge them as fallen?"

"I didn't kill anyone."

"I saw their burning bodies!"

"Who was it?" She looked steadily at him. "Who died tonight?"

Galen looked back at her, thinking of the black-stained corpse. But as before, he could not recall whose it had been.

"You can't remember, can you? You saw a body, but it wasn't anyone in particular, not that you can recall. Because it wasn't really anyone—just the idea of someone."

Galen's mind seemed to have stopped, and for a moment he couldn't formulate any response.

"I can make things appear to burn, but they're unharmed. See?" She tossed a small ball of fire into the jagged rock face, and it vanished without a smoky trace. She plucked the unburned end of a narrow stick from her weak fire and held it over the flames in her palm. The single leaf dangling in the flames shrank and crackled, but when she withdrew it from the heat, it had not so much as curled.

"Illusion," she said. "You all thought you saw dead comrades, but your greatest danger was from each other, flailing in the dark. I only made a pretty show and took what I wanted. No one was burned." A laugh bubbled up, breaking her cool explanation. "And so your good-luck token saved you only from imaginary fire." She snorted as she tried unsuccessfully to suppress her laughter. "Hope it didn't cost you too much."

Only his home and family, and all he had known.

She crossed her arms, still chuckling, signaling plainly that she considered his threat ended. Galen slumped, overwhelmed and bewildered. "Illusions," he said. "Why?"

"Why?" she repeated. "That should be evident. Why should I hurt anyone?" For the first time since his claim, her eyes narrowed on him. "Unless someone else means me harm."

He didn't move. "But don't they realize that you didn't actually... Doesn't anyone figure out that you're just using illusion?"

She shrugged. "I've worked hard to cultivate a certain advantageous reputation. Generally, groups either surrender and offer payment right off, which is easiest for all of us, or they try to mount some sort of defense, which is pretty easy to break. Then I try to push some guards one way, some another. Some of the fire is real, just enough, and in the end, people scatter. A few head to one town or another, so it takes a while to find who else survived the night, and sometimes unscrupulous characters take advantage of the chaos to do a little thieving and running of their own. By morning, some faces are missing, a chest is gone, a wagon or two are charred, a lot of ground is scorched, and my legend is secure."

"And what do you do with it?"

"My legend? Why, more and more people simply hand me a bag of money, no questions asked, no fiery display needed. No burning corpses, no tricky strategy, best for all around."

"So you're just a thief."

"In a word, yes." Her voice cooled. "Though you needn't take quite such a high tone. Deputy Alfen's bounty wasn't for your moralizing."

Galen sighed. "I'm a thief, too." He dropped to a rock and rested his chin in his hands, elbows on knees.

She looked at him and then sat down, facing slightly away. "What'd you steal?"

"The amulet."

She snorted. "The magical one?"

"It was already stolen. I just took it to keep anyone from getting killed over it. Again. But I took it." He shook his head. "All for nothing. It's a useless piece of junk."

She bobbed her head from side to side, considering. "The people you kept it from, they thought it was real?"

"Yeah."

"Real enough to hurt someone for, it sounds like?"

He nodded.

"Then it might be a worthless piece of junk, but you didn't take it for nothing. You were doing the right thing."

"The right thing," he repeated. "Which is why deputies are trying to arrest me, and why I'm sitting with the Fire Brigand."

"Can't say it always leads to adulation and honor." She looked ahead and gave a little harrumph. "Good intentions often don't work out, I think."

Galen's eyes fell on his sword, visible from his new vantage. It was perhaps two arms' reach away. He still could kill her—he might not have the protection of the amulet, but she wasn't so frightening, either. He could still capture her, bring her to Abbay.

But she wasn't a murderer, only a trickster and a thief. And just then, as he was disillusioned for the second time, nothing seemed worth the effort.

He sighed. "I should go," he said. "Sorry to bother you."

"Oh, half a moment." Her tone darkened. "I've told you things no one else knows. Why do you suppose that is? Do you think, now you know the Fire Brigand is a grand hoax, you can simply walk away?"

He stopped, halfway to his feet.

"You could break the legend of the Fire Brigand, and that would not only threaten my way of making a living but likely lead to my arrest and fairly horrid consequences. I can't just let you walk into the night and wait for your report to catch up with me."

Galen did not look at the sword, but his fingers flexed. He could have it before she could reach him, he was certain, even if she had a real weapon on her somewhere. "And you mean to stop me? With your false fire?"

Her mouth turned down. "I am a real sorceress, you know. I'm best at illusions, but it doesn't mean I have nothing else to hand." Her voice hardened. "I may not be able to burn out an entire caravan, but I certainly could ruin that shirt while you're inside it."

Suddenly the sword felt farther away. "So you think to kill me to protect your secret? And you said you weren't a murderer."

"Which of us came after the other with a bared weapon?" Her eyes remained fixed on him. "You've been dead since you announced you were here to kill me. I only wanted a laugh first."

"What do you want, then?" Galen spread his hands. "I can promise to keep your secret, to save my life, but you have no reason to believe me."

"I don't," she agreed. "You could make quite a name for yourself, bringing in the Fire Brigand. You could be famous."

"I don't want to be famous! Bounty on my head, remember? If my name gets out, my uncles find me, and that's the very last thing I want."

"Or you have enough reward money to pay off Deputy Alfen and his kind, and you lose yourself in the city."

"Are you trying to talk me into it? I'm not—look, if I turn you in, you'll turn me in. We can't afford to rat on each other."

"So quick to conclusions!" She crossed her arms again. "Tell me, what will happen if you go home?"

Galen swallowed. "If they don't kill me, I guess Uncle Parn will belt me until the leather wears out. And then Uncle Idorn will do the same with the buckle end."

She looked away at nothing in particular. "That's rough."

He didn't answer.

She stared into the small, smoky fire. "You said they might kill you. Was that a figure of speech?"

He was in the dark, with a stranger who didn't know him or his family and who had crimes of her own. If he couldn't say it aloud now, he never could. "They killed my da. For the amulet, after they stole it together. And they were going to kill each other, we all knew it."

"Fair night," she breathed, and it didn't sound like mockery. "So you stole it?"

"My mother's still there. I didn't want killing in the house."

"Boy, you really are the..." She cut off whatever word she had been going to say and finished, "That was brave."

He tried to make a little snort of dismissal, but his throat was closed and his breath short. "I don't feel brave when I think of going home."

There was a moment of quiet.

"But you know," she said abruptly, as if they'd been speaking all the while, "you don't have to go home."

He tried to laugh. "I don't seem to be doing very well for myself out here."

"But I am." Her lips curved. "You're a thief too, just as you said. If you wish to be a more successful one, you could come along with me. Both of us might benefit—my secret safe, because you couldn't betray me without betraying yourself as my partner. And you wouldn't have to worry about greedy deputies or a fireball down the back of your neck."

He stared at her. "You want me to go with you? Steal with you?"

She shrugged. "If you'd feel bad keeping the money, I'll be happy to take all for myself."

He sat down again. "I'm not really—that is, I only stole the amulet to—I don't want to rob anyone!"

She rolled her eyes. "Then don't. Go on to some cluster of dirt shacks like the ones you came from, show off your junk trinket, and find some ugly pigherd's ugly daughter and raise fat piggy babies. But you'd better hurry straight home, because if you turn toward any town large enough to boast a deputy, you won't have time even to wonder at that itch between your shoulder blades, much less explain that the Fire Brigand's a hoax."

"But—"

"And if word does somehow get out, and people who think an illusion can't hurt them try to come at me in earnest? Then I'll be forced to abandon illusion. And whatever the results, whoever dies then, that will be on your head. Right now it's a game of light and shadow, but if it turns serious and people get hurt, that will be your doing."

Galen stared at her. "You're a monster."

"I'm the Fire Brigand. And I'd rather not invent a new life again, so I must protect this one."

She was a brute. And yet for all her ferocious threats, she'd paid a bribe to save a stranger. And though she'd said she acted only from self-interest, it hadn't benefited her further to help him away, wash his face, buy him a beer. Even now, her safest action was to prevent him from talking, and instead she offered him escape. She talked far more cruelty than was in her, he thought.

"A farmer like me wouldn't be much of a help to you. You know I don't like what you do. And you would have to share supplies and additional risk. Why would you do that?"

She sighed impatiently. "First of all, because spoils are heavy. There's a coffer over there that I'd love for someone else to carry, and there's nothing like a strapping farm boy for that sort of thing. And then, if we must discuss it, I like to go into town periodically, and it's known the Fire Brigand is a lone woman so it's helpful to be seen with someone. And in certain cases the company of a man can help a young woman to dissuade the tactless. I can take care of myself, but that can attract attention. It's easier to use camouflage." She shrugged. "But I'm tired of finding new camouflage in each town, and sometimes the cure can be worse than the disease."

"That's it?"

"You seem like a pleasant enough fellow. Loyal, gutsy, and so funny, even if you don't mean to be. You amuse me. And I don't think you'll last long enough to become a bore." She laughed.

"But I don't want to be a thief—that is, not more of one."

"If you like, for your part, you could think of it as trying to reform me. Try to talk me out of robbing and scaring." She grinned. "But I'm not too worried about it. It'll give us both something to do."

"You mean, I'd try to convince you to use your power to help people instead of to rob them?"

She laughed aloud. "An itinerant sorceress doing good. I'd stop a great disaster and save a thousand lives." She shook her head, still laughing, and rubbed a smoke-irritated eye.

He still wasn't following her joking. "So, I'd just go along with you? Keep your secret because I'm your new partner?"

"Unless you have a better idea."

He did. He could go back to San and Master Highgate, apologize dearly for running, promise to make it up to them somehow. He hadn't been a coward, he'd been hit full-on with a fireball—well, he'd thought he had, anyway. But he hadn't run right away, and he wouldn't run again. He could explain.

She said nothing, sitting still, letting him consider. He thought perhaps the jokes and insults were her way of making the invitation a bit unreal, less serious, so that neither of them need feel awkward if it were refused. He thought she might really let him go.

"If I had nowhere else to go, I'd be glad of your offer, I suppose. But I have a paying position, and I need to get back to it."

She raised an eyebrow. "Sure you can?"

"What do you mean?"

"You came after me alone. Seems like an honest guard would have brought a few more along to help against someone like the Fire Brigand, even if you did think your trinket would work. But you came alone. Some might take that to mean you came to meet me, not to capture me." Her voice was level, pointed without being accusatory. "If you ran from the caravan during the bombardment, they might not be so happy to see you again."

"I'm not a coward!" Galen snapped.

"Never said you were," she answered calmly. "But you look awfully healthy for a man driven away from his duty by a fireball strike. Just for the sake of discussion, if you should be met with suspicion, and if you might find yourself in need of a way to quickly earn back favor, you might be tempted to explain how you survived the fireball that justified your flight, and that could be of very real concern to me. You do know my face."

He started to snap that she shouldn't have told him if she didn't want it known, but he bit back the words; her laughter had been better than her magic, if the amulet really was useless to protect him. She had not struck him down, though she might have—not at first, and then not once he knew her deceptions. He swallowed. "I won't say anything. At least, not about the illusions."

"You have no money, and you're desperate. Those can make a pretty strong argument for a man who knows a secret."

He shook his head. "You helped me when I needed it. And you didn't magic me into dust when I came after you. I owe you your secret."

She tipped her head to one side to regard him. "And why should I believe your bare promise?"

"Because you know I'm the kind of stupid, naïve fool who won't go back on his word."

She laughed aloud. "Now that, unfortunately, I do believe." She jerked her chin toward the darkness. "Go on then, farm boy. I trust you for today, at least. But find a new line of work, well away from caravans."

Arguing would only make her rethink her decision to let him go. He tested several salutations in his mind—*Fare well? Happy hunting? Good thieving?*—and in the end, he simply nodded toward her and turned away.

The little gully she'd hidden in ran downward toward the road, and he started down it, feeling his steps in the darkness away from her meager campfire. After a few dozen steps, he looked back, faintly worried that she might be targeting him from behind. But she was sitting by the fire, her arms crossed on her knees, her face bent into her arms, not even watching lest he return. It was a sad, lonely image, so different from his awed image of the Fire Brigand. But then she lifted her head, facing into the fire, and suddenly the melancholy was gone, a discarded misunderstanding, as she waited for her next victim.

She would have another victim, and he would say nothing to prevent it. Because she was right; if those who fought instead of delivering died to her true fire, that would be his doing.

He followed the gully in the darkness, his steps lit by the moon above as his eyes adjusted. She was wrong about San and the others; they would be glad to see him safely back. They would.

CHAPTER 13

THE CARAVAN WAS STILL on the road, wagons scattered and one overturned, but largely together. Some of their passengers were repacking goods in silence, their movements curt, while others lay wrapped in blankets, leaning against one another—not injured, as he'd thought at first, but sharing comfort.

He looked up the broken line, and he heard San's angry rumble giving orders from the third wagon. He started toward it, flexing his fingers and trying again in his mind the words he'd rehearsed since leaving the Fire Brigand. *I'm sorry—I had a close call, and I thought I was going to die. I ran. I'm sorry, I truly am. But then I thought to look for the Fire Brigand, I thought maybe I could sneak up on her from behind while she was focused on using her magic against the caravan, and when I didn't find her, I came back...*

"Thank Fortuna we have so few injured." San's voice became more clear from the other side of the half-loaded wagon. Crates were spilled around it. "It should have been much worse. I thought it was worse."

"We still missing anyone?"

"No, everyone's accounted for, since we found Mackle by the tail. Twisted ankle, but he'll be all right."

"You found Galen, then?"

Galen's head lifted as he heard his name.

But San's voice was dark. "I don't expect to find him. I saw him running, I called him, and he kept going. Boy ran like a goat, never looked back."

"Maybe he got hurt out there, same as Mackle?"

"I doubt it. You remember how he got in here with us? Slickest hustle I've seen, I'll give him that. And he's been well paid for it, between our wages and his share of the Fire Brigand's take."

Galen froze. How had she known? They thought—San thought he was a bandit? A plant among the caravan guards? But that wasn't—he would explain—

"Wasn't it Galen's idea to set the potter at the end of the line tonight? And the potter's sleeping with the jeweler, who's lost a whole coffer, just gone. Pretty clever, to set the potter at the end, knowing the jeweler wouldn't go there without her stock."

"No!" Galen burst. He pushed around the wagon, one hand trailing on the wooden slats. "No, that was Perr—I didn't tell the potter—I'm not a bandit!"

But San was already lunging toward him, snatching a handful of shirt which twisted snug about Galen's throat as San pulled him close. "Where were you? Where have you been?"

Galen gulped. "I—I ran. I'm sorry, there was a fireball, and I saw someone on the ground, and I—"

"You ran!"

"I'm sorry! I was scared. But then I thought I'd go to find the Fire Brigand, and I—"

"You thought to take her yourself? After you ran away from the fight?"

Galen shook his head. "I got hold of myself, and I thought...I thought my amulet would—"

"Your amulet?!" San's face twisted with incredulous outrage. "The same one you were fleeced for already?"

Galen had erred, blurting about the amulet. He couldn't explain now without betraying her, couldn't say he had gained false confidence in surviving the fireball without revealing he had never been in danger from it. He hesitated. "I thought her fire was—"

San cut him off by throwing him to the ground. Galen landed and rolled, flinching, ready for his uncle's fist.

But San only snapped, "Get out of here."

There were others nearby, other guards looking down at Galen, their eyes jumping from Galen to San. He didn't quite dare to glance at them, but he could feel their skepticism, could sense that none of them were stepping forward for him. They doubted him, too. "I didn't..."

He'd promised not to betray her secret, but he would give it up if he had to. If it would save him here, he would do it. She was a thief, and he was a guard.

"You're either a coward or a conspirator." San reached down, unbuckled Galen's sword belt with one hand, and jerked it free, rolling Galen a little with the force of it. "And we'll have neither with us. Get out."

"No, listen! I went to find her, I swear—"

"Shut up! We saw you run, and we won't believe your false heroics now. Get out!"

"San," said Lina. "Even if we're done with him, it's night, and we know there are bandits out there. Let him stay until morning, at least."

"So he can rob us again?" San demanded. "He was happy enough running into the dark when the Fire Brigand was beside the road, so—"

A whistling hiss made them all jerk around and scatter for shelter. Galen ducked his head into his arms as the ground a dozen paces away combusted, sending a spray of sparks over him. He unfolded and clawed to his feet, stumbling unevenly.

"She's coming to protect you, is that it?" Perr roared. "Saving her accomplice?"

Perr had a dagger in his hand as he advanced. Galen looked at it stupidly for an eternal heartbeat, not quite believing his fellow guard was about to knife him, and then another burst of flame exploded upward between them. Perr recoiled from the fire singeing his extended hand, as the flames danced protectively before Galen.

"Treacherous rat!" snarled San, coming around the wagon again, and Galen knew he would never be able to explain, not now with the fire dropping around him. He turned and ran, ran straight into the dark, and the shouts behind him changed as a wall of fire rose to block their pursuit.

His eyes, dazzled by the flames, could not adjust quickly enough to the moonlight. He stumbled over something and went down. He rolled and looked back, but no one was following.

"This way!"

A hand caught his upper arm and guided him up. He followed her to a tumble of rock behind a broken cleft. "You..." he started, but he didn't have the breath. *You betrayed me. You made them hate me. You trapped me into coming back to you.*

"Are you all right?" She glanced at him and then back toward the caravan, checking for danger. "That knife didn't reach you, did it?"

She had been watching. She had seen San seize him, throw him, disarm him.

He dropped his face into his hands, unable to shout at her. "No, I'm not hurt."

Satisfied no one was coming after them for the moment, she stepped back and knelt beside him. "I was afraid they might not understand why you were away so long. Guards can be suspicious sorts."

He shook his head. He had liked San, had liked the others, had been glad of the respect he was earning along with the wages he owed for his sword and advance. He'd only wanted to explain...

She was looking at him. "Are you sure you're all right?"

"I just lost my job," he said. "My only job, with the only people I knew. Give me a moment."

Her mouth tightened, and she stood and turned away.

He never should have mentioned the amulet. There was no way he could explain, even if he hadn't promised to keep her illusions secret. He couldn't expect San to think that he'd started to believe in the amulet again, it was so stupid after what had happened in Abbay, and so San had supposed Galen was lying to him, and how could Galen fault him for being angry that one of his guards had fled and then lied?

He never should have mentioned the amulet. He never should have kept the thing after Abbay, not once he knew its worthlessness. Only habit and nostalgia had held it, only the not-quite-faded urgency of carrying it safely away.

He fingered the chain of the amulet and then drew it out from his shirt, rubbing it between his fingers.

She yawned and stretched her neck. "That took some doing," she said with a hint of smugness. "I used real fire, because I didn't want anyone getting through to us. But I had to be pretty particular about placement, with everyone so close together. Art, I tell you." She gave him a lopsided grin. "Poetry."

Was everything a joke to her? But then, everything was a joke, after all. He'd lost his family for a false amulet and his job for false fire.

The amulet's eye felt smooth and cold in the dark.

"What are you doing?" she asked, half turning.

He licked his lips. "My father died for this. My uncles were going to kill again for this. I stole it, to protect my mother and my aunts and my stupid brother and my stupid, stupid cousins, though they'd kill me for it, or make me wish they had." He blew out his breath in a despairing emptiness. "And it's nothing. A useless bauble." He swallowed. "I guess maybe it wasn't this that caused the trouble, anyway. They would have found something else to fight over."

She was silent, but it wasn't an indifferent silence. She looked at the ground near his feet, listening.

He sighed again and started to draw the chain over his head. "I suppose I should throw this away."

"No." Her voice surprised him. It had none of the laughter or self-satisfaction of a moment ago. "No, you gave a lot for that. You sacrificed everything for your family. What you paid for it makes it worth something. Even if it wasn't as important as you thought...you should keep it. It represents who you are, now."

He looked at her. "I'm a useless trinket who only makes trouble for everyone?"

Her eyebrows rose and she started to protest, and then she caught herself. "Now you're playing dumb with me."

He nodded a confession, trying to smile. His face felt heavy.

Her expression softened. "Don't toy with me, farm boy. You know not what you may provoke. Do you have a name?"

"Galen. Galen Heelsbottom."

She snorted. "I thought I told you not to toy with me!" She waited a moment, and then her eyes widened in slow understanding. "Wait—do you mean that's your real name?"

"That's my real name."

"Fair night, farm boy, how does anyone come by a name like Heelsbottom?"

"Our farm is in the Heel, which is a spur of land near the coast, and it's...near the bottom."

"I see." She gave him a level look. "As I understand it, there's a bounty out for Galen Heelsbottom. Now I know something about bounties, and it's best not to use a name with one tied to it. 'Galen' is not so bad on its own, so you can keep that if you're attached to it. But we'd better find you something else to use along with it." She adjusted a pack beneath her cloak.

He blinked. "I don't have any idea."

"We'll work on it as we walk. If, that is, we're walking." She raised her eyebrows.

He realized he was hardly debating it. He didn't have many other options, not with an empty purse and a price on his head and his caravan master thinking he was a bandit himself. "For a while," he said. "At least until I can reform you into giving up stealing."

She snorted.

A Clash of Flames

Sayinia

CHAPTER 14

FIRE FLARED BETWEEN LISVETH and Ember, facing one another. "You can't be," Ember breathed, with more angry denial than disbelief.

Lisveth grinned. "But I am."

A scarred man ran in from the side, knife drawn. This was Ember's lieutenant, Galen guessed, ready to stab his boss's opponent for her. Galen drew his sword but could not intercept him, and he shouted as he ran.

Lisveth half turned and shoved at the new attacker even as he was a half dozen paces away, and he staggered back as if kicked in the chest by a mule. Lisveth spun back but Ember had seized her distraction.

Lisveth cried out and went down, rolling as she clutched at her arm. She gritted her teeth and rocked upward again, but she would never be quick enough.

Ember cupped her hands at her chest, cradling the blossoming energy, preparing to fling a ball of raw flame directly toward the grounded Lisveth.

Galen leaped at her and into the attack, his arms braced before him as if somehow he could block the combustive power of the fire strike. Heat burst around him like a wave crashing upon a rock, and the expanding air roared over him. Galen's skin seemed to crackle and then he felt nothing, his nerves burned away. His momentum carried him forward into Ember, and with a final desperate effort he stabbed upward and cut to the right, dragging her body as the blade struck bone.

Heat seared through his sword and into his hand, and he dropped it more by reflex than intent. The fire receded, flames licking about his limbs, and he and Ember fell together to the ground.

The air burst from his lungs as he landed, making a little grunt of pain. He wished he'd been silent. He wished he'd fallen dead, a much more striking scene than lingering in agony. He looked at Ember, her chest open. At least he had stopped the Fire Brigand, at least he had saved Lisveth.

He tried to lift his head, tried to see her. Was she all right? Had he indeed protected her?

Ember's mouth worked, but without sound. She died, but there was no rasping exhalation; her lungs emptied through the rift Galen had opened in her chest. Around them, Galen heard shouting.

Galen closed his eyes.

"Get up, you play-actor." Lisveth's voice cut through the others'. "Get away from that body."

Galen opened his eyes and saw her kneeling nearby. He felt a brief flash of anger that she couldn't just let him die in peace, even after he'd sacrificed himself to save her life, and then he regretted wasting his final moment in anger. Then he wondered why his final thoughts seemed so multifaceted and focused. Was this the clarity of mind that came with death?

"Can you hear me? Maybe that rattled your ears. I'd help you up, but I'm a bit useless at the moment. Stand up?"

He would have thought sound would grow less clear in dying, but Lisveth's voice seemed steady after the fading roar of the flames. Galen got his hands under his torso—they didn't seem to be burned, not like he expected—and pushed himself upright.

"There you go. Are you all right? You look a bit dazed."

Galen blinked at her. "I—am I all right?"

Lisveth looked him over. "You seem well enough."

"Didn't—didn't she burn me?"

"She tried," Lisveth answered, cradling one arm. "Or it looked like it, anyway. But I guess she wasn't very serious about it, if she used an illusion. Because trust me, if that had been a serious strike, you wouldn't be asking about its effects."

Galen looked down again at his hands. They were intact. "She used an illusion? But—why?"

"That's a good question." Lisveth sounded uncertain. "Especially considering she was more intentional with me." She shrugged. "Maybe she liked you. Maybe she didn't expect you to jump into her and was just trying to scare you off."

"That doesn't make any sense," Galen protested. He was starting to shake, which disturbed him. It was his nearest experience with death, and he hadn't even been near death.

"It makes more sense than you taking a real fireball to the face and coming out with just a sooty smear," countered Lisveth. "She was a conflicted murderer. She doesn't have to make sense." She looked down at the streaky-haired corpse. "I feel like I should cut off an ear or something to take for the bounty. We killed the Fire Brigand, the new one. That should be worth a tidy bonus." She adjusted her grip on her seared arm. "Now let's find Andrea and get out of here."

Galen got to his feet and found his knees were not as reliable as he was accustomed to think of them. "Lisveth," he said. "Was that really an illusion? Did I—did I just survive a fireball, or did I just kill a woman who was using illusions?"

"Hey." Lisveth's voice went sharp and cold. "Whatever she might have used on you, she was not throwing only illusions. This is my own blood I'm trying to hold in, and she did that. There's a dozen dead bodies in what's left of that caravan, and you heard her brag on that yourself. And that's just tonight. You know what she's done before."

Galen heard her words, but they seemed to swirl in his mind. He couldn't disagree with her, but it was too soon to agree, either.

"I don't know why she did something else at that last moment—but don't let her trick you into feeling guilty. She tortured people for money, Galen."

He nodded. "Right. I know. Right."

"Now, let's find this Andrea again. With any luck, she won't be too spooked of us to consider sharing the road home."

CHAPTER 15

ANDREA WAS NOWHERE TO be found.

None of the bandits were anywhere to be seen, in fact. Lisveth, still holding her arm, swore quietly. "Did we frighten them all so terribly? Some bandits, to run off when a couple of travelers take on their fire mage. Really, how did they expect to have any kind of reputation?"

"It was all hers," Galen said reasonably, "and it wasn't just a couple of travelers. You lobbed a few detonations of your own, as I recall."

"Those were in self-defense," Lisveth said righteously.

Galen held up his hands in resignation.

Lisveth stopped walking. "Do you see anything? Anything at all?"

Galen angled away and walked along the powdery dirt at the edge of the road. There were plenty of prints, faintly visible in the moonlight, but tracking away from the road was impossible as the crushed particulate gave way to rocks and intermittent scrubby growth. There simply wasn't enough vegetation or dirt to take sign, at least not that his eyes could read and certainly not in the dark.

Lisveth closed her eyes and took a long, slow breath. Galen recognized the prelude and stopped walking, holding his arms slightly away to avoid brushing any of his gear. Lisveth exhaled, just as slowly, and turned quietly in a sunwise circle, her toes pointing outward to all the points of the compass.

Galen held his breath for as long as he could, and then he began drawing it softly through his open mouth, trying to make as little noise as possible.

Lisveth continued her circle, casting her seeking magic over itself so that it spiraled outward. She completed five full rotations and stopped, her eyes still closed, looking as if she were listening to unseen music. Then she reversed her slow spin, turning once anti-sunwise, and stood still again.

Her eyes popped open. "Wow. There was quite a lot of movement; seems they scattered in a hurry. And do you remember how many there were?"

Galen frowned. "I thought perhaps a dozen."

"That was my recollection too, but now I have an impression of maybe twice that."

Galen shrugged. "Someone else came along?"

"And they all ran off together? That hardly makes sense." She indicated a direction with a nod of her head, her hand still clamped over her arm. "There's someone that way. Just one. We can ask where all the others went."

Lisveth's magic spoke the truth. They cleared the ridge she had pointed out and found a fallen bandit on the far side. It was the man who had threatened Galen with the knife, and he was bleeding hard from a leg wound.

He was trying to suppress the flow of blood with his hands, but the angle was difficult and the wound deep. Lisveth dropped to the ground beside him and pressed her good hand over his. "What happened?"

An abrasion marked the side of his head, from a blow or where he had fallen, and there were several less serious cuts on his left arm. He looked at them, his eyes wide. "You? Did you—where's Ember?"

Galen knelt and drove the heel of his hand into the thigh's soft blood vessels above the wound. "Ember's not with us," he said evasively. "What happened to you? Did the caravan guards return?"

The man stared at him in disbelief. "You think that was guards? You think they could do that to us?"

Galen shook his head, confused. "We've seen only you. What happened?"

The man's face was pale, and the blood, though slowed by Galen's pressure, kept coming. "The demons," he panted. "The demons. They found us."

Lisveth's face betrayed only the faintest incredulity. "You were attacked by demons?" She paused. "Is that the name of a rival bandit gang?"

"You stupid git," he answered in breathless irritation. "I said demons. From over the mountains. They're real." He paused to draw more breath. "We've seen them before, or their work. Looted some of what they left behind. Hadn't met them." He gasped again. "Wish we still hadn't."

"Let me take your belt." Galen shook off the various weapons and accouterments strung from it and snugged it above the wound, making him hiss and flinch. "Where are the others?"

The man shook his head. "Don't know. We all ran. Some of us together, but it didn't do any good." He swallowed and panted. "They didn't want the loot. Gerald opened a coffer, showed them the money and jewelry. They stepped up to it and cut his neck half through."

"Where's Andrea?" said Lisveth. "What happened to Andrea?"

"From over the mountains," he repeated. His eyes wandered, less focused. "We've seen what they've done."

"I don't care about your demons," she snapped. "Where's the girl Andrea?"

He looked past her, beyond her shoulder. "Andrea? I don't know. I saw her run. We all ran. I didn't see where they went."

Galen pulled harder on the belt, but the wound was too deep and too much blood had been lost already.

The man looked directly at Lisveth, fixed his eyes on her. "They're real," he said urgently. "The demons are real."

They put him in a shallow grave, more of a depression, over which Galen piled rocks to hold off the less-determined scavengers. Lisveth stood by, cradling her wounded arm. "Sorry I can't be more help."

"It's all right." Galen rolled a rock down the incline to join the growing heap. "You can keep an eye open for those raiders returning."

"Demon raiders," she repeated. "He seemed pretty insistent on that. He didn't seem—what's the word? He wasn't having delusions near the end. He was distracted, and he was unfocused, but he wasn't imagining things, don't you think?"

"Something put that hole in his leg," Galen said practically.

"He didn't have to say it was a demon. Or that it came from over the mountain." She gnawed at her lip. "You don't suppose the Selks really are coming over the range?"

"That's not supposed to be possible." Galen wedged two stones together. "You know, the magicians and the charms, and the fact that the Selks haven't been seen in a couple of centuries."

"Those men in the public house said there had been raids. This man saw the raiders and said they were demons. What if something really is coming over the mountains?"

Galen paused and propped one foot on a small boulder, breathing hard. "When I came to Abbay, some people laughed at me for believing the stories about the Selks. Said they were superstitions of country bumpkins, memories of an old war turned to bogeymen."

She eyed him. "You don't sound very convinced."

"I don't think the temple brothers would teach us superstitions. They had histories, and they had relics of war. And the stories had to come from somewhere."

Lisveth nodded. "Right." She straightened. "Whatever they are, they're killing people on the road, and I suppose we ought to try and tell someone, then. Though I suspect we'll sound like those old jabberpots in the pub. It's not like we've even seen them ourselves."

"I'm not unhappy about that." Galen glanced pointedly at the poor grave.

"And we need to find where everybody went, and find Andrea. If she's not dead, we still have to take her back—and if she is dead, we owe her father the truth about it." Lisveth sighed. "Got your things again? Are we ready?"

"Easy for you," Galen grumbled, taking up the pack he'd dropped to move the rocks. "Where are we going to look for Andrea? You can't do the magic again. You don't look well."

"I'm fine," said Lisveth stubbornly.

"You look rather less than fine."

"You're a rude farm boy," she returned. "I'll be fine once we reach a proper inn with proper food and a proper bed. And I'll have those things sooner if we find Andrea sooner."

"She'll be on the road, if she's clever," Galen said. "The demons, if they are demons, haven't been seen often. Not often enough to be more than wild rumor. So they aren't using the Octovirate's roads much. The bandits had seen their work, but they stay off the road as well. So the road is likely to be a safer place if one stays to the well-traveled stretches."

Lisveth nodded approvingly. "And now we hope Andrea, or whoever she's with, had the sense to work that out as neatly as you did."

CHAPTER 16

THEY COULDN'T GUESS WHETHER Andrea in her panic, if she sought the road at all, would have run north or south. Galen, noting how Lisveth swayed on her feet, suggested south, where the next inn was nearer.

They encountered no one living on the road, but a woman lay dead fifty paces from the western edge. She had been cut down from behind and left where she dropped. Galen glanced at the deepening sky and said he would return later with men from the village to collect the body. Lisveth did not argue.

Darkness fell, and neither of them mentioned it. Lisveth's stumbling steps came as quickly as she could manage, and Galen stayed within an arm's length in case she fell. They pressed on, hearts pounding, afraid of the dark.

They reached the crossroads town, and Galen practically ran ahead to the inn door. He held it open for Lisveth, shouted over the boisterous conversation for the landlord, and started to push a gaping tanner aside to make room for Lisveth at a table.

But she shook her head. "Over there," she said.

Galen followed her gaze and saw Andrea in the corner, arms folded tightly, curled into a chair with her back to the wall. "She made it," he said, and he heard a greater note of relief in his voice than he'd expected.

Andrea did not look up at their approach. She was rocking slightly, her eyes on her lap, and a bowl of soup sat full on the table beside her. Lisveth took the empty chair nearest her, leaning against the back and arm, and Galen sat on the opposite bench where he could face them both.

The landlord followed them almost immediately. "Fair night, what happened to you? It's been a rough time out there, no mistake. Here's some ales. I'll bring the physician—he's in the next room, playing table dice. He can see to that arm."

Lisveth made a vague protest, but the landlord ignored it. He picked up the first ale and held it out to Lisveth's good hand. "Here, have something. You need some liquid in you."

Andrea looked up, and her eyes jumped between them, wide and half-panicked. "You! It's you!"

"Just us," said Lisveth in an easy tone, somehow smoother than the voice she'd used a moment before. "Just us."

"Where's—where's Ember? Where's everyone?"

"The raiders scattered everyone," Lisveth said. "We know two are dead. I don't know their names. I'm sorry."

"We didn't see them," Galen said tentatively. "One of the men—he said they were demons. But we didn't see them. Can you tell us about them?"

She stared at him. "Demons," she repeated, and he couldn't tell if she was repeating in confusion or confirming.

"Did you see them?" Lisveth asked. "Andrea, this is important. If there are—if demons are coming over the mountain, we have to warn...someone." She looked momentarily perplexed, and Galen reflected that there was no established protocol for reporting demon invaders. Organizing the townsfolk with pitchforks seemed both unlikely and ineffectual.

"You didn't see them?" Andrea stared at Lisveth, and then she looked down at the wounded arm. "You didn't see them?"

"Ember did this," Lisveth said. "Not the raiders. We didn't see what the raiders looked like."

"They were demons," Andrea whispered.

Galen had to ask. "How do you know?"

Her eyes fixed on Lisveth's face, as if he hadn't spoken, but she answered. "They were ugly twisted things. Pointed ears, pinched faces. Human shapes, but not human." She looked at Lisveth's arm again. "Is Ember..."

"She died," Lisveth said simply.

Andrea began to cry. "I'm so sorry. I don't know... I didn't even like her. That is, of course I liked her, but... She was a mean, brutish person, and I'm crying for her, and now I'm speaking ill of the dead." She rubbed her nose on her sleeve.

"It's not wrong to mourn a death," Lisveth said simply. "Nor wrong to speak honestly."

The landlord returned, leading a man with eyebrows drawn low in concern. "This is Francis," he said, "and he can look after your arm. And I see we'll need more ales." He looked significantly at Andrea, and then he caught Galen's eye.

"She ran into some of the same trouble we did," Galen said obliquely.

The landlord nodded. "I expect the sheriff in later tonight. I'll send her this way when she comes."

Galen nodded. Well, now they had a limited time in which to organize their story of demons.

"They killed Evan," Andrea said. "We were running, and they caught him. I made the road and kept running, but I could hear... They killed him."

"And then you came here?"

"I ran until I saw the lights, and then I thought if I could just make it... I wanted the fire, and the noise, and whatever would keep them out. Demons can't come into a house, right? They can't come into a place with a hearth and lots of people?"

Galen had no idea if that was true, but if it reassured Andrea, there likely was no harm to it. Telling her there was no safety would not make her any more safe. "I haven't heard of it happening."

"Are there any traditional blocks for a demon approaching a public house?"

The new voice was familiar, and Galen turned his head as Kayvin, the handsome man with the dark red hair, took a seat on the end of the bench. Galen regarded him with surprise and a hint of apprehension; would Kayvin remember his curt attitude of their last meeting?

"Not that I've heard of," Lisveth admitted. "But Andrea, I can't see them coming here. Even a bandit party wouldn't attack the inn; it's far too visible for not enough profit. Sure, you might rob a dozen patrons of their drinking money, but then you have to get safely away before the whole mob's after you with their friends. Or you have to take hostages, and that's a lot of complications that probably aren't worth it. Easier to rob and run on the open highway."

"The demons aren't interested in hostages," Andrea said dully. "Or money. They didn't ask Evan for anything, and they didn't search his bag after—after. They just wanted to kill us."

"That doesn't make any sense," said Lisveth firmly. "There's no point in that. It's dangerous to kill people on the road, even ones running away from you. You scare people badly enough, they might fight back. And most simply put, there's no profit in killing without reason, so don't bother, really."

"But—"

"But you were frightened, and it felt to you like they meant to kill you. And maybe they did. But just because they didn't stop to loot Evan's body doesn't mean they weren't coming back to it. You had a scare, and a very reasonable scare, but... Killing for fun simply makes no sense. Killing armed bandits for fun makes even less."

Kayvin frowned but said nothing.

Andrea bit her lip. "I wish I'd never joined the gang. I wish I'd never found Ember. I wish..."

Lisveth made the words very gentle. "Would you like to go home?"

Andrea hesitated and then nodded. "If—if you say my father... Yes, I think so. I think I do."

"I think," Lisveth answered, "he would be thrilled to see you again."

"You're sure they were demons?" asked Kayvin.

Lisveth cast him a baleful look, and he flinched.

"What do we tell the sheriff?" Galen didn't want to renew the topic, either, but the question was practical and imminent.

"They were demons," Andrea said stubbornly. "I'm not crazy, and I wasn't seeing things because I was frightened. They were demons."

"Then that's what we'll tell her," Lisveth said firmly.

CHAPTER 17

THE SHERIFF WAS A tall woman with warm amber skin and a concerned expression. She took a look at Andrea, sipping at her cooling soup, and immediately led them all into one of the back rooms. "Now with a little privacy," she said, "tell me what's going on."

Andrea swallowed visibly. "Er," she started, "this is..."

Lisveth grasped the difficulty first. "Andrea was with the Fire Brigand's gang," she said. "We rescued her this evening when we fought the bandits."

Andrea looked at her sharply and then understood. If she'd been rescued, she hadn't been one of them. "That's...that's right."

"And we all were separated during the fighting, and—"

"Hold on," said Sheriff Algwire. "You fought the Fire Brigand?"

"What? Oh, yes," answered Lisveth, as if it were a mundane chore she did every day. "She's dead. That was our doing. But the other dead bandits, that's the raiders Andrea saw."

"You can't just casually drop that you killed the Fire Brigand, like it's no great thing," said the sheriff.

"Well then, it's a great thing, and we expect to be paid for it. I'm sure there's a bounty." Lisveth smiled briefly. "But you had better hear what Andrea has to say about the raiders."

"Demons," she said. "They were demons."

The sheriff stopped staring at Lisveth and stared at Andrea. "Demons," she repeated.

Andrea explained in halting words, slowed partly by distress and partly by her attempt to conceal why she was fleeing with the bandits, how she had run from Lisveth's and Galen's fight with Ember and been set upon by raiders. "They weren't human," she insisted. "They looked sort of human, but they weren't. Their faces were wrong, too skinny, and they had pointed ears."

"What kind of weapons did they use? Were they armored?"

Andrea chewed her lip. "One had a sword. I think another had an axe. I don't know what the others had. I don't know about their armor, I didn't take the time to notice."

"How many of them were there?"

"I—I only saw three. But we could hear more around us. They were chasing and killing the others."

"We found two bandits on the way here," Galen confirmed. "One was still alive and told a similar story before he died. The other was dead on the road, some distance away."

"I see." The sheriff scratched at her neck and glanced toward the door. "And what's your business in this? Did you fight the bandits too?"

Galen followed her gaze to find Kayvin leaning beside the door. He hadn't even noticed the man following. "Me?" Kayvin shook his head. "It's only my business insomuch as if there are demons invading over the mountains, I want to know all about it."

"That's hardly a reason to come gawking, and if it turns out to be the case, that's the kind of news that gets shared. Get out." Sheriff Algwire turned back to Andrea. "Well, Miss Lawson, I'll need you to file testimony against the bandits, for whatever of them we round up. And against these raiders too, for when we get a handle on them. But tonight, I think you should try to rest. It's clearly been quite a day for you."

She nodded.

"You can wait in this room; I'll speak to Hankel about a good rate, and then he'll show you to a place to sleep. And I'll come in the morning to take down your official statements." She nodded politely to her and then gestured the others out ahead of her, closing the door for Andrea's privacy.

They settled at the table they had left, with fresh drinks and hot soup. Kayvin, chastened, sat a few feet away. The sheriff frowned and sighed. "She was with the bandits, wasn't she? One of them, I mean."

Asked directly, Lisveth nodded. "Runaway. Her father asked us to find her. For what it's worth, I think she got caught up in something she didn't want."

"That's how it starts for most of them. Doesn't change how it ends for most of them." She rubbed an eyebrow. "And did you really kill the Fire Brigand?"

"No," said Lisveth. "He killed her." She nodded toward Galen. "But I helped. We can tell you where to find her."

Sheriff Algwire looked at Galen. "Well. That was a bit of work, I suppose. And yes, as you said, there is a bounty. Have to go north to get it, but if your story checks out, I'll sign off on it." She ran a thumb along her chin. "And the raiders?"

"Just as we said, we didn't see them, just found their work."

"And do you believe her?" The sheriff thumbed toward the back room.

"I'm not certain I believe everything she says," Lisveth said. "That is, I don't think she's lying. I think she believes it. But demon raiders? That's going to take more evidence than the blurry report of a frightened girl."

"Someone killed those bandits tonight," Galen said.

"You killed a bandit tonight," Lisveth pointed out. "That doesn't make you a demon."

"Strictly speaking, they're not demons," he said. "They're Selks. They live over the mountains."

"And they've crossed the range again, after centuries, just to off some bandits? Doubtful."

Kayvin stirred and spoke at last. "How would you know? If they were Selks or humans?"

"Surely there's a way to recognize them," the sheriff said. "I mean, demons or Selks or what they may be, they'd look different, right? Don't they have horns or scales or pointed ears or something? Fangs?"

"Fangs would be hard to identify in a running fight," Kayvin said practically. "Anyone concentrating too closely on an opponent's dentition isn't going to survive to report it."

Galen tried to remember his lessons at the temple. There had been a few illustrations, but they were obviously stylized, showing narrow, twisted faces with fangs and pointed ears, or nearly human figures distinguished by their position facing west from the mountains. At least, it was supposed the artists meant the westward figures to portray Selks.

The oldest tales spoke often of them, but with some dramatic license. This confusion was not helped, Brother Toller insisted, when lazy translators simply called them "demons." They were properly called Selks, which the more conscientious scholars usually translated as "the Not-Human," or "the Others."

"I think they're most likely a rival set of bandits." Lisveth looked at the sheriff. "And I wonder if there's a bounty on them."

Sheriff Algwire frowned. "Is that a proposition?"

Lisveth nodded toward Galen. "We ended the Fire Brigand tonight. I think we could be talked into tracking these down."

Galen looked at her. "You're not usually..." He let the words trail off. *You're not usually keen on killing.*

She seemed to understand him. "I don't mean we have to slaughter them, of course. We could take their leader, or just scare them and run them off to be somebody else's problem."

The sheriff considered. "You didn't introduce yourselves properly, I see. We don't generally have many mercenaries coming through here. Most of the lords who hire your kind are further north and west."

"There's no call to pass up good money when it's available. And clearly we can do the work."

"Do it, then." Sheriff Algwire nodded. "Hunt them down, and do what you need to do. I'm just one person, and even if I had backup from the town, no one here is trained for a professional fight. Make the road safe for us."

CHAPTER 18

"ARE YOU SURE YOU can do this?"

Lisveth rolled her eyes. "I have a damaged arm, salved and wrapped. It's not like I'm crippled. And I don't need to be able to handle a sword."

"No, but you use your hands for magic."

"That's a focus technique. It's not strictly necessary for the magic itself."

Galen gave her a skeptical look. "And what happens if you can't use your hands to focus?"

Lisveth twisted her mouth. "Don't stand too close to the target, okay?"

Galen shook his head. "I don't think we should be doing this."

"It's perfect this way," Lisveth said. "I'm a helpless woman walking the Octovirate's road alone—if that doesn't bring out the bad guys, what will?"

"It's not the bringing them out that's the tricky bit. I'm the last person to doubt you, but you took a pretty hard hit from that Ember woman. And these won't be single assailants. They'll probably ambush you, and we know they don't waste time in threats or negotiation."

"Then we'll have to pay attention," Lisveth said, "instead of arguing about whether or not we'll be ready."

Galen rolled his eyes. "Fine."

He followed her at a distance, walking in the dark and feeling for each step on the road. A light would betray him to whoever was watching the road. Lisveth, alone on the road with a torch to light her way, was simple to see and easy to target. It was nearly irresistible bait.

For a long while, however, the raiders or demons seemed to be resisting it. No one appeared, no spell came out of the darkness, no one shouted an order to stand and deliver. Galen thought he heard occasional sounds from the sides of the road, but he couldn't be sure if they were thieves, small night creatures, or his own imagination. He tried to walk silently, not wanting to betray his own presence, but he was afraid of letting Lisveth get too far ahead of him.

If he had not been listening so hard, he would not have heard the footsteps that nearly matched his own. But they could not keep perfect time with his irregular step, and Galen's heart began to race as he realized someone was behind him.

If he were still a caravan guard, he could just turn and warn the thief off. But their purpose tonight was to frighten away not for an evening but for a year or more, or to arrest or even kill if necessary. He could not call to Lisveth lest he betray his knowledge to the thief behind him and lose the element of surprise. He would have to make enough noise on his attack that he stunned his opponent into a moment of immobility and called Lisveth to help him.

His sword was already in his hand. He took a few more steps, breathing deep, and then whirled as he brought up the sword, shouting a battle cry.

"No! Stop!"

Fire dropped out of the sky and danced on the road between them, illuminating the red-headed Kayvin as he stumbled back, arms raised. "Stop!" he repeated.

Galen checked his rush. "What are you doing? Are you part of the bandits?"

"No, of course not." Kayvin shook his head, looking between them as Lisveth came to stand a little distance from Galen and let her defensive fire lower. "I was only following you."

"Why?"

Lisveth snorted. "I think that's obvious enough. He wants to claim a piece of the bounty the sheriff promised."

Kayvin shook his head. "I'm not interested in any bounty."

Lisveth twisted her mouth into an incredulous scowl. "Now you're lying to us."

Kayvin hesitated and then sighed. "I'm sorry. That was a stupid thing to say."

"It was," Lisveth confirmed. "And now you can go back to the village."

"Let me come with you," he said. "There are only two of you."

"And we've survived a bandit attack once already tonight."

"Not these bandits." His expression was serious. "And you're already injured. I could be useful."

It would be good to have an extra set of hands—but Galen did not like how Kayvin had followed covertly. "Why didn't you just ask to join us back at the inn? It would have looked much less suspicious than following us in the dark. Now we have no reason to believe you aren't collaborating with the thieves."

"I'm not collaborating," Kayvin snapped, and he spat the word with disdain. "Look, I—I wanted to help. You did a good thing earlier today, fighting back and getting that girl out so she can go back home. I don't want you to get killed tonight. But you two seem, I don't know, close. I didn't know if you'd let me come with you."

"We're close in that we're a partnership," Lisveth said, "a team, because we've worked together long enough to be able to work together well. You're a new factor. And you didn't know if we'd let you join us because you didn't ask."

"I should have asked," Kayvin said. "I'm sorry."

"And then you said you weren't after the bounty."

"That was dumb," Kayvin acknowledged. "Of course anyone would want to share the bounty."

Lisveth looked at Galen, the question in her eyes, and he shrugged. He didn't know what to make of Kayvin, either. An extra fighter, even a poor one, would be helpful—but an extra fighter for the bandits' side could be disastrous. He shrugged at Lisveth, ceding the decision to her. She generally had a better sense for negotiations.

Lisveth sighed. "So are you done lying to us now?"

Kayvin raised his hands in surrender. "I'm sorry. I should have asked to come with you. I should have said I wanted to share the bounty. What can I do now to make it up?"

"You can make sure you don't stab one of us in the back," Lisveth said, "because the other of us will kill you right quick if that happens."

Kayvin nodded. "That's fair."

Lisveth flipped her good hand at him. "Walk near Galen, then. But not too near."

They went on down the road, Lisveth well-lit ahead, and Galen and Kayvin picking their way in the dark behind her. Galen kept glancing in Kayvin's direction, trying to discern if the red-headed man was easing closer or lifting a weapon. Now he had more than just the sides of the road to watch.

But at least if Kayvin was a danger, he was now where Galen could watch him.

The moon rose, shedding additional light over the road. Galen looked harder into the pockets of shadow on either side of the road, keeping his eyes away from Lisveth and her torch to preserve his night vision.

The attack came from the left, a quick rush with an upraised blade. Lisveth bolted, just evading the downward sweep of the ugly weapon, and as the assailant turned to follow her Galen charged him. His sword took the attacker in the back of the shoulder, but it did not bite as it should have. The assailant was armored.

He wheeled to face Galen, sword raised, but he had the presence of mind to glance back to see if Lisveth had turned. She had, circling to flank him, one hand raised with fire licking up from her palm.

Galen kept his weight on the balls of his feet, evenly balanced, ready to move in any direction. "Stand down," he said. "We aren't paid more if you're dead."

"Dead?" He gave a high-pitched mockery of a laugh, and dark hollows showed in his cheeks. "Worry for yourselves, humans."

Humans. The word cut through Galen like a blade.

The fire in Lisveth's hand leaped higher, illuminating the figure between them.

The demon—the Selk—faced them, and Galen stared in horrified wonder. Its ears might have come to a point, just as the legends said, but they were mostly obscured by the creature's hair. Its teeth were not pointed like a wolf's or cat's, and it seemed more likely to use the ugly chunky blade it carried than to attack with claws. But it wore robes that recalled the temple brothers' garb or Galen's imagination of royal clothing, and it crouched like a feral thing, and it bore a gleeful expression unmarred by the bruising it should have felt from Galen's blow.

"You will die, humans," it snarled, and somehow the simple address underscored its otherness in a way the ears and clothing had not. "We will swarm from the mountains, we will crush you like ants."

"You've obviously never tried to clear a home of ants," returned Lisveth dryly. "Come on then, and save your talking."

Galen adjusted his grip on his sword and prepared to close.

"Wait!"

Galen did not turn in his surprise, did not take his eyes from the Selk. He had almost forgotten Kayvin in his rush to defend Lisveth—but the man had not attacked him from behind.

"Wait," Kayvin repeated. "Stand a moment."

The Selk's eyes flickered from Galen to the second red-headed man just beyond him, and his expression shifted from disdain to surprise. "My lord!"

My lord? Galen's mind spun. How could a Selk know Kayvin, and know him as *my lord?*

"You know him?" asked Lisveth, jerking a thumb toward Kayvin on the road. "Is he really who he says he is?" Oh, she was quick.

The Selk straightened and looked indignant. "Of course he is. That is Prince Kayvin, Amethyst Heir of the Rideis Bull Throne—"

White-hot magic struck him and he fell backward, twitching with the remaining energy but already dead. Galen gaped for only a second before remembering to turn and raise his sword to guard against Kayvin.

Kayvin the Selk. Kayvin the *prince* of the Selks.

Kayvin was standing on the road, feet slightly apart, arm still extended from his arcane strike. His mouth hung open slightly as he looked at the fallen raider, and then his eyes leaped between Lisveth and Galen. He looked just as Galen felt: as if he knew he should attack them, but he couldn't yet comprehend that they had suddenly become mortal enemies.

"I am sorry," he said, as if that changed anything. "Empty void, I didn't—I didn't mean to kill him." His words caught, and he struggled to continue. "I am sorry they killed here. I am sorry you heard what he said."

"You're a prince?" Galen repeated, hating the foolish words as he heard them aloud. "Of the Selks?"

Kayvin pressed his lips together. "The Rideis. Selk is a human term, and a rude one."

"And you are their prince?"

Kayvin looked uncomfortable. "I am, though that means little at the moment."

"It means everything!" Galen couldn't catch up with his whirling thoughts.

Lisveth stepped around the stilled demon with only a quick glance and came to stand with Galen, though at a distance to give him plenty of room for movement. Her injured arm hung loose, her good arm half-raised and ready to throw magic. "And you came to see if we would find your—Rideis? Your bandits?"

"Not my bandits," he said. "I wanted to find them, yes, and I thought that might be easier with you tonight. But—"

"But you really weren't interested in the bounty."

He acknowledged this with a tiny, sad smile. "No. That wasn't a lie."

"What do you want?" demanded Galen, sword still ready. "Why did you come tonight?"

"I told you, I wanted to find the bandits. They're killing people. Innocent people."

"And you have such a tender heart, you couldn't allow that," Lisveth mocked. "You're a great friend to humans. And yet you wanted to keep us from learning who you were."

Kayvin made a little nod to indicate Galen's sword. "I think you can see why."

"And what happens now?" asked Galen. "There are demon bandits roaming the—"

"Rideis," Kayvin corrected. "Not demon."

"Maybe the man we buried earlier tonight wouldn't see so much of a difference," Galen said. "But you say you're not with them. Are they here without permission? Are you hunting them down for justice?"

"No," Kayvin answered heavily.

"Then why are you here?"

"I'm hunting for something else."

"What?"

Kayvin shook his head. "Look, I don't—I don't have any—could we just talk, for a moment? Put down your sword." He stepped forward and reached for the blade.

Galen retreated and slashed.

Kayvin recoiled, clutching his forearm where blood gushed from the wound. "Empty void!" he snarled, gritting his teeth against the pain.

"Sorry," Galen said, but he didn't mean it. "Don't reach for a man's sword in a standoff."

"I forget I am no prince here. That was foolish of me. Another mistake made tonight." He adjusted his hand and pushed hard into the wound, grimacing. "I don't suppose you'd lend me your physick kit."

Lisveth raised her hand, brightening the fire. "I could cauterize that for you."

Kayvin gave her a hard, flat look. "Don't fight me, girl. I didn't want to, but I did kill him."

"And what makes you think I wouldn't have?" Lisveth kept her hand ready. "Or wouldn't do the same for you?"

"I have done nothing to harm you or your friend."

"It is not what you have done so far tonight," Lisveth said, "but you are, by your own words and his, one of the enemy, and you admit you have no interest in stopping your bandits."

"They are not my bandits," Kayvin snapped.

"But though you are a prince, you will not order them back to your side of the mountains."

"...No."

"Then I suppose we'll have to consider what a great bounty you might be worth."

Kayvin's eyes hardened, and he straightened, releasing his bleeding arm so that he had two hands available. Galen bent his knees, sword tip directed at Kayvin's eyes. Lisveth shifted her feet and brought her elbows close to her torso, protecting herself and ready to fling magic outward.

The night breeze played about them, soft on their cheeks.

Even as Galen focused on the immediate danger, his mind whirled with the greater danger they had just discovered. There were demon raiders here, really here just as all the stories had told, and everyone was at risk. The demon raiders hadn't been after gold or valuables; as Andrea had said, they'd been after life.

They just wanted to kill. Every village, every town, every farm, everyone without a city wall and the elite state mages—

Kayvin's arm moved, and Galen lunged before he realized it was only the torn sleeve shifting in the breeze.

But he was already in motion, and he struck hard with the blade even as Kayvin leapt backward and blasted him with magic. It ripped through him, tearing organs from their places and spraying behind him in a rainbow fluorescence.

But his sword connected, if not as powerfully as he'd wanted, and he drove through the motion and heard Kayvin cry out.

Galen caught his balance, shaking the starry color from his eyes. Kayvin staggered back, fresh blood from a new cut on his arm, his face twisted with pain but his eyes fixed wide on Galen. "How?" he asked.

Galen pointed the sword at him again. He didn't understand the question, so he didn't answer.

Kayvin straightened, blood slicking the palm he extended. "You—give it to me." His expression changed, a desperate greed that sat ill on his features. "I need it. Give it to me!"

"What are you blathering on about?" Lisveth hurled a magical bolt at him.

Kayvin struck it out of existence as if slapping aside a thrown apple. His bloody hand glowed as he turned on her—

A blinding flash of light made Galen flinch away, and he knew the danger even as he moved. He pivoted toward Kayvin, squinting and raising one hand to shield his eyes, ready to meet the rush or magic or whatever attack came.

There was no attack. Kayvin was ten paces away, dragged backward by a woman Galen did not recognize. "Stop!" Galen shouted, though he wasn't sure why.

"Let me go!" Kayvin demanded, struggling, but she had a grip about his chest and on his wounded arm, and he yelped as she squeezed it.

Lisveth launched another bolt of magic at him, but Kayvin lifted his good hand and countered it, the two energies clashing with a brief flash of colored light.

"Let me go!" Kayvin twisted against the woman's hold.

"Your orders have no authority for me," she snarled, "as I serve no lord stupid enough to enter combat alone and already wounded by his opponent."

"That was—that was different! Yovela!"

"If you die here, she will kill her, in the very moment the report is carried home."

Kayvin stopped thrashing. "I..."

"Come away, my lord."

"Have you been following me?" he asked, pulling upright and shrugging off her loosened grip.

"That is what a follower does."

Kayvin took a breath, and his next words were to Galen and Lisveth. "Don't come after us. And don't—well, it's probably too much to ask you not to speak of me. But I would appreciate it if you did not."

"We'll give that the consideration it deserves," Lisveth promised.

Kayvin shook his head, backing away with the strange woman, and then they faded into the night.

Galen stared into the night, refusing to think of what Kayvin really was, of the strange woman, of the presence of demons on the roads. Now was not the time for distracting thoughts. Distracting thoughts would get a man killed.

He and Lisveth listened for several long moments, straining to catch any hint of the two Selks—Rideis—circling back in the dark. But it seemed they had really gone.

Galen lowered his sword, Lisveth lowered her flaming hand, and they looked at each other. The night sky loomed large, empty, dangerous. There were demons in the world, and demons in their land, and demons among their people.

"What do we do now?" Galen asked.

Lisveth turned in place and started toward the dead Rideis bandit. "We take this back to town, for whatever the bounty might be worth."

The Downcast Prince

MANDORAL

CHAPTER 19

Two Months Before

They did not look so different, really, only a little more elongated where humans were pinched together, and the slight differences could mostly be explained as a variation of type. The tips of their ears were not so pointed as in humans' popular art and could often be missed. The humans, in their forgetfulness, called them demons, or sometimes the Selks.

They called themselves the Rideis.

They were a great people with an ancient history—but secretly, Kayvin wondered if their days of greatest glory were gone forever. They no longer made active war on each border, fighting both skin and scales, and while Kayvin practiced daily his forms and magics, he spent more hours with his music. His great-great-grandfather had led hordes into battle, but now his father passed his days and nights with his sera qadra, achieving conquests of another kind.

Most days, Kayvin did not trouble himself with these thoughts. He had his music to occupy him, and a sera qadra of his own, and if the burden of state grew less weighty by the time it descended to his own shoulders, he could hardly complain. Most days, he woke to one of his pleasure women sliding into his sleeping pit with a tray of breakfast, trained his hands in magic or music according to his mood, and then attended his father for any court business.

This morning, though, he was awakened early. "My lord prince?" The voice was apologetic, but not fearful; Kayvin was not given to fits of temper. "My lord prince, you're called."

Kayvin stretched before opening his eyes, brushing against a woman who made a sleepy sound of protest. He made a face; another candidate determined to win his favor. He rolled over and glanced up at the servant kneeling at the lip of the sleeping pit. "So early? Surely my father isn't awake yet."

In truth, he wasn't sure what time it was, though he could see daylight from the open balcony at the far side of the room, but he had a fair chance of being correct. If Gromgest had been an early riser in his days of war, he had not kept the habit in peace.

"Nonetheless, my lord prince, you are called."

There was a scrape of wood and then a hasty padding of feet, and this pricked Kayvin's worry. Why send a second servant? Had something happened—an attack, after all these years? A new spawning? Was his mother ill?

"My lord prince!" the second servant panted. Kayvin vaguely recognized him as one of his father's, though he couldn't recall his name. "You must come!"

Don't order me about, Kayvin wanted to say, but he held back the words. The servants must think it important. "I'm coming, I'm coming. What is it?"

The second servant faltered, needing a moment to form the words. "His Illustrious Excellency—the Arch Potentate—your father is dead."

The words lanced into Kayvin and stuck there, wounding him before he'd even realized he'd been struck. "What?" He twisted out of the pillows and leapt out of the pit, holding out his arms for the robe offered. "What happened? Is my mother with him?"

His father's servant was wide-eyed, not merely grieved. "It's Pasiphae Jade..."

Kayvin clenched his jaw. Pasiphae Jade was one of his father's women, one of his favorites—but she was not a wife, and she had no place at Gromgest's side before Raea.

A light robe was sufficient, he decided, in such haste. He started for the door, and the servants hurried ahead to open it for him.

Kayvin's quarters were, by his preference, opposite the Arch Potentate's in the octagonal palace. He preferred the quiet and the privacy for his music and the distance from the carousing, and he hoped the distance helped to separate him from the other royal offspring, born to concubines and courtesans instead of to the Shining Gem. In his hurry, he did not keep a dignified pace but rushed through the wide primary corridor to Gromgest's living quarters.

Servants clustered about the entrance, wide-eyed and silent. Two knelt beside something on the ground, their hands tentatively probing a bundle of clothing. Not his father, not in the doorway and so poorly dressed... Kayvin stepped through them, glancing down only briefly at the dead man, open-mouthed beneath a slick of frost.

The discordant element tore his attention from the search for his father, and memories bobbed and surfaced within his distracted mind. Pasiphae Jade had some talent with ice, and she often entertained Gromgest with pretty little snow figures and delicate frosty traces. Did anyone else in the palace have ice skill, and enough to strike down a servant?

He set the question aside and went into his father's rooms.

The apartments were much like his own, a wide first room for talking or relaxing and then several interconnected rooms—a private room containing the sleeping pit, a room where attendants slept to be close at hand, another set of rooms where the sera qadra men and women lived, a private study. Kayvin went directly to the sleeping pit.

Gromgest was there. He lay half on his back, as if rolled there, very dead, and in the center of his chest gaped a great hole, nearly the span of Kayvin's palm. His open robe was wet with water or sweat. There was no sign of a weapon, and Kayvin could not immediately guess what might have opened him in such a way.

He dropped into the pit to kneel beside him. "Father," he breathed, though he expected no answer and wasn't sure why he spoke. But he had nothing else to say, and something had to be said. "Father."

"The Arch Potentate is dead."

He looked up at Pasiphae Jade on the far rim of the pit and was caught by her cool, erect posture. She did not look like a woman who had woken to find a corpse beside her. Nor did she look like a woman who had awakened to witness a murder.

Kayvin straightened, remaining on one knee beside his father but fixing his eyes on Pasiphae Jade. She wore the fine multi-layered robes of a favorite in the sera qadra, and disjointedly he realized it must have taken her some time to dress. "Pasiphae Jade, were you with him?"

"His Illustrious Excellency is dead," she repeated. "Long live Her Illustrious Excellency."

For a moment he simply stared at her, trying to fit the words into meaning. His mother? The throne should have passed to Kayvin, Gromgest's heir—but if Raea would assume her late husband's throne instead of Kayvin, Pasiphae Jade was not the one to announce it to him.

All that he had observed, had tried to overlook, pressed irresistibly upon him. "Pasiphae Jade, did you murder my father?"

Her mouth curved into a satisfied feline smile. "All these years, I have labored to ease the burden of state which weighed upon His Illustrious Excellency. At last, I have freed him entirely from the concerns and cares of rule, taking the mantle upon myself."

Kayvin stared at her. "You killed him."

"I have just said as much." She looked at him. "You do well to kneel before me."

All the conflicting grief and outrage and fury blurred together, and Kayvin rose to his feet. "I am his rightful heir. And if I cannot take my place, then my mother Raea is the Shining Gem and—"

"It is already done, my lord prince. You are my lord prince still, and nothing more."

For a moment Kayvin couldn't speak, stunned by her audacity. But then his fists clenched, and heat burned within his palms. "This will end—"

"A moment, please, my lord prince." Pasiphae Jade spoke quickly, but without fear. "Before you act, consider those around us, who might find themselves in the way of harm. And we might desecrate the body of His Illustrious Excellency, who should be at most serene rest."

Kayvin hesitated. He did not expect that Pasiphae Jade could present much resistance, even if she had killed his debauched father in his sleep, but there was no point to needlessly endangering the servants, and she had been correct about Gromgest's remains. He should be removed and prepared for honorable burial.

He thought of the frosted servant in the corridor, and he wondered if Pasiphae Jade might wield more power than he had thought. Possibly she had more skill than her pretty ice figures suggested.

Not enough, though. Kayvin was a son of the Arch Potentate, and he had trained all his life in his own element. He would not dishonor the deathplace of his father, but he would avenge him.

"And of course, you do not want to lose your mother on the same day as your father," Pasiphae Jade continued.

Kayvin hesitated. "Where is my mother?" he asked, and he wondered if Pasiphae Jade had noticed the barest quaver in his voice. Surely Raea was unharmed. She had not been next in line to inherit as Kayvin had, and Kayvin himself had not been attacked. "Why is she not here with my fallen father?"

Pasiphae Jade shook her head. "She is not here, but she is not dead." She held up a hand. "Please, not in this place. Let us go to the Shining Gem, and we may speak of the ruling line of Mandoral."

Kayvin eyed her, distrusting her. *She is not dead,* she had said. He needed to see his mother, needed to speak to her of what had happened and how they should respond.

"I will come," he said, and he realized only after the words hung in the air that he had obeyed her.

CHAPTER 20

THE THRONE ROOM WAS magnificent, boasting gleaming marble tiles, tinkling fountains at each corner, and worked stone arches high enough to accommodate a visiting dragon.

One of the fountains was not playing. Its water expanded a few inches above the wide basin, frozen into immobility. Kayvin and Pasiphae Jade strode across the floor toward it.

"Your mother is a wise and patient woman," Pasiphae Jade said. "She did not interfere with her husband's sera qadra."

"The Arch Potentate's," Kayvin said. It was wrong to hear her speak of him without his rank.

"A Shining Gem is entitled to her own respect. But, she did not attend to her husband's needs herself, and she gave him only one son."

Kayvin's shoulders rose. It was improper to speak of the Arch Potentate this way, and awkward to hear about his own parents, and worst of all when his father was newly dead. "What does any of this have to do with my mother?" Perhaps she would be co-regent with him for a time. They would have to discuss it. What about the other royal offspring? His mother might send them away, emptying the sera qadra and the nurseries. Kayvin did not think she would dispose of them; his position was secure, and the concubines and their children would not challenge the Shining Gem's own son.

Pasiphae Jade laughed, a supple, artificial thing. "I am only explaining. If she could not be troubled to manage even her own household while he was the Arch Potentate, she cannot be expected to rule in his absence."

There was something in the up-thrust sheet of ice, a long shape that Kayvin's mind refused to accept.

"So I have relieved her of her troublesome duties, eased her mind of her grief for his passing, set you at rest for her welfare."

Kayvin stared into the basin of ice. "What have you done?" he breathed.

Raea, the Arch Potentate's Shining Gem, stared upward through the obscuring crystal. Her eyes were half closed as if she flinched backward, one arm drawn up to protect herself and the other stretched back to break her fall. But she was not falling, not anymore, frozen in this eternal instant.

"She is not dead," Pasiphae Jade assured him. "I did not lie; be at rest for her. You can be assured, for her safety lies entirely in your hands."

Kayvin tore his eyes away from his mother. "What do you want? Immunity? Mercy?"

Pasiphae Jade threw back her head and laughed, a real laugh this time, full of gaiety and incredulity. "Oh, my dear boy," she gasped, "you delight me. No, son of my lover, what I want is your unwavering obedience to my rule."

Kayvin's breath caught, his muscles frozen just as surely as his mother, his eyes riveted to the beautiful monster standing beside him. "What?" he managed, as if the word had crawled from his throat.

Pasiphae Jade traced her fingers over the block of ice, leaving a fresh trail of sparkling frost above the half-turned face. "I have many things to demand my attention, many tasks which Gromgest had let go. In truth, that is why I had to take this path. I need you for a specific work. While you serve me and this kingdom—your kingdom—she will remain safe. She is alive, and she is not in pain. You can keep her that way."

Kayvin wrestled his outrage into words. "But you are a concubine! I am the heir! She is the prime wife! The throne cannot pass to you. You killed the Arch Potentate—you cannot take his place."

Her smile faded, and she leaned toward Kayvin. "I killed the Arch Potentate," she repeated, her voice a brutal whisper, "and so I will take his place." She took a breath. "Do you think I acted rashly, without making all the preparations I would need? But ask yourself, Your Highness, what preparations you have made? Whose favor have you courted, to have their warriors at your own call? Which fine houses stand with you, confident in your promises of distinction and reward?"

Kayvin stared at her.

"But I laid my plans and bound my allies. I took his place not in mad hope, but with every confidence of success. I will do what he did not—would not. I will survive where he would have died with us all. And you will help me."

"No," said Kayvin, setting his jaw against her words. "You will be executed."

He started toward the great double doors at the far end of the hall, intending to call the absent guard, but a crystalline shattering stopped him. He turned back as Pasiphae Jade casually flung another chunk of ice to the marble tiles. It broke apart, pieces of ice skittering in all directions.

"Ice is brittle," she said, toeing a piece. She stepped on it, making it crunch against the stone floor. She looked into the basin at Raea's supine figure. "Our bodies are mostly water, you know. They freeze into ice, they thaw like ice, and they break like ice."

Kayvin's heart leapt into his throat. "Stop."

She reached into the fountain's basin, carving out a piece of ice with her hand as if scooping out snow, and flung it again to the floor.

"No!" Kayvin started toward her. "Stop!"

She did, looking at him with one perfect eyebrow raised. "I thought you were going to execute me?"

"I am," he snarled, cupping his hand and summoning heat to his palm. "I will kill you myself, and then thaw her."

"With your fire, no doubt," she answered, her voice steady and assured. "And then you will bury us both."

He hesitated. "I will melt your ice and free her."

"And kill her as you do." She gestured. "I froze her. You cannot thaw her like a piece of meat on a mountaintop; you will have only a piece of burnt meat. Only I can release her safely. Kill me, and you kill her."

Kayvin stared. "That's not true."

She shrugged, one delicately shaped shoulder rising and falling so that her gown slipped down her arm, a move she had performed a thousand times to enchant the gaze. "You may test it if you like. But I suggest you test it with something else first. Do not kill her with your love for her."

He swallowed and looked at his mother. "What will happen?"

"If you melt her free? She is ice now. She will soften and run, like heated butter."

Kayvin lifted his eyes to Pasiphae Jade. Dare he test her words? Her life depended on her ability to control him, hinged on her power over his lifeless mother and his unwillingness to harm her. Would she trust a lie to hold him?

What if he was wrong, and she spoke the truth?

There was a sound from behind him, and he turned to see Lord Fretton in the open doorway. Lord Fretton was the Second General of the East, a powerful courtier as well as a military commander, and Kayvin's heart rose in hope.

"Is everything well, Your Illustrious Excellency? We heard a disturbance."

"It is not well," Kayvin snapped. "This woman threatens the Shining Gem."

But Lord Fretton stood motionless, still waiting for a reply, and Kayvin's gut chilled as if Pasiphae Jade had dragged her frosty fingers through his core.

"All is well," she called mildly. "The prince and I are only talking. Thank you."

He bowed and retreated through the door, and Kayvin watched him go, taking all sense of order with him.

What had she done? When had she done it?

Pasiphae Jade smiled. "But if you serve me, do what I ask, then I will keep your mother safe. I will care for her in the ice—for the ice does require care, if she is to remain intact within it—and you may work toward her release."

"You need her," Kayvin said in painful disagreement. "You dare not lose your hold over me by releasing her."

Pasiphae Jade shook her head. "You think so little of me. Have I lied to you yet?" One corner of her mouth lifted, almost too slightly to be seen. "And, my prince, does it seem to you that I need you to order the court for me?"

He had left himself open to that blow, and it struck true.

But she was magnanimous in her victory. "I swear to you, I will not harm her if you are true to me, and if you serve me well, I will release her to you."

Kayvin held her eyes. "Alive."

That shrug. "Alive, of course."

"And well. My own mother, just as she was."

"Your own mother, just as she was, with only a gap in her memory where tomorrow and the next days should have been." She gestured. "But she does not have to lose much time in sleep, not if you are a willing worker."

Her words galled Kayvin. "I am not a servant. I am the Amethyst Prince, the heir to the throne."

Her lips curled, a vixen licking her lips after devouring a young rabbit. "Of course. You are heir after me, a prince assisting his potentate. And you will make a pretty speech about how I am seeing to things in your mother's place, with a formal and public request for me to take power, to reassure any who might not at first understand my position."

Kayvin swallowed against the tightening of his throat. This was wrong, so wrong, and yet there was nothing he could do. There was no one to call for aid. Even if the guards heeded his orders and seized this courtesan—and that seemed increasingly unlikely—his mother would melt into the basin like so much fountain muck, and he would lose her.

No, he had no choice but to serve Pasiphae Jade in whatever maniacal plan she had, until he learned how to free his mother from her magic and then could strike Pasiphae Jade down.

"Yes," he ground out, keeping his eyes on his twisted mother.

Pasiphae Jade's eyebrows lifted. "What was that, my prince?"

Kayvin clenched his teeth together and bit out the words. "Yes, I will serve you as your prince."

Her golden lips parted in a pleased smile. "Thank you, Prince Kayvin. I appreciate your commitment and service. May our partnership be mutually beneficial."

"And brief," he said. "Tell me what you want. Tell me how I can free my mother."

"Of course." She turned and walked to the dais and the ornate bulls-head throne that Gromgest had used for court days. She seated herself and spread her robes about her with a practiced flair. Each of her movements was studied, just as she had studied Gromgest and Kayvin and all of them and had planned this coup, had seized the kingdom in a single night, a single death.

"What is it?" he pressed, speaking so that he did not have to think about the image of her on his father's throne. "What do you want me to do?"

She smiled a cold smile, disbelieving his pale eagerness. "I want you to help me save the world."

CHAPTER 21

KAYVIN HAD BEEN COMPOSING a song for his mother's birthday. She would have been—would be—sixty-four years old. He had written delicately intertwining harmonies of the kind she loved, and his sera qadra had been practicing for nearly two weeks.

Most of Kayvin's sera qadra had been chosen for their musical talents. He did not have his father's broad tastes, and pleasures of the flesh were enjoyable enough when he must, but he preferred the pleasures of art and culture. He populated his quarters with singers, musicians, and dancers. As he had once told his mother, to her faint worry, anyone could lie in a sleeping pit, but not everyone could sing.

He could free her, he must free her, but it would require time and focus. He had no time now for music.

More, his sera qadra could not be trusted. His father had brought a courtesan too close, and it had cost him his life and his kingdom, and it might yet cost his wife and his heir. Kayvin could not risk such a betrayal.

He strode into his quarters, and servants turned anxiously to him. He ignored them—he did not yet know how to explain that he was not the new potentate—and walked through to his private rooms and into his sera qadra's quarters.

There were two long sleeping rooms, one for women and one for men, as many preferred both in a sera qadra but kept them unmingled. The women's area had more residents, but Kayvin also required masculine voices for his songs. There was a narrow common room between them, and he stopped just inside its doorway, watching them all turn and arrange themselves hastily. They too were worried by the rumors, afraid yet clinging to reassuring protocols.

Did any of them look suspicious? Did any cast down his or her eyes out of guilt rather than respect?

"You are all dismissed," he said simply. "I have no need of you now, and I do not wish to keep you where you will not be appreciated or useful. You will each be given a purse of traveling funds, and you may return to your families, if you have them, or find new employments in the city. I expect you all to be gone by this evening."

There was a moment of shock, and then several of them cried protests. One woman even ran to him and caught his arm. "My lord prince! You can't mean this. You can't really mean to send me away!"

He uncoiled her fingers from his arm. "I do. Even you, Sirina."

"But what have I done to displease you?"

"Perhaps nothing. I send you without disgrace, without displeasure. I only want you to be happy, but elsewhere."

"But I cannot be happy without you!"

He half smiled, though he felt no sympathy. She had always sought to entice him beyond his interest. "I rather think you can, Sirina."

He beckoned to his steward Arad as he exited. "They must leave their regalia of the sera qadra, but they may of course take any gifts they have received. And give each of them money enough to travel or otherwise provide for themselves for a few weeks."

They would not suffer for his wariness, not when none of them had proved treacherous yet. But neither did they have his trust.

With all the sera qadra dismissed and the servants sent away, Kayvin's rooms should have been empty. But there—again! He heard a snatch of humming from the next room. Someone had stayed, in defiance of orders—another traitor like Pasiphae Jade? But surely no assassin would hum to betray himself. He went to the carved door and pushed it back.

Inside the sera qadra common room, a woman dressed in elegant blue sat combing her long, dark hair. She was looking over his notes for his mother's song. At his entrance, she rose and faced him, bowing. "My lord prince."

"Yovela," he said. He had not thought of her in his decision to empty his sera qadra. He had only reacted.

She nodded once.

"I have sent you away."

"You have sent away your sera qadra, my lord. I remain as something else."

Yovela was merely an average singer, but she was a fine dancer. She had been brought to the palace as an exquisite offering and presented for the prince's consideration. Her dance had pleased him, and he had taken her into his sera qadra.

"I have not given you another position."

"Then I suppose you had better think of something, my lord."

This was part of why he liked Yovela. He would not brook such insolence in another—but from her, it did not sound like insolence, merely fact. "I will think on it. In the meantime, I suppose you have your choice of places." He gestured toward the women's sleeping room.

"You mean I will not share your own, now the others are gone."

Kayvin had no ready answer to that. Yovela had not fought for attention or pressured him for personal favor as Sirina or others had. That was another reason he liked her.

She didn't require an answer. "That is good. Trust no one, my lord prince, is the advice I should give you if asked. This is a treacherous time, and your palace holds treacherous people. Your father was distracted and betrayed; you should take precautions against the same."

Kayvin nodded once. He swallowed and forced a light tone. "And as you tell me to trust no one, how then should I trust your advice to trust no one?"

Yovela held his eyes. "I said that was the advice I should give you if asked. But the advice I give unasked is this." She dropped smoothly to one knee, all grace and strength as she knelt and extended her arms, wrists up. "I have no ambitions save your advancement to your own throne and service to your own kingdom, and I serve no one but you, my lord. If you trust no one else, trust me."

For a long moment Kayvin regarded her, and she remained motionless before him. She could probably hold the position for some time, if he required it; her body was lean with muscle, soft only over the belly and buttocks where beauty demanded, and she had splendid balance.

"Many are grateful for the honor of the sera qadra," he answered, trying to put distance in his voice. "They might be equally grateful for lavish rewards from a conspirator."

"I care not for the sera qadra's place," she replied without hesitation. "Many high places have treacherous footing. But you brought me into your quarters and let me dance for you." *And you did not require more,* the following silence said.

"If you stay with me, the footing will be even more treacherous," Kayvin warned. "The Arch Potentate was murdered for his throne. His heir might be next."

"If you mean to warn me of dangerous people in the palace, that is all the more reason to stay with the prince I trust."

"Even if you may become a target with me? I'm told Pasiphae Jade is already arranging her own sera qadra; surely there will be greater safety there."

If Yovela had meant to harm him, Kayvin reflected, she had already had ample opportunity. She was no different today than yesterday. But his father might have thought the same of Pasiphae Jade, who had waited years before choosing one night to assassinate her royal lover in his own sleeping pit. The fact that Yovela had previously offered no harm meant nothing.

"I have lived outside of your sera qadra and within it," Yovela said, her head bowed. "I have no interest in living outside it again, not even in another's sera qadra. I won't do it."

He frowned. "It may be that Pasiphae Jade can be very persuasive."

She kept her eyes on the polished floor. Her wrists remained turned up to him. "I have seen all manner of persuasion, my lord prince."

For the first time, he wondered if being in a sera qadra might not be an honor to all. For just an instant he thought of the expectations that chafed him, and he shrank from the thought of more.

Her words were not an assurance of loyalty, but he did not know what could be, and he was so alone in this moment. He extended a hand to her, and she took it and rose gracefully to her feet. Their eyes met, and he looked away first.

He released her and went to sit in a padded chair. "I cannot move against her," he said simply. "She holds my mother's life by a thread. If I displease her, my mother will die."

Yovela followed him and stood beside the chair. "If she kills your mother, she loses her hold over you. She cannot risk carrying out her threat."

"That may be true," he said heavily, "but I dare not test it. She has been rash before—murdering my father in his bed—and it has gone well with her. She might dare. And if she did kill my mother and so lost her ability to hold me, I would be victorious at the cost of my mother's life. I would not have that victory."

Yovela nodded. "I understand."

He exhaled and looked about the empty common room. No sound came from the sera qadra's sleeping rooms or his own chambers. The unfamiliar stillness was unsettling.

His father was dead. His mother was nearly so. The captain of the palace guard had been conspicuously absent, and other lords and officials had all but proclaimed their fealty to Pasiphae Jade. Kayvin was alone but for his household servants and a single dancer.

What did Pasiphae Jade want of him?

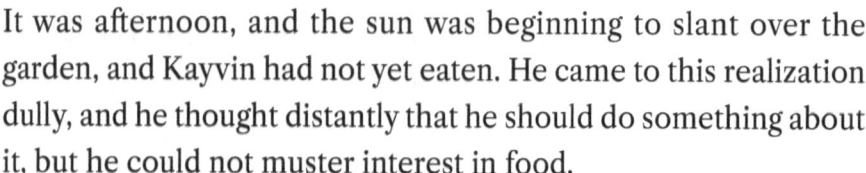

It was afternoon, and the sun was beginning to slant over the garden, and Kayvin had not yet eaten. He came to this realization dully, and he thought distantly that he should do something about it, but he could not muster interest in food.

He stood and paced across the floor. He had books, and musical instruments, and a beautiful dancer, and he could not think of anything but pacing. He turned again at the far end of his balcony and saw a figure in his room. He jumped, his fingers clenching convulsively around a sudden flare of warmth.

But the man who faced him was not one of Pasiphae Jade's guards or turned nobles. "Lord Narrim," Kayvin said, his voice mostly steady.

Lord Narrim was Kayvin's sometime tutor, a noble of middle years and greying temples, and too staid and unimportant to have been a prime target for the usurper's machinations. He was all that was right, all that had been. Kayvin took a step toward him, and for a moment his throat closed and he could not speak.

But Lord Narrim bowed once, brief but formal. "Your Illustrious Excellency."

Kayvin's chest tightened as well. Lord Narrim acknowledged him as the rightful Arch Potentate.

Lord Narrim straightened. "I hear you have emptied your sera qadra, and that was wise. When we've finished, give orders that not even one such as myself may enter here without permission. And be sure of your servants."

Kayvin did not want to think any more about the possibility of a traitor or assassin. "Surely you will always be welcome here, my lord."

"I hope so, Your Excellency—but with your permission." He pressed his lips together. "First, let me offer you my condolences on the death of His Illustrious Excellency."

Kayvin made himself nod once. "Thank you."

"Then, I have come here to tell you while that whore has her claws into the palace guard and many of the upper lords, she does not have them all, and she does not have me. You have supporters, Your Excellency, and we will not fail you now."

Kayvin wanted to be glad, but his mind was exhausted with rendering the right emotion for each turn today. "I—again, thank you."

"Be cautious for now," Narrim advised. "If you will take the word of your old tutor, do not sacrifice all your strength in an initial effort before you have laid plans and gathered your resources. That waste would undermine a more successful, more organized effort. Instead, present enough resistance that she will believe you resentful but not recalcitrant, so that she will not be suspicious. When we have prepared, we will strike."

Resentful compliance... Kayvin could do that. He was already doing that, and he was relieved to hear that it was not wholly a failure.

"She has made an enemy of your loyal supporters, and she will know it. I anticipate her downfall." Lord Narrim made another bow. "Now, please excuse me, Your Excellency, to go to those who remember their duty to you, and be cautious. I will send word when I have firm news; you may trust anything with a seal showing a left-facing kestrel."

Kayvin nodded and forced words through his tight throat. "Thank you, Lord Narrim, I am glad of your assurance and your loyalty."

Lord Narrim left, and Kayvin stood motionless in his room.

Yes, he had loyal supporters still. He had despaired, seeing Lord Fretton and others already bent to her will, anxiously angling for favor from the new potentate. But all was not lost. He had Yovela, and he had Lord Narrim, and he had the lords Narrim knew.

If Kayvin waited, if he offered the face of an unhappy prince who knew he was powerless but was reluctant to admit it, they could let her believe her coup had been successful, and they could retake power from her unwary claws. They could save his mother, avenge his father, put everything right, even put Kayvin on his father's throne.

He had only to wait.

CHAPTER 22

KAYVIN TWITCHED FULLY AWAKE with a catch of breath, shoving aside the pillows and furs of his sleeping pit as if they threatened to smother him. He shook away the half-waking nightmare. Weariness had dulled his defense and permitted his mind to finally grapple with what had happened that day. But there was too much—any of it would have been enough, the murder of his father or the abduction of his mother or the loss of his kingdom, but together it was far too much. He thought he might not sleep for a long time.

There was a sound above his sleeping pit. Disheveled and half-dressed, he stood and saw a woman kneeling at the upper edge. "Who are you?" he demanded.

She bowed low. "I have been sent to you, my lord, as you are quite alone. Her Illustrious Excellency heard that your sera qadra had been emptied, and she has sent me to provide—"

"Get out," he snapped. He wanted no pleasure woman, and certainly none sent by the pleasure woman who had murdered his father in his bed. "Get out. Don't come again."

The woman stared at him in a moment of incomprehension. "Get out, I said!"

She bowed again, backing, and scurried for the door.

"Arad!" Kayvin shouted.

His steward hurried in. "My lord?"

"You admitted a woman while I was sleeping."

"I did, my lord, as she had been sent by—"

"You will admit no one without my express permission. No one. Is that clear?"

Arad nodded. "Of course, my lord."

It would avail nothing. Even if he set a guard at his door, it seemed Pasiphae Jade already had their loyalty or at least their obedience, and he could not rely on their security.

And if it came to it, he did not know if Arad could be trusted, or if he could be threatened or bribed.

He lowered himself back into his sleeping pit, nestling into the pillows and furs as if they might shield him from more than the cool air.

Every morning, a new woman came to his quarters. Some were older than Kayvin, with knowing smiles and experience in their lithe limbs. Some were younger, fresh with youth and blooming beauty. Some were too young, and Kayvin's stomach turned to think that Pasiphae Jade believed him susceptible to such dubious pleasures.

His tastes did not run very far even along more typical lines, on the whole. He was familiar with that line of pleasure, of course; virility was expected of any man, but especially of a highborn male, and its display was a key part of social standing. But even prior to Pasiphae Jade's fateful morning, he had not devoted himself to pleasure's pursuit as his father had. He sometimes brought one of his sera qadra to his sleeping pit because it was expected; the heir's masculine suitability was a matter of court interest. But Kayvin kept them primarily for the show required of his royal station, and to sing his music.

Not all of his sera qadra had understood that. Yet Yovela had never sought to entice him as the others had, competing for attention and affection. She did not have the best voice, but she did not try to make up for that with other means.

That was something he had admired in her, he realized now. He wished he could carry himself like a prince, not straining for the approval of the court—but he was only an overgrown boy who had lost both his parents, who was failing his mother in the worst possible way, who was no nearer to avenging his father's death than the day it had happened, who was even now bowing before his father's treacherous lover and murderer.

Pasiphae Jade liked it when he bowed to her. It tickled her fancy, thrilled her with a frisson of power. It disgusted him to see it, to hear it in her throaty voice. "Good morning, my prince," she said with a languid gaze. "Did you sleep well?"

"Please stop," he said.

"Stop?"

"Stop sending me women. I do not want them."

One side of her mouth curved into a patronizing smile. "Of course."

"I have my own sera qadra, and I shall manage it as I please."

"Your sera qadra is sparse, I hear," she said, "and I was concerned for your well-being. It is not good to be too alone."

"I am not alone," he said. "And if you know I emptied my sera qadra, then you know I would be reluctant to accept any women you send."

She laughed. "You are so blunt. There's no art to what you say."

"Would art make it more true?"

"It would make it more beautiful, and I thought artists like yourself pursued beauty as much as truth." She raised an eyebrow. "But then, it seems beauty has less interest for you."

Kayvin drew a slow breath. She enjoyed toying with him, and allowing her to gall him was just another small victory to add daily to her larger one. Keeping his temper—and his mother intact in the ice—was a small victory he might count for himself. "Let us say rather, I prefer to focus my energies on achieving my greater goals, which include freeing my mother. That aligns with your own goals, for which you need my aid, and yet you have kept me waiting for days. Tell me, what work do you have for me?"

She left the subject of the women like a child abandoning a toy. "At my direction, the scholars have been scouring the records for mention of the great amulets. After the last war, they were deposited in Sayinian temples, many of them. The humans treated them as religious artifacts, I suppose."

"Amulets? From the last war?"

For answer, she opened a stiff book to an illustration. The amulet depicted was in the shape of an eye, large and iridescent green like a dragon's scale, worked all around with wire in interweaving coils and spirals. The pupil was a vertical slit, and though the meticulous artistry gave it a brilliant coloring, it was frozen and dull like the eyes of his mother.

"This is the Dancer's Eye," she said. "I will need it in our preparations, but it is not enough, not if we are to save the Rideis. You must find the others."

"What preparations? And how am I to do that?"

"Go into the human lands. Search out their temples. Find their amulets." She smiled. "Avoid their mages."

Kayvin opened his mouth, unable to formulate an immediate response. "Across the mountains?"

"Did you not hear me clearly?"

"We have not crossed the mountains in a hundred years. Two hundred."

"Then they will not be expecting you."

Kayvin swallowed. "Why me? You could send any warrior for this task, and they would be more suited to it."

She shook her head. "I must have someone I can trust. I am sending you to seek out the most precious, the most powerful arcane artifacts in all our knowledge. A warrior might, having found it, keep it for himself. Why should he return to me for reward when he holds such power in his hand?" She opened her own hand, gesturing fluidly. "I must have something of value to trade, something even more precious than an amulet. And with you, I have that leverage. Bring me the seven great amulets, and I will free your mother."

This was the first time she had specified, the first time he could clearly articulate what was necessary. He seized on it. "Seven amulets? And your scholars have found where these amulets are supposed to be kept?"

"We know where some were, years ago. We have had no word since, of course. No one has crossed the mountains—until you."

Still, it was nearer an agreement to release of his mother than he had before, and surely he could learn more as he traveled. He could pass as a human, move among them, learn their secrets and where they had preserved their greatest defenses.

The question of why Pasiphae Jade wanted the amulets troubled him. Did she plan to attack the human lands, seeking to disarm them in advance? No matter—his task was to find the amulets and free his mother. After that, they could deal together with Pasiphae Jade, including any warmongering she intended.

It would be foolish to reopen war with the humans; that could not be her intent.

But if she focused her attention on the amulets and the humans, then she would not see the plans Lord Narrim laid in the back ways of the palace. Kayvin would go along with her instructions, drawing her away from the nascent rebellion.

"You will have help," she continued, catching his attention. "I have sent others already into the human lands, with instructions to wreak havoc and create alarm. I kept you here to give them time to work."

"What? Why? Now the humans will be on their guard!"

"No, now they will be recalling their terror of us. Just as a child afraid of the dark will reach for tinder, a frightened human will reach for a weapon—and so will reveal its location. If the amulets have been well hidden, then they will need more searching out than you can accomplish alone in our limited time. If the humans are frightened, you have only to follow this distress and let them search their land for you."

Kayvin nodded grudgingly. "I understand."

"Good. But wait for my word to go; we must give them time to spread alarm. One raid or two will not be enough to require the amulets. There will be time to attend your father's funeral, after his preparations are finished."

Kayvin's chest spasmed, but he kept his voice level. "In the meantime, I will go and study what we have written of human culture and customs, if I am to blend in and win their trust," he said. "And I trust you will not distract me from my task, and I will not find another woman in my quarters tomorrow?"

She laughed. "I will not send you another woman."

CHAPTER 23

IT WAS A YOUNG man who came to Kayvin the next morning.

He was keenly handsome, with jet-black hair and the perfectly dusky skin most treasured among the varied tones of the Rideis. His clothing—an open vest over his lightly defined chest, a dyed linen kilt which barely descended to the long, lean thighs, and tiny mineral flecks over all his skin so that he flashed in the balcony's slanting sunlight—revealed him, in every sense of the word, to be a virilo. Kayvin, though a prince, had never had one of the costly specialists trained in the arts of exquisite pleasure, though he had often seen them flaunted through the palace and the nobility's parties.

As Kayvin's eyes fell on him, the young man shifted into a contrapposto posture that displayed his form to best advantage, and he bowed his head. "Good morning, lord."

Kayvin sighed. "Well, you are not a woman."

Yovela, entering at the side of the room, gave a soft snort of laughter. Kayvin ignored her. She was used to the offerings, daily rejected.

The virilo raised his head. "I am not. But if you wish, I—"

"No," Kayvin interrupted curtly. "I am certain you cost a great deal, and I do not wish to insult your no doubt formidable skill, but I have no need of you. Go back to your mistress."

The virilo's expression faltered and immediately smoothed into pleasant confusion. "It is you who are my master, if you please. The Arch Potentate chose me expressly for you."

"If you would please me, do not call her that here." Kayvin shook his head, dropping into his chair and turning to the stack of books and scrolls that awaited him. "She means to buy me as she bought you. Tell her I reject you as well."

The virilo's eyes flickered from Kayvin to Yovela and back. "But I have been sent to you, lord." He took a step toward Kayvin's desk, and then another. "I am well-trained, you will find, and skilled, and if you haven't wanted the others, I can be whatever you like." He stretched a hand to Kayvin's shoulder, fingertips brushing the bare skin above the collar.

Kayvin slapped his hand away, fingers stinging with the impact. "Don't touch me! Get away, get out of my room. Go back to the—her, and tell her I am not pleased with her mockery of a gift."

The retreating virilo bowed deeply, his pleated kilt rising high behind. "I am sorry if I do not please you. I will go as you have ordered."

"Go now," Kayvin repeated irritably, pulling a scroll toward himself. "Get out."

The virilo retreated to the door and closed it behind him.

Kayvin glanced at Yovela. "I told her not to send me any more women."

Yovela sniffed, an expression of disgust seated firmly on her features.

Despite his irritation, Kayvin smiled at her disdain. "You know you and he would occupy the same position if he stayed," he said. "Both members of my sera qadra—small as it is at the moment."

"I do not pretend to such extravagance. I dance, and I sing your songs, and I offer you loyalty in a court where few others did."

The observation stung too near. "You needn't be so honest about it." He pushed the discomfort away with a careless gesture after the departed young man. "And that makes you a suitable judge of a virilo's character?"

"A judge of an object," she said coolly. "Like a statuette, or a piece of fried dough. Something purchased, whether with money or power, and disposed of if inconvenient, is not a character."

He had neither time nor inclination to sort through her allegations. Kayvin unrolled the topmost scroll. "Whether with your pristine loyalty or with his polished haunches, I must still go to find the amulets. And so I must study instead of banter."

Yovela inclined her head in an acknowledging bow. "I will have your breakfast brought."

Kayvin had scarcely finished his breakfast, eaten slowly as he read, when he received the invitation from Pasiphae Jade. The Arch Potentate wished him to join her in her royal quarters for brunch.

Kayvin was not hungry for brunch. But he put aside his papers, dressed appropriately, and went to the rooms that had belonged to his father. He wondered when had been the last time he had been invited here, and then he immediately pushed the question away.

"Come in, come in, my prince," she greeted as he entered. "Please, join me."

She reclined on a short, curved couch on a small dais, set above a table the width of his spread arms. A bench waited for Kayvin beside the table, adjacent to and just below her place. His shoulders tightened. It was an arrangement appropriate for a formal audience or a banquet, but less commonly seen in private rooms. Still, it was not wrong, not for an Arch Potentate, and of course she would not miss a chance to emphasize her new position.

Her stolen position.

The table and seats were near the stone balustrade, looking out upon the garden below. Her sera qadra was spread through the room. One handsome young man reclined against her couch, holding a bowl of seasoned nuts. Another woman followed Kayvin to his bench and lifted a sardonyx cup of watered wine close for his easy reach. He wondered if Pasiphae Jade had inherited them as well from her murdered predecessor. He did not recognize the faces; he'd had no reason to know most of his father's sera qadra. Perhaps he should have known it better.

He took the watered wine. If she wanted to kill him, she would not have preserved him thus far, and she would not need the subtlety of poison after she had stabbed the Arch Potentate in his bed. Whatever the reason she'd called him here, it was not to murder him.

Yet immediately after the obligatory greeting, he asked, "Why have you asked me here?"

She smiled, amused by his hurry. "Don't you think we might eat together? Discuss the kingdom and its affairs? Mend our friendship? We don't know one another well, and I thought we might change that."

Not even she pretended to believe her words, and Kayvin did not return her smile. "I don't believe our friendship can be mended with a meal."

"Our partnership, then. I don't mind if you dislike that we must work together, but we must do it regardless." She dipped her fingers into a proffered bowl and selected a small ball of baked dough. "And I have wanted to give you a gift, though my efforts have fared poorly so far. I thought we might talk about that, too."

He exhaled. "I did not want what you sent."

"I know. I was so disappointed in my gifts, because they disappointed you." She took another bite and nodded toward the garden. "Don't worry; there are consequences for failures. Would you care for some pork? It's so tender, the first of the season's piglets." She indicated the approaching servitor.

Kayvin turned toward the offered platter. The meat was white and moist, sprinkled with finely diced herbs. He selected a slice and glanced up as he lifted it. He jumped in his seat, nearly dropping the meat.

The woman holding the platter faltered, more visible in her posture than expression. Her face was too swollen to convey subtle emotion, her cheeks red and purple with bruising. Her lips were split and scabbed. She dropped her eyes from his gaze.

Kayvin stared.

"You remember Fiera, don't you?" Pasiphae Jade said, choosing a piece of fruit. "But perhaps you don't recognize her, though it was only yesterday. You saw her so briefly, and of course she does not look quite the same."

"Yesterday," Kayvin repeated, and dimly he realized: This was the last woman he had sent away.

"It is such poor service to displease a prince so quickly. I had her slapped for it."

"Slapped?" Kayvin was only repeating her words, but he could not get ahead of the conversation.

"Oh, thirty slaps, enough to warn against future failures but not enough to disfigure. She'll be fine in a week or two, and more attentive to her work." Pasiphae Jade sat back on her couch, and the woman fled with the pork. "Now, the young man you sent away this morning, that's another matter. He likely won't look entirely the same again, no matter the care taken. And that's a shame, with that lovely skin. But, after all, there must be standards."

"What? What do you mean?"

"A virilo should be the most pleasing prize of all, and I took such pains in choosing him. But he earned your dismissal in mere moments. So quickly! A virilo, with so much careful training, should do so much better. I will have him flogged."

Kayvin was aghast, and still struggling. "Did you—did you do this to all the women I sent back to you?"

She continued as if he had not spoken. "I was sorry to hear of your displeasure this morning, and so I invited you here to see how it's corrected." She gestured again toward the garden. "They should be nearly ready."

Despite himself, Kayvin followed her eyes. There was a wooden frame with triangular supports assembled on the plantings below. "Why would you flog a man for that?" he demanded.

"I paid a great deal for a trained pleasurist. He has not performed as expected."

Three guards led the young man across the garden. He looked confused, but he did not resist; he did not understand what awaited. Kayvin looked back to Pasiphae Jade. "A virilo is too expensive to scar in spite."

She gave a disappointed shrug. "He's already proved worthless. It's not as if I could recoup the price of a virilo who does not please."

The handsome young man had realized something was wrong, and he drew back, but the guards forced him over the crossbar. They secured his wrists and ankles at the base of the triangle, exposing his thighs and haunches. The virilo argued in a quick, worried tone, but they ignored him. One stepped back and lifted a whipping wand from the ground.

"Don't do this," Kayvin said, his own voice growing tight. "He has done nothing wrong."

She shook her head. "In your own sera qadra, you might keep whatever disappointing or useless servants you wished. But while it is my reputation he soils with his incompetence—"

The wand hissed and struck, and the young man cried out with surprise and pain.

"Stop it!" Kayvin looked between the Arch Potentate and the bound virilo.

The wand hissed and struck again, and the virilo twisted against the restraints. He pleaded with the guards, his words indistinct. Red streaks blossomed across his thighs.

Kayvin was standing, leaning forward over the table. His anger vanished beneath his horror. "Stop this!"

She turned from the garden balustrade toward him, her face expectant. The young man screamed again.

"I'll take him." The words tumbled from Kayvin, rushed and conceding. "Just stop this." He was squeezing the emptied wine cup too hard, threatening to break it.

"What was that?" she asked, though she smiled with the answer.

Kayvin sucked a breath. "You offered him to me. Let me have him; he should be mine to manage as I see fit."

She had outplayed him. That hideous, devious, fox-faced harpy had outplayed him, unwilling to be thwarted even in her most frivolous whims. Even her outrageously expensive jest of a virilo could not be turned away.

Now he had accepted her lavish gift and admitted her creature into his private quarters.

Pasiphae Jade turned to call toward the frame and the guards. "Unbind him and deliver him to the prince's rooms." She reached for her drink. "I'm glad that's worked out so well. Now you'll have someone to accompany you at the coming banquet, as is proper for a prince. I was worried you might come with only one attendant."

Kayvin sat down heavily on the couch. A lovely woman refilled the wine cup he released, but he wanted neither food nor drink.

"Now, don't look so upset." Pasiphae Jade took a sip from her own cup. "Did you think I wouldn't have someone to watch for me in your rooms? Won't it be better if you already know who it is?" She chuckled. "This is simpler for both of us."

Kayvin's stomach churned. "This was unnecessary."

She held his eyes, and the veneer fell from her voice. "Do not cross me again."

CHAPTER 24

KAYVIN WALKED NUMBLY INTO his rooms, only half seeing the familiar shapes. How many had suffered for his refusal of Pasiphae Jade's wishes? Surely she had not punished each of the women he had sent back—surely she had not? She would have admitted it—boasted of it—if she had, wouldn't she?

He flung himself into a chair, waving away the servant who peered at him.

The men and women serving in Pasiphae Jade's brunch had not seemed appalled, Kayvin thought. She had not drawn her victims from that pool, and they knew themselves secure in the Arch Potentate's circle. She had purchased the virilo specifically for him.

Kayvin had no cause to know the going price of a virilo, but it was a luxury impossible for most purses. A virilo was a proof of high status for his master and for those with whom he was shared in diplomacy or business. Yet she had been willing to ruin that costly purchase to force Kayvin's concession. How much more willing would she be to sacrifice the inconvenient dowager wife of a deposed monarch?

Her display had been cruel and wasteful, and yet it was the most secure purchase of Kayvin's cooperation.

There were voices at the door, and Arad led in a guard and the virilo, carrying a trunk between them. "My lord, I was told to return this one to you," the guard said, lowering his end of the trunk and nodding toward the young man.

Kayvin nodded curtly. "Your task is done. Leave him with me."

The virilo stood in the doorway, almost exactly where he had stood that morning. He did not take a contrapposto stance now but stood rigidly with his feet together. His legs trembled with pain and exhaustion, and rivulets of blood ran down his calves. The glittering sheen was gone, and his jeweled vest hung askew. He pushed a hand across his face and bowed toward Kayvin. "My lord."

Kayvin did not want to deal with this.

Yovela entered from the side door. She paused, looking darkly at the virilo, frowning at his bow and his blood.

"I am sorry I displeased you, my lord. I'll endeavor to do better." The virilo spoke to the floor, still bowing.

"You did not displease me," Kayvin muttered, looking down.

The surprise from the young man was palpable. "But—you had..."

"That was not me," Kayvin said firmly. "That was—a misunderstanding." He made a curt gesture to dismiss the question of the punishment. "What is your name?"

"Dielo, if it pleases you, my lord."

"And if it doesn't please me?"

"You may call me whatever you like, my lord."

"Shut up." Kayvin was angry, angry at Pasiphae Jade for winning this round of her twisted game, and at himself for falling to the manipulation he could so plainly see, and at this slave for being a part of it all.

The virilo sniffed quietly.

"And stand up."

He straightened and rubbed quickly at his face.

Kayvin sighed. "The sera qadra quarters are there, behind Yovela. I expect you'll know how to settle in."

The virilo bowed, lifted the trunk with a little effort, and crossed to the side door. Yovela inched aside, eying him. He dipped again toward Kayvin and then escaped through the door.

Kayvin looked at Yovela, who stood with her mouth turned down. "Go with him."

"Me?" But she nodded and went out the door.

Kayvin put his head into his hand. Now he had Pasiphae Jade's spy in his rooms, and despite the virilo's ostensible role, he could bear no love for Kayvin after his flogging. Still, as Pasiphae Jade had suggested, there was some relief in having it all openly known. He could be cautious around the virilo.

He needed to return to his books and scrolls, to focus on finding the amulets and rescuing his mother. He hoped for another kestrel-marked note from Lord Narrim hinting that another alliance had been made. He did not need distraction by a pretty boy in a sparkling garment, sent to entice him from his duty or flaunt the prince's deficient interests.

Kayvin let his head fall back, his vision blurring on the gold and silver inlay of the intricate ceiling, and groaned his frustration.

"Stop crying," the woman said from the doorway. "It's over now. You got what you wanted."

Dielo jumped a little with the sudden harsh words. He looked up from the floor of the men's sleeping room, where he was kneeling gingerly. The woman in the doorway—Yovela, the prince had called her—was lovely, but her face was set in taut disgust.

He was not crying. But he could have been forgiven if he had been.

Dielo swallowed against the tightness in his throat and answered honestly in his confusion. "I did not want this."

"I saw your look this morning. You were anxious to become a prince's bauble."

Dielo shook his head. "Not like this." His words were coming too fast, and he could not control his speech as he'd been taught. He twisted and probed gingerly at his seeping leg. Panic made his heart race. "I am scarred. Worthless."

"Heh," she bit out. "So you will no longer be a costly plaything, but only like the rest of us. You'll dress in ordinary garments instead of prancing about in gauze and glitter. You have nothing to cry about but your lost pride."

Dielo stared at her, stung anew.

She drew a breath and looked away as she spoke again. "Arad is the steward. He can take you to a physician. You can leave your things for later; there's no one else in the sera qadra but me, and I don't want a virilo's case of fancy clothing and tricks." She turned in the doorway with a scuff of sandal and disappeared, presumably to the women's sleeping room.

Dielo looked after her. No one else in the prince's sera qadra? But it was true, this room was empty—not merely unoccupied in the moment, but completely empty, with no personal belongings and an air of disuse around the empty sleeping pits. But even if the prince had no male members for his sera qadra, surely he had more than one woman? Dielo had never imagined such a situation. Any man wealthy enough to acquire a virilo would already have a few courtesans.

But he could sort that out later. First, he needed treatment for his legs. Perhaps they would not scar much, if he was quick and diligent with medicine. And maybe his first duties wouldn't strain them.

He left the trunk, trusting to Yovela's disinterest, and went to find the steward Arad.

CHAPTER 25

"HE IS PASIPHAE JADE's creature. You cannot trust him."

Yovela checked her step, hearing her thoughts spoken so clearly in another's voice. She did not fully intend to listen, not deliberately, but she did hesitate in the corridor.

"I'm well aware that she's placed him here to watch me and report to her."

"More than that, she has put him in your household to humiliate you." This was Lord Narrim's voice, firm and disdainful. "It is no secret that you skirt the expected manly practices. A virilo is meant to bring honor to his master by publicly illustrating his master's masculine power; this one may do the opposite, at her bidding."

Yovela could not be caught listening in the corridor—but she was a woman of the sera qadra, and it would be expected that she would accompany her prince as he welcomed guests, and expected that she might attend in all but the most sensitive discussions. Suspicion of the new man forced into Prince Kayvin's quarters could hardly be a secret.

She went away long enough to drape a gauzy scarf over her shoulders and to pick up a tray of incense, and then she entered the prince's receiving room with a quick, graceful step.

"I can take precautions," Kayvin was protesting. "I will tell him nothing of our plans. I will not allow him close enough to pry secrets from me."

"Forgive my late arrival," Yovela murmured. "I did not know of my lord's visit."

Lord Narrim hardly looked in her direction. That was no more than she had expected; she was not truly here, not in the argument. "You cannot afford not to allow him close to you! Don't you see, that is her whole plan?"

Yovela knelt across the room and began preparing the incense burner.

"I don't have to invite him to my sleeping pit," Kayvin said, irritated.

Lord Narrim's mouth firmed into a disapproving line. "You are the Amethyst Prince. You are the heir to the Bull Throne. But already rumors start that you are nearer a steer, my lord, and failing to use your virilo appropriately will spread more of the same. You are trying to reclaim a throne! How can the nobles rise to follow a prince who is no man? Who has a sera qadra of one?"

"Two, now," Kayvin muttered, but weakly under the assault.

"If you do not let this virilo serve you, then you sabotage your own resistance by further weakening yourself in the eyes of the court. If you let him close, he is a more valuable spy to her." Lord Narrim shook his head and made a gesture of despair. "You make my work to raise support very difficult, my lord, by bringing this virilo into your household."

"First you say I must have a visible virilo, and then you say I shouldn't," Kayvin snapped. "You cannot have it both ways."

"It would have been different if you had maintained your own sera qadra as expected. You could have been the powerful prince all would have wanted to follow, instead of keeping singers and artists and then sending them away when you most needed the appearance of strength."

Kayvin glared. "So you say if I had kept my courtesans close, as my father did, I would not be in this perilous position now?"

Lord Narrim rolled his eyes, a gesture few could have dared with the Amethyst Prince if not a trusted tutor—or making an argument for his public weakness. "Do as you will, my lord. But know that every night that your pit is lonely, you push away the recovery of your throne. If you cannot dominate even your own sera qadra, you cannot command the warriors of your nobles or the court of the Bull Throne. If no young man will serve you, if even no woman will bow to you, then you cannot ask the noblest houses to bow, either."

Yovela fanned the rising incense smoke with restrained fury.

Lord Narrim rose from his cushion and looked down on Prince Kayvin. "There are recipes, if you have need of—"

"Enough of that," Kayvin growled, his eyes on the floor. "I suffer no lack of function."

"Only a lack of will or strength," Narrim replied.

Kayvin said nothing, but his jaw bulged.

"In better news, I have had discreet inquiries," Narrim said. "Not everyone is pleased with Lord Fretton's assumptions, and I have even received an offer of funds for our endeavors. So keep your spirits up."

"Who? How many?"

Narrim shook his head. "I won't know how many until after the banquet. I will take you to meet them then. But I can tell you now, this first promise is no small thing. So you must show yourself a true prince, one who will draw the right lords to his banner."

Yovela ducked her head and did not look at Kayvin's chided embarrassment.

"In the meantime, think about what I said, and try to decide how you can use this virilo in public view without letting him come close enough to ruin you."

Yovela waited in the side corridor, counting her breaths to keep them steady. Then she heard footsteps, and with a nod of determination she stepped out, putting herself in Lord Narrim's path. She looked down, holding the thin scarf to her shoulder and chest with one hand.

He stopped and eyed her. "You're the one that's left."

"Yes, my lord. And I want to help him."

"As you should."

"Please tell me what I can do to aid him. I will do additional work for you and your faction, carrying discreet messages or whatever you might need."

He gave a little huffing chuckle. "You are a woman of his sera qadra. You cannot move discreetly; all the palace will know if you are lent to different sleeping pits." He scowled. "And he cannot afford any more speculation on whether his own pit is lonely."

Yovela had nothing to say to this.

Narrim fixed his eyes on her, appraising her from hair to feet and back. "Is it you? You have enough to offer, but perhaps it's not a satisfying whole?" He stepped forward. "Are you a cause of his weakness?"

The wall was uncomfortably close, pressing against her back, and his herbed breath brushed her cheek. Yovela fought to keep her voice steady. "I serve the Amethyst Prince."

Lord Narrim's mouth twisted. "Foolish girl. As if I could be tempted by a bland little piece unable to hold even a young man's attention. I do not take other men's leavings."

Despite her discomfort, the words stung, setting a measure and at once cutting her short of it.

"And even if somehow I wanted you..." His mouth turned in a faint sneer. "You could not refuse me. Your prince is adrift in a wide sea, and I am his only chance of reclaiming his throne."

It was true. She had to rely upon a protector, and her protector could not protect her from the one he needed to protect him.

She stood against the wall, hardly breathing, with nothing to answer.

Lord Narrim took a step back. "If you would help your prince, then show his court the man they must see if they are to join him."

He walked away, leaving her uneasy and helpless.

CHAPTER 26

THE BANQUET HAD BEGUN.

Kayvin stood close to the corridor wall and took a measured breath to calm his queasy stomach as servants filed through the arched door bearing trays of fruits and sweets and delicacies. He had no appetite, but it would be rude manners to refuse food at the feast, and Pasiphae Jade would miss no opportunity to mark his inappropriate behavior for later remonstrance or to discredit him before the nobles.

The elite had all been seated, and only the royals remained. Kayvin ground his jaw. His mother was royal, more royal than the whore who sat on the Bull Throne now, but of course she would not be attending. Kayvin would enter first, Amethyst Prince and heir, and then Pasiphae Jade would take her place as Arch Potentate and giver of the feast, and all would praise her and affirm her place, and Kayvin would be forced to watch and endure.

How he hated her.

"My lord?"

He turned to see Nala, a servant from his apartments. She extended her palm to show a golden ear cuff. "I found this on the floor, and I thought you might want it."

He did not much care whether he had one more or less bauble, but she had done what she thought right, and he smiled and nodded. "Thank you." He fit it onto his right ear and then adjusted the elaborate stick in his pinned hair.

He wore the gilded hair stick his father had given him, on his pinning day, in the hope it would display his royal heritage and regard. He did not hope much, though.

Nala smiled, pleased to have been of help, and retreated down the corridor again toward his rooms. He wished he could go with her.

"We are ready, my lord."

Kayvin set his expression and nodded. Dielo and Yovela stepped into place, two steps behind on either side of him. They were resplendent in their court attire, all draping silk and worked metal, with the glittering coronets of their sera qadra station upon their ornately twisted hair.

They entered the feast hall. The floor was carpeted in petals, mingled red and white and yellow, deep enough to cover his sandals as he walked. Here and there the tiles were left bare to show a particularly fine mosaic and to provide a safe footing for performers, but already the scent from the trodden petals was overwhelming.

His place was on a dais a little apart from the nobles' tables, where he could look over them and they could easily observe their prince. He sat in the great chair, and Yovela and Dielo stood on either side. They eyed each other, and Kayvin recalled belatedly that he should have chosen one to sit at his feet, a typical mark of favor and of display. He had not thought of it in his consternation, and neither of them had asked, which would be seen as grasping after position. He might even now gesture one or the other into place, but he could imagine the bitter insults that would come of it, no matter how he chose, and he would not subject himself to more this night. He left them on either side, flanking him.

Now Pasiphae Jade swept into the hall, gown streaming around her and a phalanx of professionally beautiful men and women trailing her. She was devastating and exquisite, with her hair twisted high and sparkling with jewels and her clothing wrapped and folded to most flatter her well-preserved form. The nobles applauded her. She gave them a dazzling smile that passed over all the room except for Kayvin's seat.

He burned with anger and fresh humiliation. By custom, each royal was accompanied by his or her sera qadra, and now Kayvin almost regretted emptying his. Beside Pasiphae Jade's decadent entourage, settling about her chair in various aspects of service and aesthetics, his meager accompaniment made him look abandoned. It was hardly a way to win back support from the nobles.

Kayvin was such a fool. He had never paid attention to the court games, while Pasiphae Jade had learned well the arts of appearances, and now he was forfeiting battles he hadn't known he should enter.

Or, he mused, he could own his error and make it intentional. He had only two attendants, perhaps the mark not of a forsaken prince but of a powerful warrior who did not need fawning servants. Even now a young woman held Pasiphae Jade's jeweled jasper cup for another to fill; he would pour his own drinks, take his own meat, sit alone. It would look deliberate, intentional, a rejection of the sumptuous decadence that had led to his father's downfall and a return to the fiercer heritage of their people.

Beside him, Dielo presented a plate of carved fruits, and Kayvin waved it curtly away. When the servants brought the meat to his seat, he took a piece for himself and sat back in his great chair. He looked over the dining hall and tried to recall the arrogant sprawl his father had displayed at feasts.

Or was that a poor image, as his father had been killed? He knew so little of court games. Why had he played at music and magic instead of learning what mattered?

Maybe he should be seen observing his nobles, weighing their worth, as if his opinion of them might still matter. Or did they all know his consideration meant nothing, and would they privately laugh at his posturing?

He drank deep of his wine from his goblet of carved amethyst and wished the feast were done.

A handsome young man sat at the edge of Pasiphae Jade's dais, resting his arm on a raised knee and leaning back against her chair; Kayvin thought it was the same who had held her bowl at the coercive brunch. She toyed absently with his hair as she observed her feast.

At Kayvin's arm, Dielo held out a handful of dark berries. "Try these, my lord," he prompted.

Kayvin pushed the hand away. "Let me be."

Dielo hesitated. "I only want to be of use."

On his other side, Yovela snorted. "He wants to bend backward and let you graze them off his belly." She gave Dielo a withering look.

"You squabble like children," Kayvin said wearily. In truth, it was always Yovela who spoke cruelties, but he was equally tired of the virilo's meek acceptance, as if he invited the barbs. He suspected

Dielo had been trained not to argue lest it be unbecoming, but to Kayvin it looked more spineless than seductive.

Now Dielo only looked down at his berries and then across the room to where Pasiphae Jade sat with her coterie of men and women. Kayvin growled to himself and took another drink of wine. He would be drunk before they finished, but the night might be easier to endure.

Dielo had seen feasts before, though he had never sat so high as with a prince. He had accompanied a seated guest only once before, and that merely to fill out the visible group of servants. A man looked more important when attended by so many. Standing beside the prince tonight, a royal virilo, should have been an achievement.

But he felt no achievement this night. At least Prince Kayvin had not given Yovela the position of honor, but that seemed more an oversight than an indication of their respective standings. Prince Kayvin was ignoring his sera qadra instead of allowing them to attend him, as was their role.

Dielo looked toward the group around Pasiphae Jade, and his eye met another's. Riolo, sitting beside the Arch Potentate, rotated his wrist slightly to better display his bare upper arm.

Dielo and Riolo had come together to the palace when Pasiphae Jade had called for virilos. Riolo knew Dielo had been sent to the prince and had been rejected. Though Dielo had chosen long, loose trousers for tonight—he had not been able to find the laced tunic he wanted to accompany them—Riolo knew Dielo had been disfigured for failing to please and now served a master who did not want him. Riolo, his eyes coldly gleaming, knew he served an empress, while Dielo could not win a word from a displaced prince.

Dielo's pulse pounded and he caught up a handful of berries. He ran practiced fingers over them and selected the best, taut with ripeness and dark with flavor, and turned to his master. "Try these, lord."

But Prince Kayvin pushed his hand away without so much as a glance.

The gesture—visible to the entire room—hurt like a blow. Dielo had one role, and Kayvin had negated it. Dielo took a breath. Perhaps his lord was distracted, perhaps he did not think of what he did. Dielo tried again, prompting gently, "I only want to be of use."

Kayvin did not respond, staring straight ahead. It was Yovela who answered, but speaking to their lord. "He wants to bend backward and let you graze them off his belly." She gave Dielo that look of disdain she had perfected, an eloquent opinion on the difference between them even if they were both pleasure servants in the sera qadra.

The words sliced Dielo. It was not true; if his master did not wish to use him for that sort of pleasure, there were other ways Dielo could serve, and proffering berries was the least of these. Only, he needed something, some service, some appreciation, some use.

He looked toward Pasiphae Jade's dais and saw the others there were watching; they had seen. Riolo caught Dielo's eye with a smug, disdainful smile, though a few others offered pitying glances. Both burned like the sting of the cane.

All his life Dielo had trained to please, and now his efforts were pushed aside like a discarded piece of fruit. Humiliation scorched him, and he kept his eyes down, as if play-feigning modesty. He took one of the berries and chewed, but he tasted nothing.

He looked up as two servants brought an enormous platter for Prince Kayvin's choice, and he saw Pasiphae Jade herself looking at him. He flushed with fresh emotion, but she only observed him distantly as if appraising an animal at market.

Riolo took a fig from the platter Pasiphae Jade's servants were assembling, lifted it and waited to be certain Dielo saw him, and then bit into it with a flash of white teeth.

Dielo turned away, but Kayvin was refilling his own drink, and Yovela, beautiful in her silks, was looking forward as if no one else in the noisy room could interest her. Dielo swallowed and tried to look at ease.

A virilo who sat unnoticed to one side was a contradiction, a failure, a figure of laughter. He had to draw attention, to bring honor to his new prince and to demonstrate his worth to him.

He left his master's side and threw a sidelong glance at the musicians in their corner. They were well accustomed to events of royal decadence, and that was all the communication needed. The drummer struck up a rapid staccato run that culminated in a sharp strike, and Dielo took his place at the front of Prince Kayvin's dais, snapping his limbs into a posture of controlled power, a held breath in visual form.

Then the drum and plucked strings began together, and Dielo began to dance.

This was not a dance to seduce or a dance to overawe. It was a dance to display his prowess, to show his training. It was a dance to highlight his skill, flaunt his educated culture, to make the other guests envious of Prince Kayvin's prize.

He danced through his injuries, determined to show himself well. He leapt and bent like a sapling, and he turned and rooted like an oak. He inclined his head and he tossed his hair and he set his eyes across the room in an intense dare. He stretched long and contracted. At last he slid to his knees in front of his prince, arms extended.

The long table of guests cheered and applauded, whistling their approval.

He had done well; he had brought attention and praise to his master. Dielo rose smoothly, lifting his eyes to see if he had won the prince's approval as well. But he saw Yovela moving from her place, coming forward on the dais. She lifted one leg and held herself in perfect balance, demonstrating flexibility and strength Dielo could only hope to match, and then leapt into a wild display.

The musicians scrambled to keep up with her pace as she spun, bent, leapt, lifted. She was a flower petal on the breeze and the wind in one's hair, and Dielo's heart sank as she continued. He was too well-trained to betray jealousy, but he had lost this chance to win his master's favor. Dielo was a virilo, trained in many skills for pleasure, for relaxation, and for entertainment; Yovela was a dancer, specialized beyond his ability.

She finished with a mad spin, faster and faster in place, hair and skirts flying, until at last she came to a perfect halt with a clap over her head. The room erupted in applause.

Useless. Dielo lowered himself beside Prince Kayvin, careful of his healing legs, and wondered what he had done to offend queen, prince, or god.

CHAPTER 27

IT WAS LATE IN the night, nearer dawn than dusk, and Kayvin's head pounded with the wine, the endless music, the overloud laughter, the intermittent dancing by beautiful servants and stumbling, grinning banquet guests. He rested his head on his fist and hoped he did not look too disengaged. If anyone bothered to look at him.

His sera qadra did not draw the eye as did Pasiphae Jade's rotating coterie. Neither Yovela nor Dielo had done much since their consecutive dances hours ago. They looked good, though; even in his alcoholic misery, Kayvin could observe that. They performed their roles better than he did his own.

He thought he might have another cup of wine.

There was movement at the far end of the hall. The room gradually quieted in anticipation as an upright wooden frame was wheeled into the great room. A man dangled from his bound wrists, his toes just skimming the base crossbeam, stretching to take his weight first on one foot, then another as he swayed with the frame's motion. There was a hood over his head, but the rest of him was bared to the drunken hoots of the banquet diners.

Pasiphae Jade stood, muting the speculation. "Just as salt will bring out more sweetness, it was a custom of old to season a feast with blood, so that the guests might enjoy their own pleasures the more. But many consider it too barbarous these days, and so we no longer have bouts of combat or a criminal's whipping or bound races about the hall. That's just as well, for none of us love cruelty or waste—but I wish to show you how I mean to preserve Mandoral in the time-honored ways, and so I have brought you an old custom in a new service."

Kayvin did not understand, but the lords at Pasiphae Jade's long table were intrigued.

"Tomorrow we place the water-purified bones of His Illustrious Excellency into the royal mausoleum. It was once traditional to send a servant into the afterlife with an Arch Potentate. I have selected a retainer to again accompany our late lord, and tonight we will prepare him for his duty."

The man was gagged beneath the hood; with the music stilled and the guests quieted to listen to their new Arch Potentate, Kayvin could just hear his muffled protests.

"Rest easy, for this man chose his own fate. He assured me he had no desire to serve the new Arch Potentate, and he swore he would dedicate his remaining life to Gromgest's memory and legacy."

The banquet guests were drunk, and so it took longer than it should have for the realization to work its way through the room. This man was not chosen at random; this was a noble who had not supported the new potentate and so had to be removed.

Eyes began darting about the room as guests tried to calculate who was not present at the table. With over a hundred seated in long rows, and with bodies swaying to look back and forth, it was not an easy exercise.

"Will you not tell us his name?" This was Lord Scallong, seated high at the table and flanked by a half dozen beautiful hangers-on. Probably at least a couple of them had been dispatched by other lords to vie for attention and favor. Kayvin squeezed his cup and wondered why he had ever thought this reasonable.

"Be patient, I beg my lord." Pasiphae Jade's tone did not beg, despite her words, and Kayvin thought there was an extra bit of crystalline edge to her voice. "Or have you missed someone?"

"I? No, of course not." Scallong spread his hands to indicate the beauties on either side. "I'm only curious."

"Then wait a moment, and all will be revealed."

"All, you say?" Scallong raised an eyebrow and took a calculated sip from the jeweled goblet presented by a dusky blond. "Then, by all means, proceed."

Pasiphae Jade swept her eyes over the rest of the banquet. "We will not sully his brave sacrifice with much blood, nor will we disturb your merriment, but we will honor the ancient traditions with a brief exercise." She nodded.

One of the guards who had brought in the frame took a whipping wand from its place on a supporting beam. He slashed the bound man once, bringing a long streak from far shoulder to near hip. Then as the man twisted and whined, he crossed to the other side and repeated the blow, opening a similar welt in the opposite direction, so that a large X was formed over the man's back.

A few guests cheered or jeered, emboldened by the alcohol, by the certainty that their own friends were visible at the long table, and most of all by the relief that it was not them dangling from the frame.

"And now, we send this loyal retainer to enjoy his loyalty forever at his master's side, honored in the place he has chosen for himself."

She gestured, and the other guard stepped to the prisoner and garroted him. It was not a quick death, and the prisoner struggled and choked, but at last he stilled and dangled limply, his toes knuckling over when they brushed the floor.

Kayvin stared, feeling ill. He should have done something. There was nothing he could have done.

The display—public humiliation, pain, death—was working as intended. The lords about the table had turned upon the prisoner, jeering at his death, putting as much conceptual distance as possible between his gooseflesh-covered body and themselves.

"Cut him down," Pasiphae Jade ordered.

The body dropped deep into the flower petals in a disorderly heap, painfully lacking the calm repose of a ceremonial death. The guard bent and tugged the hood free, pulling grey-black hair loose.

Lord Narrim.

Kayvin wanted to be sick, but his stomach seemed as paralyzed as the rest of him. *Wait for us, my prince. We will not bow to a usurper.* And now he lay dead and mocked on the banquet floor.

Something brushed Kayvin's fingers. It was Yovela, gathering his hand into hers and pressing it, all the consolation she could safely offer in the treacherous theater of the banquet. A heartbeat later, Dielo took his other hand, not recognizing the significance of the dead prisoner but perceiving the effect on his prince. Kayvin was aware of them, but he could not respond.

With Lord Narrim died any alliance. Kayvin was alone, utterly alone.

In sudden hopeful desperation, he looked toward the head of the long table to where Lord Scallong sat, in case the lord's questions had indicated a secret concern and possible alliance with Narrim. Scallong would be a powerful ally.

But Lord Scallong reclined on one elbow, a smirk visible over the piece of cheese he held. Any fear or regret in the room belonged to the Amethyst Prince alone.

The mess was cleared away, and more wine was brought. Kayvin sat still, not looking toward the high seat where Pasiphae Jade had resumed her seat. He knew he was too numb to feel yet what had happened; that would come in merciless waves as the wine wore off.

CHAPTER 28

FUNERALS HAD ONCE INCLUDED songs. Kayvin knew this because he had studied many classic compositions once written for state funerals.

There was still music, this time, but it was staid and rote, a traditional piece Kayvin remembered from funerals when he was a child and from a couple of minor nobles' services. It was not performed in honor of the deceased but played by musicians to one side to fill any awkward gaps of silence and to permit quiet whispers among the mourners. It was a safe piece, not too emotional and intended to blur into the background of the rituals. That was somehow fitting, as Kayvin's father was removed from his position and hidden away in a mausoleum.

Kayvin did not weep as the water-ashes were placed, first a grand cinerary urn for the Arch Potentate and then a smaller, less decorated vessel for Lord Narrim, following his ruler into death and leaving Kayvin alone in the usurper's court. He did not weep as Pasiphae Jade bowed a final respect to her lord, lover, and predecessor. He did not weep as the courtiers dropped their white flowers upon the path and then turned to follow her back to the palace.

He did not follow. He stood, staring into the dark opening of the royal mausoleum. Generations waited there. Some had been great, by any definition of the word. Others had inherited greatness. Others had claimed it by association rather than by deed. At last the line had come to Kayvin, who only stood in the cool morning and watched as his father's murderer placed him into a stone cell for the rest of time.

The laborers waiting to replace the sealing stone squatted behind the musicians. They could wait. On either side of Kayvin, Yovela and Dielo stood silent, near enough that he could almost feel the pressure of their arms but without touching him. Neither moved but for the motion of their silks and gauzes in the breeze.

The musicians finished the stale threnody and rested their instruments. They should have played as long as Kayvin stood a mourner, but even the hired players knew he was a prince in name only.

His flower had crumpled in his warm grip, and he tossed it forward to the mausoleum's threshold, where it lay lonely and misshapen. Kayvin blew out a quick breath and turned away. Yovela and Dielo moved with him in perfect cadence.

Safely returned to his apartments, Kayvin held out his arms for the stripping of his funeral finery. Then, with the eyes of his servants and his small sera qadra silently following, he drifted in search of a place to sit. He did not want the garden, too bright for his mood and in this season inducing sneezes. He did not want his sleeping pit, too clearly a retreat. He did not want his desk, too closely tied to his readings for Pasiphae Jade and his lessons as a prince.

Dielo was arranging cushions and pillows on the balcony, where two walls came together. As Kayvin paced near, he stood and gestured. "I will bring you some refreshment," he offered quietly.

Kayvin took the pile of cushions, for lack of anywhere else to go, and sank into the soft corner. Hanging vines gave a sense of enclosure even in the open air. The virilo had guessed his unspoken discomfort and met it; that was his purpose, after all.

But Kayvin would not want his refreshment. He had suffered a chronic queasiness since the banquet. He did not want to be coaxed into happiness with sweets, not on the day of his father's interment.

Yovela sat beside him and adjusted a pillow to lean upon. She laid an open hand near him, palm up, available if he wanted it. He was not sure if he did.

He was grieving, he knew, but he was not grieving only his father. He also grieved his mother, who was not dead but who was certainly gone, and who hung in danger with every day that he did not please Pasiphae Jade. He grieved Lord Narrim, who had not been close but who had been loyal. He grieved the prince he had been, carefree and lost in amusements, and he now grieved the prince he could have been, astute and prepared.

Yovela's hand wrapped about his forearm, loose but warm. He let out a small breath.

Dielo returned and uncovered a plate. "I asked the kitchen to have savory meat buns ready for our return. There are three fillings, I believe."

Kayvin shook his head. "I'm not hungry."

"My lord, you have hardly eaten your meals. You had little at the banquet."

"I had wine at the banquet. I'm still feeling it." That probably was not helping his queasiness.

"Then try—"

"I don't want it." Kayvin waved his hand. "You two eat them."

Dielo dropped his head. After a moment, Yovela took one of the buns and bit into it.

It smelled good—he could recognize the richness of the aroma even if he did not want the bun, in the same way that he could appreciate the sensuous beauty of the sera qadra or the athletic allure of a dance or the cool refreshment of a pool he did not wish to enter. He closed his eyes. He wanted to tell them to leave him alone, but he did not have the strength for the words.

Yovela settled nearer him, her shoulder against his arm. She said nothing. It was pleasant.

After a moment, there was a rustle of fabric, and then Dielo arranged himself on Kayvin's other side. He sat close, not quite touching. After a moment, there was another burst of spiced meat in the air. Kayvin kept his eyes closed and drank in their stillness.

He was keenly, painfully aware of his extravagant prerogative in this moment. He could eat the exquisite buns with their costly spices. He could request the services of his sera qadra, who would massage his aching head or bathe his feet or simply share their warmth against the creeping bone-deep cold of loss. He grieved in luxury.

But what he wanted was not soft fingers in his hair or flower petals in his bath or tasty morsels proffered by beautiful servants. What he wanted was a life that did not leave his stomach churning with fear for everyone he knew.

CHAPTER 29

DIELO DID NOT LIKE sitting alone in the empty men's sleeping room.

His entrance to the palace had been nothing like he had imagined. First he had been selected and brought to the Arch Potentate—a thrilling achievement, full of promise—and had been selected again for the Amethyst Prince. But that exhilaration had been brief, for then he was rejected. Rejection was unthinkable, but it did not compare to the humiliation and punishment that followed. Finally he had been sent to the prince again, but he had not been welcomed.

Stop crying. You got what you wanted.

He recalled those words, spoken from the doorway into his empty room, more than he liked. He had not been crying, not really; he'd only been in shock with the unexpected flogging and then his distinctly chilled welcome into the prince's court. Yes, he'd been wiping his damp eyes, but that was not so unforgivable as he also wiped seeping blood from his thighs.

It had shaken him beyond imagination—not only the physical pain of the moment, but the shocking realization that he was not protected even in his prized status. He was suddenly as vulnerable as any of the palace drudges, if with prettier words for his vulnerability—and perhaps even more so, as his new master did not seem to want him. Everything he had trained and hoped for had proved a fragile wall against danger, and he stood disoriented and afraid in its wreckage.

He'd hardly believed at first that the prince's sera qadra was almost entirely empty. He had assumed Yovela was jealous, a pleasure woman threatened by the arrival of a virilo.

I saw your look this morning. You were anxious to become a prince's bauble.

Dielo blinked against the memory and paused his pumice stone to examine his work. Whether called to his lord's sleeping pit or not, he had to be presentable for public and private events. A virilo should be an object of envy; it was his task to bring honor to his lord.

Now, that meant wearing draping trousers instead of kilts. He'd had good legs, and most had liked the expansive display of his perfect skin. Even his chit depicted him in a short kilt. Now the wounds on his legs had mostly closed, but the streaks remained, vivid reminders that he had not pleased.

He approved his freshly smoothed skin and began buffing a fingernail. It would not do to have a careless snag disrupt a moment of closeness.

Yovela had good cause to be jealous, as Dielo had not yet seen her called to the prince's sleeping pit. But all knew the conquest of a man signified greater potency than the conquest of a woman; that was why virilos had first come into service, highlighting the most elite and capable. The only oddity was that Dielo had still not been called either.

In all his years of training, he had never imagined being wholly unwanted.

He licked his lips and whispered to the empty room, "My lord, what might I do to be of better service?" There was an edge to his voice, a rasp that betrayed the urgency of the question even in rehearsal.

I am trained in many skills, my lord. I danced for you, because I did not know you already had a dancer. But I have practiced many arts for pleasure and entertainment. I can provide an aid to relaxation against worry and distress, and I have noticed my lord is often—

No, that would not do. Admitting he saw the prince's conflicted obedience to the usurper of his throne would not win Dielo favor.

Is there nothing I can do for you? I can serve many preferences, I can—

No, that was too near pressuring a man who clearly rejected such enticement. And if Pasiphae Jade had been a courtesan who murdered her lord in his own sleeping pit, as was whispered, Prince Kayvin could view insistence only as a threat.

But Dielo had to find a way to serve him.

A virilo was chosen and trained for service. A virilo did not simply enable an act of physical pleasure but practiced an art to bring the greatest experience to his patron. He did this not in exchange for coin, but for a place of honor, bringing greater status to his patron and by extension to the virilo. Dielo had been so trained from a young age: He would earn his status and security by pleasing the powerful.

But now he was scarred, and no other would find him handsome. His training, everything he had studied to make himself desirable, was unused. He dressed himself in his most alluring garb, and the prince asked instead for his opinion on a chorus.

Prince Kayvin did not think himself cruel, but he had made Dielo worthless and helpless.

It was your training that made you worthless and helpless.

The harsh words came in Yovela's voice, though she was nowhere in sight. He wondered how she had pierced him so deeply that she could mock him even in the empty men's quarters, even within his own mind.

His breath whined in his throat.

He knew the argument he imagined now in her voice; he had heard it before, from others jealous of a virilo's power and prestige. They said that he was never chosen to be valued, that he would always be disposable. Virilos' chits were arrayed before elite men, and all represented fresh youths, never men past their first looks. He was not appreciated for himself, only for what he could make the elite feel for a time.

But that was a cynical view that thought poorly of a virilo's ability. They were well cared for precisely because they were valuable. A skilled virilo could accrue gifts enough to support himself once his career was over. And some even stayed with their masters for years, despite sagging muscles and starting paunches. Dielo would never let himself go in that fashion, but that some could was a testament to the power of committed appeal. Some earned love.

He blew out his breath. With determination to clear his mind, he turned on the floor and began his bodyweight exercises—arms only for now, until his legs had finished healing. He dared not strain the new skin.

He had bought salve for his thighs. Perhaps they would not scar much, if he was diligent with medicine. He would be healed enough to be ready for whatever was needed. But first, he would do his duty to his lord. Perhaps Prince Kayvin did not want that sort of physical pleasure, not now, but Dielo had many skills and he could see that his lord suffered. He would serve however he could, for now. And someday the prince would recognize him and repay him with favor.

CHAPTER 30

KAYVIN HAD ALWAYS PRACTICED magic.

Magic was expected of elite sons, a nod to days of war and glory—but in tasteful moderation, of course. There were other ways to display one's prowess in court, more pleasurable and less difficult, and most sons grew out of their magic phase as quickly as possible, leaving off facing imaginary sorcerers and instead pinching the serving girls. It was far easier to flaunt power with a beautiful sera qadra than by refining bolts of energy for hours upon hours.

There were traditions for a prince, however, and anyway Kayvin found more satisfaction in magic than in preening for display, and he had kept the practice throughout his youth and into manhood. For his pinning ceremony, marking his coming of age, Kayvin had asked for a book on fire spells. He'd had the sense to ask privately, and in the end his mother had quietly given him the book herself after his father had made a more public affair of his son's finely engraved spearhead. Kayvin had been embarrassed at times, and even nearly ashamed, and he did not often speak to others of his hobby. But now Kayvin regretted nothing.

Since his father's death, he had spent hours in his little courtyard, practicing his forms. He had composed a program of fire exercises to challenge all his skills, not just those he enjoyed, and he ran through it dozens of times each morning to build strength, endurance, and control.

He told himself it was like practicing scales. He needed his magic to be fluent and available without conscious thought, so that when he had the chance to kill Pasiphae Jade, he could do so.

He wanted that chance.

He had never thought of killing before. Yes, his tutors in magic had taught in terms of attack and defense, and yes, he knew their history of warring with magic. But he had never before grappled with the idea of actually killing someone, and he wondered if he could.

Whenever he wavered, he thought of his mother, trapped in ice, waiting for him to rescue her.

Pasiphae Jade had used magic to steal a kingdom and his mother, and he would need magic to face her. Until then, he would need magic to travel safely in the dangerous human lands.

He trained each morning in his garden, bending fire to his will. He kept a series of upright poetry stones to make the garden correct, but he turned the poems outward so that he had a half-ring of stone targets he could use with less guilt than if he scorched the ancient literature.

When had Pasiphae Jade practiced? Even a sera qadra woman had time of her own, but where had she found the privacy to train?

Tiny ice figures, to build control and to appear harmless. Repeated in humorous variations, to amuse and to build endurance.

Each morning Kayvin practiced until sweat poured from him, from his fires and his exertions, and then he retreated into his rooms. Arad or Nala—today it was Nala—would meet him with a cooling drink, and then he would bathe, and then he would sit to read historians' and scholars' notes until his eyes ached.

Still he was held here, waiting to be released to search for the mages' amulets. He should have been chafing under the restriction, but in truth he was afraid of what lay before him. To go into the human lands? To try to pass himself off as one of them? And even if he managed to blend in, how could he hope to track down the amulets? What if they were scattered across the human realm?

What if he found them all, and Pasiphae Jade still did not release his mother?

But she would. Her safety, her position, depended on promising Kayvin what he wanted, and if she lied, she lost all of that.

He wished for music, but that was a luxury to be rationed while he worked to free his mother. There was music in his magic, too; he could not explain it, and it was not literally true, but he felt the sweep of notes in the sweep of energies.

It was not that he did not mourn his father. But Gromgest was gone, and Kayvin could do nothing for the crushed bone already consigned to the burial grounds. Gromgest had not taken a close interest in his children, trusting that tutors and tradition would prepare his heir. Raea could still be saved, and Kayvin would not lose time to mindless grief instead of working toward her release.

He sat up from his desk and stretched, trying to bend his neck and spine backward as if that would cancel out the posture of reading. He passed a hand over his face, closing his eyes briefly.

But there was no time to waste; he had to find the amulets, lost in human lore. He picked up the tablet of bound pages and tried to settle in a different position.

He heard someone pass through the room. The footsteps slowed at the point nearest his desk—Dielo, probably—and then continued. Kayvin sighed and turned the page.

Dielo entered the royal room and stood waiting. He was not dressed in his finest, not the gauzy robes and kilts meant to display to best advantage, and he still could not find his laced tunic, a good choice for answering a potentate's summons, but he had dressed well. He had dressed to cover the streaks on his legs that ensured he would never command a virilo's price again.

The prince had said he had not ordered Dielo flogged, but that could leave only the Arch Potentate. The prince had said it had been a misunderstanding, but that also strained credulity. The order had been so extraordinary, so unthinkable for a costly virilo, that surely it had been questioned. So who had given the unfathomable order?

Now Pasiphae Jade had called him to her own chambers.

Young men and women were scattered about the room in various stages of draping costume, performing minor tasks or simply waiting like animate art. Pasiphae Jade had been a courtesan herself before her rise, and she knew what was expected of a powerful ruler.

"Dielo," she said, reclining on a cushioned couch with a document in her hand. "I'm glad you've come. I have questions only you can answer."

Dielo stood straight, grateful for the years of training that molded him into an aesthetic posture and gave him the proper role to play. "I am glad to serve, but what could I answer for you, Illustrious Excellency?"

"You can tell me how your master spends his time. He is reluctant to speak with me, and when he does his tone is most intemperate. So I am forced to turn to you, his virilo, to tell me how his preparations proceed for going across the mountains."

Dielo's heart quickened. "A virilo cannot speak of his master, Illustrious Excellency," he said, smiling with just a hint of affront. "His role is to be a refuge, and a confidant cannot share a confidence."

Pasiphae Jade listened, nodded, and then gave a sweep of her hand across the room. "Leave us. I need to speak to Dielo privately."

The pretty men and women gathered themselves and retreated to the sera qadra's quarters, leaving Dielo alone before the potentate.

Pasiphae Jade put down the document and sat upright, braced on one hand. "Let me be frank with you. I was once like you; I have learned better. But you are young, and you are still foolish, and I can see you may need your eyes opened to the truth."

Dielo controlled his breath, kept his posture, reminded himself that he was not hers. He served the prince, and she could not have him whipped again. He did not think she could.

She half smiled. "Oh, Dielo." She twisted on the couch to the little cabinet behind her, with a row of tiny figures upon a shelf.

She took one out, identifiable by its deep-black hair and perfectly dusky-gold skin, interrupted only by a short kilt.

She still held his chit. Dielo served Prince Kayvin, a lent luxury, but at Pasiphae Jade's command and pleasure.

She noted his recognition and replaced the chit. "I am sorry if your current position is not as fulfilling as you might have expected."

"I am glad to serve the prince," Dielo answered automatically.

Pasiphae Jade shook her head. "I was something like you once. But I earned my place and my status, because I understood what my role was."

Dielo waited, unspeaking. She did not seem to require an answer.

Pasiphae Jade fixed her eyes on Dielo. "Do you know our role? What service we provide to our masters?"

"We provide a respite from the trials and pressures of life, and pleasure—"

"Wrong." Pasiphae Jade cut him off with a curt tone and gesture. "That is what you were taught to say. It is what they think, and it is even what we may think, but it is not the truth."

Dielo swallowed. "What is the truth?"

"We provide power." Pasiphae Jade rose, her robe slipping over her shoulder with practiced ease. "We are prey to be caught, which makes them feel dangerous, or we are weaker souls to be protected, which makes them feel strong, or we are trophies to be displayed, which makes them feel envied or respected, but we are always a means to power."

Dielo watched her move. What she said made sense, and it was not incompatible with all he had been taught about pleasing those who could give him a better life and a secure position.

But then there was always the ultimate enticement, hanging invisibly in the air for every virilo trained to be more than a common prostitute. "But there is love."

"Is there?" Pasiphae Jade laughed. "Maybe there is, I can't say. But when we use the same mechanism for power and for love, it's possible the two are confused."

Dielo did not speak.

Pasiphae Jade faced him and leaned forward. "Listen and think clearly for once," she said. "You were trained from a young age: Be pleasing, be charming, be agreeable, be attractive. You will earn status and security by earning a powerful man's attention, and you will please him to keep that position."

Dielo nodded, almost against his will. His training had been clear.

"I was not so costly a plaything, but I had the same role, the same purpose. We understood our options, you and I. We could please our masters, making ourselves cherished objects, or we could be without position or security. Am I right thus far?"

Dielo nodded again.

Pasiphae Jade held him transfixed. "And now, your master has said he does not want you. With a few careless words, he has stripped the only worth you had, your only currency in bartering for safety, position, affection, even love."

Dielo's breath caught in his throat. She echoed what he thought in the dark of the night, alone in the sera qadra quarters.

But his training did not allow him to admit to his traitorous thoughts, not yet. "He has taken nothing of me."

"In taking nothing from you, he has taken everything from you," she said. "Like anyone else, we do not live by meat and bread alone—we must have purpose and respect, or meat and bread rot in our mouths. And now you have neither."

Dielo's chin jerked in a tiny, involuntary nod.

"You have one currency, virilo, and it's one most would sell themselves to carry, and he is a moneychanger who will not accept it. After your lifetime of training to be the richest of gifts, he has made you penniless."

Dielo's stomach churned uncomfortably. It was true, true in the prince's brushing him away, true in Yovela's disdain, true in how he sat useless and lonely in the empty sera qadra. Even if he were envied, that would be something to claim, to hold, to believe of his own worth, that he could be envied. But this emptiness...

"And this man, who has made you less than nothing, this is the man you want to protect? When I ask you not personal or intimate questions you should know by the rightful position he's denied you, but only to confirm that he has not done treason? Why would you defend a traitor who has also betrayed you?"

"He is not a traitor," Dielo said, his words rushing too quickly. "He is anxious to do what you have commanded him."

Pasiphae Jade smiled. "See? That was a simple thing to say."

He had answered her question, and he had not meant to. She had tricked him into answering. Tricked him by repeating his own thoughts aloud and sharing what she had also felt in a powerful man's sera qadra.

Dielo's stomach turned again. He did not know who had ordered him whipped—but he could almost forgive that punishment more easily than the debasement of Kayvin's continued rejection and Yovela's contempt. His torturer had cut his flesh; Kayvin and Yovela had cut his soul with their disregard.

Pasiphae Jade's eyes read him and used him, and he did not care, because using him meant acknowledging him.

"I will answer your questions, Illustrious Excellency."

CHAPTER 31

KAYVIN ENTERED THE THRONE room silently. He had every right to be there—more right than Pasiphae Jade—but he did not want to argue in his defense, not this evening.

He moved in the dark across the tessellated tile floor until he reached the end where the great Bull Throne sat on its dais, empty. Kayvin, too, felt empty as he looked at it. He turned away so that he could not imagine Pasiphae Jade sitting upon it.

He went to the silent fountain. Its base was filled with a single block of ice, expanded above the lip of the basin. Kayvin crouched at the edge and leaned to look at the woman imprisoned within.

Mother.

He did not say the word aloud. Somehow it seemed it would be worse if he spoke and she did not answer him.

Her eyes were half-closed, flinching away from the magic she had raised her hands to ward against. He could read her final moment so clearly.

No, not her final moment. She would recover. Pasiphae Jade had promised she would release Raea when he had completed his tasks. His mother was not dead, and he would have her back. He would free her with his efforts.

I'm trying, Mother. I'm doing what I can, what I must. I'll free you soon.

She would yet hear her birthday song.

He had not finished it. It did not seem right to work on it while she was frozen here, and he could not concentrate when he thought of it. It was a choral piece, anyway, and Yovela and Dielo were not enough.

Could she see, frozen in the ice? Could she hear him? Was she aware of where she was, how she was trapped? That would be worse, so much worse. He wondered if he should speak to her, just in case she could hear him through the ice.

But he could not listen to the silence where her answer should be.

He began to hum. He could sing for her, and if she heard him, she would know he was thinking of her, and she would not need to answer a song.

He hummed a new melody he was developing. It had no words yet, but he did not need words here.

A light flickered at the door, and he wheeled to his feet. Pasiphae Jade strode toward him, carrying a golden lamp of oil. "Oh, don't stop on my account," she said, her voice dripping with condescension.

Kayvin clenched his fist and tried to ignore the flush of hot embarrassment that swept over him. "I did not think you would have reason to visit her tonight."

"Visit her," Pasiphae Jade repeated. "As if she is receiving an audience." She gestured into the empty air.

Kayvin did not allow himself to follow her gaze. "Can she hear?" he asked, hating himself for asking but wanting the answer. "Can she hear me? Us?"

Pasiphae Jade laughed. "Not a chance."

Kayvin had been prepared for that answer, had even expected it, but still it struck him like a physical blow. He clenched his teeth and forced air through his throat.

Pasiphae Jade set her lamp on the fountain's iced rim and looked down. "She had a birthday coming soon, didn't she? Well, at least she won't be getting any older. Bit of a gift, really, to an aging wife from the concubine who replaced her."

Kayvin nearly struck her. His hand clenched, his arm spasmed, he nearly hit her. But her position leaning over Raea was too close, Raea too vulnerable.

He reached for the lamp, too near his mother. "You said fire would kill her."

Pasiphae Jade raised an eyebrow. "Yes. But not so small a fire."

He set the lamp on the floor.

Pasiphae Jade smiled and ran her palm over the wide block of ice as if soothing it, laying fresh crystals over the surface. "Do you come often to visit her?"

Kayvin did not owe her an answer. He kept his eyes on the lamp, though it felt as if he were abandoning his mother to the usurper's hands.

"Do you always sing to her?"

He did not answer.

"I know you are an artist of song."

He jerked his head once, a nod of acknowledgment.

"The Rideis were mighty warriors, fearsome and feared, who built palaces of their spoils and trained in warcraft," she said. "But now our palaces are too luxurious, our spoils from battles long finished instead of freshly won, and the royals indulge their considerable skill no longer in war but in escalating decadence. And the prince himself practices music." She traced a circle of frost over the fountain. "How is that serving your mother now?"

Kayvin stiffened, his fists clenching.

Pasiphae Jade faced him, her expression now open disdain. "Art! As if that will save you, or her. You waste your skills and your time playing at music. You should be honing your magic, studying your weapons, making yourself ready to fight. Trying to save your people and your mother."

"I practice my magic," he growled, wanting to defy her but too stung to argue well. "Why do you delay me?"

"It is not that I will not send you," she said. "It is that I have not yet been able to send you. We are waiting for the path through the mountains to be cleared, as it has been blocked for two hundred years."

Kayvin frowned. That made sense; they did not keep the passage open between spawnings, and there had always been fewer skilled with earth, even in the glorious old days.

"I regret that I cannot send you immediately, but I waste nothing, certainly not time. Your father... Your father wasted himself right into his death." She clenched her jaw, angry beyond their simple exchange. "I had no choice but to kill him, if we are to survive. He could not be ready, no matter how I pressed him."

"Ready?" repeated Kayvin. "Ready for what?"

She gave a frustrated snarl. "Ready for them," she snapped. "Ready for the spawning!"

Kayvin stared. "The spawning? But that won't—"

"It's coming! That is what I told Gromgest, again and again, and again and again he ignored me or laughed at me or told me to be quiet, disregarding me just as you do now. He would not prepare for it. Rather than let us all die, I took his authority so that I could make us ready. Because I know it is coming."

Kayvin's mind spun. If the spawning— Her military preparations, her extensions into the human lands, even her desire for the amulets made sense now. "When?" he asked breathlessly. "How do you know?"

Her face shuttered instantly, distrustful. "I don't ask you to believe me. You have only to do as I say to win your mother back."

"I am still a prince. This is still my kingdom, and they are still my people. I don't want them to die unnecessarily."

She crossed her arms and lifted her chin, a queen dispensing knowledge. "It has been thought that the broods come on a cycle of years," she said.

Kayvin nodded. "Two or three hundred years. The count is not exact, but it is always a cycle of time."

"Not always," she corrected darkly. "And if one looks beyond the count of years, one sees another pattern, one to which the broods adhere much more closely. It's a pattern of storms, of sun, of seasons. It has to happen in precisely the correct order. It is not the years, but the weather that hatches a brood."

The foreign explanation lodged in Kayvin's mind a moment before he could take it with the rest of her words. "Oh..." He had never thought of it—had never studied it—but what she said made some sense, or at least it wasn't immediately ridiculous. It could explain the variations in the long and irregular counts of years. "How would you calculate it, then?"

She picked up the lamp and began walking. "You have seen the great hordes of locusts. They darken the skies and sweep over the land, covering all they touch, from chairs on your balcony to bushes in your garden to the farmers who try to beat them from their crops."

He went with her, an arm's length from the pool of light. "Yes, of course." They did not come often, a blessing, but they had come three times during Kayvin's lifetime.

"Do you know that sometimes the hordes are hatched, but they do not cover the sky? Those years they are mostly eaten. We do not see the locusts, so we do not think of these as horde years, and so they are generally not recorded with the same imperative."

Kayvin followed. "If they are not horde years, why should they be recorded? What eats them?"

"What eats them is another brood hatching deep in the earth. They feed on the locusts, and then they surface to feed on larger prey."

Kayvin stared, an incredulous suspicion building in his mind. "Are you speaking of the spawning? Are you saying it comes with the locusts?"

"Only with the locusts we don't see," Pasiphae Jade answered. "But the relevant fact is, if we allow that the years in which we recorded a spawning are also the years in which we should have recorded a horde of locusts, then that gives us enough years to, together with collated weather diaries, establish an approximate prediction cycle for the locusts. We can guess with reasonable accuracy when the next surge will be." She stopped and opened the door that led to the royal quarters. She set down the light and went into the Arch Potentate's study.

Kayvin nodded. "I see how that could be useful, especially to the farmers and to the council that sets the taxes for the following season. We could adjust the tax rate more precisely, as we already do for rainfall."

"True. But I am not thinking only of taxes." She lifted a thick sheaf of papers, filled with tables, plots of dotted lines, detailed notes, a chart of stars. "We can predict the spawning."

"Calculated like a season's rain."

"The spawning comes to the surface after they have devoured the locusts," she reminded him. "In a horde year, there are enough to satisfy the appetite. In a hatching year without locusts, the hatchlings starve—or, I wonder if they might simply remain in their eggs another year, waiting for a sufficient food source."

"I don't understand."

"It means that if we could accurately predict all locust swarms, with whether it's a large or small brood, we could breed cave monsters as efficiently as cattle—and we may predict the spawning with enough accuracy to have people out of their way. And I know they are coming soon."

He was silent a moment, trying to balance what she said against the knowledge that she needed him to believe her and obey her. What she argued here was so contrary to what he had been taught, and surely all of his tutors had not been wrong about something so important...

She regarded him with contempt. "And while I studied the histories and learned of our impending doom, our Arch Potentate played with his sera qadra and drank and whored himself to sleep each night, and our prince sat in his room and plucked strings to make pretty sounds. As if swarming death could be held off with music instead of by combat and magic."

Kayvin heard her bitter insult, but he was counting back through what little agricultural history he remembered. "Why didn't you say so?" he asked numbly. "Why didn't you tell someone?"

"Tell someone? Why didn't I tell someone?" She stared at him in incredulous disgust. "Do you think I didn't? Did I not just say that I studied while my royal master gorged himself on food and drink and pleasure? I pleaded with him to listen, but of course no one would. What was a sera qadra woman's word worth?" Her mouth curled as if she were trying to smile and spit at once. "They won't listen until you seize them by the balls, pin them against the wall, kill a king. Do you pretend you would have listened to me, before I had your mother here in my fountain?"

Kayvin wanted to argue with her, but he could not. She was right: She would have been only his father's concubine, and he would have been absorbed in his own pursuits, with no reason to acknowledge a concubine's insistence that his father was wrong in his most important duty.

"So I did what I had to do," she said, straightening and calming her voice. She placed a hand on the stack of documents. "I took the authority I lacked and found the leverage I needed, and now I will survive, as will most of our people. And how can you tell me I was wrong?"

Kayvin looked at her and thought of the dying generation that she might now save, and he also thought of his mother entombed in ice and his father cooling in his sleeping pit with an icicle through his heart. He said nothing.

Her mouth firmed. "You should be more grateful for the chance to live."

"I don't know yet that I will," Kayvin said. "We are not ready for a spawning."

"Which is why I will push you so hard. When you bring the amulets, we can slow them, even turn them back with their own magic."

"The amulets can stop them?"

"My prince, the amulets were made to counter dragons. They will stop hatchlings."

Kayvin nodded. "I understand."

"And yet you sit here, singing nighttime ditties to a fountain that cannot hear you, resenting my request for what I need to keep us—all of us—safe."

The words pierced Kayvin. He did not pardon her cruelty, but he could no longer hate her orders, could no longer delay to spite her and mark his remaining pride and freedom. "I will bring them."

CHAPTER 32

KAYVIN CLOSED HIS EYES against the blurred page and rubbed at them. They had been itching for the last hour or two, and now they burned as he tried to focus on the endless words. The problem was, they did not burn any less when he closed them.

He wanted to fight Pasiphae Jade. He wanted to rescue his mother, to avenge his father, even just to not let her profit so openly from her treachery. Everything felt wrong. But he was weak, and now without support, and he was unprepared to be any sort of prince other than a spoiled and useless one.

Pasiphae Jade was a murderer, but she knew how to save his people from a disaster they had suffered before. He could not. The greatest act he could choose now as a dedicated prince was to remain quiescent and let her render the help she had promised.

He reached for the cup of hollowed amethyst on his desk, filled with cool fruit and water. Nala had brought it some time before, in her usual anticipating way. He fished a slice of sweet citrus from the cup, knowing his fingers marred the drink.

Amethyst Prince. The amethyst was honored for its purity and its resistance to outside influence. Kayvin, meekly bowing to the indulgent extravagance expected of him and bending to the will of his father's killer, was a joke.

"My lord?" It was Dielo's voice, from the doorway.

Empty void, of course he would arrive just in time to spot Kayvin nursing a headache. Kayvin straightened. "I'm fine. Just tired of reading." He had spent most of the day reading through treatises and monographs on human culture and history, and the scholarly script had begun to waver in the candlelight. "The season always makes my eyes more sensitive and my head throb at times. My physicians tell me it's probably a flower in the courtyard, a scent undetectable at this distance but still affecting. But the reading is making it worse."

"I could read aloud for you, my lord."

Kayvin started to refuse out of habit, but he realized the offer did sound helpful. "Thank you, but you might put me to sleep," he said reluctantly. "It's not exactly scintillating material."

"If I summarize it, perhaps?"

Kayvin kept one hand over his eyes and used the other to push the bound tablet forward on his desk. "Take a look."

He heard the tablet scuff across the wooden surface. "Give me half an hour, my lord, and I'll have this into a story for you. Not one of the best stories, but easier to hear than to pick out of this text. Go and bathe, and I'll be ready when you've finished."

Kayvin shook his head. "I haven't called for a bath, and I don't want to wait. I'll just lie down for a few moments."

Dielo brought the bound tablet with him to the sleeping pit in case he needed to remind himself of a detail or was asked questions. Prince Kayvin was there already, reclining with eyes closed, and Yovela sat behind him, massaging his head as it rested upon her knees.

Dielo fought down a twinge of frustration. He could have offered such a service, only a massage, but the prince would have declined. He permitted Yovela such intimacies, however.

Still, Dielo was serving the prince now, reading for him. He would gain trust and favor a little at a time.

The sleeping pit was of a royal size; Dielo might stretch out fully along the long axis of its oval, with his arms overhead, and his fingers and toes would not quite reach the ends. It was too spacious for coziness, and so Kayvin had made himself a smaller nest of pillows and furs at one side. Dielo took the far end now, giving the prince and the sera qadra woman space, and settled on a spare pillow. "Shall I tell you now, my lord?"

Kayvin did not open his eyes. "Go ahead."

"The piece you gave me speaks of the equinox ritual at the Vernal House in Atalasu City." Dielo rested the tablet on his lap, not yet needed. "The Vernal House is the primary temple in Sayinia; strictly speaking, all other temples are chapter houses. Each spring, there is a ritual to welcome home the gods to the temple and reset the circles of protection."

"Where do the gods go over the winter?" asked Yovela, amused.

Her fingertips were rubbing small circles into Prince Kayvin's temples. Dielo knew that was pleasant, but with the irritation Kayvin had described it would be more effective to focus on the bones around the eyes, starting with the eyebrows. He wished he could demonstrate.

"They are gods, so presumably they go where they wish," he answered lightly. "Three gods are enshrined in the Vernal House. They are considered to bless the temple when they return in the spring from walking through the land, and that is what the ritual acknowledges."

"What circles of protection did you mention?" Kayvin asked.

"Sayinian temples have virtue circles marked out in the courtyard of the primary entrance. Each circle represents a virtue—love, peace, self-control, and so forth—and adherents may walk these circles as an act of meditation. In the spring bells ceremony, the circles are ritually renewed, refilling them in the spirit of the season's renewal and rebirth after a year of adherents passing through."

Dielo lifted a hand to catch Yovela's eye. He then put his fingers to his face to demonstrate pressing the space between the eyebrows and working outward. She frowned, took a moment to consider, and then adjusted her hands to mimic his.

Kayvin grunted. "How can an eyebrow be sore? Tell me about the bells."

"There are invisible circles too, as well as the virtue circles. These are concentric rings of holiness, and this ritual of renewal holds real power—or so these writings report."

"The bells?"

"I'm coming to that. In the ritual, a chosen vessel will invoke the blessing of the returning gods and will lift a cutting from the temple's sacred apricot tree from the highest tower. The branch will burst into bloom, witnessed by all the faithful gathered in the courtyard below. As the flowers open, all the bells in the temple and within the reach of the holy circles begin to ring, without any hand to set them to movement."

"That sounds fascinating," Yovela commented, and at first Dielo thought her words were sarcastic. But she seemed interested, looking across the pit as if imagining spring blooms and bells.

Dielo dropped his eyes and read aloud, "It is common to wear small bells on one's clothing or tied to a wrist at the festival. These will tinkle throughout the day with the wearer's movement, but at the time of the ritual's climax, all worshipers will stand still, perhaps with arms slightly extended, to allow the bells to ring of their own accord without interference or influence."

"Oh, that would be incredible." Now Yovela sounded wishful. "I would like to see that."

"If it happens at all," Prince Kayvin said dryly. "These are old reports; they might no longer be accurate, if ever they were."

"It seems to be an ancient ceremony," Dielo replied. "With centuries of tradition even at the time of this writing, it might well be still honored today."

Prince Kayvin had been bowed over his desk for hours. Dielo indicated to Yovela the small muscles at the back of the skull that would be strained. She did not answer, but she did work her hands around and beneath the prince's head. Kayvin made a sound of discomfort and appreciation.

"With any luck at all, I will not be in Sayinia in the spring," Prince Kayvin said after a moment. "I hope to find these amulets as quickly as possible."

It should not have been Yovela who received the credit for Dielo's thoughtful suggestions. But if his duty was the care of the prince, not his own appreciation, then he had done his work even if he was not acknowledged. He could take some small pleasure in knowing how he had served the prince even at a distance.

He could also carry to Pasiphae Jade a report of what the prince studied.

CHAPTER 33

KAYVIN WANDERED THROUGH THE palace by night.

He wandered the terraces, open to silver-cold moonlight streaming low over the railings and casting long, bleak shadows upon the tiled floor. He wandered through the corridors, his bare feet silent and his eyes strained wide to see the way. He wandered around and around the entrance to the throne room, never quite working up the courage again to enter it by night, to see her frozen in icy moonlight, eyes half-closed in eternal flight from a fate she could never escape. He wandered until Yovela and Dielo came wordlessly to find him, silently leading him to his quarters and bringing him to his sleeping pit, where they stationed themselves on either side of him so that he could not escape again without their knowledge.

By day, he waited for Pasiphae Jade to complete her calculations and he waited for word that the passage to human Sayinia had been cleared. He read. He read until he could no longer focus on the crawling script. He picked at melodies, he criticized and threw aside old compositions. He found his only daytime solace in practicing his fire magic, honing his skills as he built up the power of his combustions and perfected his aim in throwing bolts of arcane power. His courtyard became a plaza of ashes and blackened stone, and the palace gardeners gave up replanting.

But he waited, and orders did not come. While orders did not come, he did nothing toward freeing his mother. And he felt more and more helpless before the crushing weight of inaction.

Kayvin woke suddenly, breath coming fast, heart pounding, blankets and furs flung back against the walls of his sleeping pit. He did not clearly remember the nightmare that had wakened him. He knew it had ice, crystalline shards piercing him with biting cold and hot pain, ice entrapping him so that he could not move, must lie in eternal prison with spears through his torso—

He jerked sharply to the side, rolling into himself as if he were back in his egg. He inhaled for a long count of six, held his breath for four, exhaled for six, repeated. He closed his eyes against the dark and made himself see the notations as he counted, black ink against textured paper, notes and rest marks, pulling each sheet aside to count up as he inhaled, laying them down again as he exhaled.

He sat up, his pulse still fierce in his chest but no longer deafening. He needed music.

He got up from the sleeping pit and walked half-dressed through the moonlight to the cabinet where he kept small instruments. He selected a horned lyre and padded back to his bed. The deep pit would keep the sound mostly to himself if he played quietly.

At first he played an old tune, a fragment of folk song with a progression he had always liked, just to get his stiffened fingers moving. Then he began picking out a new melody, letting the notes come to him singly, the rhythm irregular and imperfect as he experimented. After a few moments he began repeating, choosing the best from the variations that came to him and setting them in order, picking a refrain, linking the bars together.

"My lord?"

He jumped where he sat against the wall and looked up at Dielo, leaning over the border of the sleeping pit. He wore a silk robe tied loosely about the waist, the open chest gaping aesthetically. Kayvin wondered if the virilo had deliberately tied it so, or if the training was so ingrained that he did it without thinking, or whether the sleeping robe was cut in such a way as to always hang most provocatively.

"My lord, can't you sleep tonight?" Dielo asked.

Kayvin sighed. "I don't want your services," he said gruffly.

Dielo's face nearly didn't falter. "I can offer many kinds of companionship, my lord," he said, his voice only a little hopeful.

Anger flushed Kayvin with heat. Why did the virilo always have to make Kayvin feel so guilty? He hadn't wanted the man in the first place, he shouldn't feel ashamed to put him away instead of using his body, he shouldn't feel guilt at keeping him at arm's length. His father had been murdered by a concubine. Even if he wanted someone, Kayvin would be beyond foolish to open himself, especially to a lover sent by that same concubine.

"I'm sure you have many talents," Yovela's voice offered, and the sarcasm dripped in the darkness.

"Hush, both of you," snapped Kayvin, unwilling to listen to her belittle the virilo. He did not want the man, but that was not the man's fault. "I'll lose the melody."

"Are you writing it, my lord?" asked Dielo.

Kayvin did not answer but returned his attention to the lyre, repeating the phrases he had chosen. Yovela disappeared into the dark room and returned a moment later carrying paper, ink, and a shielded lamp. She climbed down into the sleeping pit and began noting the music.

After a moment, Dielo descended as well and made himself a little pillow seat of furs and blankets opposite Kayvin. He watched and listened for a moment, and then he began to hum, following Kayvin's melody. When Kayvin reached the end and began to repeat, Dielo left off humming and began to sing wordlessly, staying with the melody for a few bars and then splitting into a rising harmony that ran fluidly along with the song.

Kayvin lifted his head to look at the virilo, but he kept playing. He glanced at Yovela, who nodded once as her pen flew over the page, taking down both lines of notes.

When they reached the end of the new song, Kayvin set the lyre down. "You did not tell me you sang."

Dielo smiled, a little embarrassed or shy, or trained to appear so. "A virilo is trained in many things, lord. As I said, I can offer many forms of companionship."

Yovela's mouth flattened into a line, and Dielo turned slightly away from her.

Kayvin sighed. "Can the two of you harmonize?"

Yovela's eyes widened. "My lord?"

"Can the two of you sing together as I play? Work with the melody?"

Her shoulders relaxed. "I think we can, my lord. I am not so good at improvising harmony as he seems to be, but I will do my best."

Dielo nodded, looking from Yovela to Kayvin. "Yes, we'll try."

Kayvin picked up the lyre again and set his fingers to the strings.

Kayvin woke happily warm, with a sense of comfortable pressure all about him. He was wrapped in blankets, reclining against the wall of his sleeping pit. On either side of him leaned Dielo and Yovela, similarly cocooned and curled against him, their heads pillowed on his furs. An arm's length away, the lyre lay on a neat stack of musical notations, a record of the song they had completed.

Kayvin did not want to move. He did not want to disturb the sleep of his companions nor disrupt the hazy peace he felt for the first time since his father's death. He did not regret sending his sera qadra away, but he had not realized how wearying isolating himself had been. Sharing space with Yovela and Dielo—even sharing only space, with each of them bundled into their own warm shells—had warmed a part of him he had not known was growing numb.

"Are you awake?" breathed a voice beside him, and he turned his head to see Dielo's eyes watching him. At his movement, the virilo shifted and sat upright. "Good morning," he whispered.

Kayvin guessed he was watching for clues on how his master liked his mornings after, even if they were mornings after nothing more than singing and composition. "Good morning. I'm sorry if I woke you."

"Oh, no," Dielo answered. "I didn't want to disturb you."

Yovela stirred, wriggling a hand free of her furs to brush her eyes. She looked around, blinked at them, and then pushed her loose hair back from her face as she rose from the blankets.

Dielo drew back and pushed himself upright against the sloping wall of the pit. "What would you like for breakfast, lord?"

"My lord!" This was Arad, shuffling into the room with a discomfited scowl. "My lord, the Arch Potentate calls for you. She says to tell you the passage is newly cleared, and it is time."

Kayvin stiffened. "Time? To go, at last?"

Yovela's expression did not change, but he thought something radiated from her, some dark blend of worry and anger.

Arad replied, "To the human lands, yes, my lord. What shall I bring out for you to wear to her?"

It did not matter what he wore; she would not be fooled by his princely garments. He gestured, and Dielo nodded and rose. He would choose something fitting. Kayvin would need to change his wardrobe entirely anyway, to blend in common human society.

His heart was racing, though he had not yet moved. It was time.

REPORTS OF DEMONS

SAYINIA

CHAPTER 34

IT TOOK SOME TIME for Galen and Lisveth to convince Sheriff Algwire that they were not simply playing for a larger payoff, that the Selk bandits were real and more, that there was a Selk prince roaming the countryside. But at last after she had examined the dead bandit more closely, she agreed that while she had no stomach to examine the rest of his physiology for differences, there was at least a slight tip to his ears, and she would send a message to the local lord, who could alert his own lord, who could tell someone in authority.

"But look at this," she continued. She rubbed hard at the dead bandit's face, and her hand came back with a darker shade. "These cheekbones are his own, but they've been shadowed. Nose, too, and the temples. Someone wanted this face to look more gaunt and angular."

"Are you suggesting that he made himself up to look more like a demon?" Lisveth asked.

"It does weaken any argument that the Selks are really here." Sheriff Algwire sighed and shrugged. "Doesn't explain why the other one would kill this one for going along with the plan, though. None of that makes sense. And he does have the ears. I'll report it."

It was nearly dawn before Galen and Lisveth retired to the room the inn's landlord offered. It was a fine enough room, with two beds with real straw mattresses. Andrea was sleeping in the next room, the landlord assured them, so they could escort her home as soon as they were ready to go.

Galen dropped onto the first bed, flinging his arms wide and letting his abused shoulders stretch and pop. Fights were exhausting things, even short ones, and he had also buried one bandit and carried another back to the village. It had been a brutally long day. "Good night."

"Not yet," Lisveth said. She sat on her bed, a hand wrapped about her bad arm, but she did not lie down.

Galen groaned. "Can it wait until morning?"

"I don't know."

Galen turned his head to squint at her. "We killed the Fire Brigand, found a missing daughter, fought some bandits both human and inhuman, and tangled with the prince of a legendary evil that seems to be renewing an ancient war, and you've got something else you want to talk about?"

"You're not dead."

Galen huffed, too tired to laugh, but then he realized she was serious. "Well, yeah," he agreed. "I thought that was evident already."

"That impostor, Ember or whatever her name was, hit you with a fireball."

"Yes, but you said she didn't really, seeing as I didn't burn to charcoal." He was so tired. Why couldn't she just go to sleep?

"I didn't see exactly what she did," Lisveth said slowly. "I was busy staying alive myself. I didn't see her spell, so I assumed it hadn't been anything very strong because it didn't do much to you."

"Well, it knocked me down pretty hard. It felt different than your fire illusions. But that could be a difference in personal techniques, I guess."

Lisveth wasn't listening to him. "But I was watching with full attention when that Kayvin hit you as you went in for him. That was no illusion. That was pure energy."

"It gave me a decent wallop."

Her voice was hollow. "It should have ripped you apart. It should have sprayed you over the road like sowing wheat in a windstorm."

It was her tone, more than her words, that caught at Galen's chest. Lisveth's voice always held a note of sarcasm, or exasperation, or disdain, or laughter. He had not heard it before with fear.

He rolled to face her. "What are you saying?"

"Galen. I'm saying I should have watched you die, and you did not die. You survived killing magic that should have destroyed you, and maybe twice in one day. Why?"

He blinked. "Why? How should I know?"

"It surprised him, too," she said. "Kayvin. He asked how, do you remember?"

Galen frowned. "But I don't know how."

Lisveth leaned forward, reaching for his neck where his shirt gaped with his sprawl. She tugged the amulet into view. "What if it's this?"

Galen laughed despite his exhaustion. "This thing? The protective amulet that let me get beaten so badly that some soft-hearted girl had to drag me down the street and prop me up? Somehow I don't think so."

"What if it's not physical harm? What if it protects you from magic?"

Galen snorted and shook his head. "Nope, I tried that too, remember? When I decided to go after the Fire Brigand all by myself?"

"And I was using illusion. Not real fire. You thought it protected you from magical attack, but there wasn't any real magical attack."

"Right. So it didn't protect me—" Galen stopped, his tired brain finally catching up.

"It was never tested with real magic. We just assumed it was junk. But now—junk couldn't have saved you, not tonight."

He stared at her. "Are you serious?"

"Galen, I couldn't have stopped that strike tonight. Whatever he is, prince or Rideis or whatever, he's good with magic. I couldn't have done a thing to stop him from killing you. And yet you're sitting here, laughing about your stupid useless amulet."

Galen looked down at the iridescent eye staring sightlessly at the ceiling. "What do we do?"

"Let's test it," Lisveth said. "Let's see if it's real. Tomorrow, away from town."

They had to go away from town, Galen realized, because Lisveth intended a proper series of tests.

First, she studied the amulet in the daylight for a long while, turning it over in her hand, running her finger along the coils of wire, polishing the stone eye with her finger. Finally she shrugged and shook her head. "I can't make anything of it," she admitted. "It might be a great artifact, or it might be a junk trinket. It's got no signature at all when I touch it." She set the amulet on a stone and piled the loose chain behind it. "Let's see what happens when we set it on fire."

Galen thought briefly about protesting, but he decided against it. It was a memento, but he did not need it to remember. If it was nothing more than junk metal, it would not hurt to be rid of it. If it was something like what they suspected, fire would not harm it.

Lisveth walked twenty paces from the rock and turned to face it. She took a breath, and Galen recognized the signs of her preparing non-illusory magic, the kind that always took more from her. She breathed slowly, extended her good arm, focused her eyes on the amulet and stone, and flung a stream of fire.

Galen flinched back from the heat and shielded his eyes. After a few seconds, the flare ended. Lisveth wavered in place, and then she jerked her head toward the stone. "Come on."

The ground was blackened and smoking. The rock was the same brown-grey it had been before. The amulet was unsmudged, unmelted, its lines unsoftened, the stone forming the eye uncracked.

Galen reached out and tentatively tapped the rock, then placed his hand flat on it. "It's warm," he said. "But only warm."

Lisveth touched the amulet. "Same here."

"Is that proof? Or would it be warm either way?"

"I don't know. I don't usually burn rocks and junk to have a comparison. Anyway, if it's real, it wasn't meant to be used on rocks." She frowned. "Where did you get this, again?"

"My father and uncles stole it from a temple."

"Temple. I guess it could be the real thing, maybe, though what it would be doing all the way out in the Heel is anyone's guess." Lisveth sighed. "We need a more conclusive test."

She turned back to the pack she had carried out and opened the drawn top. She reached inside and drew out a brown rabbit, its legs trussed and its nose working nervously.

"Oh no," Galen said. "What are you doing?"

"We have to test it," she said. "I bought this out of the landlord's kitchen this morning." She looked at Galen. "You think I'd rather test it on you? And no, farm boy, I know you can't be so soft about a rabbit. He was going to be lunch anyway."

"Right," Galen admitted, "but usually we just twist their necks, and it's over."

"Trust me, if it goes poorly for him, it'll be over quick enough." Lisveth put the rabbit on the ground and wrapped the amulet about its neck, tripling the chain so that it stayed close to the furry body.

She stepped back, put out her arm, and then she went unnaturally still.

That last was not part of her usual casting. Galen hesitated and then ventured, "Are you—"

Her lips drew tight and thin, and she looked for an instant as if she might be sick.

"Lisveth—"

She hit it with fire. The rabbit screamed, a terrifying sound of agonizing fear, and Galen cringed.

And then the fire was gone, fading into the air, and the rabbit lay kicking on the ground, wide-eyed and gasping and its fur not so much as singed.

They stared. Galen felt his mouth fall open.

Lisveth gulped air and then reached out to stroke the panicked rabbit. "Easy, little fellow. You're all right." She removed the amulet, and then she took the knife from her belt and held the rabbit still as she cut its trusses. "And I think you've earned your reprieve from being lunch. Go."

The rabbit bolted, bounding zigzag across the terrain and disappearing.

Galen reached to take the amulet, cradling it. "I didn't know. How could I not know?"

"We haven't exactly been fighting a lot of magical bandits," Lisveth answered. "And you did know, at one point. You just didn't know the whole truth, and so you let yourself be talked out of any of it." She gestured. "Put it back on. And don't take it off. Ever."

Galen dropped it over his head and hid it within his shirt, feeling as if the metal chain were not enough. The amulet had somehow become larger and heavier and more solid, without ever changing size or shape or weight. How had he ever thought it worthless junk?

After two years of his thinking it useless, what did it mean now?

CHAPTER 35

LORD BRYUKI WAS THE local authority, and Sheriff Algwire had sent ahead word that she was bringing an urgent report. She led Galen and Lisveth into his fortified house. "He's a reasonable man," she told them. "He'll listen to us."

The house was part home, part fortress, like many of the nobles' holdings in the east. People here remembered the wars with the Selks. It was entirely of stone, to resist fire and magic, though some newer extensions and outbuildings were of wood.

They were escorted to the central hall, a serviceable but well-decorated room that could seat several dozen diners or stage several dozen warriors. Galen gratefully rolled the long bundle in dark grey from his shoulders to a tabletop.

Lord Bryuki entered the hall with a ledger still in one hand and an apple in the other. "Sheriff Algwire," he greeted with a nod.

She bowed. Galen followed her lead and tried to peek to see if Lisveth did.

"I hope this isn't about those same bandits," he said, taking a seat at the end of the room and setting the ledger neatly to one side. "I told you, I haven't enough soldiers to send a proper expedition against the Fire Brigand. And fair night, why is there a body on my hall table?"

"It is not about the Fire Brigand," Sheriff Algwire began.

"Leave off what it's not about," he said, "and get to the part about the dead body on my table. Is that a dead bandit?"

"Yes. But not one of hers."

Galen took his cue and unwrapped the sheet about the head end, exposing the dead Selk. The body looked a bit more inhuman in unflattering death.

Lord Bryuki rose to his feet, leaving the apple on the table. "Fair night. What is—is that...?"

"Selk," Lisveth said. "Or Rideis, as they're also called."

Lord Bryuki sucked in a breath. "How many?"

"There was a group of bandits on the road, and then with this one there were two. But we know—"

Lord Bryuki held up a hand. "Two?"

"Yes."

"And this was one of them? Did you kill the other?"

"He was injured, but escaped. But—"

His shoulders dropped an inch in relief. "Then it is not so bad as I feared."

Galen twitched, but Lisveth spoke first. "My lord, how can you say—"

He shook his head. "No, you did right to bring this to my attention. But two Selks are not an invading force. They are outcasts, rogues who crossed mountains because they could not stay in their own land, but they are not an invasion."

Galen straightened. "The survivor was the prince of the Rideis."

Lord Bryuki froze. "What?"

"We engaged with this one," Lisveth said, pointing at the dead body, "because Sheriff Algwire had offered us a bounty on the local bandits."

Lord Bryuki nodded. "Yes. We don't have a standing police force for the roads."

"You had two groups of bandits, human and Selk. Then there was another Selk, in disguise as a human. We didn't kill this one—he did, when this one recognized him and revealed his identity."

"So he claimed he was the prince of the Selks?" Lord Bryuki looked ready to happily dismiss this as a rogue fantasy.

"No. He killed to keep this one from saying it. But not quickly enough."

Lord Bryuki looked equal parts disappointed and worried. "Oh. That could still be a trick, but...but it's less plausible." He started walking about the table. "But why would a prince of the Selks be in our lands, and disguised as a human instead of coming in his own prestige?"

"An espionage tour," Sheriff Algwire offered. "He is preparing to invade."

Lord Bryuki shook his head. "I have men and women to do my spying for me, and I'm only a march lord. There is no reason to send a prince himself into enemy territory."

"We don't need to know his reasons," Lisveth said, "not yet. The point is that he's here, that he's been moving unknown through the kingdom. The Octovirate needs to be told."

Lord Bryuki frowned. "If there is an invasion coming, then definitely, of course. But if there is not, then I cannot be an alarmist drawing attention from more urgent matters. Politics are at a sensitive point just now and—"

"More urgent matters?" repeated Lisveth. "What could be more urgent than another invasion and its war?"

He gave her a reproving look. "Nothing, if indeed that's the case. But we don't know that's the case. We have one dead Selk and his unreliable word that a second Selk is improbably royal, roaming alone and unattended through our land."

"Not entirely alone," Galen said. "A woman pulled him away."

"Another Selk?"

He shook his head. "I can't be certain. It was dark, and she wasn't close. But she said she was his follower, and she called him *my lord*."

"She pulled him away from a fight with you after he was injured?"

"Yes."

Sheriff Algwire grimaced. "That does lend more support to the prince story."

Lord Bryuki swore in apparent agreement.

In the silence that followed, Galen re-covered the dead bandit. He wasn't contributing much to the conversation.

"It could be there's a political schism in the Selk kingdom," Lord Bryuki said. "Something happened that exiled the prince—a prince—and he had to flee with a few retainers over the mountains. So he's here, but not leading an invasion."

"Even if that's the case," Sheriff Algwire said, "we know they're raiding here. People have died. We still need to address it."

Lord Bryuki sighed. "I know."

"But you're wondering how much help to ask for," Lisveth observed.

"I am a march lord. I can't go to the Octovirate and ask for an army for a few bandits."

"Could you go to the Octovirate with the news that the Selks have thrown out a prince? That if we could capture him, we could learn more than we have known in centuries, and know our risk of future invasion?"

Lord Bryuki scratched his chin and then gestured to the table. "Sit down with me, all of you."

CHAPTER 36

THERE WAS A LONG corridor between the guest rooms and the kitchen. This was good for defense in case of attack, but it was annoying when one was hungry. Galen was hungry.

Lisveth had stopped for the latrine and told him she'd catch up. They had spent hours repeating their story for Lord Bryuki and his close advisers, trying to convey the truth of their account and the necessity of taking the information further. Galen was not sure how successful they had been.

"I hear you hid behind a girl."

Galen turned at the voice before he had properly registered the words, and he mentally kicked himself for thus entering what could not be anything but an unproductive conversation. "What?" he said, for lack of a better comeback. He kicked himself a second time.

There were two men behind him, not much older than himself, both in the livery of Lord Bryuki. One of them sneered. "You heard me. We heard you hid behind a girl during the fight with the bandits."

"That's not true," Galen said, and he started to turn back and go on his way.

"Hey! If you didn't hide behind her, how come you aren't even marked up, if this bandit is really a demon? While she's injured?"

Well, the word was out about the Rideis.

Galen sighed. "First, it's not a demon, he's a Rideis. Or a Selk, if you want to use that term. No one except back-swamp inbreds calls them demons. Second, she was injured earlier in the fight with the Fire Brigand, not in the fight with the Rideis. And third, I'm not injured because I hit him before he hit me." He hoped that was enough posturing to end this.

It wasn't. "So he's supposed to be this all-terrifying threat that we have to call out armies to face, and we need the Octovirate's mages to be ready for him, but you beat him single-handed?" The man laughed. "If you're so amazing, you could probably take both of us right here in this hallway, right?"

Galen raised his hands, palms out, the universal gesture of placation and dismissal. "I'm not interested in scrapping with Lord Bryuki's men," he said. "That's not what we came for, and there's no benefit to it for anyone."

"Heh," said the second. "So you did hide behind a girl."

"Woman," said Galen. "My friend. Beside me."

"Picking at words instead of defending yourself? Seems like you're still hiding behind her." The first man grinned disdainfully.

A scratching sound interrupted the taunt and made the three of them glance toward the floor. A cockroach the size of a hunting spaniel crawled between them, stretching its forelimbs for the first soldier's leg.

He leapt and swore, kicking at the insect. But its hooked feet caught the fabric of his trousers and wrapped around him, pulling itself upright and humping his leg like an overexcited dog.

The man shrieked and shook his foot as if it were on fire, and then he turned and began kicking the insect desperately into the wall. "Get off! Get it off! Fair night, get it off me!"

Another oversized cockroach crawled toward the second soldier, its feet clicking against the stone floor, and he swore and bolted down the corridor, abandoning his friend. He sprinted past another figure in the corridor. "Kill it! Kill it!"

"Kill what?" asked Lisveth, her eyes wide and innocent.

The soldier wheeled and pointed at nothing, at the empty floor and his companion still smashing his leg into the stone wall. "There was..." He trailed off.

"A man hiding behind me," she completed. "Yes, I saw. A big tough one, who tries to pick fights and then squeals like a piglet."

The first man stopped kicking, staring in confusion at his empty leg. He grimaced and put a hand gingerly to his bruised knee.

"Galen," Lisveth called, "do you want me to step aside and stop shielding this piglet behind me so you can answer whatever he was trying to say to you?"

Galen shook his head, smothering a smile. "Probably not worth the time, thank you."

"All right. In that case, can we get something to eat? I'm starving." She walked away from one soldier and past the other, looking at neither, and Galen joined her to continue on their way.

He waited until they were out of earshot. "You can be remarkably petty, do you know that?"

She snorted. "They don't know you well enough to pick a fight, and we aren't staying long enough to sort pecking order. It was foolish of them, and rude."

"A leg-humping cockroach isn't rude?"

"A guest should follow her hosts' lead."

"You are the worst."

"I know. That's not even how cockroaches mate."

CHAPTER 37

"IT'S AN ELEGANT SOLUTION for all," Lisveth said patiently. "You need someone to confirm the presence of Selks on your roads. You can't send your house forces to wander the roads looking for trouble, because if there are Selk bandits you'll need your defenses here at home. And for reconnaissance you'll need someone familiar with magical fights, ideally someone who has already survived a few. Meanwhile, Galen and I will need a new job, once we collect the bounty on the Fire Brigand. As we have to escort Andrea home, we'll be on the roads anyway, and it will be no trouble to take a few side routes after we've settled her. What do you think the arrangement lacks?"

Lord Bryuki shook his head. "If I did think it lacked anything, I'd hardly be able to recall it with you talking like a market day cattle seller."

Lisveth raised her hands in mock defense. "Then I'll say nothing, and you can tell me your own plans."

Bryuki flapped his own gesture of dismissal. "That won't help. I don't have a better idea. As you point out, I cannot spare the guards if there may be Selks coming. Not just for this house, but for the nearest towns." He frowned. "How long will you be, taking that girl home? Could we put her into the care of a passing caravan or something?"

"With respect, I doubt a caravan will trouble to bring back our payment to us. Her father hired us to find her."

"How long, then?"

"We were thirteen days on the road to get here."

Bryuki swore. "I can't wait a month for a report. Thanks, but I'll find someone else."

"You could give us a letter authorizing us to ask about the bandits. That will get you more answers than sending someone around locally after the bandits have already been scattered."

"I can manage, thank you."

Lisveth let her breath escape in a nearly inaudible little sigh, but her expression remained pleasant. "We'll look in after a few weeks, then, and see what you've found."

Galen had long kept the habit of letting Lisveth negotiate their hires, but as he followed her out of the hall, he let his surprise show. "You think his work won't pay as well as Andrea's father?"

"Not yet. But give it another month, and it'll pay better." Lisveth shrugged into her pack. "Lord Bryuki is trying very hard, despite Sheriff Alwire's efforts, to forget there were two packs of bandits. The Fire Brigand is gone, and he wants to wallow in that relief for a bit before he faces the greater concern of Selks on his roads. He's a man holding blinkers to his head so he doesn't have to see the more frightening part, and that will last until he's had to listen to a few more reports of attacks. Then he'll want someone to research and inform."

"It's too bad that people will have to get hurt before he passes word of the threat."

"That's always how it is. And Lord Bryuki knows he isn't widely admired, and he'll want the credit for disposing of the Fire Brigand before he carries fresh bad news. Best to separate them."

"You figured that out quickly enough."

"Eh, they're mostly the same. More self-preservation than imagination."

"So we're back with Andrea, then."

"With a half day's detour to pick up our bandit bounty, yes."

Andrea looked better than she had on the night of the attack, but she remained willing to return with them. Galen supposed she hadn't many other places to go, and it was daunting to set out when truly alone. He might have given up, too, if only his wounded pride deterred him.

But wounded pride was sufficient to worry Andrea. After the side trip to collect the Fire Brigand bounty, they made it as far as Greentown, where they stopped for a meal and the night. As they ate around a small table, surrounded by chattering townsfolk, Andrea asked abruptly, "He didn't seem too angry, did he? When he sent you?"

"Who, your father?" Lisveth asked, as if she hadn't fully understood the question. She returned to her plate. "He was upset, sure, but not angry. Mad that you were gone, but not mad at you, if that makes sense."

It made sense to Galen. It was a fantasy for some, but a kind one, and probably real enough for Andrea.

"How much does he have to know?" she asked after a moment. "I mean, about where I was. What I was doing. He—he was a lawman, you know."

Galen cleared his throat. "He told us where to find you," he said. "So he already knows."

Her face crumpled.

"But he knew when he asked us to find you. So that didn't change his mind about you."

She thought on that a moment, and then she nodded once. "Maybe the town... I don't want to shame him. Not everyone would understand, and they would speak poorly of him if they knew about me. I don't want that."

Galen had no answer. Neither did Lisveth, who usually had, if not an answer, at least a comment.

"If the dread is the hard part," Galen said after a moment, "we could cut south and take a riverboat. It would cost a bit but save a few days."

"Oh, no." Andrea shuddered. "I don't like boats." She shook her head. "I'm sorry, it's silly, but—I can't swim."

"Neither can I, but boats are for people who don't want to swim." Galen smiled to make it a jest.

"No, I understand." Lisveth folded her hands on the table. "I once happened across a place when they were fishing bodies up from an accident. They'd been down a couple of days, and—that sticks with you." She nodded toward Andrea. "Made me consider that no one can accidentally overturn a road."

Andrea flashed a quick, embarrassed smile. "Thanks. I know people ride all the time, but..." She blew out her breath and glanced toward the rear of the public room. "I hope the privy is reasonably decent."

"I'll come with you to find out," Lisveth said.

"I'm not going to go anywhere," Andrea protested quietly. "I'm not running away again."

"Then it will just be for company." Lisveth rose from the table. "Come on, let's go."

Galen pushed his spoon through his cooling beans. A moment later, a man approached the table. He nodded after the departed women. "I've seen you two around before. You're the ones for hire."

"That's right."

"Is she with you, now?"

He meant Andrea. "Just for a few days. We're giving her safe escort to her destination."

"I guess that's why she needs watching." The man grinned. "After that, you'll be looking for another job?"

Galen nodded. "Most likely."

"I'm looking to hire." The man nudged out the opposite bench and sat down. "I've got an idea that will pay big, but it needs more hands than I have."

Galen began to feel uneasy. "Not all—"

"My friend doesn't feel right about robbing kids," Lisveth cut him off.

Galen turned, startled she'd returned so quickly.

She sat down on Galen's bench. "Or people with kids. Or people who shouldn't be robbed." She glanced at Galen. "She's fine. It's a nice privy, even fenced from outsiders."

"No worries then," the potential client assured them, leaning forward. "No kids, just lots of treasure."

Galen scooped his beans together. It still sounded like robbery. "Go on."

"I don't know if you've seen all the town, but there's Brighthill Temple at the end of the market, and it's got this treasure room in the center that—"

"No," Galen said flatly.

"No," Lisveth said simultaneously.

Galen glanced at her in surprise.

The man looked between them. "What? It's not hurting anyone—the temple doesn't need such a lot of fancy pots, and it'd be fast enough to dispose of the gold. It's not like they're using the money to feed kids, you know. It's just sitting there. We could be in and out quick enough, with the right tools and skills."

"No," Galen repeated.

"I'm afraid you've mistaken us for some cheap crooks," Lisveth said in a dry tone. "I'm sorry you've wasted your time. Have the rest of your evening."

The man scowled and left.

Galen scraped the last of his beans from the wooden bowl. "I didn't expect you to turn that down so quickly."

"Yeah, well, maybe you're rubbing off on me." She took another bite of vegetables.

"Or maybe you were once a temple maiden, and now the idea wouldn't sit right with you." Galen chuckled.

Lisveth snorted. "You wouldn't wish me on a temple, would you?"

She scraped her bowl clean as Andrea returned. Galen shouldered their bags, and they all went up to the room they would share.

Lisveth scanned the morning traffic. "So no Selk near here yet," she mused. "No one's talking about it in town. And it's early yet, I suppose, but the imposter's survivors haven't regrouped, either, or that fine avaricious fellow would have locals to engage."

Galen nodded. "There's so much territory, though, nearer the mountains. Selks could spread north and south and still be nearer the border if they wanted to retreat home."

"Mountains need passes; it's not all the same distance. Still, you're not wrong."

Andrea crossed her arms and said nothing.

They came to the market, and Galen's steps slowed as he looked around. "There's the temple."

"Yes," Lisveth agreed amiably. "We won't be burgling it."

"We could tell them someone else is thinking of it."

"Do you have a way to do that without implicating us?"

"They can't come after us for refusing to rob a temple, can they?"

"I'll do it," Andrea said abruptly. "I can tell someone and then leave. I'll tell them I overheard it in the public room. I don't look like..." Her voice trailed off. It was true, she looked the least bandit-like of the three of them, and the irony was not lost.

"Be quick," Lisveth advised.

Andrea was quick. She trotted up the shop-lined path and found a priest within the yard, still visible to them. They saw his confusion and then consternation, and then she disengaged herself and trotted back to them. "Done. He believed me, I think."

"That's all we can do, then." Lisveth crossed her arms. "Thanks."

"It was easy enough," Andrea said, but Galen looked across at Lisveth curiously.

They made good time, and the morning of their expected arrival Andrea woke nervous and irritable. She fussed at her equipment and complained of small matters until, as they neared the town's outer buildings, Lisveth finally snapped at her. "There's no need to make such a fuss of it. You've come all this way, and he's waited so long for you, and you don't want to ruin it all by grumping over your boot buckle. Think maybe of how you're going to look, coming home all surly and making him regret sending us out for you."

"Nobody asked you," snapped Andrea. "And that's pretty high talk from someone who doesn't go home herself. Or are you an itinerant mercenary with a family you visit every new moon?"

Lisveth blew out her breath in exasperation. "That's it. Galen can take you home; I have better things to do."

Galen looked at her in surprise. Lisveth rarely had something better to do than collecting money owed. "It's not that big a town." Besides, he already felt uncomfortable, anticipating witnessing a homecoming that he would never have.

Lisveth shrugged. "I need to have my knife sharpened, and there will be a smith. You can find me when you're done; as you say, it's not that big a town." And then, true to her word, she drifted away from them and down another lane.

"The smith is another street over," Andrea muttered, but not loudly enough to call Lisveth back. Instead she nodded for Galen. "We go that way."

Her pace slowed twice as they walked, and for a moment Galen thought she might abandon her return and try to bolt, but she stayed on course and at last led him to a pleasant house. Galen knocked—he did not want her to feel the awkwardness of knocking at her own door—and stepped to the side, partly so that whoever opened would see her first and partly in case she had a last minute change of heart and tried to run. Lisveth would never forgive him if he lost their quarry and payment in the last moment.

Andrea stood stiffly on the stone step, her breath faintly audible, and when a moment passed without answer, her fingers clenched hard. Galen knew this delay meant little; the family was only out for a time, that was all, and there was nothing unexpected about that. But she had worked herself up for this moment, and it was hard to have it come to nothing.

"Andrea!"

She and Galen turned together, and her father stood in the street behind them. He let a basket drop to the ground and rushed forward.

"Papa—" she started.

He continued into her without pause and crushed her in his arms, pulling her close. Small sobs broke from him, and her resolve gave way into matching tears.

Galen looked down, kicking his boot toe into the step and blinking warmth away. His father would have welcomed him home this way. His mother might, too, if she could. But she couldn't stand up to Idorn and Parn, and Galen protected her by staying away.

At last they broke apart. "Let's tell your mother," Andrew Lawson said. "Come inside. You, too," he added, looking at Galen.

There were more tears inside—her mother had been in the kitchen out back, not hearing the door—and Galen tucked himself against a wall and waited uncomfortably. Lisveth would have known how to break into the happy reunion with a reminder, gently if not tactfully, and he would not be trapped here in this whirlwind of joyful embraces.

And then Andrea's mother turned and hugged Galen close—"Thank you! Thank you for bringing her safely home!"—and his stomach turned over. When she drew back, he felt as if his skin stretched like warm candy with her fingers.

How many years had it been since he'd been embraced?

Now Andrew Lawson could spare a few thoughts for Galen. "I must thank you, indeed," he said, extending a hand. "Your partner...?"

"She's fine," Galen said. "She had some errands in town. She trusted us to make it up the final street unattended."

Andrew laughed. "Let me pay you what I owe, and you can treat her to a fine dinner tonight."

"What are you saying?" demanded his wife. "They're invited to dine with us tonight, of course!"

Galen shook his head. "Oh, no," he said before he could think. "I couldn't think of intruding. You have so much to—" He checked the ominous words *talk about* and instead finished, "to share, as a family. We couldn't stay."

"I'll send you with a packet of tarts, anyway," she assured him.

Lawson counted out the money, and Galen thanked him and wished them well, and then he fled into the street with the tarts still warm in their bundle. He walked up the street, not caring where he went so long as he got out of sight of the house.

CHAPTER 38

LISVETH WAS AT THE end of the street, sitting on the edge of a fountain and buffing the small knife she usually wore at her belt. Galen rarely saw her use the knife, but today was apparently the day for sharpening and cleaning it. Clearly the task had preempted the delivery of Andrea to her waiting parents.

She saw him and slid the blade into its sheath. "Hello! All has ended well?"

"Paid, which is what I think you mean." He tossed her the little pouch of coins.

She snatched it from the air and grinned at its heft. "Well done, us."

"He told us to have a nice dinner."

"And we should." She nodded down the cross street. "How does the Figgy Libertine sound?"

"It sounds unclear, but I'm willing to try it."

The Figgy Libertine had a large room and a lean musician in the corner, picking out melodies on a long-necked instrument but not singing aloud. Lisveth and Galen took a seat. "Large portions," Lisveth told the maid who came to the table. "Whatever it is, large portions."

"Good choice. It's Maria's lamb cuts tonight."

"Then we're in luck."

"Is there a room available?" Galen asked.

"We've got just the one left. It's got two beds, soft but skinny." She looked apologetic.

"That'll be fine."

"All right, then. Room three, and I'll tell them you're taking it."

Galen put his chin in his hand and looked at Lisveth as she watched the musician. He wanted to ask her why she had not come with them to Andrea's house. The question was so simple, and that frightened him. Why was he reluctant to ask something so simple?

Sometimes it was better to leave alone a simple question than risk a less simple answer.

They were brought ale, and he sipped at it. Andrea's homecoming had raised other questions, too. He did not know the exact circumstances of her departure, but he'd seen her welcomed home warmly enough. But then, she hadn't stolen the family treasure when she'd gone.

Galen did not think often of home; there was no coin in that, as Lisveth would say. His uncles would test his assertion that the amulet was useless against ordinary threat by letting him wear it as they wore out their belts, and even if he were proved right, they would not forgive him for stealing it from them.

And, if he was honest, he was afraid of what he might find if he went home. Maybe stealing the amulet had not been enough to end the fighting. Maybe it had not united them against him but had provided another excuse for more fighting. That might be worse, to know he'd given up his whole life to have accomplished nothing or even made things worse.

And maybe he would learn whether David had known what their uncles had done. His mind shied away from the question like a spooky horse.

The musician snapped out a louder chord. "Are you ready for a song?" he asked the room with a crooked grin.

General enthusiastic assent came back, and he nodded. His elfin-thin fingers worked over the strings, beating out a melodic introduction, and then he started a gentle tune about walking along a road and sighting a strikingly colorful stone.

The lamb cuts arrived, and Lisveth and Galen began to eat. The bard sang about the magic rock and the narrator's discovery of its power to grant bravery. The lamb was good, its popularity justified.

The song's narrator worked his way through his village, exercising his newfound bravery in successive verses: first passing a nesting goose, then apologizing to the baker for taking an extra loaf, then opening his own shop. Galen's chewing slowed with the singer's words as he worked through the confession to the baker, asking forgiveness with the courage granted by the magic stone. Then the chorus picked up the tempo again, and all was well.

There was no magic stone to let Galen go home again. Not even the one he'd taken.

Galen had known what to expect; he would farm the same land his family had farmed, and one day he would marry a farmer's daughter, and then they would farm together. He had never thought to question it, not until the ridiculous idea of stealing the amulet had come to him.

Now he barely questioned his new life, either.

The song's narrator at last worked up the courage, clutching his stone, to bare his love for the miller's daughter, and she requited it, and they moved together into his new venture. The chorus ended with a little flourish of notes, and the listeners put down their spoons and applauded. Lisveth signaled for another ale.

Now he expected nothing, Galen realized. The song's narrator had a shop and a bride; Galen had nothing to look forward to, no plans to realize, no intentions to work toward. His life was the same, this month and last month and a year ago and probably the next, varying with the next task presented him but without structure or purpose. The thought alarmed him; he was a leaf, unmoored, drifting down a stream without a rudder or even an idea of where he wanted to go.

Fair night, I'm a cow. Grazing in whatever pasture I'm in today, never doing different, never even trying for something different.

"What about you?" he asked Lisveth suddenly.

"What?" She gave him a confused look.

"Was there something you thought you'd do? Did you have any expectations?" He tried to soften the abrupt question. "Surely you didn't grow up thinking you'd be a highwaywoman or a sorcerous mercenary."

She shoved a mushroom across her plate. "It's good to live in the moment. Thinking too much can make trouble."

"You don't mean that. You're thinking all the time. You already know how much you're going to pay for this dinner, and how much that will leave, and how far that will get us, and what you'll ask Bryuki for when we get back."

She nodded admission. "And all of that is thinking forward, not backward. Never look back."

He shrugged. "That's easy to say, but we can't help it. We are what we are. You can take me off the farm, but I'm still a farm boy, as you often remind me."

Her mouth tightened. "Never look back."

It was good advice, and yet...

The musician was circulating among the tables, laughing and nodding and accepting coins. Galen did not know how many songs he'd played before their arrival, but the man was good at his craft, and so he fetched out a few small coins as the musician approached. "Thanks for the music."

"Thank you, neighbor! I'm glad you liked it. May you find all the courage you need for whatever it is you need it for." He funneled the coins into a purse.

"Well, my magic stone doesn't quite work as I'd hoped."

The musician laughed and drew his hand out from his coin purse, dropping a pinkish pebble on the table. "I always keep a spare."

It was an ordinary piece of gravel. Galen chuckled. "I'm not sure I should take it from you. You must need it, too."

"Oh, anyone can have a rock of courage, if they only pick one up." The man winked. "I should be more careful with my secrets, though, or you'll steal my song and my audience."

"What? Oh, no." Galen chuckled nervously. "Even if I could sing, I wouldn't try in front of people all staring. No thank you."

"Oh, you know there's a trick to that, too."

"Imagine them all sitting there naked?"

"Fair night, no. That's far more terrifying." The musician shook his head. "No, I imagine they've all come particularly to hear my song, and they've only picked up the beer and ale to fill the time while I tune my strings."

"The pebble of courage."

"It's easier to trust in your magic pebble if you also have skill," Lisveth said a little curtly. "Or if you already have reason to believe the miller's daughter will say yes."

The musician nodded. "True enough. Sometimes it's easier." He walked on to the next table.

Lisveth huffed out her breath with an irritated sound.

Galen gave her an annoyed look. "He was making a living."

"He was making the rounds."

"It's the same thing, for him."

"I know that." She looked across the room.

Galen crossed his arms. "Don't worry about it. It's over. Never look back."

Her mouth tightened, but she said nothing.

This was not like them. They had just finished a job of weeks, and it had come off much better than it might have and netted them an additional bounty besides, with the acclaim of having taken down the Fire Brigand. They should have been celebratory.

Galen was feeling a little sharp with the reminder of home; maybe he was pushing that onto Lisveth as well.

"Is this what we're going to go on as?" he asked, trying to moderate his voice so that he did not sound demanding.

"What do you mean? Tonight, or forever?"

"Either. Both." He tried to put his frustration into words. "I'm sorry for being testy. I just—she got to go home, and it made me think of things."

Lisveth said nothing, but he thought he saw her expression soften.

"And it made me think of us, wandering and looking for odd jobs, and I realized that maybe—"

"Maybe what?" The tension was back. "You got someplace else to be?"

Galen had tried to be reasonable. "I wanted to do what I thought was the best thing, to help the most people, and now I'm wandering with you, living out of a bag, and not a particularly roomy one."

"I'm sorry I couldn't offer more luxury or better company."

"I'm only saying, this isn't how I thought I'd be living my life."

"It might be hard to believe, but I didn't plan this, either."

It was a rare allusion to her life before she had met Galen, and he almost pressed questions. But her arms were crossed and she was scowling at the far side of the room, and the opportunity was already gone.

"Look," she said after a moment, "we're both out of sorts, and it's not going to get better. Let's take some time and then come back when we've both cleared our heads. Fair?"

"I have a question first."

"Ale!" She held up her empty cup and then turned skeptical eyes on him. "If it's so important."

"Let me ask it while we're already irritated, just in case." He took a breath; it was harder to voice than he'd imagined.

She jerked her head toward the table. "There's your helpful rock."

He ignored this. "A while back, when we first—early on, I wanted to send a letter. Just to check on things. It didn't have to be carried too far; we could have made it within striking range of the Heel in a few days."

Lisveth's lips tightened.

"But you didn't want to carry a letter for me. Not even a day or two out."

"I told you then, I didn't want to find that they didn't want your letter. I wouldn't want to be that witness or carry that news back to you."

"I understood that. But then, today—"

"Today what?" She turned and lifted her cup again. "Ale!" She turned back. "You agreed at the time your letter was more hope than anything else. You were just being wishful."

"That's also true. But today we knew we were bringing her home to—"

"And we were two days out, at least."

"We've walked farther to carry a letter."

"We were paid for that, and we knew the recipient wouldn't try to kill us."

"Anyway, I thought I might write now. It's been a while, maybe long enough, and—"

"Why do you want to do that?" Her cup thumped hollowly on the table. "Your stupid sheep-loving cousins aren't going to be happy to hear from you. Your uncles aren't going to thank you for making them fools over an amulet they can't use. You think that news would make them love you? Rather than admit they murdered their brother for nothing, they'll tell themselves you sold the real thing and came back to lie to them, and they'll kill you too. Fair night, I'm trying to protect you, and you won't stop badgering me about it. Where's that ale?"

"Right here," said the woman with the pitcher, and Lisveth slumped a little in embarrassment and frustration as she refilled the cup.

Galen chewed on her words. He had not thought it through as she obviously had, and she might well be right. Shaming his uncles would not win their welcome.

Maybe she was right. Maybe it was gone forever. Maybe there was nothing left but the drifting.

She drank half the cup and then set it down. She blew out a breath. "Look, I'm sorry. I didn't know you were still thinking about it."

He hadn't known, either.

"They put a bounty on you. They didn't invite you home. They won't welcome you in."

"I could just send a letter," he said doggedly. "Just to see. Just to know, for certain."

"Do you think that will give you peace of mind? Knowing for certain they still want to string your teeth on a wreath?"

"My mother is still there."

"And she chose that! She's a part of that. Of everything you left. You left to help her, and now you want to go back. You think it will be easier on her if you kick up fresh fracas with your uncles? Of all the idiotic, selfish things to—how dense are you? Stupid red idiot." She snatched up her drink and drained it.

For a moment Galen sat still, stunned into silence. Then he pushed back from the table.

She watched him stand, and her mouth opened, but she did not speak. He picked up his knapsack and walked away, to the door, out into the street.

The cool air struck him, washing away the heat of her words. *Stupid red stupid idiot red red...*

He had not been prepared for that. He had heard those words from Uncle Idorn; he had not expected them from Lisveth, at least never in that tone. And not *red*. She had jested a hundred times and more about his idiocy and his muddy farm origins, but not *red*.

He walked to the fountain and scooped cold water over his burning cheeks.

Darkness was settling over the streets, herded into alleys by lamps lit at intervals. He did not know the town, but it was probably safe to walk for a bit yet.

Stupid red...

That had been unfair. He had not deserved that. And she had no reason to be so angry. It was Galen who risked rejection in the letter, not her. It wasn't that she was so wrong in her assessment—if Galen was honest, she was probably right about his uncles. But she had never met them, so how could she be so certain of it? It was as if she wanted to believe the worst of his family.

And today, bringing Andrea home, there was no bad news to fear. Her parents had cried while welcoming her. Galen and Lisveth had known the outcome, because they had been hired to bring her.

The implication struck him like a snowball to the face. It wasn't the rejection she meant to avoid—it was the welcome. She was afraid they would want him back.

It was full dark, and none but a cutthroat or an idiot would be on a strange street now, and so Galen went up the inn's stairs with his bag over one shoulder. He stopped at the third room, and he stared at the door.

He could turn and walk away, and that would be easier than facing the woman inside. But if he walked away, it would be harder still to return later. And it was getting late.

He tried the door, wondering if it would be locked.

The latch shifted.

Inside, two narrow beds sat against the right and left walls, with an equally narrow gap between. Lisveth sat on the right-hand bed, her back to the wall and her knees to her chest. The lamp burning low on the stump of a table cast more shadow than light on her face.

"Hey," Galen said, his voice strained.

Her chin moved upward and her eye caught the light, gleaming. "Hey," she returned, gruffly.

Galen dropped his bag on the empty bed. "I did some thinking."

"Oh?"

She should be the one to apologize. She was the one who had said the words. But Lisveth would never apologize. It was not in her nature. Even now she was still, defensive, gruff.

Galen sat on his bed, facing her. The lamp was too near the far wall; it glared for him and did not light her. "Today was about wanting to avoid Andrea's happy homecoming. Back then, you weren't trying to protect me from rejection, you were afraid they would ask me to stay."

She was a still, dark shape, eyes gleaming at him. She didn't move.

"You should have said something. You took me in when I needed it; I wouldn't have left you alone."

There was a small, shaky sigh, as if the boil of her irrational fear had at last been lanced. "Oh." She exhaled, almost like a relieved laugh. She shifted on the bed and lowered one knee.

"Tonight, you didn't have to say that to keep me from them."

Her knee froze halfway to the mattress. "I was—I wanted you to stop. I didn't want you to try it, so I just said..."

"You said the worst things you could think of."

"No. No, I—said the things that would hurt you worst."

The words hung in the dark between them.

At last she said, "I didn't mean them. Not really. If that's worth anything. I only wanted you to stop, and that's all I could do to stop you."

"You can't say words that have no meaning."

"I know." Her voice was subdued. "I shouldn't have said that. Any of it."

That was as much of an apology as he would get, and he should accept it for what it was. He blew out a long breath. "That lamp needs attention." He stood and reached for it.

Her hand shot out to rest on his arm. "Wait."

He waited. He understood; some things were easier to say in the dark.

"You're not stupid." Her voice was soft. "I know I say that a lot, but as a joke. You know when it's a joke. Tonight—you're not stupid. Or an idiot."

"Thanks," he answered quietly.

Still red, though.

A moment passed, but her hand remained on his arm. He waited.

Finally she said, in a voice nearly a whisper, "Thanks for coming back."

He looked at the crest of her hair, all that was visible. "Didn't you think I would?"

She did not answer. Then she pulled her hand back.

He drew the lamp forward and adjusted the wick so that it lit the room properly. He avoided looking at Lisveth and turned back to his bag, opening it for a few items he did not need. When he turned back, she had unfolded and was squeezing the pillow critically.

"Did you ask for a breakfast?" he asked.

She cleared her throat. "No breakfast. We can go out to the market."

"That'll do." He set his bag on the floor and spread his cloak to supplement the blanket.

CHAPTER 39

GALEN SLID ONTO THE barber's stool and showed a fistful of hair. "I want it gone."

"I can see that," the man said, and Galen's stomach sank a little. It was bad enough without hearing such ready agreement. "I can take it short, or very short, or down to the skin."

Gone, Galen wanted to repeat, but even in his frustration, practicality stayed his hand. Shaving hair to the skin lasted only a short while, as his bristly chin and cheeks could attest, and it wouldn't be the solution he wanted. Instead, he would be cold and scruffy as well as red.

But he could cut it down to something more easily hidden beneath a hood. "Very short," he answered. "Easily covered."

"Just a few moments, then."

His shears were only a little smaller than the ones Galen's family had used for shearing sheep, and the box they came from smelled as if it had been left in a barn. The barber's other tools for bloodletting, tooth pulling, and other minor physical repairs were clean at a glance, but something must have been spilled in the base. The barber took a handful of hair and, bracing the shears against Galen's skull, began to cut.

Galen leaned against the pressure of the tugging, trying to stay upright. The shears squeaked beside his ear. His scalp began to feel cool, and cold air brushed the back of his neck.

The barber switched the shears for a smaller blade, and he began to work his way around Galen's head, evening the rough cuts. He nicked the tip of Galen's ear—"Sorry, there"—but worked quickly, scattering a little rain of red trimmings over Galen's shoulders and lap.

Galen had not had his hair cut since his mother had done it for him, fussing over each little bit while his cousins sniggered as they passed through or made pointed comments about all the chores they were doing while Galen sat on the stool. Perhaps his mother was more conscientious about her work, or perhaps it was more work to trim about his ears and shoulders than to shear it short, or perhaps she had lingered over the task because Galen was her youngest, or most likely the barber was just more practiced. The process took less time than he'd expected.

"I've got a mirror for you to see it," the barber said, producing the object. "Careful with that, and don't drop it when you look different."

Galen did look different. His forehead was broader and his face seemed wider, and he wasn't sure if he'd always had such prominent freckles or if they were more visible now that they weren't competing with the red of his hair. All around his scalp, a finger-width of fringe still showed his natural color, but controlled.

He pulled his hood up and appraised the result in the mirror. Yes, he could nearly pass for a man with ordinary hair. It would do.

He paid the barber and brushed the scrap hair from his clothes as he went out.

He left his hood down as he walked down the street, trying to surreptitiously watch the passersby. Were they looking at him? Were they looking at him more or less than usual? Did he remember how others looked at him? Did he mind, after so many years, if they did?

Did it matter? Few on the street had mentioned his hair color aloud. Only Lisveth, and she would still know the truth.

He had been stupid. Cutting his hair had changed nothing, not really. But...

A young woman with a basket of root vegetables balanced on one hip gave him a smile as she bent toward her wares, and his heart quickened as he smiled back. She had seen him—not his hair. Would she have smiled if he'd still had his own longer hair? It was impossible to say, but it was certain she had smiled at him without it.

He didn't have to change entirely, after all. He could change how he presented himself, and that would be something.

He bought a small vegetable pie and ate it as he walked, licking his fingers. He slaked his thirst at a public fountain and shrugged his bag back into place. He wandered through the leather market, fingering belts and bags and sheaths laid out on display.

He was stalling.

At last he went back to their room. He climbed the stairs, each one squeaking or groaning, and put his hand on the latch to their door. He went inside.

Lisveth was sitting on her bed, her elbows resting on her crossed legs, her head bent over a sock heel. She threw a cursory glance toward the door and looked back at her darning. "You're back. I was beginning to wonder."

Galen went to his bed. "I got something to eat."

She nodded. "I should. I haven't gone out." She put her thumb on the sock heel, as if to mark her place. "What did you—"

She stopped as she looked at him.

Galen resisted the instinct to move under her gaze, to flinch or shift or look down. He tried to sit casually, as if nothing was out of the ordinary.

She stared at him. "You..."

She knew why he'd done it. He could see it in the tiny downturn of her mouth, the instability of her chin, the way her eyes flicked to his scalp and away and back, anywhere but his eyes. She looked as if she might be sick.

Galen felt a twinge of regret. He hadn't done it to hurt her in return. Still, it was right that she see what her words had done. Maybe she would think before calling him "red" again. But then, she had already regretted the words, and he had cut his hair for his own sake, not just for what she had said...

It did not matter; it was done. The hair was cut, the sight was seen, the rebuke was received.

Lisveth stood up suddenly, her eyes on the floor. "I need to go out for breakfast," she said in a tumble. "I might be a bit."

Galen leaned forward. "I can—"

"I'll be fine. I'll be back later." And she fled, nearly slamming wisps of her own blonde hair in the door.

Galen waited a moment to see if he would feel better. He did not. Before the visit to the barber, he'd had red hair. Now he had red hair, if shorter, and a partner who hated herself for driving him to change.

He pulled his hood up again, as if he could hide his cut hair, and began packing the clothes he'd left to air. It didn't take long. Then he turned to Lisveth's bed and tucked her dried wool socks into her bag. He would carry it down and meet her when she returned.

Her remaining sock, mid-darning, was lying where she'd left it on the blanket. He sat on the bed and picked it up. The sock was a faded yellow, probably a goldenrod dye. He finished the darning and wove the loose tail back into the outer stitching. Then he packed the needle and darning stone back into their kit and the sock into Lisveth's things.

When he went downstairs, he paused and looked across the public room. "We're going," he called, hearing movement in the back room. "Thank you." He tugged his hood up over his cropped hair.

The maid who'd served the supper leaned through the door. "Thanks, and safe journey."

Lisveth came in from the street. She had a packet of cheap-paper, and when she looked up and saw Galen, she extended it toward him with one hand, taking a bite from the other. "I didn't know if you'd had any."

He could smell it from the base of the stairs. It was a yeasty fry bread, savory and stuffed with cheese. It was one of his favorite treats, and he'd not seen it when he'd gone out, so it must have been on another street.

He closed the distance between them and took the fry bread. Herbs had been cut into the dough, making a colorful scatter over the surface. He folded back the cheap-paper and took a bite.

Still warm. It was delicious.

"You've got both bags?" Lisveth asked after a moment.

"Both."

"I had a darning needle out."

"I packed it." Galen slid her pack from his shoulder. "Are you ready?"

"I can walk and chew."

They started together up the street.

CHAPTER 40

DIELO WOKE MOST NIGHTS listening for a whisper of music through the wall. But the prince was beyond the mountains, and Yovela had disappeared, and he was alone in the prince's quarters.

Not truly alone, of course. But Arad and Nala and the other servants kept their own society, and they had little reason to seek out a discarded virilo.

When at last daylight crept over the windowsills, he breathed a silent sigh of relief that the long, empty night had ended, and he rose to face the long, empty day.

He had known Prince Kayvin would leave at the Arch Potentate's order. He had bid the prince farewell and wished him success on his quest. He had known he would not accompany the prince; this was not a mission of diplomacy and statecraft, where an ostentatious display of wealth and power would be of use. Dielo would serve by ensuring Prince Kayvin's homecoming was warm and welcoming.

But then Yovela had gone, too. It took Dielo a full day to realize she was not merely avoiding him in the prince's absence but was no longer in the prince's quarters and, he thought, no longer in the palace. It was unthinkable that a sera qadra member would run away, especially one who had defied Prince Kayvin's clearing of his sera qadra and refused payment to leave. She must have gone after the prince.

The realization had stunned Dielo. He stood still for a moment, half in shock at her daring and half wishing he dared to do the same.

Dare he?

It was different for Yovela. She was a sera qadra woman and nothing else, so if she followed her lord, she was blameless. While Dielo was also in the prince's sera qadra, he was a virilo, and the chit of his ownership did not rest with Prince Kayvin, but with Pasiphae Jade. If he left, even to follow his master, might he be fleeing his service? Leaving to follow Prince Kayvin meant breaking the rules that bound him, spoken and unspoken.

And Yovela had been something else before she entered the sera qadra. Dielo had been trained from youth as a virilo, and he knew how to make a chamber comfortable, how to please his master, how to prepare dainties, how to entertain, how to make his lord feel loved and admired and missed. And all of those were good skills, to be sure, but they were unlikely to retrieve any of the amulets they desperately needed.

He was exquisitely prepared to be useless when his lord had actual need of him.

With a start, Dielo realized just how useless he was. He had been trained to be a pet—perhaps a useful pet, as a cat might also keep mice from a kitchen, but a pet. He did not know how to travel in the world outside. He did not have any useful skills to barter other than the skills of making a pleasant retreat.

You are an object to them, a pretty jar or fancy box, nothing more.

Yovela's insults hurt more than ever now that they were proved true.

But Dielo was fulfilling his duty here, even in the prince's absence. He would keep the instruments in tune, and he would wait for Prince Kayvin's return, when he would provide a warm welcome and prompt refreshment. In fact, after a couple of weeks had passed, he should think of having some treat that could sit at the day's temperature, ready and waiting each day, just in case.

He had at least a couple of weeks to wait, though, and likely longer, so for now he could sit and wait.

He sat. The sunbeams crept across the tiled floor.

He could not remember when he had last been so completely unaccompanied. Since childhood he had been supervised, watched in education and in leisure by his tutors. He had lived in a hall filled with sleeping pits, first in training and then in waiting for his assignment, and of course once he had a place as a virilo, his life centered upon his master. What time he had for himself was spent in quarters with other virilos or sera qadra, talking as they worked on wardrobe items, browsed new ornaments from sellers, exchanging ideas or gossip. He still could not quite grasp the idea of this empty room.

He'd never been in a room so empty.

The prince's soaking pool was set between the apartment and the garden. Like most of the garden, it was shielded from other palace eyes by clever architecture and plantings. Dielo toyed with the idea of using the pool. As a virilo, he occupied a twilight realm of privilege, and while one of the ordinary servants like

Nala should not be caught using the prince's luxuries, Dielo might expect access, if not with the same attention from the servants.

The soaking pools were heated with deep waters that came steaming hot to the surface, occasionally pocked with tiny mineral petals. When the waters smelled too strongly of minerals, the soaking pools were sweetened with flowers and oils, but often they could be taken as they were. The pool would be as isolated as the empty room, but it would be a pleasant way to pass the time.

Dielo went to the pool and began to fold back the heavy wooden cover that trapped the heat, releasing a cloud of steam into the air. The fading steam briefly obscured his view of the garden, and then he saw two figures among the plantings. The gardeners glanced at him and then went on with their work repairing the burned beds near the turned poetry stones.

Dielo dragged the lid back in place, feeling self-conscious. He might be permitted to use the soaking pool, but to be seen doing so upon the prince's departure might look as if he took advantage of the prince's absence. He could not afford disparaging talk.

He went back to the sera qadra's rooms. He sat.

No one would come into the sera qadra men's quarters but to clean, and only when Dielo was away. He could hear servants moving about the prince's apartment. They would respond politely if he greeted them, but then the exchange would halt awkwardly until Dielo made an excuse and moved on. He could ease the awkwardness by offering his greeting in passing, as if he did not wish to linger either.

So he nodded and spoke to Arad and then to one of the maids who wiped the dust from the floor, and he fled to the palace kitchen.

He did not need to come here himself; as a member of the prince's sera qadra, he could expect his meals to be delivered.

But a virilo might come himself to the kitchens to select a special treat for his master or to make a special request, so his appearance would not be unusual. He could consider what specialty he would have waiting for the prince, and he might strike up a conversation with a friendly servant.

But the kitchen was full of activity; palace kitchens did not sit quietly in the mornings. The crush of breakfast preparations had ended, but there were plenty of pastries and cooked grains in progress for lunch. Dielo eased his way through the busy room, trying to stay out of the traffic paths while peeking into the larger pots. Vegetables, rice, something that was probably a mushroom filling for a pie.

"Are you looking for something in particular?"

He turned toward the voice and saw a girl seated at a table near the wall. She was dicing fruit. "No," he admitted.

"Did you come for something?"

"No," he repeated, feeling foolish.

"If you're just looking for company, I can talk while I chop." She nodded toward the bench opposite her.

Dielo slid onto it, putting his back to the rest of the kitchen. Her cutting board was bright with mango and plantain. "You won't be scolded for chattering with me?" He tried to make the question a jest.

She rolled her eyes. "I'm already scolded. That's why I'm here, cutting fruit. I'm not a kitchen maid; I usually do the north rooms." She continued cutting, and even to Dielo's inexpert eye, she was not efficient. "I'm making a fruit salad, but I fear I'll be at it until evening."

"Can I help?"

She shook her head. "I've got just the one knife, and someone like you can't risk cutting a finger." She gave him an upward glance, her mouth crooked at the corner.

She was a few years younger than Dielo, somewhere in her mid-teens. She was pleasantly attractive, if not beautiful, and could have been more so with a few attentions. "My name is Dielo. I serve the Amethyst Prince."

She nodded, her eyes bright. "I guessed by your clothing."

Dielo was not in his finest garb today, not for a day when he would entertain no one, but even the most mundane of his pieces were still fit for a virilo's wardrobe. He looked down at himself and smiled. "I should have been disappointed if you disbelieved me."

"I've seen you before. I knew your position, just not your master." She rolled a shoulder. "I don't work in an apartment with a sera qadra, but my aunt was in one. I'll never be pretty enough to enter one, but it's fun to imagine."

This admiration from afar of the glamour and prestige was more of what Dielo had expected, and after Yovela's cool disdain, even this mild praise was welcome. "You are pretty, and that's true whether or not anyone brings you into a sera qadra."

"I wish someone would. It would save my fingers." She pushed the knife through another piece of plantain.

"So what do you do when you are not cutting fruit?"

"I carry linens, and clean rooms, and wipe floors, and polish knick-knacks. I look forward to a long year of more of the same." She sighed. "But there are bright days, too. We have our own occasions, you know—the servants, I mean. We bring our own special dishes and tell stories, and there's music and dancing. I don't suppose you attend those, being too much in the sera qadra."

"It sounds fine," Dielo said, and he wondered if she heard wistfulness in his voice.

She scraped diced fruit into a pile and scooped it into a bowl. "I could bring you. There's—"

"What are you doing here? Did you need something for your master or mistress?"

This was the second cook, a tall woman with an expression that could curdle cream, though her tone was level. Dielo found himself half rising to answer her. "No, I came for nothing in particular. Not today, anyway. I wanted something special for another day."

"You'll have to tell me what you mean by special." She jerked her head. "Come this way, and start by saying sweet or savory."

Dielo explained that he wanted something that could sit for a few hours without losing flavor or texture, and that he would need the dish daily once it drew nearer the time Prince Kayvin might be expected. She was predictably irritated at the request to have uncounted days of extra planning and diverted kitchen labor, and in the end Dielo offered her compensation from his own spending allowance. What was that for, anyway, but to help him to better serve his master?

He did not think of the fruit maid again until some time later. He had not gotten her name, but that was all right. Now he had someone to watch for as he walked the northern palace corridors.

CHAPTER 41

DIELO ROLLED OVER AND adjusted his pillows, glancing up at the rim of the sleeping pit to check the light. There was none, so it was probably hours yet until dawn. Or it might be even longer; he had gone to bed early, as there was nothing else to occupy him in the evenings.

He closed his eyes and willed himself, eventually, back to sleep.

When dawn lightened the windows, he twisted and got up from the pit. The men's sleeping room was eerie in its emptiness, and the small sounds of his dressing echoed. He wondered if an empty day could echo as well.

A virilo was never meant to be alone. His orbit should be fixed about the prince, and with the prince gone—no, if he was honest, even when the prince had been there, Dielo had been adrift.

He had known the prince would be gone on his mission, but he had somehow imagined the absence to be days, perhaps a couple of weeks. He was coming to fully realize at last that Prince Kavyin had to explore the country of Sayinia, and without clear knowledge of his targets. Dielo was foolish to plan welcoming refreshments just in case; it might be months before the prince returned.

Months of waiting, useless, alone.

Pasiphae Jade held his chit. No one would think twice if Dielo went to the royal quarters, as he had done on occasion to speak with her about the prince's progress. He might pass some time chatting with the men and women of her sera qadra, or even speak again with the Arch Potentate herself. If he made himself agreeable enough, she might take him back into her own sera qadra, even if only for the time that the prince was away.

Some distant part of him remembered that she might be the one who had marked him. She certainly had told him that he strove to offer a sense of power and of being envied, not love. He could not hope for respect or affection from her.

But he did not know how to be alone.

He dressed with care and, after a long moment, left off the lavender silk sash that marked him as a member of the Amethyst Prince's household. He went the long way around the palace, to take more time and to allow for the outside possibility of finding something else to occupy him. He passed through the north wing, watching the side corridors.

"Dielo!"

He turned and saw the young maid he'd seen in the kitchen, trotting toward him with a basket in her arms. She was smiling. "I did not expect the prince's virilo to be in the north wing. Did you come to see me?" She dipped her head in shy teasing.

He could hardly have admitted it, but he could return her jest. "How could I not? Are you freed from your extra kitchen duties?"

She rolled her eyes. "At last. Until Parris finds something else to complain about."

Dielo groped for conversation. "He's a stickler, is he?"

"You have no idea." She adjusted the basket in her arms. "Oh! Do you remember what I said about our servants' parties? There's one coming soon. Would you like to go with me?"

He was ashamed of how much he wanted to. "They won't think themselves too fine for a virilo to attend?"

"Oh, no. We'll be happy to have you." She tipped her head to one side and smiled. "I'll vouch for you."

"Well, that's all right then."

"Four days," she said. She glanced over her shoulder. "And I have to get back to work, or it'll be more fruit salad. But we'll talk before then?"

"Of course," he agreed without thinking.

She gave him a broad smile and then hurried away, glancing back once with her head tipped over her shoulder.

He still hadn't asked her name. Next time, when they were not in such a hurry.

Well, he was not in a hurry. He walked on, completing his circle of the palace, no longer looking for a potential conversant. His feet slowed and he paused several times to examine the palace art.

But at last he arrived. The guards at the Arch Potentate's door knew him, as he expected, and he was admitted to the dog-legged entrance for her chief servant's approval. "I have not come on any urgency," Dielo hastened to explain. "I only come to see if I might be of service in her household today."

The servant gave Dielo a knowing glance and then returned his eyes to the thickly lined agenda. "Her Illustrious Excellency has a busy day."

Dielo nodded. "Yes, I'm sure. But I can bring drinks or set a more comfortable seat as well as any, and my chit is here, so it is only natural that I should return here while the prince is away."

The chief servant made a show of consideration, but he could not argue the matter of the chit. "It took you long enough to come back, then," he allowed. "Go on, then. Make yourself useful."

"Thank you." Dielo should not have needed to thank this man for admittance to his rightful place, but it was good to keep relations pleasant. One never knew when he might need a genuine favor or a recommendation.

The Arch Potentate's quarters were bustling with the usual morning activity. Two women were dressing her beside her sleeping pit, as she listened with outstretched arms to a man reading from a sheaf of notes. Others were bringing in breakfast trays and pitchers, or arranging new flowers, or setting scents in the rooms.

Riolo was carrying pillows across the room toward Pasiphae Jade's study. He was wearing Dielo's missing tunic.

Dielo was too well schooled to let slip his first thought, and he closed his mouth on his outrage. But it was all clear, now. Riolo had taken it from his trunk while Dielo was led into the Arch Potentate's garden to be beaten. Riolo had seen that Dielo had fallen out of favor, and he had used Dielo's misfortune to thieve from him.

Dielo followed the other virilo into the next room. Riolo set down the pillows and turned back, startling slightly at seeing Dielo with him. Dielo spoke quietly. "Give it back, and I'll keep my voice down."

Riolo's mouth twisted. "What makes you think it wouldn't be just you getting yourself thrown out if you didn't?"

That was a good point; Riolo had been serving in Pasiphae Jade's sera qadra, and she would naturally favor one of her own, and Riolo might have earned extra consideration, especially against the one she had sent away. "Still, she would hardly appreciate the disruption, and your part in it."

Riolo scowled. "Fine. I don't like the hand of this fabric, anyway. But I'm not going to strip it off in the middle of the morning tasks and walk about looking as if I forgot to make myself presentable."

That was fair. Going with bare skin was acceptable, but going undressed was not.

Riolo pointed down a short corridor. "There's a room at the end. Wait there, and I'll bring it to you. Then you can go out the throne room corridor door without carrying your laundry through the Arch Potentate's quarters."

Dielo nodded. "That's acceptable."

He went to the end room. It was a little larger than the study and comfortably furnished with facing seats, a cozy room for talking rather than for working. Dielo assessed the seats and decor in a sweeping glance. This room was somehow more private than the study or even the personal living space.

He waited, and Riolo did not come. Of course, he had to change his clothes and jewelry, and he might take some time. Still he did not come. Dielo sat on a bench against the wall, behind the two chairs with tall backs. He closed his eyes. He had lain awake a long while the night before.

Riolo still had not come with his tunic. Had he forgotten? Of course he'd not forgotten. Did he hope Dielo would give up? Dielo should have followed him into the sera qadra's quarters. He would go there now if he had to; the Arch Potentate would not overhear there, and Dielo could rummage through Riolo's things if he was out. He would take only his own, of course, but...

He leaned his head against the wall. Five more minutes, five minutes of resting his eyes, and then he would go get it himself.

He came awake with a small jerk. He was lying on his side, his feet still on the floor, and Pasiphae Jade had just entered the room. The closing door had woken him. He tried to gather his thoughts.

She didn't look toward the bench on the wall, and he remained still. He was partially concealed behind the seats; she might not notice him if she was here for only a moment. He had not done anything wrong, in the strictest sense, but he did not want to present himself again to her service by being found napping in her private room. She was not going to a chair, only walking across the room toward the opposite shelf, so perhaps she only retrieved a book and did not mean to stay.

But at the far wall she operated a latch and opened a door, admitting a young woman. "Did anyone see you?"

"No, of course not." Barely a woman, a girl, really; Dielo could hear her youth in her voice.

Realization struck him. *Did anyone see you?* Dielo was not meant to see this, either. The last drowsiness drained from him.

They embraced. Dielo drew his legs onto the bench, curling them against his torso. He could not see them clearly, with the chair between, but that meant he was also partially hidden from them.

Had Riolo meant for him to be discovered in the Arch Potentate's secret meeting?

"How has it been? Does anyone know?"

The girl shook her head. "No, no, everything is fine." She wore the clothing of a palace maid. "I came by a long way."

Dielo knew her voice. This was the maid from the kitchen.

My aunt was in a sera qadra. Oh. *Was*, not because she had retired or died, but because she had risen to a new station.

And she visited her illustrious aunt by a private entrance to a private room, away from the eyes of even the sera qadra. Pasiphae Jade kept the girl unknown for her safety. Dielo was never meant to have seen this.

Riolo had sent him here knowing this room would be forbidden.

"Has he been back?" The Arch Potentate's voice was warm and concerned. Dielo had never heard it so unvarnished.

"No. I haven't seen him even in the corridors."

"Good. If he comes around to you again, let me know. I'll have him butchered for fertilizer."

"Don't you think that would give up the secret of our relation?"

The Arch Potentate gave a sniffing laugh. "Don't underestimate me. I can be vengeful and protective, true, but I can also be secretive and misleading in how I dispose of a brute."

"Don't do anything, please. As I said, he's gone. I wonder if—"

"Wait." Now Pasiphae Jade's voice was quiet and firm, cautioning. She had spotted Dielo on the padded bench.

He could not plead ignorance of the room's forbidden status; that would mean nothing if she believed he had seen something he shouldn't have. Nor could he promise discretion; Riolo wouldn't have sent him here if she had not warned her sera qadra away from the room, so she did not trust discretion. With sudden insight, Dielo saw that ignorance was his only hope, and as he was not ignorant, he would have to lie to the holder of his chit.

The two women had gone still, and he could feel their eyes on the shielding chair. He did not move; movement would acknowledge their suspicions. He must be ignorant.

"Go," Pasiphae Jade said quietly, and the maid slid out the door. The Arch Potentate started toward the bench.

Dielo closed his eyes and made his jaw go slack. He breathed, counting slowly in counter to his pounding pulse. *In, two, three, out, two, three.*

It would not be enough. She would see through such a shallow trick.

"Who's there?" she demanded, coming around the chair.

Dielo pushed a glob of saliva out his barely parted lips, letting it run over the edge of his mouth and onto the padded bench. It was counter to everything he had learned—he knew how to arrange his head so that he neither drooled nor snored when he stayed to sleep—but Pasiphae Jade expected that a virilo would never knowingly let himself be discovered in so unattractive a position.

She stopped beside the bench, and he could feel her presence, and he poured all his concentration into counting the same steady pace for his breathing. He hoped she could not hear his pulse, which surely must be only a little softer for her than the pounding in his own head.

"Dielo?"

There was surprise in the voice, and suspicion too. Of course she did not expect to see him in her apartments, but she was more jealous of her secret, and he was a hair's breadth from disaster.

He was not sure if he could even do it—he had never attempted it. But lying on his side, with his knees drawn up... He clenched until he produced a small spurt of gas, just enough to be audible.

He heard her small catch of breath, and hope raced through him. No virilo, the perfect aesthetic piece for pleasure and display, would fart before the holder of his chit and the highest elite in the land. No greater proof of his uncomprehending sleep could be offered.

She slapped his cheek. "Dielo!"

He jerked back without thinking, shielding his face, but that reaction was natural. He sat up, one hand to his cheek and the other rubbing the offending saliva from his mouth. "My lady!"

He was grateful for the slap. It gave an excuse for the wide eyes and uneven voice he could not conceal with mere counting.

"What are you doing here?" she demanded.

That was not as accusatory as it might have been. Dielo gulped and offered honesty. "I came here to serve because the prince is away. Riolo told me to wait in this room." It was true, it was plausible, and it deflected blame to the one who had set him for disaster. "I waited...I don't know how long, but I fell asleep. I am so sorry, Your Illustrious Excellency. I am so sorry." He rubbed with pretended surreptitiousness at the damp spot on the bench's gleaming fabric.

"Riolo sent you here?" She turned. "Follow me."

This was promising, and he started to think he might have succeeded. She would be angry, but she did not suspect him of seeing her secret.

He followed her out of the little room and into the primary open sitting room of her apartment. Men and women looked up at her entrance, but only one face held a small smile for himself instead of for his mistress.

That smile faded when she snapped his name and beckoned him to join them. Without waiting to watch, she turned and went into her study. She sat in a padded leather chair rather than at her desk. Dielo stood opposite her, trying to guess his best posture for this moment. He should look concerned but not worried; he had displeased his mistress but it had not been his fault, and she was about to sort out the trouble.

She did not wait long once Riolo came in. "I found Dielo in my private parlor, and he said you had sent him there."

Riolo, still in the laced tunic, shook his head in surprised indignation. "Of course not! You have told us we are not even to go to the far end of that corridor. I would not have put him in your way." He cast an accusing glance at Dielo. "He must be trying to distract you from his creeping about in your private quarters by implicating me."

Pasiphae Jade sat forward on her seat. "Ordinarily I would accept the statement of my virilo without distrust. But here we have two virilos, both mine, and their statements cannot both be true." She jabbed a finger toward Dielo. "I have already flogged him. Why would he risk lying to me in something so simple?"

Dielo missed Riolo's reaction in the shock of what she said. She had indeed been the one to mark him—and because he had not won the prince's favor quickly enough.

Riolo shook his head. "No, my lady, it was a misunderstanding. I did tell him to wait, and that I would tell you he'd returned, but I sent him here, to the study. He must have misunderstood me, if you are certain it could be nothing else."

Dielo's heart was still racing. This was escalating far beyond anything he'd imagined when he had come here.

Pasiphae Jade sat back on her chair, her eyes narrowed. She was more than familiar with the rivalries of the sera qadra, but she would see no reason for Riolo bothering to peck at someone who had already lost standing. She could not be certain if Riolo lied now about where he had sent Dielo.

She looked at Dielo, who hastened to offer, "I am very sorry. I would never have entered if I had known." He gambled and provided a reason. "I only waited for Riolo to bring me my things."

"You said you came back to serve, not to retrieve what you should have taken with you to the prince's rooms."

"I did, my lady. But I also asked Riolo for the return of my tunic, which he is wearing now." He kept his tone neutral, without actual accusation of theft, but the suggestion was there.

Pasiphae Jade was a courtesan who had murdered a monarch. She would use her sera qadra for display and for leisure, but she would not bring even a virilo close enough to duck all suspicion. Dielo hoped he had judged her correctly, and her inherent caution had prevented Riolo from becoming a favorite who could not be found wrong. If she could be suspicious, she would see Dielo had no reason to enter her private room and every reason to fear displeasing her, while a theft provided Riolo with a reason to send Dielo there. Still, she could not be certain if he lied.

"This is mine!" Riolo protested.

And with that outburst, Dielo drew a breath of relief. Dielo had only apologized for waiting in an inconvenient place. Riolo, in his sharp denial, had transgressed the chief code of the virilo, which was to make his mistress's life pleasant and without disruption or agitation. By protesting and placing the dilemma of decision before her, he had defeated himself.

Pasiphae Jade scowled in disgust and waved a hand desultorily. "Give him the tunic, and anything else he should have. And be more careful of any directions you might give in the future." She stood and walked out.

Riolo glared at Dielo, and for a moment Dielo thought Riolo might count on Dielo's inability to bring complaint again without disturbing their mistress, and he would refuse to return the tunic. But he appeared to reach a decision and turned to leave the study.

This time Dielo followed him to the sera qadra quarters. It was a lively place, neat but full of people and possessions. Another young man was doing bodyweight exercises near the shelving. Riolo drew the tunic over his head and then shooed the exerciser out of the way to open a chest. "There," he said shortly, tossing the tunic toward Dielo. "And there." He pulled an ear cuff from the chest. "You know I saw them first, when we were choosing pieces. But I suppose you're going to end up with them."

Dielo barely caught the ear cuff, the worked metal pricking his palm. He straightened from the catch and said, "Thanks for returning them."

He carried them back to the prince's rooms. He would present himself again to the Arch Potentate's chief servant to be assigned a new place, but first he should put away the things he carried: a tunic, an ear cuff, and a secret Pasiphae Jade might kill to keep.

CHAPTER 42

"Buy a scent for your wife?" A vendor shoved a glass vial into Galen's path.

"Don't have one," he said genially, pressing the vial out of the way. "Thanks, though."

"No wife? Whyever not?" The young woman gave him a warm smile. "Maybe this could help you get one."

Galen could not be certain that his shorter hair was resulting in more attention and friendly overtures, but he liked to think so. He shook his head. "No one waiting for that chance, either." He grinned in what he hoped was a casual manner.

"Well, you just try some of our oils, and we'll see what can be done about that."

Galen decided this was more about the products for sale than his newly short hair, and he shook his head. "I'll take my chances, but thanks."

When he turned away, Lisveth was smirking. "She almost had you taking a sample, I think."

"Not really."

Lisveth didn't tease him further, but after a moment she asked, "Why didn't you marry, then? You were the right age for it, weren't you? I've heard farmers marry young. Or weren't you interested?"

Galen shook his head. "I was still young, even by Heel standards. And I hadn't found the right person."

"Takes a lot of time to get to know the whole dozen villagers in the nearest town." Lisveth gave him a mocking grin.

"A dozen and a half," Galen retorted with a matching grin.

There had been another reason, too. How could he have expected someone to come home to his family's house? Galen had no prospects for starting his own household. Better not to marry than to bring a wife into that cauldron and let her see how Idorn and Parn and the others shouted at Galen.

"Well, cheer up," Lisveth was saying, looking down the street. "Now you're spoiled for choice, traveling through the country like this. You might pick out a wealthy baroness and leave me for a small castle."

Galen snorted. "Quite likely." He quickened his step. "What about you? Did you ever think of marrying?"

"Fair night, what a romantic you are," Lisveth said easily. "Can you imagine any young gentleman wanting to take up with a highwaywoman? My standards couldn't accept anyone who could be interested in me. Look, there's the temple. I hope they've kept up security."

It was probably the would-be burglar's suggestion that made Galen think of the temple treasury. "Say," he began, slowing, "we could look in at the temple."

Lisveth gave him a startled look. "What?"

"It has a treasury."

"Many do. Still won't be robbing it."

"Right. But we could see if there was another amulet."

Lisveth drew her eyebrows together in dubious consideration.

"Mine was in a tiny farmlands temple far out in the Heel. Barkerton is at least a proper town. It's not a ridiculous idea."

"It's not," Lisveth agreed. She looked across the market to the vendor-lined path toward the temple, but she didn't move forward.

Galen's boot scuffed in the dust. "What are you waiting for?"

"Just looking." She crossed her arms and stepped to his side. "We can be quick."

They had passed a great number of temples in their travels, but Galen had not entered one since he had left the Heel. It felt wrong, now that he carried something stolen from one of them, and he regarded his temple lessons as another thing he had left behind when he fled home.

The temple that stood before them now, its gate framed by painted pillars of stacked and snarling faces, was little like the rural temple he had visited in the Heel. Galen was not sure if the faces were supposed to represent demons or the Rideis, nor why they were at the temple gate.

"Well, let's get on with it," said Lisveth sharply beside him, and they started forward.

Inside the gate from the city street was a tiny courtyard, wider than it was deep, with boxes of plants set about for greenery and with a few late spring blooms still showing. A second gate opened to the temple itself.

Lisveth raised her hand to her mouth as they crossed the tiny courtyard, as if shielding herself from a smell Galen couldn't catch. As they stepped through the second gate, she reached to set her hand flat against a worn spot on the paint, though her eyes remained fixed forward.

The inner courtyard was laid out in a fashion more familiar to Galen. The dimensions were different, but the symbolic circles were there, set linearly along a long rectangular court. Galen and Lisveth crossed Love and had just entered Joy when a priest intercepted them. "Good midday! Have you come to service, or can I help you find your way somewhere else?"

Lisveth drew out a letter on heavy paper and opened it to display a signature and seal. "As you can see, we're investigating bandit activity. We have come to look among your artifacts, if you would be so kind as to take us to your vaults."

The priest blinked. "What could Lord Bryuki want with our vaults?"

"Specifically, we are interested in the guardian amulet that is here."

Galen's heart quickened.

"At the moment, he only wants for us to examine it," Lisveth answered. "Please, show us the way."

The priest smiled. "I would be glad to show you to our abbot."

As they followed, Galen glanced at the letter Lord Bryuki had refused to give to Lisveth. He reached to pinch the paper between his finger and thumb. It felt real enough—the paper had good texture and weight—but Lisveth could suggest physical sensations if she wanted.

Abbot Alyak welcomed them courteously, and then he showed a bemused interest in the letter. "Why does Lord Bryuki have an interest now in our amulet? It's been two years since that boy was spreading his tale."

Galen and Lisveth exchanged glances. "What tale?"

He gestured for them to follow deeper into the temple. "Didn't you—? I thought it must be why you've come. It was one of the local boys who come in for lessons. He went into the treasures room and found the amulet—on a dare, typical boy foolery. He swore he did not come with the intention to destroy it. That came later."

"What?"

"He had the amulet in his hand, he said, when—well, of course he must have been drinking, though he says he wasn't. But he admits he was on a dare, and you know how boys can get."

"What happened?" Galen asked. "Or, what did he say happened?" Surely no one had broken into the temple, put the amulet about the neck of a rabbit, and fireballed the treasures room.

"Oh, he said the amulet looked at him. It's in the shape of an eye, you know. He said he was holding it and it looked at him, and he got scared. But obviously it must have been a trick of candlelight in the dark, and he was already nervous from sneaking in, and of course probably drinking."

"Obviously," Lisveth agreed.

"You said he tried to destroy it?" Galen prompted.

"Tried, but did not succeed, thankfully. He started by stomping on the amulet, trying to crush the eye, and then he carried it into the courtyard and tried to crush it with a rock. It was scuffed and dented, but those were cosmetic damages, and we were able to repair them almost completely.

"Since then, we've kept everything locked up more tightly, but we've had no further reports of the amulet making eyes at anyone." The abbot laughed. "Look, it's just here."

The treasures room was set below the main level of the temple, with a stair spiraling downward into it. Abbot Alyak unlocked the gates at top and bottom and gestured them in.

Most of the temple's treasures were treasures of scholarship rather than of monetary value. Books, scrolls, and picture tablets were stacked and shelved around the circular room, a well of knowledge into which temple visitors could dip their curiosity and desire to learn.

There were also small statuettes, a few coffers that might contain more precious books or scrolls, and a narrow display of golden jewelry. In the center of this lay an amulet upon a fabric backing.

It was very like Galen's, though he resisted the urge to draw his out to compare them side by side. This one had a deep violet eye, not blue—though the eye was just as iridescent and brilliant, with a sense of depth unlike any of the semiprecious stones found at a common market. What stones had been used to create such an effect?

The eye stared unseeing at the ceiling.

"What boon does it confer upon the wearer?" asked Galen. "To aid in battle?"

"According to what I've read, it enhances a sorcerer's magical skill. Of course, no one in living memory has worn it, and there are not so many sorcerers around to try it." He looked between them, curious but polite. "Is there something in particular you wish to know about it?"

Lisveth reached out to rub her finger across the vertical pupil. "How long has it been here, in your keeping?"

"Oh, about three hundred years, I think," he answered. "I'd have to check the records to give you an exact figure."

She looked at him. "You have a record of its commitment to the temple?"

"Of course."

"May we see it?"

"The original is in poor condition, but I have a copy I can let you read."

"We would be obliged. And, if you please, could we have the name of the student who broke into this place?"

CHAPTER 43

"WHAT DOES THAT MEAN?" Galen asked. "The amulet looked at him? What are they?"

Lisveth shook her head. "It means the boy was drunk and nervous. At least he's done some good; they'll have tightened the treasury security since he broke in to have a staring contest with an amulet. That will have helped against the thieves, too."

"You're still thinking about that?"

"Stealing from a temple, sure," she returned irritably. "Don't act as if I've never held the moral high ground. That letter from Lord Bryuki was real, wasn't it?"

"Was it?"

"Of course—can't you tell?"

He shook his head. "Not always. Fire usually, now, but not other things."

"Oh." Lisveth patted her bag. "It's real. He thought better of my suggestion and sent the letter before we left. It seems he does want additional eyes." She shrugged. "The letter doesn't mention amulets, of course, but if the Selks want one so badly, it's part of investigating bandits, I think."

"And you didn't mention this letter?"

"It hadn't come up. I didn't know we were going to look through temples."

They walked on. It was only a couple of hours more to Lord Bryuki's house; they would arrive by dusk.

"You really can't tell?" Lisveth asked abruptly.

"Isn't that the whole point of illusions?"

"Yes, of course, but...I thought you might know the difference. By now, anyway."

"Are you going to tell me the secret?"

She shrugged. "For magic? You can just... If you know the sorcerer really well, you can kind of get a taste of their magic. You don't recognize the spell so much as the caster."

Galen shook his head. "I don't have the slightest idea what you're talking about, so I'd have to say I've never done it."

She fell silent, and Galen thought there was an unhappy note to it.

That was unfair. Galen had no natural skill in magic, and no training in it, and no way to recognize what might be real and what might be untrue. It was wrong of her to disdain his inability.

They had by unspoken agreement not mentioned again their argument in Andrea's hometown, but the root of it was still unresolved. Lisveth had selfishly kept Galen from reaching out to his family; what else had she done?

A wagon was coming toward them on the road. Galen and Lisveth drifted to the side to make room for it. Galen returned the driver's wave. They left the grassy verge for the road again.

Galen cleared his throat. "Have you ever used an illusion on me?"

"What?"

"Not *on* me, like the fire, but... You know. So I would see something else, something other than what was."

"No. Well, once."

"Once?"

"You came back from the privy sooner than I expected. I was half-dressed."

He snorted. "Well, I suppose that's all right, though you could have just said something. Any other times?"

"No. Like, for what reason?"

"I don't know, to make me think you were going one way instead of another, or looking at something else."

"No?"

Her answer had come easily, but Lisveth's answers always came easily. He pressed. "Why not?"

She shrugged. "It's effort to use magic." She rolled her head to stretch. "You could throw hay up into a loft, but it's heavy, and you wouldn't do it for fun. There'd have to be a compelling reason."

"So maybe there's a reason." He hated the words as they came out, but he couldn't stop them.

Lisveth gave him a look somewhere between irritated, skeptical, and concerned. "Like what?" She tugged an arm across her chest, stretching. "Why are you so fixed on this?"

Galen did not have a better answer, so he gave her the truth. "I just want to know if you're lying to me."

He hadn't realized until he said it aloud how true it was, and how harsh it sounded.

Lisveth stopped walking, and she turned on him. For a moment, she said nothing, her face bloodless. When at last she spoke, her words were fast and clipped. "Look, let's get three things straight. First, my illusions may be lying of a sort, but it's awfully rude to call them that outright. They're not always for deception or manipulation; sometimes I just make pretty fountains of fire to make you look good. Second, what your family did has no bearing on what I do, so don't confuse us. I'm not your uncles."

He knew that. On some level, he knew that, only it was hard for the rest of him to believe.

"Third, you're my friend, and I don't lie to you. I lie to you less than to myself. Don't belittle that."

It was easier to protest this than to weigh her previous statement. "How do I know you don't lie to me?"

She jabbed him in the chest, and it hurt. "Where was I born?" She drew her hand back, as if embarrassed, but her voice continued fierce. "What's my family name? Why am I out here on the road instead of married to a rich merchant and raising chubby pink babies? You don't know any of that, and I could have told you any plausible story and you would never have doubted it. Maybe that would have been smarter. But you don't know anything, because *I haven't lied.*"

Galen drew back from her anger. He had not meant to insult her, though it could not have sounded any other way.

Lisveth turned and plowed up the road, shoulders hunched. Her hair hung heavy down her back.

She was right, and he'd been unfair.

He followed her. "Wait."

She did not slow.

"Lisveth." He jogged to catch up with her. "I'm sorry. I didn't mean that the way it sounded."

"I don't know how else you could have meant it."

"It was just a question."

"It was just a question of whether you could trust me. And now you've made me answer that you cannot." She did not look at him, eyes fixed on the road ahead.

That was true. She had said she did not lie, but she had equally pointed out she did not tell him the truth.

"Lisveth..." He reached a hand to her shoulder. "Wait."

She slapped his hand away.

"Stop it. You're being unreasonable." He hurried to get ahead of her and turned to face her. "It was a fair question about your illusions."

She stopped, looking at his chest instead of meeting his eyes. "Get out of the way."

"Not yet." He took a breath. He had started this with his foolish question; he would have to end it. "I'm sorry. I did not mean that the way it sounded. I have lived the last two years with you—maybe because of you, because Fortuna knows I wasn't cutting a straight furrow when you picked me up in the street. I do trust you."

She continued looking at his chest, her cheeks pale, her expression resistant. He placed his hands gently on either side of her head, inviting her to look up at him. "Lisveth..."

"Stop," she said, her voice rasping. She took a breath. "Close your eyes."

Confused, he did. A few heartbeats later, he felt damp beneath his thumb.

Realization struck him hard, and he jerked his eyes open. Lisveth did not move, staring at his chest, her face reddened and streaked with tears.

"That's the secret," she said in a low, hard tone. "Don't look. Your eyes will mislead your other senses, but you can usually get around an illusion by not using your eyes."

He dropped his hands and stared at her, his stomach twisting.

She stepped around him and kept walking, now wiping her eyes. Galen turned and caught up with her, now on her other side. "I'm sorry."

"Forget it." She shoved the heel of her hand across her face. "You've learned something about magic. It was a good day."

He blew out his breath. She was going to need some time. He fell into step, easily matching her hurried pace, and walked in silence.

But Galen could not stop the argument from echoing in his mind. His question had been inconsiderate—not the question about illusions, but whether she lied to him. She could not have been other than offended. He understood that.

But he had seen Lisveth offended by tavern boys, and that usually brought knife-slick insults and a disdain thick as honey. This response was unexpected.

They had gone about two miles when she broke the silence. "What did you do for fun?" she asked in a deliberately casual tone.

"What?"

"Before you met me, what did you do for fun?"

He shook his head. "I did farm chores. It wasn't exactly fun."

"That isn't what I meant." She lifted her chin and looked down the road. "I know there were three minutes in a day when you weren't pulling turnips or milking a goat, and even if you didn't do something else, you at least thought about it. And I know you don't want to tell me now, because back then you were told it was stupid, or a waste of time, or not appropriate for someone like you were supposed to be, and you believed it and stopped saying it aloud." She glanced at him and then forward again. "I'm asking you what that was."

She was trying to bridge the chasm. Galen looked down the road with her. "I liked going to my temple lessons."

"That's a weaselly answer."

"It's true! I did like my lessons. I loved the stories of history, and I was glad to learn about more than which weed will make the cows sour, and yes, I was told it was a waste of time for a farmer. I did not get to attend as much as I would have."

She nodded. "All that's true, I'm sure. But there's something else, too." She crossed her arms and took a breath. "I liked blown glass."

Now he looked at her. "Blown glass?"

"I loved watching the shapes form—so hard, so malleable, so fragile... Colors coming out of fire... It was a kind of magic, without magic. I even had the opportunity to blow a couple of pieces. With help." She laughed. "They were small, ugly things, but I was so proud of them."

This was her overture, revealing a fragment of the past she had never yet lied about. Galen nodded. "That's fascinating; I have no idea how glass is done." Glass was expensive, and glass art must be even more so; he wondered briefly if she had been a maid in a noble house. But aloud he said, "I suppose you're a missing princess, then. We didn't have glass-blowing in the Heel. Where are your glass pieces now?"

She gave a huffing chuckle. "I don't know. Probably burned."

Galen wanted to ask, but he sensed a line drawn invisibly around the revelation. This much was offered, but no more would be given.

He should meet her soft overture. After a moment he confessed, "I made up stories in my head."

"What?" She turned a delighted grin on him. "You—"

"No, I won't tell you any," he interrupted firmly.

"Just one?"

"See, this is why I didn't want to say anything."

"Because some fumble-headed cousin told you it was stupid and a waste of time."

Galen shrugged. "They wouldn't have been wrong if they did. They're just silly stories."

"The stories at the temple were your favorite thing."

He didn't reply. That meant only that his favorite thing at the temple was equally silly and useless.

"Well, maybe someday you'll tell me a story."

He snorted. "And maybe someday you'll blow me a glass cup."

"That's not fair. Glassblowing needs all sorts of supplies and equipment, while you can tell a story anywhere."

"When glassblowing is done, at least you have a useful cup."

She elbowed him but otherwise let it go, and he was content. She had extended a hand, and he'd taken it, and they were all right again. She was, if not forthright, at least honest with Galen, and she lied to him less than to herself, she'd said, and that was enough.

Though he did wonder, as they walked together: What lies did she tell herself?

CHAPTER 44

GALEN AND LISVETH SAT together in Lord Bryuki's spacious kitchen, with the space nearly to themselves since the evening meal had finished. The march lord had accepted their brief report of few bandits, human or otherwise, to the east. As luck would have it, the Octovirate had elected to consider the Selk problem, and their commission would be meeting in a few days, and Lisveth and Galen were invited to explain their experiences.

Galen had not expected so significant a response, especially after their time away in the mundane task of escorting Andrea, and this seemed to herald something great and terrible.

A few servants worked still, cleaning dishes and starting the next day's bread, but they kept their own conversation near the fire and work tables, and they left Galen and Lisveth to themselves at the far side of the room.

"What do you think?" Galen asked her, keeping his eyes on the indifferent servants and his voice low. "The Octovirate... Could we have made a mistake?"

"We didn't make a mistake," Lisveth said firmly. "Maybe *he* made a mistake, Kayvin or whatever his name is. Maybe he isn't a prince of the Selks, maybe that other Selk just made that up on the spot and Kayvin decided to kill him because he was so embarrassed for them both, and then that other woman just happened to show up on a lonely bandit-infested road in the dark of night and went along with all of it in the flush of the moment, even to jumping into a bloody combat that did not involve her. But no, we did not misunderstand what was said to us."

Galen rolled his eyes. "You know what I mean."

"I don't, actually. Did you mean that we made a mistake about the amulet? That we were mistaken about the rabbit not being dead?"

Galen nodded a concession. "No, I don't see how we could have been mistaken about that."

"Then what do you mean?"

He sighed. "I don't think we made a mistake. It's just—it's so enormous, we *must* have made a mistake. Do you understand? Because if we didn't make a mistake, then the Selks—the Rideis—are coming over the mountains, with a prince to lead them through land he has scouted for weeks or months."

She exhaled slowly, her eyes on the table. "I know. I know exactly what you mean."

They sat still a moment, shoulder to shoulder, the legendary invasion looming over them.

"But even if it's just a political schism that has thrown Kayvin over the mountains," she said, "and he's not really leading an assault—even if that part is a mistake, we still had to tell someone. We had to try to warn people."

"Of course we did."

They sat another silent moment.

"May I see it?" Lisveth asked.

He did not have to ask what *it* was. "You said never to take it off."

"I think it's all right to let your sorceress partner look at it."

With a cautious glance toward the kitchen workers, who were giggling together and slapping puffs of flour in some sort of game of bakers' tag, he drew the amulet over his head and set it on the table before Lisveth.

She took it in her hands and cradled it, as if it were a delicate speckled chick instead of a stone and metal eyeball. "It's so strange," she said. "If this is imbued with that kind of strong magic, I should be able to feel it. We can load magic into certain items, but there's always an aura, a signature. This has nothing."

"Maybe it's subtle? Or hidden? Could it be magicked to conceal the magic?"

She shook her head. "Concealment magic is still magic and would leave its own signature. If it were subtle enough, I suppose I might have missed it when you were just wearing it casually, but I couldn't miss it while I'm looking for it and holding the object in my own hands." She shook her head. "It's just not there."

"What if it's only magic when magic is touching it?" Galen asked. "Like, it's just a piece of jewelry until it gets struck by magic, when it becomes magical and absorbs it?"

Lisveth gave him a flat stare. "I know you don't know much about magic, farm boy, but let me save the time of explanation and just say that's impossible. And ridiculous. You can't just store a spell that turns on and off. Either it's got a spell, which has to be powered and hold power, or it doesn't."

Galen shrugged. "I'm just trying ideas."

"I know. But I'm telling you, this thing is impossible."

"Maybe it's not impossible. I mean, obviously it's not impossible, you're holding it. But maybe someone else would understand it—a state mage in the capital, maybe."

Lisveth shook her head. "I don't think so."

"Well, you shrugged that off quick enough."

Lisveth didn't raise her eyes from the amulet. "They don't know any more."

Galen frowned and sat back. After a moment, he ventured the question, "Did you know a state mage? In the capital?"

She jerked a shoulder. "The capital is full of mages and would-be mages. Some of them even know a little magic."

Should he ask? "Is that where you learned magic?"

She snorted. "That's where I learned I didn't want to be a state mage." She leaned forward over the table, face closer to the amulet, blocking him with her bent shoulders. "There has to be something to this. It's inert, just metal and stone. But let's see if magic touches it, like if I run this little spark into it—"

The eye blinked and swiveled in the coiled wire socket.

Lisveth screamed and shoved backward, flinging the amulet away from her across the table. Galen twisted away, and together they flipped the bench backward and sprawled upon the rush-strewn kitchen floor.

The cooks paused in their chatter and turned to stare at them, and then they burst out laughing, covering their faces too late with floury hands.

Lisveth swore, fast and furious and not caring if they heard her. They turned away, still laughing, and returned to their bread loaves and rolls.

Galen extracted his legs from the bench and set it upright. "What was that?"

"It blinked." Lisveth stared at the table, looked at him, looked back at the table. The amulet lay on the far side, unmoving and unblinking. "Fair night, Galen, the thing *blinked*. The eye moved. It *looked* at us."

Galen swallowed and nodded. "We both saw it, then."

"Yes."

"Just like the student at the temple."

She nodded. After a moment, she seemed to gather her courage and stretched across the table for the amulet. It sat still in her hand, lifeless as ever.

"Well, at least it answers one question," she said after a moment, sinking back onto the bench.

"What's that?"

"I said an inert object couldn't hold a spell without power. But this is not an inert object with a spell put upon it." She set the amulet on the table. "This is not a piece of jewelry, or at least it is not just a piece of jewelry."

Galen swallowed. "So it is not holding a spell—it is reacting when it is touched by magic."

Lisveth nodded. "Which answers one question, but begs another."

Galen stared at the amulet. "Whose eye is that?"

CHAPTER 45

FOR THE FIRST TIME in a long, long while, Dielo did not know how to dress.

He should not go to this servants' party. A virilo had little place with maids and servants, and he might bring embarrassment to his prince if he were discovered there—though it was unlikely the prince's elite peers even knew of servants' events, much less who attended them. More importantly, he should not attend with Pasiphae Jade's niece.

She had found him again in a long corridor between the Arch Potentate's room and Prince Kayvin's. "Dielo! Wait a moment!"

He had, though his heart had quickened. He had not known who she was in the kitchen or in the north wing. He would continue to claim ignorance. But if Pasiphae Jade spotted them together, would she guess Dielo had seen what he should not have?

"We're having that occasion the night after tomorrow. We're going to use the servants' dining hall behind the kitchen. You'll come, won't you?"

He should never have hinted he might. "I don't know that I'd fit with your friends," he managed. He could assert rank if he had to, but best to start more gently.

She shook her head. "I've already told some you'd be there, and everyone is pleased."

"You've told them you're bringing me, and I don't even know your name?"

"Oh!" She laughed. "I'm Lirin. And now you know, so now you must come." She gave him a coy glance.

"What if we're discovered?" Oh, that was a poor way to put it—it sounded as if there was something to discover.

She laughed. "It's only some eating and dancing. You're making too much of it."

And he so wanted to go anywhere with music and laughter, and hugging and perhaps even kissing, and where someone would speak to him, and where he could pretend for an hour or three that he was not alone.

"You remember that you asked me to this occasion, some days ago?" he prompted. "A week ago? In the kitchen?"

"Yes, of course," she answered, giving him a confused but tolerant smile. "How could I forget?"

So she could assure her suspicious aunt, if ever asked, that she had approached him, and before he had ever been in that private parlor. He could plead, if it came to it, that he had only gone to a servants' event as asked, and he had never sought out her niece.

It might not be enough, if he were taken with Pasiphae Jade's niece. But he would not be taken. She wanted the relationship secret, secret enough that the girl was scolded and given extra chores, and so there would be no palace guards at the servants' party.

And how he wanted to go.

So now he knelt beside his virilo's trunk, assessing pieces of his wardrobe. He did not want to be too fine; this was not a place to be ostentatious for his master. He did not want to dress too invitingly; he was not meant to entice this night. He did not want to look as if he tried to appear something other than the virilo he was; deception was not his intention.

At last he chose a long tunic with an open chest, loose trousers, and a multi-branched silver ear cuff that climbed and pinned one side of his hair in place while the other flowed loose. A light silver chain net over his chest and upper arm would compliment the ear cuff and draw attention. He applied a bit of kohl to his eyes, adding definition without glamour, and dabbed a fingertip of crushed garnet onto a cream over his eyelids, where it caught the candlelight. After a moment's hesitation, he put another dab on the center of his lips.

It was not an extravagant look for a nobles' banquet or a private assignation with someone he was meant to impress and sway to another faction, but it was enough flash and flare to delight the maids and scullery servants, raising their party in gratitude for including him.

The dining hall behind the kitchen was not hard to find, and Lirin was waiting for him there. Her face lit when she saw him approaching, and his own heart jumped a little. It felt good to be wanted.

"I'm glad you're here!" she said. "It's already started, so let's go in."

She had waited outside for him, though he hardly could have gotten lost on his way to the dining hall. He was glad he'd come.

The servants' dining hall had been transformed from its usual serviceable demeanor. Instead of the overhead chandeliers, lamps had been placed in little clusters on tables or along the walls, casting deep shadows and creating separate pools of warm light. Most tables had been drawn aside, but for a few which bore trays of tidbits, leaving space for dancing and for numerous piles of cushions. Musicians sat in a circle, facing one another to collaborate. The floor even had a scattering of flower petals, probably taken from the fading bouquets of nobles' rooms.

Lirin grasped him by the hand and drew him into the room. "I'm sure it's nothing like the feasts you attend, but it will do for tonight, won't it?"

"It certainly will."

"Dance with me?" She did not wait for a reply but tugged him into the open space.

He was more accustomed to dancing alone, but his training had of course included partnering. Lirin led him to a forming circle and they fell into place. The dance was not one Dielo knew, but the steps were simple and he quickly matched the others. There were many eyes on him, and he gave gracious smiles all around.

When the song ended, Lirin beckoned him to the side. "Oh! Let's sit for a moment and catch our breath."

Neither of them were winded, but Dielo agreed amiably, and they sank to a pile of cushions. Lirin settled against Dielo's arm, and he braced himself to hold her.

"Hello!" said a woman as she sat beside them. "I'm Farah. And you are?"

"This is Dielo," Lirin answered before he could.

"Nice to meet you," Farah said. "I'm sure this is the first we've met, because I feel I would remember."

Dielo automatically gave her a knowing smile. "Likewise."

She gave a little laugh.

"Oh, Trent!" Lirin hailed a passerby. "I want you to meet Dielo. He had no other obligations tonight, so I've brought him here."

"As well you should," Trent said with an appreciative grin. "Hello, Dielo."

It was like sweet wine, the attention and the welcome. Dielo melted into it. Lirin pressed warm against his arm, and he breathed in the scents of her hair, the petals crushed beneath the dancers, the drinks, the validation.

"Oh!" Lirin tugged her hair against the fine chain around his upper arm. "Help me?"

"Hold still." He used his other hand to work her dark hair from the tiny links, picking strands apart. She remained in place, face slightly upturned, lips slightly apart as she watched him.

"I think you're free now," he said.

But she did not move. "You haven't said anything about how I look tonight," she said softly.

Everyone liked to be appreciated, and he should have said something, if only in thanks for inviting him. "You look lovely." He brushed her eyebrow with his thumb. "I see you've added some color for tonight. It serves you well."

Her expression relaxed into a self-conscious smile, and she looked down, pulling her hair against his hand.

"Would you care to dance again, or shall I bring us something to eat?"

"Bring a drink," she said, and her voice caught slightly. Then she added, "I'll come with you."

Dielo got to his feet and made his way to the tables, with Lirin's fingers lightly around his arm. She smiled around at the others as he poured two cups of wine. It was not nearly as good as the prince's wine, but he presented it to her as if it were in a jasper goblet.

They drank, and then they danced again. Dielo enjoyed the dancing; he thought about his presentation and form, of course, but there was a freedom to dancing for himself and not for the gaze of others. They continued as the musicians reeled through song after song. Lirin kept him close, leading him through the partners' dances rather than where men and women danced singly in a loose group, but he did not mind that. She had asked him here, and he owed her accompaniment.

At last they sat again on a pile of cushions against the wall, a light sheen blooming over both their faces in the warming room, and she laughed and leaned against him again. "Your hair," he warned, and he tugged strands from the links of his arm chain.

She tipped her face up and took a white flower from the drinks table an arm's length away. "Braid this into my hair for me?"

He didn't mind. He took the flower and held it over her ear, judging its placement.

"Oh, the other side," she prompted, moving his hand away from the wall and toward the open room.

He complied, choosing an angle and making a small loop of hair to mark the place. "Now turn away and I'll braid it."

She turned, and now the flower was nearer the wall. She pulled it free. "I'm sorry—this side, please."

"All right," he agreed, a little confused but amenable.

He replaced the flower on the side toward the open room and began to plait her hair. It was odd that she had switched sides twice, but maybe she thought there was better light coming from the room's center, or—

Or maybe she had considered the visibility.

His fingers slowed as realization began to coalesce. The actions should have been familiar, as he'd been trained to consider them. He had to braid her hair where it would be visible to the room. The glances over her shoulder, the upturned face, the clinging to his arm, the plaiting of her hair... He had not recognized it in its crude form, the clumsy flirting of an untrained and inexperienced girl.

He could not permit such a thing. She was too young, too inexperienced. She was a palace maid, blinded by the glitter of Dielo's position. And she was the secret niece of the Arch Potentate, who would surely not permit the interference of a virilo. He would have to dissuade her gently.

His sinking heart reached his stomach and heaved uncomfortably. But Lirin was not merely flirting; she had drawn him to the center of the room, guided him away from less visible seating, kept a possessive hand on him throughout the night. She had brought him to display before her fellow servants, a catch of a virilo, a triumph. She also used him for her own advancement, even in the servants' petty games of rank.

Even a friendly maid used him.

She reached up to tap his motionless fingers on the flower. "Did you lose your place?"

He resumed braiding. "Nearly done."

It might be that he misunderstood. Perhaps she had asked him here because she had liked him for himself, and he did her a disservice by imagining such motivations.

She brushed the flower. "Thank you!"

"It's a perfect addition for you." He sat back on the cushion. "I'll go and bring us something to eat. We could stand something sweet after so much dancing."

"I'll come with—"

"I'll be right back. Let me surprise you." It felt wrong to cut her off, but she was not one of his elite guests, and he wanted to know why she had brought him here. If she only flirted with him, wouldn't she wait to see what he brought her?

He made it to the table and began filling a small plate with treats—nuts, tiny dumplings, and a hard sweet pastry with red icing.

"You're the virilo, aren't you?" The question did not require an answer; the speaker's smile was confident. He nodded at Dielo. "I must say, you add a touch of excitement to our gathering. I'm surprised you find anything here to entice you, when you must be accustomed to much greater entertainment."

"I met him in the kitchen one day, and we've talked, and then Dielo was kind enough to accept my invitation," Lirin explained, slipping her arm about his. "I hope he'll make a habit of it. Oh, dumplings! Thank you."

Dielo passed her the plate, long training making the motions automatic as his chest tightened. She had not left him alone, and she had promptly claimed both credit for his presence and a sort of possession of him. She might flirt with him, futile as that would be—a virilo would not dally with a palace maid—but she certainly meant to display him as a prize.

Even the servants thought of him only as an accessory.

Dielo led Lirin to another seat and held the plate for her. He had no appetite to sample the dumplings. He looked out at the dancing. He wanted to rejoin it, but it would feel different now. He would no longer be dancing for himself, as he had briefly imagined.

"Dielo? Are you all right?"

He glanced down. "I'm sorry—I was distracted. And that is both inexcusable and incomprehensible." Rote apologies came to him, words meant to flatter, and he regretted them.

"I'll forgive you if you dance another round with me."

He was a virilo. He had always known the object of his affections would be chosen for him, and it was his duty to both compliment and complement. But no one had assigned him to this maid, and even if she thought only to flirt and dally, he had to put her off. They could not indulge even a bit of romantic fun. "I think my dancing is done for tonight," he said gently. "I'm sorry, I'm not feeling well now." That was true; his stomach felt hollow and acidic with disappointment deeper than he had imagined. "I will go."

"But—do you have to go? You could stay, and we could just sit?"

She wanted him to remain visible in the room with her, even if he felt ill. His stomach sank another inch. "I don't think that would be wise. I'm going to go and sleep, and maybe that will help."

"Oh. Well, I'm sorry, and I hope you feel better soon."

He made himself nod and pressed the plate into her hands. "Thank you for asking me here tonight." He thought he could mean that, at least on some level. It had been wonderful while it lasted.

The prince's apartment was dark and silent. No lamp had been left burning low in the men's quarters, so he had to shuffle across to find his sleeping pit. He pulled off the ear cuff and body chain, leaving them on the floor, and coiled into the pit without changing clothes or washing the cosmetics off. It did not matter. No one would see him in the morning, either.

CHAPTER 46

"SINCE WE'RE FLUSH FOR the day, I'm going to buy a new shirt," Lisveth announced. "I think this one's older than the child who sold us this morning's meat pies, and there's not enough left to hold the next round of patches."

Galen nodded; they both looked more than a little worn, but he could hold out another few months, barring an accident. "Are you carrying enough for it, or do you need some of mine?"

"I should be fine. But I don't need you to sit around a shop waiting, so do you want to walk around a bit? I can meet you at the public room down there." She pointed to the far end of the street, where a sign jutted over the traffic.

"I'll be there."

Galen watched her slip away in the stream of passersby and wagons. She disappeared quickly, too short to track for long.

He turned back and continued down the high street. At one time this bustle and noise would have felt overwhelming, but he had seen a few towns since that first arrival in Abbay. The markets occasionally still seemed a kind of wonderland, dazzling with choices and offerings, but he no longer had to conceal his awe. The farm boy had become quite sophisticated.

He browsed a collection of dye samples he didn't need and shouldn't spend for, and then he examined a pair of socks he could justify. He purchased a small, sturdy patch for a weakening spot on his boot. Then he saw a thickening in the traffic, a cluster of watchers, and he edged over to look with them.

A man crouched in the street and pointed to three wooden vases, each about the height of Galen's spread hand. They were painted in red, yellow, and blue. "Now watch the vases," he instructed loudly. "Note they are three different colors. Young man," he addressed a small child in the front, "can you tell me what colors they are?"

"Why are they wooden?" the boy asked.

"What?"

"Our jugs at home are clay, with a glaze on them."

"I'm using these in my show, and so they have to be easier to carry without breaking. Now, what colors are they?"

The boy rolled his eyes, disappointed in the ignorance of adults. "Red, that's yellow, and that one's blue."

"All right. Now, keep watching them, because something is going to happen."

Galen had to admire the cheerful persistence of the performer. It had to be a challenge when even the smallest of your audience doubted your intelligence.

But the crowd obediently watched the vases as the sorcerer made a series of probably-useless gestures over them. And then, as Galen watched, the colors shifted, bleeding into orange, green, and purple. A few gasps and "oooohs" of appreciation marked the first change, and then as the colors became more dramatically different, applause broke out.

"Now," called the performer, "does anyone have a half-kerl to spare?"

After an awkward moment, someone produced the coin. "Can you turn it into a full kerl?"

"For the price of your half-kerl, madam, you may choose the next set of colors."

She wrinkled her face in indecision and at last surrendered the coin, seeing no way to retain it after admitting possession. She held up three fingers and counted the colors off. "Bone, chalk, and alabaster."

The street performer's expression faltered, but he recovered quickly. "Three white vases, I understand." He turned, made his complex and flowing gestures, and the wooden vases began to lighten, arriving at three very similar whites.

"That's not bone," another woman chuckled, but the crowd laughed and applauded. Galen glanced toward the woman. From the side of his eye, as he turned, the vases looked brightly colored, but when he looked back they were white again.

"What's next?" the magician called, turning to solicit suggestions.

Galen gestured toward the nearest vase. "Could you change their texture, maybe to make one feel like wool instead of wood?"

The street performer gave him a flat look. "No busking your jokes while I'm working here, friend jester, as this corner's already spoken for. What colors will someone suggest next? Young man, please choose between dots and stripes."

"Yellow dots!" shouted the child. "And blue! Blue is my favorite color!"

"Yellow dots and blue stripes," he amended. "And what else? Can you think of a shape for red?"

"Green stars!"

"Yellow, blue, and green, then, in dots, stripes, and stars. Here it comes!"

Galen waited, watching as coins were put in and the street performer worked his craft. He knew to stop before the novelty began to fade, and he bowed and thanked the crowd, extending his hat for additional donations.

Galen held out a coin, and the performer gave him an irritated look as he came by. "You didn't have to try to make me look bad," he said in a low voice, though he took the coin. "I don't come by your workshop or vendor stall and tell your customers to ask for impossible things."

"I'm sorry," Galen answered automatically, a little stung. "I have a friend who does illusions like that. I thought it would be impressive to influence another sense to change as well."

"No, you don't have any such friend, because yes, it would be grand for a show, but it can't happen." Someone came by to drop another coin in the hat, and the man thanked her with a quick smile. Then he turned back to Galen, dropping the smile like a mask. "Five adults left after you said that, newly disappointed in real magic I was doing because it wasn't magic no one was doing. Comments like that cost coin."

There was no guarantee that the people who left would have donated if they had stayed or would have stayed if they hadn't heard Galen's question, but he didn't bother to argue; frustration often didn't heed facts. Instead, Galen gestured up the street. "Could I buy you a drink to make up for my mistake?"

That stopped the street performer mid-complaint, and for a moment he hesitated awkwardly. "Um, well, yes, actually, I'd like that. Just let me pick up my vases."

They sat at a small table in a room mostly empty at this time of day, and the landlady brought them each an ale as well as a loaf of brown bread to share. Galen buttered his slice thickly and bit into it. The bread had a rich, nutty flavor, and something in it made Galen think of the bread made at home, in the farmhouse in the Heel. For a couple of heartbeats, he wondered what it was like there now, and whether he had made a difference by leaving. Then he shook off the indulgent wistfulness and took another bite of bread and butter.

The street performer was on his second slice before Galen had finished savoring the contrast in textures. Galen began to suspect the root of the busker's hope and irritation. "What do you do when you're not coloring vases in the street?" he asked, keeping his tone friendly.

"I'm a charcoal burner," he answered. "I will be again in a couple of weeks. There's a narrow window when folks have the spare time and the decent weather to stand in the street to watch colors change."

"But in the meantime, you can make better money as a busker?"

"A bit. And it's less heavy carrying, anyway. Tiring, but in another way."

Lisveth was often weary after working magic other than her illusions. Galen eased into his question. "You said I had no such friend who could change other senses."

The man laughed. "I'm sorry, my lord, but I didn't recognize you in your cunning disguise." He shook his head. "No, unless you're a noble from the capital, slumming here in the villages for your own reasons, I doubt you have such a friend. That's state mage material, at least."

"Is it?" Galen turned up his hands. "I have no magical skill or training; I don't know how to judge the skill."

"If your distant friend wanted to explain it to you, he'd say illusions are difficult things. It's easier for most of us to imagine something looking somewhat different, so that's an easier illusion—in a manner of speaking, as if any of them are easy. And it's not as if you're also holding it and able to feel the difference between blue and red, I mean. Leading someone to perceive a piece of wood as looking and feeling like wool—two senses at once—would be fine work indeed. Hence, state mage practice, because anyone who can do that certainly isn't busking for coins in a village in the middle of nowhere."

This was clearly said in good faith, and Galen accepted this without argument. The busker was a charcoal burner and probably had little contact with more talented magic users. It was easy to be impressed when one's own skills were minimal. He nodded and shifted the subject. "I'm Galen, by the way."

"Michael." He extended a hand, shook Galen's, and picked up a third slice of bread. "It was good of you to offer a drink after I grumped at you."

Galen waved off the comment. "I was coming here anyway. I'm to wait for a friend."

"Your same friend who does tactile illusions?" Michael grinned and buttered his bread. "My granddad was a state mage, actually. Family lore says he retired and moved out here after dandling with the wrong daughter in the capital, but I don't know if that's true, and I don't like to think of him as a dirty old man. He was the one who taught me how to use my magic when it first appeared."

So Michael had known a skilled sorcerer after all. "Oh?"

"My mum didn't inherit much, so he was pretty delighted when I started showing signs. He taught me until he passed, when I was seventeen. I'm a little glad he didn't live to see me coloring wooden vases in the street, though. I don't think he'd find it very dignified, not after he'd served the Octovirate."

Galen turned this over in his mind. Michael had not been a very young child, too small to learn much and left too impressionable. "Could you do an illusion of, I don't know, flying? Could you make me think I was flying?"

Michael laughed. "Of course not. I'm no bird."

"You made me and all those others see colors that weren't there."

"I know what blue stripes look like. But I don't know what it feels like to fly. In order to work an illusion, you have to know it well enough to make it believable." He finished the slice of bread.

"But you can imagine what it might be like to fly, right? Wind on your face, the ground far below, arms tired?" Galen grinned.

"Oh, throw in some scents and sounds while you're at it!" Michael snorted. "No, that's not enough. Look, can you swim? Have you ever been in a pond or something?"

Galen shrugged. "I've splashed about in a pond, but I don't know how to swim."

"Good enough for this example. I've also dunked my head underwater and floated. That's why I can do this." He gestured about them, a much less elaborate movement than the ones he'd used in his performance, and the air grew wavy. Light seemed to ripple about them, and colors shifted slightly. A brown-green fish wriggled past their table.

But it wasn't as compelling as one of Lisveth's illusions. Galen didn't instinctively hold his breath, and the sounds of the nearly empty public room were not muffled as if his ears were filled, and he didn't feel the cool wet against his skin. He would not have needed hours of practice to move through this illusion.

Michael dropped his hand, and the pond-light shifted back to normal. He grinned proudly. "Neat, huh? When my granddad did it, you could see waves, as if someone was jumping in behind you. He was good."

Galen nodded as if impressed. "I see."

"Well, thank you for the drink. I'm off to catch the next crowd." Michael stood. "Try not to spoil my show if you stop by again."

"I'll be good as gold." Galen gave him a wave.

He was still musing when Lisveth slid onto the opposite seat. "Found you! And bread!" She tore off a piece and popped it into her mouth, muffling her next words. "Like my choice?"

Her new shirt was linen of deep green, with curving seams for shape and texture. "Very nice," he said, and he meant it. "Bit of a splurge?"

"That's the best part. It was made on order by someone who paid half down and then took sick with something, and no one else in the family was petite enough for it. She let me have it for what was owed."

"Very nice."

"You said that already." She gave him a scrutinizing look. "What's on your mind?"

"I met a busking magician," Galen said without preamble. "He told me about illusions."

"That must have been fascinating," Lisveth commented dryly. But her eyes slid to Galen's, wary.

"He said illusions were difficult and could affect only the vision, not other senses."

"Well, of course he did."

"He wasn't just a poor magician; his grandfather was a state mage, so he's seen real magic. Good magic. He still said illusions were frail. But that's not true, is it?"

"What? Of course it's true, yes. Or didn't you see any of his busking tricks?"

"I did. He changed the colors of some vases. But that isn't anything like what I've seen you do."

"Fair night, I didn't..." She stuffed a hunk of bread into her mouth and spoke while chewing. "I didn't know how much you didn't know."

Galen's ears burned hot, though he had done nothing wrong. "What do you mean?"

"Look, farm boy, when I tell you—" She stopped, frowned, tried again. "Why do you think I was able to be the Fire Brigand for so long without anyone fighting back?"

"Because they thought the fire was real."

"Every time? Even when no one was actually dying?"

"Well, people were panicking in the moment, I suppose." But it sounded unconvincing even to Galen.

She shook her head. "No one thought it could be illusion because it *couldn't* have been an illusion. It wasn't a possibility to consider. No one has ever seen illusions like that."

He shook his head. "But..."

"Look, remember a few months ago when we rescued those books for the collector? Imagine you're sitting in a courtyard garden reading a book, and in the story you're reading, there's a rainstorm. While you're reading, the sky darkens, and then drops begin to fall, and then your hair gets wet and starts dripping down your back, and your shirt sticks to your shoulders. Which is easier to believe, that it's a very gripping story, or that there's a real rainstorm over your courtyard?"

"Well, obviously rain doesn't come out of books."

"And heat doesn't come out of illusions." Lisveth tapped the table. "What you're describing—affects sight only, holds for a bit if you don't squint too hard—that's what illusions are. The idea that something you can see and hear and feel and smell could be just a suggestion, well, that's madness."

"But it's not madness," Galen said slowly.

"It's madness to everyone but you and me." She gestured. "Your busker, his state mage—for them, it's just a momentary vision, and one more likely to amuse you for a moment than convince you of anything. That's why my illusions worked so well; it was incomprehensible that they could be illusions, so they had to be real. Which is a kind of illusion itself, I suppose. The mind sees what it's sure it's seeing."

Galen stared at her. "So you're very good at illusions."

She placed her palms on the table and leaned forward, grinning crookedly. "Farm boy, I am very, very, very good at illusions. That fellow's grandfather has never even heard of someone else even half as good at illusions." She shrugged. "I've got no special standing with anything else, barely average on most, and I'm probably on a level with that busker on some things—but illusions, I can do." She nodded with a smug smile.

"So why are you out here doing small tasks for farmers and merchants? Why aren't you in the capital? You could be a state mage, maybe."

She scowled. "Or I could go back to robbing terrified people on the highway, and be able to sleep at night." She took a slice of bread and began to tear it into pieces. "Butter, please."

Galen was startled at the stark finality. Not a state mage, then. He passed the butter.

AN UNFORTUNATE FAILURE

MANDORAL

CHAPTER 47

KAYVIN'S ARM WAS NOT healing as he thought it should. The skin reddened around the slice from Galen's sword, growing hot and puffy, and while Yovela helped him to wash and bandage it daily, it throbbed and ached in the days of their travel, making it hard to think.

He had been told to follow the bandits' trail of attacks and seize the amulets brought out to face them, but he had found little organized resistance to the bandits. Not only were the human armies not drawn up to face them, the humans hardly seemed to believe the Rideis were invading. Pasiphae Jade's plan had not worked.

He could not wander Sayinia and hope to stumble upon the right temple holding an amulet, and his arm was swelling, making his reddening hand ache with pressure. Yovela announced that she was taking him home, and frustrated as he was, he did not countermand their retreat.

He could have tried again to find Lisveth and Galen. He was sure Galen had something like an amulet, or how else could he have survived their fight? But it was impossible that a wandering mercenary would have such a treasure himself. It must be some other charm with a similar effect.

Or, loath as he was to admit it, perhaps Kayvin's magic had been less effective, held back after the accidental killing of the bandit.

He had not meant to do that, and his stomach twisted whenever he recalled it. He had struck far too hard in his anxiety. He must have over-corrected when striking Galen next.

He might have learned more if not for Yovela. She had dragged him away, though he should have fought Galen and ascertained the nature of his protective charm. He had not known Yovela had followed him. How foolish of her. How kind of her.

Yovela urged him through the mountains once more, pressing him to eat though his fever dulled his appetite. Despite the fever, he often felt cold, and she pressed close to him when he slept and shivered. She regularly gave him water, pressing him to drink, and though he protested, he always found himself thirsty once he started. He wondered if his fevered arm might be more worrisome than the mercenary's cheap charm.

He did not remember much of their passage. His shoulder was stiff, and his swollen arm sometimes had a smell like ram's urine. He did not know if he imagined that or if somehow a sheep had soiled him while he slept, as he did more and more. Yovela had to prod and scold him into getting up from each rest.

His return to the palace was a satisfying blur of greetings and concern, as guards guided him to his rooms and sent servants running to inform the Arch Potentate and fetch physicians. He remembered Dielo rushing toward him as he entered his quarters, and he remembered settling in his sleeping pit, grateful at last for furs and pillows instead of road dust and stones.

He woke with his arm freshly bandaged, with the scents of honey and myrrh indicating his treatment. He drew a deep breath of the medicinal smells, and at the other end of the pit Dielo sat forward. "My lord? Are you awake?"

"I think so." Kayvin's voice croaked. It was dark, with only a candle sitting above the pit. "How long has it been?"

"You've slept the day through," Dielo told him. He ascended with easy motion, returning with a goblet of fruited water. "Here—the physicians said you would be thirsty."

They had been right. Kayvin sat up and took the drink with his good hand. "What else did they say?"

"They said you should sleep as much as you wanted, and that your wound should be dressed twice daily. I have rose oil and honey ready. And you are to eat as much fruit as you can. I have a tray of cut pieces for you."

His arm felt a little better already, and his hand was less swollen. They must have drained the wound. "What did she say?"

"Yovela reported that she had found you in combat, and then the two of you—"

"Not Yovela."

Dielo pressed his lips together. "Her Illustrious Excellency has been given a report of your arrival and condition, and she wishes you a rapid recovery."

And then she would want to know why he had returned without an amulet.

Empty void, the physicians were good, or perhaps it was just the relief of safe sleep away from the danger of human society, but he already felt clearer in his mind. It would be difficult to explain how in his muddled state he had decided to retreat instead of pursuing the possible amulet.

How could he ever find Galen again?

Pasiphae Jade's eyes narrowed as Dielo entered her study. "Where is your master?"

Dielo bowed. "He is recovering still, Your Illustrious Excellency. His physicians advised him to rest."

"He traveled all the width of the Sung Mountains with his injury. He could make it across the palace to my rooms." Pasiphae Jade's mouth turned down. "Must I go to him, then?"

Dielo knew how that angry intrusion would unnerve Prince Kayvin, already nearly imprisoned in his rooms within his own palace. "I'm sure you need not trouble yourself. I have come today to carry your words, and the prince will attend you soon, perhaps as soon as tomorrow."

"We do not have so much time to spare," the Arch Potentate grumbled. "And unless you bring me more useful information than that he has suffered an injury to one arm, you are equally useless to me."

This was Dielo's role now. He could shelter his master from the Arch Potentate's anger, letting her vent it safely upon Dielo instead of Prince Kayvin. He had been told he must make his master's home a haven. He had not realized then what that might mean, but this was his service now. "Your Illustrious Excellency," he said, bowing low, "I have done my best, as you must know. What can I bring you other than the news I have?"

And if he served well, if he did this for the prince, then Kayvin might not leave him behind the next time.

"You could tell me whether he has managed at least to locate any amulets, even if he could not bring one."

If Prince Kayvin could have presented any semblance of success, surely he would have done so immediately, regardless of his injury. Dielo had to divert her. He bowed again, and lower. "If he has good news for you, he will wish to present it to you himself. In the meantime, surely my lady knows any secret shared with a virilo is secure."

His quiet provocation worked. "Look at you, young and pretty and ignorant." Pasiphae Jade's tone dripped derision like acid. "You think you know so much, because you had lessons to tell you how much more clever and more beautiful you are than your rivals. As if a distinction of words could make you any different in truth."

Dielo knew better than to answer her. His teachers had told him to expect these accusations from courtesans and spouses, explaining that jealousy often manifested as rage and disdain, and he knew to let the words wash over him, secure in his place. Tapping her anger now would drain it before it reached the prince.

"It's easy for you now," Pasiphae Jade hissed. "But wait until age softens your figure and dulls your features. It does not matter what you can do in the dark if they are not pleased to look at you in the light. You are an ornament, and you know that, and when you cease to be an effective piece to display, you'll be discarded. Don't pretend I speak in angry lies—you are not so stupid that you don't know the truth."

She was not entirely wrong, even in her hate. It was never explicitly taught, but Dielo had, like other virilos, listened and observed, and he knew, like other virilos, that his time of service would be limited, possibly to fewer years than he had spent in training for it. Those with more foresight kept back a portion of their gifts and allowances, seeding a portion to live on when they were sent from their masters.

But Dielo had not worried about such things. He was young and more than conventionally attractive, and he had been placed into high circles, now achieving even the royal palace, and he would live well in his position.

And even if he would age—a long time from now—he did not expect to be quietly cast aside as happened to so many. He had done his lessons well, and he had dedicated himself fervently to his purpose. He would find love, not just service, and his master would keep him even when his jaw softened and the cut of his waist blurred. And Dielo knew how to keep himself fit, and he knew how to mask small faults with cosmetics and dress and stance. His place would be more secure than the places of those who needed to squirrel away for abandonment. And he had more standing than those who were chosen for looks and a single night or few of service; a virilo offered more. Dielo should not be afraid of her warnings.

I don't want you, the prince had said, and then he had left.

Dielo shoved the icy clamp of fear away. It was fear, only fear, not rational thought. Dielo had years of training, he would be good enough—quiet enough, welcoming enough, comforting enough to soothe and win the prince's alarmed heart. And if the prince truly did not want him, well, it was only a matter of time before he formally sent Dielo away, and then he could find someone else to love and keep him.

Pasiphae Jade regarded him as if she could see his inner debate laid out plainly before her. Her lips curled in sad, hateful sympathy. "You poor boy. You have been so convinced. But I tell you, they do not value you as you believe they do."

"We are not courtesans," Dielo answered firmly.

"Not in name," she agreed. "But it is not your ideas they want. It is not your insight. Your prince likes music—could you give him a different song than he asked for? Tell him you'd rather not sing that night?"

Dielo, back on firmer footing, wanted to laugh at her ridiculous misunderstanding. "That would be to fail at the basic purpose of a virilo. We provide peace, respite, and comfort; we do not offer strife and rebellion."

"And you interpret such a small thing as rebellion. As if having your own preference of song is strife. And if you wished to do more than sing? What if, while you waited for your prince to finish his duties, you had preferred to craft your own pieces to sell?"

Dielo blinked with the absurdity of it. "Why would a virilo wish for another trade? That suggests distrust in his master, that he will not be provided for in an appropriate manner."

"Hm." She tapped a finger to her chin, smug as if he had not rebutted her challenge. "Or even to study?"

"Of course we might study. It is good to sharpen one's mind and skills, to better entertain—"

"I don't mean study to better please your master. I mean study to serve another purpose."

Again, the absurdity of it. "A virilo does not have another purpose. We were meant for this."

She shook her head and sighed. "I studied. There are many hours outside of a bed, and I filled them with books and charts and calculations. My master was amused, and he even said he liked having a clever woman to show off. I continued to study, and I made sure it did not take from my time with him. I made my own charts instead of simply reading over the old ones, and I compared charts no one had thought to put beside one another before, and I found something no one else had noticed." Now she sat up and looked directly at Dielo, all the smugness and the disdain drained away. "I found how the hatching could be predicted, and I found what we could do to guard against it. And I went to the Arch Potentate, the most powerful man in the land, with the ability to save thousands of lives, and I showed him what I had learned."

And you made him uncomfortable, Dielo thought. *You did his work, and so you took away from his power. You brought his anger upon yourself.*

"And he did not understand my insights, and so he belittled my work. He said it was foolish and unproven, said it disagreed with what his counselors knew. He said if it were so, then someone more qualified would have thought of it first. And he told me to stop dreaming of scholarship and keep to his sleeping pit."

Such a thing wouldn't happen to Dielo. He knew his skills and his purpose; he wouldn't bring his master's anger upon himself.

"He told me to keep to what I was good at." She barked a bitter laugh and spread her hands. "And yet I seem to be good at all this, yes? If he had listened, then I would never have sat upon his throne. I owe him thanks, in a way."

She had done his work, and she had taken his power, and then she had taken his throne. Dielo would never do such things. Dielo knew how to please and he knew how to soothe. He bowed again. "Indeed, Your Illustrious Excellency."

She reclined in her chair, her hand resting upon her notebooks. "You think your master will be ready to see me tomorrow?"

He would have to be. "I will tell him you are expecting him, Your Illustrious Excellency. Is there anything else I should convey to him?"

"Suggest to him his injured arm does not hamper his walking. Tell him he is losing time."

CHAPTER 48

IN THE MORNING KAYVIN went to Pasiphae Jade's quarters—once his father's—and pushed back the servant who tried to politely block his entrance while asking if he would like to be announced.

"I will announce myself, and my intentions," Kayvin snapped. "Pasiphae Jade! Where are you?"

She had redecorated. His father's large padded chairs and couches were gone. Her room was comparatively bare. She was not in it.

Two young men, dressed alike in silk and gauze and jewels, lounged in the summer room, artfully sprawled across floor and couch, looking up at him curiously. Dielo was not the only virilo she'd purchased with royal funds.

He turned from them and walked toward the corridor of smaller rooms. "Pasiphae Jade!"

"*Arch Potentate* is my title," she said coolly, looking up from her desk. She had redone this room as a study, and stacks of old books, scrolls, and tablets walled its edge. "*Illustrious Excellency* is my address. Pasiphae Jade is my name, to be used by family and lovers. Which are you?"

Kayvin did not try to disguise the wave of disgust that rolled through him. "Neither, so help me. But you have promised a way if I did what you wanted, and I have done my best. Your plan did not succeed. If you will not tell me what remains, then nothing remains, and you will return my mother to me."

Pasiphae Jade wrinkled her face in disgust, twisting her reddened lips. Irrelevantly Kayvin wondered why she had painted her face even for study in her own rooms. "Are you recovered from your injury, my prince? Enough to press on beyond the first difficulty, when the object of your quest was not neatly presented to you? Then I can send you back to your single task."

Kayvin wanted to break her neck. Surely it would not be so hard—a step forward, a quick grab, a savage wrench—

"If you kill me," she said, her eyes on her papers without concern, "she dies. If you disobey me, she dies. If you fail to fulfill my orders and we do not counter the spawning, she dies. You can kill her with ice or with scale and fang, but you will kill her in the end."

His heart burned in him like a live coal had been dropped into his chest. He imagined that with only a little effort, he could exhale fire. "You are a monster," he snarled.

"I cannot help what I have been made," she answered. "But I am the monster who is going to save this kingdom."

He fought down his anger, clenching his fists around it and squeezing it into tiny diamonds of rage, crystalline fragments to put away until he could indulge them.

And one day, he promised himself, he would indulge them.

But for now, he took a long breath, and then another, and made himself face the woman he hated for the sake of a woman he loved.

Pasiphae Jade rose from her desk, setting aside the scroll she had been reading so that it snapped together and rolled across the open surface. "Kayvin," she said. "Prince. Son of my lover. Why must you make this so hard for both of us?"

"I do not see how it is hard for you."

"Do you think I want to wrestle with you at each step? Don't you think I want to focus my attention on the crisis facing us, the imminent danger that we know can destroy us, instead of constantly wrangling to keep your obedience? I would so much rather have you on my side."

"I am on the side of my mother and my people," Kayvin said firmly. "If that is the side you are on, instead of your own, then we will work together. But I mistrust you."

"And there is our problem."

"Why wouldn't I mistrust you?" Kayvin shook his head. "You have murdered my father. You expect the impossible."

"Nothing is impossible." She walked around the desk and toward him. "You need to look beyond the moment, beyond what we have both lost. You need to think of the future."

Kayvin was thinking of the future, of the day when his mother would be released from the ice.

And then what will happen? came Yovela's persistent voice. *Do you think she will leave either of you alive once she no longer has a threat to protect herself?*

Kayvin shoved the thought from his mind. He could not think of that, could not even consider it. If saving his mother was not possible—

He could not give up all hope. Not yet.

"If we stop the spawning, then our kingdom and our people will have a future," Pasiphae Jade continued. "You must think of that time."

After his mother was free.

"This, this overturn, this interruption—" Pasiphae Jade gestured, as if to encompass the whole of her treachery and murder. "It need not be the end of your dynasty, you know."

Kayvin stared, distrusting his ears. Was she going to return the rule to him? If she had truly acted only to stop the spawning, did she mean she would cede the throne to Kayvin once safety had been achieved?

"Your descendants could hold this forever."

Kayvin's tongue clung to the roof of his mouth.

"They should inherit." Pasiphae Jade moved forward and touched his chest. Kayvin flinched at the unexpected contact, jerking away as she spread her fingers against his chest. She lowered her chin and raised her eyes to his, her movements fluid and beckoning with all the training of her profession. "Give me a child."

Kayvin recoiled and slapped her hand away, revolted. "What?"

She rolled one shoulder, poetry in flesh. "Give me a child, who will inherit after me. Then your line, your father's line, will continue. The dynasty will be unbroken, the heir legitimate in every way."

"I will not legitimize your usurpation!" Kayvin tasted bile as he fought down a fresh surge of fury. "You are a murderer, and nothing you do will change that."

"I am the salvation of our people, and nothing you call me will change that." Her eyes blazed with anger and then amusement. "But I am sorry to learn you find me so repugnant. Your father didn't think so."

Disgust twisted within his stomach. "My father did not know what you were."

"He knew more than you think. He liked a little danger in his bed."

"And he died in that bed."

"At least he died doing what he loved." She gave a crooked smile.

Kayvin could not bear this any longer. He turned to leave, not waiting upon etiquette.

"Prince Kayvin," she called after him, "do you know your servants?"

She would not turn him against Yovela and Dielo. He would not allow that. "I know my friends."

"That's not what I meant. Have you seen your servants lately?"

He turned back to her. "What do you mean?"

"I have heard you dismissed most of your staff. It seems a sad, isolating way to live."

"It seems a safer way to live," he said fiercely.

She shrugged, two shoulders this time. "I only thought you might want to keep an eye on those closest to you," she said. "But I suppose you know best. Do you even remember what they look like?"

He did not understand her, and he thought it was best that he did not. She only meant to confuse him, to distract him, to lead him to distrust those few he could trust.

His fever was gone, and he had healed enough. "I will leave again for Sayinia in the morning," he said curtly.

"I'm glad to hear it."

He turned and stalked out of her rooms—his father's rooms—and returned to his own safe chamber.

CHAPTER 49

KAYVIN SET ASIDE A sheaf of music, starting a new stack on the floor, and noted a reminder on the list beside him. Across the room, Dielo entered. He'd adopted more subdued clothing, abandoning the sheers and draping silks, but it was still finely cut to display his form. Kayvin supposed distantly his entire wardrobe was, of course.

Dielo began to hum a harmony with the tune Kayvin was trying under his breath. He knelt and pushed a small tray across the floor. "I've brought your medicine."

"Thank you."

Dielo looked down at the several stacks of notated music. He picked one up, abandoned it as not matching the song, and glanced curiously at Kayvin, who traded him the annotated page he held for a steaming cup. Kayvin drained it and then asked, "Are you familiar with Ason's work?"

Dielo shook his head. "No. But the melody progresses much like one of Demfast's."

Kayvin nodded. "I hadn't thought of that, but you're right. They were writing in a similar period."

Dielo ran his eyes across the stacks, weighted with pens and small objects against the occasional breeze from the garden. "Are you sorting them by period?"

"No, I'm trying to choose..." Kayvin hesitated. It was a difficult thing to say aloud. "I am trying to choose a concert program. And I know that should be the least of my concerns just now, as it does nothing to advance the retrieval of the amulets or the release of my mother or the return of my throne—but as I cannot accomplish any of those this day, I found something I could." He looked down at the music in his hand. "Sometimes, when I make music, it feels like it's not me at all, but the music coming through me. It's a relief to be something else in that moment. And I know how foolish that must sound."

Dielo shook his head quietly.

"When I do guide its flow, when I decide whether to modulate or to segue into another piece, then that's at least something I can do when I cannot do anything that matters. I know it sounds beyond ridiculous, but..."

Dielo nodded. "I understand."

For a moment, looking at him, Kayvin thought he might. Wasn't that Dielo's entire training, in fact? To distract the overburdened with pleasure and achievement and amiable agreement?

Dielo looked down at the music Kayvin had left to one side. "You do not like Tegon?"

"There are some beautiful contrasts. I'm just not sure his style blends well with what else I'm considering."

Dielo shrugged and placed a finger on the ruffling sheets. "I thought perhaps, since there is a breeze, you had better choose Demfast before Tegon."

Kayvin stopped and stared at the virilo. "Did you...did you just make a terrible pun?"

Dielo tried first to suppress his grin, but at last he gave in, very embarrassed and a little proud. "I have waited two years for the opportunity."

"That was not worth two years." Kayvin found himself fighting a smile, too. "That was hardly worth the breath to say it. Those are great composers, justly famous, responsible for some of our finest music."

Dielo's face was innocent. "And yet my lord laughs."

Kayvin chuckled aloud before he could stop himself. "All right, yes, I confess a laugh. But you should have been taught better entertainment than base puns."

"That was why I had to wait for years. I could never have tried such a jest with my tutors."

"And yet you thought me worthy of it."

Dielo's grin faltered. "I—I did not mean..."

Kayvin waved the worry away. "It was no offense. Indeed, there is precious little laughter in my household now, so thank you."

Dielo nodded, his expression sympathetic and a little sad. "If I could help... That is, I know what you do not want, my lord. But I can do other things. Music, massage—"

"Or more puns?" Kayvin shook his head and set the music aside. "Actually, I might bathe." It had been a long time since he had indulged in the ritual soaks to cleanse mind as well as body. "But..."

Dielo understood. "But with a different attendant, my lord. Nala, perhaps."

"Yes." Kayvin thought it was clear there was nothing between them, but it would not hurt to wait a little longer before Dielo joined him for anything other than a state dinner or help with music. "But I suppose," he continued, trying to ease the rejection, "you will make a jest about drawing my bath?" He lifted his pen.

"No, of course not." Dielo rose. "But if my lord will only wet a moment, I will prepare the pool."

Kayvin needed a second to realize what he had done. "You—"

"Water do you think about the rose scent, my lord?"

"Dielo."

"My duty is al-waves to please."

Kayvin groaned. "Stop."

Dielo was smiling now. "I'll be so careful of my work, there's snow chance of the water being too chilly."

Kayvin shook his head.

"Icy that you will freeze so—" Dielo stopped, the humor draining abruptly from his face and leaving horror.

At Dielo's sudden shift, Kayvin went cold where he sat, seeing ice in a fountain, seeing his mother's hand stretching as if to break the frozen surface but never moving.

"Empty void, I'm sorry," Dielo whispered. "I didn't mean—I'm sorry."

Kayvin shook his head, a tight, small movement.

"I will call Nala to attend you." Dielo bowed, hiding his expression of horrified regret, and then hurried from the room.

Kayvin's soaking pool was near his garden, and the area it overlooked was blackened and singed instead of green, thanks to Kayvin's renewed practice. The water was steaming warm, and Nala had scattered flower petals over much of the surface.

Nala was nowhere to be seen now, however. Kayvin dropped his robe and slipped down into the water. His arm's wound had nearly closed, but the new skin prickled in the heat.

His soaking pool was deep enough to stretch fully while keeping the surface area small enough to hold heat, and he savored the hot water and floral scents as he rolled his head back and let his toes brush the base. Carefully shaped stones supported his neck and elbows, keeping his nose above water without effort as he lay back and let the warmth seep over his ears, his scalp, his cheeks.

Dielo had not meant to offend, and Kayvin had enjoyed their moment of levity and regretted its end. Pasiphae Jade's chilling reach extended even to his own quarters.

But now he should forget her and take a few moments of ease. With his eyes closed against the light, and the water blocking most sound, and the sweet warmth wrapping him, he could put aside for a few minutes the frustration and grief and constant wariness. He let his muscles relax, little by little, with little twinges of pain as they let go one by one. He drew a deep breath and finally sighed.

He lay in the warm quiet for a long while.

When at last he lifted his head and broke the surface once more, it seemed he even breathed more easily, although that could have been an effect of the flowers and oils and his reclined head as much as the bath itself.

A moment after he surfaced, he heard Nala's voice behind him. "Would you care for massage, my lord?"

It was a privilege to lay out the prince's clothes, massage his shoulders, dress or undress him, but his new sera qadra was less interested in privilege—well, Yovela was less interested, anyway. He suspected Dielo would be glad, and even if he was an informer, it would not matter if he reported to Pasiphae Jade that the prince bathed. But with his reduced sera qadra, some duties fell to other household servants.

Today, he had Nala to attend him.

Her hands took each side of his head, and suddenly he felt again all the tension he had not released in the soak as her fingers pressed the tender points around his skull. She was not so skilled as a trained attendant, but it was enough. He let his head fall back, the sharp scent of the massage oil penetrating.

"That's helpful," he said after long minutes of relief. "Please do my feet as well."

Her fingers jerked in his hair. "Oh! I'm sorry, my lord."

"It's all right. The feet, please."

"Um...yes. Just lie back and close your eyes, my lord."

He already was lying back, and his eyes were closed. "Mm."

She left his head and padded around the pool. He heard her sit and slip her legs into the water, and then she cradled his right foot. Her thumbs began rubbing, and little frissons of released tension ran through him. She was not well-trained in massage, but he was in a state where every touch helped. He drew a long breath, and his back cracked as his lungs expanded.

He shifted, and her fingers closed about his foot. "No, my lord, stay there!"

Her words might have been meant to soothe him, but her tone did the opposite. Kayvin pulled his head up. "What are—"

She flung his foot away from her, splashing. She bolted from the pool and ran into the garden. He had only a glimpse of her back disappearing into the sooty pillars.

"Nala! What are you doing?"

She did not answer.

Annoyed, Kayvin stood in the pool, shivering as the water ran from his shoulders. "Nala! Come here!"

"No, my lord. Don't—don't ask it."

What was wrong with the girl? He had never taken her for a sera qadra member or harmed her in any way. "Nala! Come out. Now."

"My lord—"

"I order it." What had upset her? "Have you done something you're afraid to confess?" That wasn't like her. He shivered again, and he reached for the robe lying ready at the side of the soaking pool.

Nala emerged from the blackened garden, dragging her feet so that each step took too long, her head lowered. Small, quick sobs shook her, barely audible through the arms wrapped over her face. "No, my lord, no. Only, Her—Her Illustrious..."

"Nala? Whatever is wrong?"

She came to the end of the pool, holding herself and looking at her bare feet, and she cried more loudly, losing restraint.

"Nala!"

She lifted her head, facing him. Her face was mostly as he remembered, but the upper portion had been stretched downward and back, distorting her left eye. Her skin was pulled like soft sugar candy. As if it had been melted—

Ice wrapped about his heart, just as it must have wrapped about Nala, and for a moment he could not breathe.

She took his silence for horror—which it was, though not at her face. It was horror at what had been done to her. But she folded into fresh sobs.

"No," he said uselessly. He wanted to be sick. "Nala, when?"

She choked on her tears.

Pasiphae Jade's voice echoed in his mind. *If you melt her free? She is part of the ice now. She will soften and run, like heated butter.*

"Oh, Nala."

I only thought you might want to keep an eye on those closest to you. Do you even remember what they look like?

She turned and fled into the garden, and he did not call her back.

This was a warning. Pasiphae Jade had melted his servant's face to remind him exactly what was at stake and to renew his obedience.

CHAPTER 50

KAYVIN STORMED INTO PASIPHAE Jade's apartments, striding through the chief servant who rushed to intercept him and pushing into the dog-legged entrance passage. Two guards stepped forward as if to physically block him from proceeding, but he pushed aside one's polearm and went on, his heart in his throat. The guards hesitated—it seemed Kayvin had not fallen far enough to be struck or seized outright, which was both a small surprise and a great gratification—and then followed after him, calling for him to wait. He did not.

Pasiphae Jade reclined with Lord Fretton at a well-appointed table, sera qadra sprawling about them. Kayvin struck aside the guard's hand that obstructed him and marched upon the dining couple. "You lying termagant!"

She looked up at him from her couch, impassive but for a trace of disgust. "You're dripping on my carpets."

He had come directly from his bath, wrapped in his light robe. He had intended his immediate response to underscore his righteous anger, but now Lord Fretton was staring at him in frank disdain, and the sera qadra was trading little smirks.

Kayvin pressed on. "My household was to be safe. You have your spy in my rooms only because you assured me he was safe there from you."

"Oh, is that what this is about." The question held no interest. She sat up, passing the pastry in her hand to a young man sitting near her. "Go on, let's have it done."

Kayvin's fury rose, newly provoked. "How dare you harm someone in my household?"

She waited, and then she cocked her head to one side. "That's it? That's all you have to say?"

He felt Lord Fretton's eyes. He had timed this poorly; Lord Fretton's audience weakened his protest, as he and the sera qadra outnumbered Kayvin in disinterest and made him ridiculous. Kayvin ground on. "You are not to touch my people!"

"And you are not to storm into my sitting room and interrupt my meeting with one of my courtiers, and yet here you are." She looked at Kayvin, and for the first time she seemed to take his challenge seriously. "You should remember that I am not the greatest threat to your people. Shouting at me will do nothing to protect them; you need the amulets for that, and you have brought none. While that is the case, your people—the population and your own servants—are not safe. And you had forgotten that."

He clenched his fists in helpless rage. "Then if you feel free to attack the servants in my quarters, why should I keep the spy you sent me? When I took him only to spare him?"

She was already looking again at the dishes, choosing her next morsel. "Send him back, if you prefer." She took a honeyed roll. "Now, will you sit with Lord Fretton and me, and we can finish our meal?"

He should have done it. He should have sat down, despite his wet hair and damp robe, and conversed with them as if nothing were out of the ordinary, as if he had every right to be there, as if he had his own dignity of position and had not been dismissed as an overtired toddler in the midst of a tantrum.

But he did not have it within him, not then. "I have my own meal." It was a weak line, and his skin burned as he said it. He stepped back from the table and into someone.

"I beg your pardon, my lord," said the young man, drawing back. He bowed and extended a folded object in both hands. "I've brought you a towel."

Lord Fretton sniggered. Kayvin shoved past the smirking servant and went out of the room, gritting his teeth against the imagined scene behind him. Pasiphae Jade would be bestowing an approving laugh on the servant's jest, while Lord Fretton preened.

He nearly barreled into Dielo in the entrance passage. The virilo scurried from his path and then fell into step just behind him. "My lord?"

Kayvin said nothing. He couldn't risk speech; he was somewhere between cursing and crying, and he was not sure which would erupt if he opened his mouth.

Once safely in his own apartment, he sank into a low crouch, forearms resting on his knees and cradling his face, and groaned. He was an idiot. He was a powerless fool. He was useless.

A scuff of fabric drew him from his self-loathing. There was a cushion beside him, waiting. Dielo knelt on the other side, holding a cup of what appeared to be wine.

Kayvin slouched onto the cushion. Yovela came out from the sera qadra's corridor. "What is it?"

"I've..." Kayvin let the words trail off. He did not know how to explain it.

"He went to protest the harm done to Nala," Dielo said quietly. "He challenged Her Illustrious Excellency as she dined with Lord Fretton. He called her to account for her encroaching into his household. He was not heard as he deserved."

It was the kindest possible way to represent the disdain he'd met, and Kayvin almost marveled at Dielo's gentle rendering of the scene. But the retelling meant that Dielo, who must have followed him, who must have waited behind them, had heard Kayvin call him a spy.

It was true, and they all knew it to be true, but there was something worse in the admitting of it aloud in his hearing.

Yovela came and sat on Kayvin's other side. "Thank you for going."

"It did no good," Kayvin muttered. "It might be worse for my going."

"It will not be worse for Nala."

He dropped his face back into his hands. "Nala. And for nothing she's done. Only to goad me into actions I am already obligated for." He shook his head. "When did they take her?"

Neither of them had seen it happen. Kayvin should ask Arad, who as chief servant should know if the Arch Potentate's guards came for one of the prince's household.

Kayvin blew out a breath. "Where is she?" They would not know. Yovela had been in the sera qadra's rooms, and Dielo had followed him. "Call Arad."

The chief servant was apologetic. "She's been in the servants' quarters since the bath. She won't come out—though I'm sure she'd answer Your Highness's summons, of course."

"No. We needn't drag her out, not yet. But there's no more of this, Arad. No one else will be taken from my rooms. No one."

It was an unfair edict—what was Arad to do if guards were sent? But Kayvin had to say something.

Arad nodded and bowed, and Kayvin brushed the bandage on his arm. "And I must go back across the mountains. But also..." He looked at Dielo.

The virilo looked back at him, his face open as if he had not heard Kayvin call him a spy, as if he had not heard that he was a member of the prince's circle only in pity. "Yes?"

"The Arch Potentate cannot afford friends. Lord Fretton is her ally only by purchase, and that meal had all the earmarks of a negotiation. I want to know what they are negotiating."

CHAPTER 51

KAYVIN COULD NOT DEPART for Sayinia as he'd intended. Pasiphae Jade called him to her study shortly after midday to inform him curtly that the passage was closed.

"Closed?"

"Not with rocks. The way is still clear, so that's all well. But a magoran has been sighted."

Kayvin felt a little thrill of wonder despite his anger. "I did not know any remained here."

"At least one, or so we are told. As much as I hate to delay your mission, late is better than never, and trying to pass a magoran is a risk too near to never." She sat back at her desk and blew out her breath with a little irritated sound. "I have asked for daily reports, so we will know when it has moved on. In the meantime, please do not bring this up with others. I do not wish to alarm the populace, especially if we will need to warn of a spawning in coming days."

Kayvin was not likely to go into the marketplace and speak of dangerous beasts with the vendors. It was an easy concession, and he nodded.

"You will use this additional time in full recovery, and be ready to depart when the passage is open."

Kayvin clenched one fist behind him where she would not see. "So if you order me now to stay, what was the point of marring Nala's face?"

She scowled at him. "Pettiness is not regal. I did what I thought needful in your ambivalence, and I had the consideration to take someone outside of your sera qadra."

The words chilled him. He had not thought that Yovela might be a target. "Leave them alone."

"Do not disappoint me again." She gestured for him to go.

When he returned, seething in his useless rage and frustration, Nala was in the summer room with the others. Her reddened cheeks showed where she had cried recently, but she was not crying now. She sat beside Yovela, her face lowered, and Dielo sat an arm's reach away, facing Nala's marred side.

Kayvin went directly to them, taking a seat opposite and gesturing for them to remain where they were. "Nala. I'm so sorry."

"My lord," Nala blurted. "I have family in Demkest. I want to go home." She looked startled and a little frightened at her blunt speech.

But Kayvin nodded. "I understand." She would not feel safe here—she was not safe here. "You'll have traveling money."

"They'll mock me." Her voice was nearly inaudible. "The others... They said people would throw stones."

"No one will throw stones," Kayvin countered at once, before he considered the statement. He did not know what people might do. Some might be cruel, whether with stones or with words.

But there was nothing to do but to provide for her journey to her people. "You'll have money," he repeated, as if that could be enough. "Thank you for your time here, and I wish you well at your family's home."

She nodded, eyes down. Dielo slid forward on his knees, and he opened his arms in quiet invitation. After a moment she inclined slightly toward him, and he embraced her, pulling her shoulder into his chest. Nala sagged into it, letting her head droop. One hand came up from her lap to squeeze Dielo's arm.

Kayvin rose and went to his desk to write a pass for Nala's exit from the palace. She was a servant, not a slave, but the abrupt departure of a servant who did not ordinarily leave the grounds, especially with a sum of money, might draw attention and suspicion. She needed no more stumbling blocks.

Kayvin wrote next an order for the palace librarian. He had been selecting Kayvin's reading material on Sayinian culture, so this summons would not be unusual. Kayvin would have to work out the wording of his request so that more treatises on magic and counter-spells would appear to be further research for his assigned quest, rather than an investigation into how to overturn Pasiphae Jade's magical stranglehold on her hostage.

Dielo came half an hour later, dressed in a more extravagant display. Gauzy fabrics floated over his torso and the wrapped trousers. Golden chains wound about his open chest and upper arms, drawing the eye along his lightly defined musculature. "My lord, may I have two days to go down to the market, and money to arrange Nala's departure?"

The request seemed incongruous with his change in clothing. "I will have Arad do it."

"If I may, this is something more." Dielo pressed his lips together. "To stop the stones."

Kayvin put down his pen. "You can do that by going to the market? What, will you lecture the merchants to be kind?"

Dielo shook his head. "Two rinds of silver should do it, and this afternoon and tomorrow morning."

It was a considerable sum for a day of shopping, though perhaps not for a virilo. But Dielo had also felt the brunt of Pasiphae Jade's brutal manipulations, and possibly that drove this odd request. Kayvin waved his hand. "Arad will provide it, and take the afternoon and the morning. If it will ease her mind."

Dielo nodded and bowed. "Thank you, my lord."

Dielo spent the afternoon shopping. He made an overt display of each stop, fluttering his floating fabrics and lifting high each new garment he examined for drape, sheen, and hand. "Don't you have anything in a purple silk?" he asked. "This is for the Amethyst Prince's household, you know."

"What about this vest?"

"Oh, no, it's not for me. This is for a young woman." Dielo gave the man a knowing look. "A particular young woman."

After circling the shops in a pretense of considering all, to be sure he was thoroughly observed, he finished his purchases and returned to the prince's apartments and his empty room. He took out the dark purple scarf from his selections, fetched his sewing kit from his trunk, and got to work.

Kayvin stared. "What?"

"The concubines have all been dismissed," Arad repeated. "She kept them long enough to determine none were preparing to set eggs, and then she sent them away."

"And the children?" Kayvin was the only surviving child of the Shining Gem, to the disappointment of the court, but there were seven born to concubines, across a spread of ages.

Arad shook his head. "The women were not permitted to take their children with them. The Arch Potentate is careful not to allow any potential heirs out of her grasp."

Kayvin did not bother to rebuke his use of the title within the apartments, busy with horrified speculation. "Has she killed them?"

The chief servant shook his head. "We have heard nothing to suggest that. The wing is securely guarded and well-staffed, and there would be no need for that if the children were gone."

"Unless she wished to conceal their murders," Kayvin muttered. But he realized he did not believe it. Pasiphae Jade had hardly bothered to deny her killing of Gromgest, and concubines' children, though technically royal offspring, were not so closely regarded in court eyes. Pasiphae Jade would not face more outrage for their disappearance than for the Arch Potentate's.

"Ask in the kitchens," Kayvin said. "Find out if the children's wing is requiring enough food to suggest they're still there."

Arad's expression stiffened, as he probably resented being thought of as a kitchen servant or an informer. He gave a curt nod.

But Kayvin needed his help and his loyalty. "Thank you for telling me of this," he made himself say. "I'm not glad of the news, but I'm glad I have someone to tell me."

Arad nodded again, less stiffly. "We're glad you're back, my lord. And glad you're feeling better. Shall I bring you anything now?"

"No, thank you." Kayvin was not hungry, and he did not look forward to the empty day. He would read, and he would practice his magic, and he would dwell on Nala's injury and what else might come if he did not find a legendary amulet in a haystack the size of an entire country.

Then Dielo spoke from the study doorway. "My lord? Will you come?"

Kayvin sighed at his gratitude for this small diversion and followed the virilo into the summer room.

A woman waited there, dressed in sera qadra finery. White sandals marked her as a person of distinction, unaccustomed to walking in the dust. Her dress and robes were layers of white and lavender, descending through deeper hues to an amethyst under-sheath that shifted tantalizingly into view at the collar. On her head she wore a deep purple scarf, which slanted over most of her face and ended just above her reddened lips, so that Kayvin caught himself unconsciously inclining his head in an effort to see past it. The veil was pierced with a purple gauze inset over the eyes, permitting the wearer to see out more clearly than the beholder could see in, and a cascading chain of silver links and pendants draped the forehead and left cheek, weighting the veil against any sudden breeze.

"Nala," he breathed.

The reddened lips curved, visible only for an instant as she ducked her head.

Dielo, again in unmistakable virilo finery, bowed. "If you will permit me, my lord, I will escort this favored lady through the market for what she still requires before delivering her to her caravan."

Kayvin wanted to peer beneath that veil and see what beauty was promised by the rounded chin and red lips, partly hidden by the veil's worked edge. He wanted to marvel at the magic Dielo had worked in making this servant girl an object of fascination. "Of course. Nala, be well on your journey."

"Thank you, my lord." She had a little awe in her voice as well.

Yovela emerged from the women's quarters and gave a little gasp. "Who—Nala?" She came around them to gaze at the full effect.

"Let's go now, to have plenty of time before your caravan departs." Dielo gestured and gave Nala a tiny bow, as if indeed she were an elite lady.

But Nala first bowed low to Kayvin. "I am sorry to go, my lord. I wish you well. Thank you for your kindness." Then she went out with Dielo.

Yovela stared after them. Kayvin turned to stand beside her. "What do you think? Isn't it marvelous?"

She pressed her lips together. "He has made her a trinket like himself."

Her sour words deflated Kayvin's mood. "She will have a lifetime of plainness. Is it so bad to give her a day or two of admiration and wonder? He is putting her in no danger. If anything she may be at less risk of bother, now that she is presented as a prince's favorite."

"Hn." Yovela did not clarify her response.

"Go down after them, then," Kayvin suggested. "Then you can tell me how it went off."

Yovela did not smile as he'd hoped. He realized he did not see her smile often, certainly not as often as a sera qadra woman should. He wondered if he'd trusted her because she did not dissemble even to suit her position.

"Please go," he said. "I would like to hear of it."

She nodded once. "If you wish."

He supposed she was gratified that he'd asked for her report rather than Dielo's. He wished he could order their enmity away. It was a thorny thicket he did not need in his prickly life.

Yovela returned first. "Nala is away," she said. "Gone safely with the caravan."

Kayvin looked up from his picture scroll, grateful for the interruption. "How did it go?"

"She seemed to have a marvelous time," Yovela said without inflection. "Everyone made a great deal of her, inviting her to try honey cakes or asking her to consider bolts of fabric or offering her a prime seat in a wagon. She was overwhelmed, a little flustered, but she seemed happy about it." She crossed her arms. "She's never had so much favor in her life. She's a trinket for today, but you might have been right that she would enjoy being one."

"It won't last, not as long as her scarring, but at least she won't fear being mocked while she's alone." Kayvin pulled one arm over his head, stretching his shoulder.

Dielo entered, slightly out of breath and with a light sheen of sweat over his face. He carried a paperboard box. "I'm sorry—I thought I might catch up, but I wasn't quick enough. My lord, I've brought honey cakes." He came forward and opened the box, proffering it over Kayvin's desk.

"Careful!" Kayvin started.

"Mind the honey!" Yovela snapped, pushing it back from the precious documents.

Dielo jerked the box back and to the side, away from the stack of books on the desk's front edge, and a corner of the box caught the tall bronze vase at the corner. The vase rocked and, evading Dielo's frantic grab, tipped off the desk. It clattered on the tile and spun, sending polished stones in a spiral across the floor.

"I'm sorry!" Dielo gasped. He dropped to his knees and began scraping stones together.

Servants appeared, drawn by the noise. Two squatted beside Dielo, gathering spilled stones. Kayvin sighed to himself and abandoned his reading. He stood and left the desk, going to look over the garden.

Yovela brought Dielo's paperboard box. "A cake, my lord?"

Kayvin did not want a honey cake. He wanted safety for Nala, and the return of his mother, and a full night's peaceful sleep, and a sense that he could make some sort of difference if he tried hard enough. But he could not obtain any of these things. He took a honey cake.

Dielo came to his other side and looked at the box in Yovela's hand. He said nothing.

Kayvin pressed his fingers into the inner corners of his eyes. He was so tired, in a way sleep could never cure.

Dielo's voice came a little subdued. "Shall I read for you, my lord?"

It was not the reading that wearied Kayvin. But Dielo had been kind to Nala, and he deserved some recognition. "Yes, thank you."

"Would you prefer that I read directly to you or summarize?"

The decision seemed too large. "Do as you like. Summarize. Summarize it, please."

Yovela stepped to the side, silently leading Kayvin away. He could follow her and listen to her play, losing himself in music for a few minutes. He moved after her to a low couch, while she selected a small lyre.

She sang a low folk song that made the most of her voice, and he hummed a harmony, experimenting with different intervals. The measured breaths felt good.

He could not rectify what had been done. But he would see that it was not done again. If Pasiphae Jade wanted amulets, he would bring her amulets—all seven of them, even if he had to go to the far borders of Sayinia and beyond.

A History Forgotten

CHAPTER 52

GALEN SPOTTED THE SHOP first, identified by the needle-and-thread sign swinging within arm's reach of the door. He led the way through the market crowd and pushed inside.

It was not busy, even with the market outside bustling, which was probably a bad sign for the shop but which served their own purposes well. "Hello," Galen said to the grey-haired man seated at a work table, as Lisveth turned to survey the room. "Is Harold in? We'd like to speak with him."

The man sighed. "He'll just deny it, whatever it is."

Galen hesitated. "We only wanted to ask him some questions. He hasn't done anything, not that we know of."

"Then you don't know much." The man leaned back in his chair and shouted into the rear room of the shop. "Harold! Some people here for you!"

"Who is it?" came the answer.

"People!"

"I don't want to talk to them."

"I don't want to box your ears, either, but one of us is going to have to do something that displeases us."

There was a loud bang, as if a chair had gone against a wall, and then Harold came into the front room. He was close to Galen's age, but lean where Galen was muscular. He crossed his arms and eyed them. "What do you want?"

The grey-haired man, once again stitching, commented stiffly, "What a manner you have with the customers, Harold."

Harold jerked his head. "If they were customers, you'd be talking to them. You said they asked for me. That means they're not customers. So, what do you want?"

Lisveth could match his scowl. "We came to talk to you about the eye in the temple."

Harold stiffened. "I don't need anyone telling me again I made it up. I didn't go in to smash it. I smashed it when it woke up."

"You didn't make it up," Lisveth said.

Harold tipped his head, eying her suspiciously. Then he looked at Galen, who did his best to look impassive and credible. Then Harold jerked his head toward the rear room. "Okay, we can talk. For a minute or so."

The rear room was full of bolts of cloth stacked against two walls, with thread, buttons, pegs, needles, and more organized along a third. The fourth wall contained the door and a tall series of pigeonholes filled with patterns, notepapers, and such.

"I don't like to talk about it in front of Da," Harold said, his tone much lower and less antagonistic. "He doesn't believe me. Says I was drinking."

"Were you?" Galen asked.

"No. Yes. A little. But it wasn't the drink." He looked at Lisveth. "You said you believed me."

Lisveth nodded. "We've seen it, too. With another amulet, not that one. But it happened."

Harold nodded, and he looked oddly relieved. "Then—then it was real. I didn't imagine it, I didn't make it up." He looked up, a little sheepish. "I mean, I knew I hadn't. But after so long, with everyone saying it was impossible... You know."

"I know," Galen agreed.

"What magic did you use?" asked Lisveth.

Harold's face closed again. "What do you mean?"

"You put some magic into it, or it wouldn't have reacted. What magic did you use?"

Harold's mouth compressed. "I'm not supposed to have any magic," he said. "Mama had some, but Da didn't like her using it. It wasn't useful stuff, just silly things like pushing around the steam on a cup of tea. He said if she couldn't earn a living off it, it wasn't worth doing."

"And what could you do?"

"Not much more. I could stir the tea a little. Not enough to blend the honey."

Galen recalled the gift of the violet amulet. "So you tried the amulet, to see if it could increase your ability."

Harold flinched. "Yes. I did."

"Did it work?"

"I don't know. When that eye started rolling around and looking at me, stirring up a drink was the last thing on my mind." He gave them each a pleading look. "I've never told anyone about the magic."

"Not to worry," Galen assured him. "We don't need to tell anyone else. We just needed to confirm what had woken it."

"And what do you mean, woken it? What's awake?"

"We're still working on that," Lisveth said. "Thanks for your help."

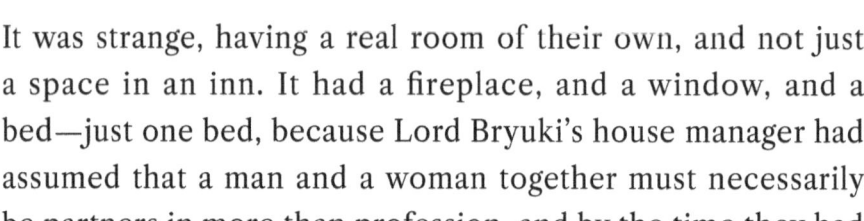

It was strange, having a real room of their own, and not just a space in an inn. It had a fireplace, and a window, and a bed—just one bed, because Lord Bryuki's house manager had assumed that a man and a woman together must necessarily be partners in more than profession, and by the time they had realized the error, it had been too late to correct him without awkwardness.

They had shared many nights on the road back to back when they were the only people within miles, and they had shared rented rooms. Sharing a room in a nobleman's house with strangers on either side should hardly be more intimate. But it still felt faintly odd.

It wasn't that Galen had never thought of sleeping with Lisveth, but she had never seemed interested. Galen was no expert with women, that was plain, but he felt he could read the signs well enough if one *was* interested.

And most importantly, he did not want to break what they had, whatever it was. They were each other's only friend and family. That was too important to risk.

His hair was growing out to an annoying length, too short to draw back into a tail and long enough to flop about his face and fall into his eyes. He pushed his hand through it, a necessary new habit, and went to the stool beside the fire.

He held the amulet in his hand, as he did so many nights now. The eye glistened in the firelight, almost as if it were alive and reflecting, but the pupil remained fixed and sightless.

"Do you suppose this is a real eye?" he asked. "I mean, did it come from a real creature, and a sorcerer enchanted it, or did a sorcerer somehow make an enchanted eye?"

"I don't know what would have an eye like that," Lisveth said, coming to sit on the floor beside him and stretching her stockinged feet to the fire.

"It's a big eye," he said, rocking it so that the light played across its iridescence. "Horses have the largest eyes, but no horse ever had an eye like this. Not any horse I'd care to meet, anyway."

"Horses? Really?" Lisveth tilted her head. "I never thought about it. So if it's a real eye, it must come from something bigger than a horse."

"That doesn't stand to logic. There are larger animals than horses, but they don't have larger eyes than horses." Galen frowned. "Still, it must be something large. And it has a vertical pupil, like a cat."

Lisveth frowned. "Then that's not something large."

"What?"

"Large animals don't have vertical pupils. That's a predator, but a small one."

"Really?"

"Do wolves have vertical pupils? No. But foxes do."

Galen opened his mouth, closed it. "I didn't know that, but I think you're right. I suppose between us, we know nearly enough about eyes."

She laughed and leaned against his leg with the indifferent comfort of familiarity. "So it must be a small but large predator, with an eye that can live on independently for centuries." She turned up her palms. "I've got no idea."

"So the sorcerers made them themselves, or they took them from an animal we don't have now." Galen turned the amulet over in his hand. "I wish we knew where they came from."

"The sorcerers?"

"The amulets. Or the sorcerers. Anything."

She tipped her head up to look at him. "But we do."

"What?"

"The amulets. We know where they came from, or at least who made them. Didn't you learn that in your history?"

"No," he admitted. "But how would I learn that? I'm just a witless farm boy, or so I've been told."

She made a face. "Have I ever actually said *witless*?"

"Pretty sure you have."

She sighed. "Well, let's amend that to *uneducated*. You've shown remarkably good sense in business partners."

"Fine. Now tell me how an uneducated farm boy should know the history of these amulets."

"Because it's part of the history of the wars."

Galen stared at her. "All that knowledge was lost. Only the artifacts remain."

She snorted. "Lost in the Heel, maybe."

Galen remembered a temple brother talking about books being burned or stolen or lost—and he realized what as a boy he had not, that such a loss had beggared their own region, but not the world beyond, a world he had barely considered before he had run away to it. "Tell me."

"The king's mages made the amulets for the Selk wars—or the Rideis, I suppose we know now. Their names were...oh, I'm not going to remember all of them. I remember Noquiexis, because it was so much fun to say. And Windora. And a half dozen more, I think. Anyway, they all worked together to craft magic greater than any one or three mages could work alone. They made seven amulets to support the defense against the invading Selks."

"Rideis."

"Whatever. When I learned this, they were Selks, and that's how I can recite the lesson."

"When was this?"

"This was long ago, about eight hundred years, during the reign of Ferdinand the Greater. But the amulets were kept after that war and used during the next, and the next. They were also used between war with the Selks—Rideis—in wars with other humans. Because once you have a magical amulet, why wouldn't you use it?"

"And that's how they spread across the country," Galen said. "Because there would be no need of a weapon against the eastern Rideis all the way west in the Heel."

"Right."

"And then someone lost it—maybe his opponent hit him with steel instead of magic—and it stayed in the temple until it was stolen." The magnitude of it came to him. "The most powerful sorcerers in the history of our kingdom, maybe of the world, worked together to make this, and my uncles kept it in a wooden box in the hallway so that neither of them could guard it."

"No accounting for uneducated farm boys," Lisveth said.

"But we still don't know what they really are. How did these greatest sorcerers of history make the amulets?"

"If I could tell you how," Lisveth said pointedly, "I would be one of the greatest sorcerers in history."

"Instead of one of the greatest bandits?"

"You're cute. Anyway, I can give you the general idea of infusing protective magic into an object if you're willing to sit through a lot of jargon, but it's really not the same, because it's not on the same level at all. This can *absorb* a tremendous amount of magic. And it has been working for hundreds of years without maintenance. To be perfectly honest, I haven't any idea how that kind of spell could be made."

Galen turned the eye over again. "What if the eye is part of it?"

"What?"

"You said it would be hard to infuse that kind of magic into an object and maintain it. What if the eye was magic to start with?"

Lisveth grinned. "A magical horse with a vertical pupil?"

He shrugged. "Why not? Do you have a better idea?"

"No, I don't."

They stared into the fire. Galen's leg was starting to go numb with the pressure of Lisveth's shoulder, but he didn't want to make either of them move.

"What if," Lisveth began slowly, "what if it wasn't the sorcerers who made it? What if it was the Rideis?"

"What do you mean?"

"They're good at magic. They're really good at magic, better than we are. Only our best sorcerers can take on the Rideis, according to the stories. So what if they made the amulets?"

"Why would the histories say the sorcerers made them?"

She made a face. "Sorcerers tend to say whatever makes them most popular. Or, I suppose, they could have taken the materials from the Rideis, or some of the magical theory, and still claimed the final working even if they borrowed the start."

"So the story you learned was partly true, but the sorcerers obtained the amulets from the Rideis. How would they do that?"

Lisveth shook her head. "That's too much speculation for a question that might not be valid itself." She pushed herself from the floor. "I'm off to bed. Tomorrow we're meeting with the general, and we can guess about the amulets then."

CHAPTER 53

"DIELO?"

He recognized her voice, and while he was sure his outward demeanor did not change, his stomach sank a little. There was disappointment-tainted hope in that voice, and hesitation, and self-doubt, and everything he had been schooled to anxiously correct.

He turned back, scanning the corridor for other eyes that might see. But it was only Lirin standing there. "Hi," she said, subdued. "I haven't seen you again in the kitchen."

"No, I—"

"I suppose with the prince returned, you have less time away, then." Her hasty explanation precluded any other.

She was only a few years younger than him, but she was so young. More worldly, and less so. Striving to be something she thought she should be, and lacking the training he had been given.

"I hope you're feeling better now." This had an undertone of accusation.

He took a breath. "Can we talk for a bit?"

She brightened. "We can—"

"The prince's garden," he said quickly, before she could complete her suggestion. It was forbidden enough that she would probably agree for the excitement of it, but it had one end clearly visible from the palace walkway, where they could sit at opposite ends of a bench and be overtly nothing they should not be.

As he had hoped, the exclusive location intrigued her. "Could we? Yes!"

He led the way, taking her by an alternate entrance so that they did not pass through the prince's apartments directly. But as virilo he had a key to the secondary gate, which the gardeners used to avoid disturbing the royal quarters, and he let them in just below the open walkway. She had probably looked down upon this section before, but still she looked about her as if fascinated.

"Come here." He selected a bench divided by a box of blooming violets. He took one end and half turned to face her, gesturing to the far side.

She sat down on the opposite end of the bench, looking at him. "You're going to tell me that we cannot see one another."

"No. That is, you're right, we cannot, but that's not what I was going to say."

"It doesn't matter how you say it. I know that, I always have. It wasn't that I wanted you that way."

He knew that, too. "No, that's not what... I want to tell you something else." He took a breath, trying to find words to express what he had heard but could himself yet barely understand. "The strength of attraction—it's not true strength."

She stared at him. "What?"

She had wanted him to enhance her own status, but he did not want to tell her he knew that. "It isn't the place of power it might seem. It can be dangerous."

Her expression darkened. "I'm not as stupid as you think I am!" she snapped. "I know what I'm doing. Didn't I tell you my aunt was in a sera qadra? Do you think you're so much better, as a virilo?"

This was going all wrong. "I'm only telling you to be careful."

"That was why you left me with that sudden sickness story? Because you wanted me to be careful—after all that dancing?" Her eyes sparked with indignation.

"I'm sorry. I didn't want to lie to you. But..." He could not explain that he had been insulted—hurt—by a maid's leverage of him.

"I'm not dumb," she insisted. "I know what the stakes are. Do you think palace maids are untouchable?"

He supposed they were not. Even a full sera qadra could not sate some appetites, and there were others who did not keep a sera qadra.

"You think I'm stupid," she repeated. "I know that my aunt—that I'm watched. That someone is protecting me more than the other maids."

"What do you mean?"

She shrugged, a jerky motion that betrayed what she meant to conceal. "Teth made a joke at supper one night. He said... It was a joke, he said, but he shouldn't have said it. Two days later he came in with his hand all bandaged and wouldn't talk about what had happened. Said he closed his fingers in a door, but that couldn't be true, not for what... Anyway, there was another one, a man who followed me down one night. He was a noble, I won't say which, and he kept coming back, watching for me. I'm not being vain, he was really watching for me, and I kept trying to avoid him. And then he was gone, and I never saw him again. And nobles don't just lose interest, at least not before they're satisfied."

No. I haven't seen him even in the corridors.

Good. If he comes around to you again, let me know. I'll have him butchered for fertilizer.

"She thinks she can protect me by choosing someone for me, someone important enough that no one will take me from him." She curled a lip. "But I don't want to be *given*. Does that make sense?"

It did. In a courtesan's logic, finding a place for her niece with a single powerful nobleman was the safest thing for her. But Lirin feared what that could be, and she was not wrong in that, either.

"It makes sense," he said softly. "But understand, if you barter yourself, you are still bartered."

"That's some talk from a virilo! And what do you suggest instead, if you're so clever? Should I cross my fingers and my legs and simply hope I'm overlooked?"

He did not have an answer for her, and he wished he did. Not having an answer did not mean he was wrong, but she would not see it that way.

"Just be careful," he said uselessly. He stood. "You shouldn't stay here in the garden."

"What about you?" She jutted her chin at him. "Are you too good for me now?"

He gave her a flat look. "You weren't afraid to use the good dishes when you wanted others to see your place setting."

That gave her a moment of pause, and he watched her consider for possibly the first time how he might have seen her actions. "I didn't..."

"You did. You thought I was a stepping stone. I was a prize."

"And how is that so very different than at your finer banquets? Is it because I am a maid and not a prince?"

It's no different at all, and that is exactly the point. But Dielo could not say that aloud, not even to himself, much less to her.

He pointed toward the gate. "I need to lock it behind you."

"Fine." She stood, took a step, stopped. "Look, if I...if we talk, and just talk, and not in front of anyone..."

Dielo knew better. She was young, and she was Pasiphae Jade's niece, and she was confused, and Prince Kayvin had returned.

But the prince would go again, soon, and if he did not take Dielo with him...

"Just to talk," he said, regretting the words as he said them. "Not in secret, not with anything to hide, not with anything to display. Just to talk, in the kitchen or the passageway where we happen to meet."

She nodded. "That's fair." She gestured toward the gate, and he followed her to it.

As he locked it behind her, she gave him a tight smile. "I'm sorry. I don't have many friends who aren't—you know."

He wasn't sure he knew, but he thought he might guess a few possibilities. "Nor I."

"Well, I hope I see you around sometime."

Almost, he hoped so, too. Almost.

CHAPTER 54

KAYVIN HAD DISAPPOINTED HIS parents.

If he had not been the only son of the Shining Gem, he would have been a prince, but not the Amethyst. There were other ranks for sons who would not take the throne.

As it was, he wondered now, looking back, if he had still been in danger of losing his position. It was not unprecedented for a courtesan's son to inherit. That might explain the times Kayvin's mother had come to him, kind and concerned.

"Don't you think it might be time to take up other interests?" she had suggested. "You can still practice your music and magic. Just keep them as hobbies for quiet moments, and let the court see you pursuing more—traditional pastimes."

Kayvin, sixteen and already aware of the general disapproval, had shifted uncomfortably on his seating cushion. "I have my own sera qadra already. Everyone knows that."

"And you have them sing in the garden. How many of them serve you more closely?"

Kayvin had become a man, after his father's teasing encouragement, and as far as he was concerned that should have been enough for the rest of the court. "Do the ministers mean to come and observe for themselves?"

She sighed. "I'm concerned for you."

"There's nothing wrong with me." There were days when he questioned that, less interested in what seemed to be the primary obsession of all influential men in the palace, but he was not about to admit that to his mother.

"That's not all that I mean." She pressed her lips into a thin line, thinking, and then she gently warned, "The Bull Throne is a seat of strength and vitality. The nobles will not follow a prince who lacks these traits, and they will not support an Arch Potentate without them."

Kayvin knew. This was a sera qadra's purpose, displaying and illustrating a man's power. A man who could not leave his legacy was not fit to have one. He looked down at his plate, busying himself with pushing a piece of bread through golden oil.

"You must be seen as strong, Kayvin, and a strong man does not spend his time in books, or in learning to fight at a safe distance without closing hand to hand with an opponent. A strong future ruler does not waste his energy in art and music rather than honing useful skills."

"I bring my sera qadra to court events," he protested irritably. "Do you want me to paw some of them openly while Father is making a speech?"

"Perhaps," she answered, matching his defiant tone. "If that's what you can manage."

Kayvin did not reply. She thought him deficient, too.

"I'm worried for you," she said more gently.

Kayvin understood. His capability, his worth, his future, all were determined by how frequently his sleeping pit was occupied, and by whom. Aloud he said, "I know you're only thinking of helping me."

She gave him a small, relieved smile. "Choose one of your prettiest or most handsome to sit beside you tomorrow night, at your father's dinner. It will be good to be seen."

"I will."

He had.

Still, it had not been enough. When Pasiphae Jade had seized power, no one had turned to Kayvin to stop her. Even Lord Narrim had acted on his own, choosing Kayvin as the face of his resistance but expecting little of Kayvin himself. Kayvin had been a legitimizing excuse to cast out the interloping woman, not a compelling cause as the rightful ruler.

Yet today it meant he had little to lose. He could clear his sera qadra and only confirm what was already rumored. If music was heard from his balconies at night, no one would be surprised. He could no longer disappoint anyone.

It had been his mother who first taught him about magic. There was an irony to that, he thought. But it was acceptable, even appropriate, for noble young men to learn a little about magic, just as they learned to read but would never waste themselves as scholars. Too much schooling made them susceptible, distracted them from more important virtues, and a confident warrior would not use magic instead of proving his courage and his prowess with muscle and iron.

Was it her fault, then, for not discouraging him in his early interest? He had sat in her flowered courtyard at dusk, watching her make candle flames dance. "I can do that, too," he had told her.

She smiled patiently. "Maybe, one day."

He opened his fingers and squeezed his eyes and forehead into wrinkles in concentration. A little spark danced in his palm, and she gasped. He beamed at her reaction. "See?"

"That's wonderful!" She opened her hand to show another candle flame wavering alone over her skin. "You'll have a proper flame in no time."

He had been eight. Too early to be a man, and still permitted to indulge in childish things. Only, he'd not given all of them up when he'd become a man.

Others continued in their studies. There were scholars, professional readers who prepared to advise a ruler when necessary. There were mages, though far fewer than there had been, according to what Kayvin read in the older books. But those men did not have to worry about tainting their reputations. They accepted their destiny as supporters of the powerful.

The older history books, thicker than the ones his tutors brought him, suggested magic had been a much greater part of their past. This made sense; some of the great wars must have included arcane as well as mundane weaponry. They had fought dragons, after all. But magic had gone wrong, or been used by the wrong people, or something else that wasn't quite clear, and the Rideis had learned to rely upon their own might. Magic was an antique art, something an educated man knew a bit about but rarely used. Personal strength was the only reliable power, and unlike magic it was easy to achieve and easy to display. And it was far safer for an Arch Potentate to direct the youngest crop of ambitious lordlings at gathered women than to risk them experimenting with magic and studying the history or legitimacy of his reign.

But Kayvin sometimes wondered, as he cast his thoughts about for any less prickly resting place, if things could be different.

CHAPTER 55

IT SEEMED ABSOLUTELY INCREDIBLE that ordinary life went on while Gromgest was dead and Raea was imprisoned in ice, a hostage displayed before the entire court. It was inconceivable that Kayvin was expected to carry on as if he had not had his life torn away. But Lord Trerin's second wife had borne him an egg, and there were social protocols to be kept.

Kayvin held his arms out for the servants to finish dressing him. It was not a truly formal affair, but the prince should be well-attired for an official visit to an egg lying-in. He would also need his sera qadra in attendance. Once more he regretted sending so many away, reducing his apparent status when he needed it most. But of course he could not trust them near. Perhaps he might have kept them in another wing, brought out only for necessary court appearances.

Too late now.

He shook his head and pushed it from his mind. What was done was done, and now his sera qadra was all of two members, who bickered like toddlers and who might embarrass him before Pasiphae Jade and all the court.

No, neither would embarrass him. They knew their public roles. But their resentment brought him no solace, either.

The servants fastened the last bits of chain and braid, and they stepped away. Kayvin went out into his primary room. Dielo was already there, in a glorious costume from his virilo wardrobe, all draping cloth cut at improbable angles to sweep his torso and flare as he moved. Delicate gold chains wrapped his shoulders and slid over his bare chest. He turned, so that cloth and gold shifted and shone, and he bowed. "Your Highness."

Kayvin was impressed despite himself, and for a moment he wondered if the virilo outshone him in his princely garb. But it did not matter; it was the duty of a virilo to be flashy and vivid, like a brightly colored songbird. The prince was still a hawk. "You look well. Has Yovela come yet?"

But of course Yovela would not have waited alone with the virilo. She was probably just around the corner, ready to hear Kayvin's voice and arrange her entrance.

"I come!" A breath later she came around the corner, fiddling with bangles on her arm as if she had only just finished. She was dressed well, too, in blue and green silk and trailing scarves. She was not as overtly striking as Dielo, but eye-catching just the same.

Kayvin decided to be kind. "What does it matter if my sera qadra is small when it is so impressive? You both look stunning."

Dielo beamed beneath the praise, making another small bow. "Thank you, Your Highness."

Yovela's response was pleased but more understated, merely a quick nod as if the words embarrassed her.

"Well, then, let's go." Kayvin led the way to the door, and they fell in on either side of him and two steps behind, a living train of fabric and jewels.

Lord Trerin's seasonal house, the one he kept while attending the court, was in a cluster of luxurious homes reached by a raised walkway, shielded from sun and common eyes by a series of trellises and arches all artfully overgrown with heavily scented flowering vines. They were not alone as they walked over the courtyard and the palace garden; many were visiting Lord Trerin today. Kayvin kept a steady litany of greetings and nods, until he felt his head might come loose.

At last they came to Lord Trerin's home, its doorway decorated with traditional hake flowers and little piles of polished stones. The doors were open, and servants proffered drinks and sweetmeats as Kayvin threaded his way through the gathering.

"Your Highness! Welcome, welcome. Thank you so much for honoring my home with a visit."

Kayvin nodded and greeted and made the appropriate wishes to the egg-father. Kayvin was playing a script, picking out the notes of a melody he had been assigned, but the performance was important. Lord Trerin was a senior member of the council. He was also now a supporter of the interloper Pasiphae Jade.

Behind him, Dielo and Yovela stood in perfect poses, tiny smiles on their faces as they listened and observed and flattered with their attentive gazes. They had harmonizing parts to play, and they were better at it.

The courtiers around him laughed and talked of amusements and fashion, markets and alliances, and Kayvin wished it were possible to leave without providing insult. Trerin's sera qadra passed through the crowd like slim golden fish through a pond, proffering trays of refreshments.

At last one gauze-draped woman came about with another tray, larger and piled with bright yellow hake flowers, and Kayvin saw relief in sight. After the presentation of flowers and stones, he could take his leave and safely retreat to his own rooms once more. He selected a bright yellow flower the size of his palm and fell into the queue that was forming.

"Flowers? Stones?"

Dielo took a smooth river stone from the next tray, bequeathing his dazzling smile upon the sera qadra member bearing it. Yovela took one as well, ignoring the exchange of bright teeth.

The visitors passed singly through the corridor and into the laying room, where Trerin's young wife sat beside her egg on its stand of carved and gilded wood. She kept one hand on it in a traditional gesture of protection as, one by one, each guest placed a flower on or beside the egg, or set a polished stone at its base.

The line moved slowly, with each guest exchanging formal congratulations and well wishes with the new mother. At last it was Kayvin's turn. She dipped low as he approached. "Your Highness."

"May happiness fall upon you and your new family," he told her. He set the flower on the egg, where it slid to the side. "I wish for a safe brooding and a healthy hatchling."

"Oh, thank you, Your Highness."

Beside him, Dielo knelt with a graceful flourish and used two hands to prop his stone against the gilded base. "May your child grow well and hatch strong, sweet lady."

"Thank you."

Yovela stood beside him, a little stiff next to Dielo's fluid movement. She did not speak to the woman, and her knuckles were white on the stone she held.

"Yovela," Kayvin prompted, and she bent to put her stone on the floor, rocking gently in place. She made an obeisance to the wife and looked down.

It would do. Kayvin led them out of the laying room, made his farewells to Lord Trerin, and fled back into the shaded passageway, now darkening with the evening.

None of them spoke until they reached his own princely quarters once more. Kayvin extended his arms, and servants appeared to remove the surplus sumptuous garments. "At last, I can go back to my song," he said in a light tone. "I have never known precisely what to say at a lying-in."

"Will you have us with you, my lord?" asked Dielo, and Kayvin could hear the faint hope in his voice.

"Not for this," he answered. "I want to concentrate on the bridge, and I can do that better alone. Take some time to yourselves."

Dielo nodded, any disappointment well concealed, and Kayvin went in to his instruments and music.

CHAPTER 56

Yovela did not speak, but the prince did not notice how her jaw was locked into place. In her place two steps behind and to the side, her quick blinks and stiff shoulders went unnoticed. None in the house of honor would have noticed or, if they had, would have thought on it more than an instant—only a passing disapproval of a sera qadra member looking other than her best. Now Prince Kayvin had gone in to his music, now she was safe in the women's quarters, now she could unbend. Now she might let herself reach out enough to push feelings away.

But when at last she stood alone in the women's quarters, no longer surrounded by protective duty, her breath choked in her throat. Without the social obligations to occupy and protect her, it all rushed upon her, icy-hot memory lancing through her careful walls. Her defenses crumbled beneath a yellow flower.

She laid a small yellow hake flower, the first of the season, on the egg stand, tucking it into the drying mud. She could not afford the hothouse blooms and had thought she would have no flower at all, so she had been delighted to find this ambitious bud near the stream. There she had also found a river rock, a little larger than her hand and oblong with the smoothing path of water. She set this at the base of the stand, narrow end up, and stepped back to judge the results of her efforts.

Yovela was ill with clenching her muscles around memory and grief. She sank slowly to the floor, and without bothering to strip her formal finery she curled into herself, clutching a pillow to her abdomen.

The sick feeling did not pass but settled deep in her stomach, deep in her soul. She buried her head and squeezed her eyes shut, but still the slanting light hurt her head, blinded her, smelled of blood and feces and rotting earth.

This is your only choice. This is the only way.

What have you done?

Blood coated her fingers, hot and sticky, and she rubbed her hands across the dirt but it was blood-soaked, mud made of blood and other things, and now she was smearing her child through the mud and she was screaming. She screamed and she made no sound, she could call no one to help her or to witness these deeds, and she only clawed the mud where she knelt.

Someone was there. She jerked with sudden awareness, pulling away. Her breath wheezed in her throat.

"Shh," someone soothed in the dark. "It's all right. You're safe."

She was on the floor, her arms wrapped about herself, still in her visiting clothes. Blankets lay over her.

"It's Dielo."

He lay on his stomach facing her, his chin on his wrist, the other hand outstretched so that he nearly brushed her blanketed arm.

She froze, every muscle freshly rigid, her breath caught in her lungs.

"I could hold you, if that would help." He put a hand on the blanket without touching her skin. She wanted to pull away, but she also wanted to feel its weight. "I heard you," he explained softly. "Are you—awake now?"

She had not had the lurid nightmares for a long time. "Where did you bring me?"

"I heard you here. You're in the women's quarters."

He was not allowed to enter here.

She pushed herself upright, and her stomach turned. She began to shiver despite the blanket.

He sat up beside her, slowly. He drew one knee to his chest, a buffer between them, and he wrapped another blanket around her and pulled the ends tight, embracing her without arms and cocooning her within the furs and quilts taken from the sleeping pits. "Are you all right? What happened?"

Memory came down upon her like a blow. She flinched and squeezed her eyes against the smell of it. "Stop," she whispered.

He released the blanket and pulled his arms back. "I'm sorry."

"No." No, she hated him, she despised him for being what she was—but she was in the dark and the blood, and touching someone, even him, helped to keep her here in the palace.

He tightened the blanket again, shielding her back with his drawn-up leg, waiting. She clung to herself, unwilling to hold to him, unable to hold nothing.

"I can't," she whispered incompletely.

"Be still," he soothed. "All is safe now. There is no hurry. Just breathe."

He was holding her, though he did not know her. He did not care for her as a lover or a friend. He was trained to cater, taught to soothe and comfort, coached in the words to say, the gestures to use, the tone to voice. All of it was false, and hollow, and better than her empty pit of blood.

She relaxed into his leg, letting him take some of her weight, and the knot in her stomach loosened. He tipped his head to the side, and she could feel his slow, measured breaths. The shivering slowed. Her gut uncoiled, and she began to breathe more evenly.

She was leaning against him. The thought came distantly to her, but she was too exhausted to move. She started to slide, and he braced her with his forearm, his hand open and loose beside her.

It was only a few minutes that they sat together in terse silence, but it seemed to drag forever, as she hated herself for letting him help her even as she wanted to stay close. She kept her eyes shut, blocking out his presence. She would be angry, so angry, when they drew apart, but for now she was desperate for any kind touch where she could pretend—

Dielo jerked backward, and she fell to the side. She caught herself on one hand.

"Get away from her!" Kayvin snarled.

Dielo was already retreating. Yovela turned, shedding blankets. She faced the prince as Dielo folded to the floor in formal apology.

The sera qadra was for the prince alone, not for outsiders and not for one another. Though nothing had happened—though nothing would happen, though there had been nothing in the touch but terror and desperation, and there had been no actual touch—the prince would be within his rights and power to punish them both.

That was not Yovela's greatest concern.

Kayvin looked between them, his eyes enlarged in the twilight. "Have you two been playing at rivals before my eyes so that I would not know—"

"No!" Yovela shook her head

"No, my lord, no," Dielo protested, his face lowered.

"No, of course not." Yovela looked at Dielo, in his alluring garb and draped with jewelry and trained to pose in this flattering and obsequious manner, and she hated him and herself. "I would never."

"Then, Dielo, did you approach her?" His voice was controlled, but angry.

Yovela had never been afraid of Kayvin, but just now she could not bear to hear any anger, and her breath caught. "N—no, my lord."

"Yovela, you have been crying."

This was the moment. This was when she could cast Dielo out forever, rid herself of his dark eyes and endless posturing, his constant plea for attention. All it would require was a word.

She did not speak.

Kayvin looked frustrated and expectant. "What happened here?"

Dielo bent low, caught between her secret and honesty. "I heard a noise, my lord, and I came to see what had happened."

"And you fell in the dark and landed in a tumble with Yovela?"

"It was me," she burst. She hated him, but she would not destroy him unjustly. "I was dreaming. A nightmare. He woke me."

This surprised Kayvin. "A nightmare?" He looked at Dielo.

Yovela could hear his skepticism, and she knew the unspoken rest of the question. *But she is cruel to you, despises you. How could you go to her?*

She pressed on before Dielo could answer more than she wanted. "He woke me, that is all. It can take a moment before I'm fully myself. That is what you saw."

Kayvin searched her eyes, and she was grateful for the poor light. What she said was the truth, as far as it went, but she did not want him to see the rest. At last he nodded.

She looked at Dielo, kneeling on the floor, and she hated him—hated him for seeing her weakness, for guessing her secrets, for keeping her privacy under Kayvin's questions and indebting her to him. She glared at him with the salvaged fury of her interrupted nightmare, and she thought she saw him flinch.

Kayvin sighed. "I need someone." There was just an edge of reproof in his voice, but it was the closest he would come now that he believed her. "I've finished the bridge, and I want someone to take it down as I play."

"Of course, my lord," Dielo volunteered. "I'd be glad to."

He would, and then he'd be glad to take more down when they had finished with the notation, hoping to play all sorts of instruments as the night grew late. Yovela crossed her arms and despised him.

Kayvin nodded. "Come along, then. Yovela, you'll be all right? You haven't changed."

She cast her long, rumpled sleeve out of the way and nodded. "Go on. I will be fine."

She would not be fine.

CHAPTER 57

WHEN PRINCE KAYVIN HAD finished with Dielo—finished with music, for surely he was not accepting anything else—Yovela was called to him. "Will you dance?" he asked, but his expression hinted at other questions to come.

Yovela danced as he played, but her fire had burned low. She was weak and drained after the episode in the women's quarters, and she knew her dancing was barely competent. After only a moment, Kayvin stopped playing and put his instrument aside. "Come here."

Her heart sank, and she obeyed.

He pushed himself across the floor to the wall, couching himself against a pile of cushions. She followed, coiling into the space beside him, facing him to preserve a little distance.

But his expression was not that sort of expectant. "Tonight, when I found you and Dielo... Are you all right?"

She shook her head. "He told the truth. I had a nightmare."

"In the early evening."

"I fell asleep after the visit."

"In your formal clothing." His disbelief was gentle, less a challenge than an invitation to explain.

She wasn't sure she wanted to explain. "I didn't feel well, and I didn't take the time to change."

He waited, and she pressed her fingers through a silken tassel, concentrating on the texture of it against her skin. She wished for one of the sleeping furs to wrap about herself.

"What was it that troubled you?"

She shook her head. "I just didn't feel well."

"Yovela," he said in a gently chiding tone. "You despise Dielo, you torment the poor man day and night, and then I saw you weeping in his arms. Something happened."

She did not answer. Why couldn't he have forgotten this? No, of course he would not forget. But...

"Tell me." It was too soft to be a command. Nearly a plea.

"You will not want to hear it," she answered stiffly.

"I want to hear it," he assured her. "I want to know."

She looked down. When she answered, she could hardly hear her own words. "You will send me away."

"Yovela. You are the only sera qadra member I kept. Even when my father was killed by a courtesan."

And that was why she did not want to tell him. She did not want to frighten him. She did not want to lose her safe place in his sera qadra.

"Let me help. You were upset. I can't do anything about it if I don't—"

"You can't fix this!" she snapped. "You can't save—"

But she stopped herself. No matter how upset she was, she could not tell him that he could not save her any more than his mother in the ice.

But he sat still, his gaze level upon her, and she had no more excuses she could say aloud. She took a breath and looked down, avoiding the honest concern of his eyes. "I was a dancer."

He nodded. He knew this; she danced for him.

"I was born into a performing family. We had our own troupe, dancers and players and musicians, often traveling but occasionally staying in one place for the winter season."

He nodded again, letting her settle into her narrative at her own pace.

"I had a father—of course I had a father, but—my father was... He began to come to me, at night. I did not like it, but what could I do?"

Kayvin's eyes widened. "Did you not ask for help?"

Hot anger flared within her. "Do you think I never wanted help? But he was the leader of our troupe. I tried once to tell, but she thought I was carrying tales because I was angry at something else. My stepmother knew—I could see in the way she looked at me, in the way she would be angry at me in the mornings. How could I ask her for help when she knew and only despised me?"

He did not answer.

"So this continued until I felt the egg coming on. We were wintering on the outskirts of a large town, and I built an egg stand in the little house we were staying in."

She had crafted it of mud and straw, uncertain of her technique but trying again and again until she had a functional stand. The storeroom would be barely warm enough in the winter months, so she built the stand wide and low, with thick mud walls to hold the heat she would add while she was away for practice and performances and a deep hollow to keep the egg secure beneath its thatch covering.

Kayvin looked unhappy. "I never knew you had a child."

The words burned her like acid, and she did not answer.

"Were you afraid? When your egg came?"

"I did everything I could," she said. "I hugged it with my own body heat. I put embers in the mud stand. I found one last hake flower out of season, and I picked my own river stone. And I planned."

She'd planned to give her child all that she did not have—choices, freedom, safety. She would take her child and leave the troupe, would find new work far away from nighttime visits.

"Planned for what?"

"I planned to go away." She did not want to tell him. She did not want to say this, to expose a wound more tender even than her father's appetites, a failure worse than her failure to protect herself. "But they did not want me to keep the child."

It would be difficult to care for a child as she worked. She knew this, but she was a good dancer, often earning extra coins when the troupe performed, and she would find a way. She repaired a wide scarf into a sling for after the hatching. Again and again she refused to give up the egg, no matter how her father and stepmother shouted or pleaded.

She made promise after promise as she cleaned it or warmed it or simply held it. She would be a good mother. She would keep her child safe, protected from all harm. She would be all that she'd wanted and not had, and she would make herself better for her child's sake.

"So you did not." Kayvin's soft voice startled her.

"What?"

"You did not keep the child."

How had she ever thought he might understand? Rage and frustration boiled within her, fury at him and at herself. "No."

She had told no one else of the egg, but once her child hatched, there would be questions, they argued, and it was unfair of her to sabotage her father's reputation. She was a whore and he had responsibilities to the entire troupe, didn't she realize, and she shouldn't risk the others' livelihood by drawing aspersions on their troupe, that would be selfish.

She came back from a performance, weary, clutching coins tossed to her though others thought she should share them amongst the troupe. She had saved so much now—not enough to spare, it would not be easy, but she thought she could go out on her own soon and without so much fear. It would be only another couple of weeks.

But when she went into the storeroom, someone was there, standing over the egg stand. The straw covering about the egg stand was scattered. The stand itself was cracked, dried mud flaking like chaff, and her egg...

Her stepmother raised the axe again and brought it down. The egg collapsed further, thick yolk stringing over the side of the broken stand. In the basin of the remaining shell lay a small, dark lump in a slowly diminishing pool.

Yovela screamed and rushed forward, and her father caught her. His grip was scalding iron on her arms. "It has to be done, Yovela."

"No!" She writhed and kicked at him.

"Yovela!" Her stepmother shouted at her as if she were an unreasonable child demanding a sweet. "People would know, and they would think ill of your father. And you cannot raise a child. How could you dance with an infant strapped to you? Or do you expect us to watch your child for you?"

"Did you give him up?" Kayvin pressed gently.

"He—he died."

In the storeroom, Yovela drove her teeth into her father's wrist, and as he yowled she twisted away. Her dancer's legs carried her across the room and under the next swing, where she caught the haft of the axe and wrenched it free with a quick sidestep.

"I'm so sorry," Kayvin said, beside her on the pillows.

But Yovela gave a little shake of her head. "My stepmother killed him. She smashed the egg."

Kayvin's mouth opened silently.

"They would have known!" her stepmother explained furiously. "They would know what he did. There would be no hiding it with his child in plain sight."

"Think, girl!" he roared behind her. "You know this is for the best, for the troupe and for you!"

Yovela did not know if what she remembered was what had happened, or only what she imagined afterward to be what must have happened. She could not be sure how many times she struck, or if she had truly pursued a crawling form through the storeroom door and into the little yard behind the house until it crawled no more.

She remembered clearly sitting between the three corpses, sobbing. Then she moved to gather up the contents of the egg, cradling the broken incomplete form, trying irrationally to scoop the precious golden yolk together, keening her disbelief and loss.

She remembered clearly hearing her father's voice. Remembered her blood going freshly cold. Remembered his weak movement, defying death, and his call for help. Remembered looking at her child, who had to die to protect his reputation. Remembered getting to her feet as he began to curse her and taking up the axe once more with numb fingers.

"And then I killed my father."

Remembered his terror when he saw Yovela take a step forward.

Yovela sat unmoving, hardly breathing, caught as if the events were happening to her once more.

"Yovela?" Kayvin touched her arm. The contact made her jump as if their skin had sparked. She looked down at his hand and then to his face.

There were tears in his eyes. "I'm so sorry," he whispered. "I'm so sorry that no one came. That no one fought for you."

This was sympathy too late, good for nothing but weakening her to the memories. She shook her head. "I left that night. I went to another city where we had never performed. I looked for work, but there were few positions for a lone dancer." Especially not for one with hollowed eyes from never sleeping through the night and a terror of every city guard or street performer who came by.

"What did you do?"

She had done the work her father had prepared her for. It usually paid, and she was what he had made her, after all. "I found a manager."

But she had clung to her dance, practicing it to salve her soul and scrub out the memory of the work she did. Through it all, she danced.

"Then a procurer spoke with my manager, looking for young women for the palace. He wanted to see me dance."

He'd wanted to test her, and she was no more than she had always been. But then he wanted to see her dance, and she danced for him and the entire tavern. She had danced her story, danced the hidden visits and the shame, danced her hope for escape with her child, danced her fury at their betrayal and the horror of the murder. She danced her revenge, danced its shallow, meaningless victory, danced her despair, danced her plea. She danced her story, confessing all without words and pleading for absolution or aid.

The man understood nothing but that she was beautiful and talented and could be worth a great deal of money at the palace.

"And so I came to your sera qadra." She looked toward him, not meeting his eyes. "And now you know what I am, a whore and a murderer and nothing fit for a prince."

He was silent, and that silence sliced her keenly. He had cleared his sera qadra when his father's courtesan had killed; how much more readily would he do it again when it was his own? He would be right to fear. He could get anyone to sing his music. He owed her nothing.

But there were still tears in his eyes as he shook his head. "If you were tried in a court of law," he said, "an honest judge would not call what you have done murder, or at least not murder in cold blood. If somehow a conviction were brought, I would intervene with a pardon." He shook his head, his face drawn tight. "They killed your child."

She wept.

Kayvin opened his arms, and she moved into him, sheltering into his embrace that asked nothing. It was the way Dielo had held her as she shook off the waking nightmare. It was a way she had never been held by any man until today.

"I'm sorry," she said thickly, and she could not have explained why. She was sorry for bringing the story into his princely quarters, for not telling him and for telling him, for leaning against him now without offering herself as payment for the warmth and strength he provided.

Dielo had also sat with her, and she had owed him nothing. Prince Kayvin could take his payment at any time; Dielo could never. Dielo, whom she despised for permitting and embracing to himself all that had been done to her, had held her in her distress for nothing at all.

How she hated him.

CHAPTER 58

MORNING LIGHT SLANTED THROUGH the windows, slipping over the lip of the sleeping pit and painting warm streaks across Yovela's arm. Still she did not move. If she lay still, if she refused to get up, then perhaps the previous day would fade from memory into misty nightmare.

She had broken apart, and in the most terrifyingly visible ways, and before the people from whom she needed most to hide her shame. She had cracked and cried before Dielo—Dielo, whom she despised, who had not only seen her helplessness but aided her through it—and then she had confessed her guilty story to Kayvin, the Amethyst Prince, her protector, who must believe the best of her if she would stay safe in his apartments. She had come apart, for the first time in a long time, and she had revealed her worst secrets to the man she liked and the man she loathed.

If Kayvin sent her away, as he had sent away the others, she would understand. She would more than understand.

And Dielo... She did not pretend she had been kind to him. He was everything she hated, about herself and about those who had made her what she was. And now she had given him the weapons that pierced her the deepest. If Kayvin somehow did not send her away, Dielo would make her life a living hell.

As long as she remained in the sleeping pit, she could wish that she had dreamed it all, and she did not have to face either of them.

The sun slid along her arm, warming first her elbow and then her shoulder. It touched her neck. It nudged toward her chin.

A brush of skin on wood or stone came from the door, and the pit walls seemed to close about her. Someone had come.

"Excuse me." It was Dielo's voice, and her heart sank even further. Was this worse than Kayvin? She wasn't sure which of them she feared more to face.

The footsteps came closer. They seemed curiously obvious; she wondered whether she was too sensitive to his approach or whether he was scuffing slightly to alert her to his presence.

"Yovela? I've brought you something."

She must look terrible—her eyes red and puffy, her face streaked, her hair tangled, her robe and blankets in disarray, and not in the artful disarrangement he could readily manage. She would be vulnerable anew.

"Yovela? Here's breakfast." Dielo squatted low, and he looked across the pit rather than down at her. "May I bring it down to you?"

It was an over-formal request. Her sleeping pit was not so deep as the prince's, and Dielo might have stepped down easily with the tray if his balance were good, as it surely was. She pushed herself up and ran a hand through her dark hair, pulling it back from her face.

He seemed to take this for assent, and he sat on the lip of the pit, legs dangling, and lowered the footed tray. It looked familiar, with a pitcher and a plate of cut fruit, arranged neatly. "This is the prince's breakfast," she realized dully. "Did you bring me His Highness's breakfast?"

"No, no," he said quickly, but without defense. "I made two. His includes his medicine."

It had been arranged with care, a spiraling spray of petals cut from fruit. Dielo had prepared the breakfast ordered by the physicians against the blood poison in the prince's arm, and then he had made this for her, and he had arranged it as carefully.

Despite herself, her chest constricted. It didn't matter that it had surely been only habit and training—it felt like an act of kindness, and it cut her. Tears burned her eyes, and rage at those tears burned her lungs.

"I did not know if you'd want to go for your breakfast this morning," Dielo explained in a softly neutral tone. "I asked His Highness if I might bring you a tray, in case you wanted to sleep in or take some time to yourself."

Empty void, they had talked. About her.

But Dielo had brought her a breakfast tray.

She realized he was gently addressing the opposite wall of the sleeping pit rather than her, and he had not stepped down to deliver the footed tray. His infuriating caution drove her to greater anger. How dare he pretend that this meant nothing, that he did not know the advantage he now held, that he was merely being considerate of her—

"Why?" she blurted hotly, and immediately she was horrified by the word. She shifted quickly to cover the slip. "What do you think this will win you? Will he think more of you for making nice at me?"

Dielo pressed his lips together and kept his eyes on the far side. "I thought yesterday must have been difficult for you. That is all." His throat moved, and then his voice dropped slightly. "But you might not understand that."

"What wouldn't I understand?" she demanded, hating how strident she sounded and unable to stop herself.

Dielo's eyes dropped, and his voice lowered to a near whisper. "You so plainly hate me."

Empty void. It was true, yes, but she had never meant for it to be said aloud.

For a moment she did not know whether to deny it uselessly or to savagely confirm it. She bit her tongue until she thought it might bleed, and then she took a breath and tried to be both reasonable and honest. "It is not you I hate. It is what you are, what you have let them do to you."

"Them?"

She gestured, encompassing Dielo, the room, Pasiphae Jade's wing, the palace, the world.

His expression showed he did not understand.

Of course he didn't understand. The words came boiling to her mouth, bursting into the air. "I resent what they did, and you believed in it."

He stared at her, surprised. "Believed?"

"I know better than to expect something I'll never have. But you, you give everything you have and more, all for the lie that it will make someone care for you." She gulped, too far in to stop now. "They'll never love a market trinket! I at least knew that, and knew what I was. But which is worse, to know there's no hope, or to wish for something that will never come? Maybe you think it's better to hope, even if you hope in vain. But for that, you lie to yourself every morning."

The words burned her. Such words were never meant to be said aloud. These words were broken glass, dangerous when held and dangerous when spilled.

Dielo's wide eyes remained on her, his face still in silent shock or affront or horror.

She had gone too far. "I'm sorry," she managed. "That was poor thanks for a plate of fruit."

He shook his head slowly, looking away from her again.

She waited, but he said nothing. Frustration swelled in her again, anger at him for his silence and at herself for her speech and at the world beyond for everything else. "Well? You're not going to say anything to all that?"

He shook his head again. "You are still upset, and justly so. I will not argue with you while you're upset."

He said it so evenly and softly, without judgment or reproof, and it was so level-headed and so peaceful that it made her rage flare anew. "You let them use you and discard you. You let them, and you're grateful for it! My state of mind does not change whether that is true."

"You deny that there is love."

"There is no love! There is perhaps affection, yes, at times—but not love. Love sacrifices! Love thinks of the other before oneself, and when will someone holding your chit put your needs before their own?"

Dielo smiled patiently. "Their needs are always before mine; they are the head, and I am the—"

"We know what you are," she interrupted savagely. "And that is something any two dogs in the street can do. That is not love."

"Love may look different in different roles. My master has a role of responsibility, and I have the role of support and encouragement. Physical pleasure is a part of our role, of course, but we also provide respite, and entertainment, and refuge from the difficulties of the world."

She had goaded him into replying after all. "And if this is all for the gift of relieving the pressures of life," Yovela asked curtly, "why do you serve the wealthiest?"

"We help those who face the greatest challenges, those who order business or govern. The greatest—"

"A woman hoeing cabbages fifteen hours a day, or a man hauling heavy water until he's at the point of collapse, to earn enough coin to feed crying children in a tumbledown hut—surely these might benefit from some tenderness. When they must choose between buying bread for a sick child or paying the rent on their leaky shack, they surely deserve entertainment to distract them from the cares of life and their difficult decisions," Yovela said sourly. "Surely these suffer more than a courtier who has left his estates to a steward and is playing for advantage by shuffling seats at royal banquets. Why don't you put their heads in your lap, and stroke their hair, and sing them songs?"

Dielo's mouth twitched, but he did not answer aloud.

"They took your whole life from you, and they taught you to want to please them."

"I was tested," Dielo said quickly. "My parents were so proud when I was identified. I had always been helpful, one of those children who likes to assist and always quick with a hug and a kiss when someone was upset. That was what first started them speaking of it. And then when I was in consideration, I was given pictures of sera qadra men and women in court finery, and I was asked which were beautiful. I told the selectors both the men and the women were beautiful."

Yovela rolled her eyes. "A child. You were a child, shown shiny baubles."

"The man who showed me the pictures was a trained virilo, able to recognize signs you would know nothing of—"

"A man anxious to deny what had been done to him and what he did to others, who dared not upset the weight of a whole *industry* or speak against the ranks of his community."

Dielo's lips thinned, and at last his tone sharpened. "You are angry, and hurt, and you speak in ignorance. It is natural to feel jealousy of status, comfort, prestige."

"They taught you that, too," snapped Yovela. Her words tasted like poison. "They taught you to divide the world and consider others too different to understand, lest you recognize yourself in me. Do you think your decisions were your own? That you were not shown bright baubles to grasp at?"

Dielo stared straight ahead.

Tears rose in Yovela's eyes, not of sorrow but of frustration. Nothing she could say would matter. She would not be understood, she would not be believed. Everything would persist as it was, and no matter how great her anger, she could change nothing—not for herself, and not for anyone else. The anger swelled and rose and burst from her in hot tears, and she hated herself for letting them free, for they would be seen not as fury but as weakness.

But she *was* weak. She could change nothing. It did not matter if Dielo saw that; he already knew. He was a cog in the great milling machinery, not caring if the gears ground around him and over him as long as he was safely in the mill and not abandoned on the roadside.

He looked at her, and she loathed him for his patient expression, his brown-eyed concern, his distress at her tears despite his dismissal of their cause.

But when he spoke, the poison with which they had filled him spilled out. "We are not rivals for his affection."

Fury took her. "That is right—we are not rivals. I do not want to tempt him away from who he is. You, however, are meaningless without him. Worthless. And that is why you'll do anything, tolerate anything, give up anything."

His jaw hardened, and his mouth compressed into a line. She wanted him to shout back, to fight anything, even her, if it meant he would fight at all—but he said nothing.

"You still think we're different," she spat at him. "But only in what we know. They used me more quickly, and they did not pretend I am anything but a crumpled flower, a soiled and discarded rag. It was cruel, but it was the truth." She choked. "That's the difference between us. They told me exactly what I was, but they lied to you."

Dielo slid from the edge of the pit onto the blankets below, and her heart jerked in its race. He turned on one knee to face her, and she recoiled against the wall of the pit, trapped before his anger and regretting that she had said too much. But his hands did not rise to strike her, only caught her clenched fingers and folded warm over them.

"They lied to us both," he whispered, his voice urgent. "You are not discarded refuse. They lied to take your hope, and they were wrong about you."

For a moment Yovela could not breathe. She tried to stare at him, but she could not meet his eyes, too close, too concerned.

"Look at you," she sobbed, her eyes on their folded hands. "Look at you. Even after all this, you still comfort. You're still quick when you see someone upset."

Dielo sank a little over his knee to catch her lowered eyes, and he offered a small, tentative smile. "What is that supposed to mean?"

She shook her head. "It means they didn't have to lie to you to make you kind."

Dielo did not move, but his smile wavered.

Yovela squeezed her eyes shut so she would not see the desperately hopeful boy inside that wavering smile. "Imagine what you could have done for others, if you'd chosen yourself to help them."

Dielo's hands slipped away from hers, leaving them cold and unshielded. She heard the soft scuff of his stepping out of the pit. She sat for a long moment, feeling as if she had very nearly caught a rope tossed into the sea and her fingertips had slipped across it, and now it was twisting away in a current and she would not come across it again.

CHAPTER 59

YOVELA WAS STILL CRYING quietly when Prince Kayvin came. She looked up with a little catch of breath as he crouched at the far edge of the pit, and she hurriedly wiped her face with her hands. "Your Highness."

"Yovela." The word—her name—was so much more tender than she had expected, and it nearly started her sobbing again. But he continued, "Did Dielo do something today?"

Dielo had believed and perpetuated—but that was not today's work, and she could not explain her despair anyway, and so she shook her head. Then she sucked a bracing breath. "I know my lord did not want to keep a sera qadra he could not trust. With my—"

"I want you to stay," he said firmly. "Unless you prefer to leave. But do not put words in my mouth."

She hesitated, surprised and hardly daring to hope against the expectation she had braced for hours to hear.

He extended a hand into the pit, offering to help her up, and without thinking she took it. He drew her upright and onto the floor.

"I want to apologize," he said, and it was something she had not expected a prince to say. "I should not have pressed you to explain anything last night. I was worried—I was afraid something had happened, and I wanted... But I should not have insisted, and not while you were so shaken. I'm sorry."

She shook her head quickly. "You have every right—a prince should know who is in his apartments, and—"

"I need only to know if you are a threat to me," he interrupted, "or to others in my household. I don't believe you are. That should be enough."

It should be. And yet...

She sniffed and nodded once. "Thank you." She wasn't sure exactly what she meant by it, whether she thanked him for the apology or the trust or something else, but it was something to say that was not wholly out of place.

He still held her hand. Kayvin looked down at it, and he did not look up again. After a moment he said, "Of course I'm upset by what you told me. What happened—what was done to you—was horrific. And, I should be upset at what you did as well."

This was what she had feared.

"But this year, this year I have seen my father killed, I have seen my mother imprisoned, I have seen my sole supporter executed at a banquet, and I have felt myself helpless to avenge them or to right the upset of my kingdom. I have lost my place to a murderer. And I find myself wishing—I don't wish for murder among my people, of course not. But no one else defended you or your child." He drew a shaky breath. "I wish I could have defended my mother or Lord Narrim, even by violence if I had to."

"You know I killed. Deliberately."

"And I hope if I came upon someone harming a child, I would do whatever was necessary to stop it. You were too late to stop it, but you did not kill for your own profit. I think that is different."

She nodded slowly, agreeing because he was her prince and she was too exhausted for decisions.

"And Dielo," he said after a moment. He still held her hand. "I know you don't like him, but—is there anything else? Has he done anything?" He looked at her closely. "He asked if he could bring you breakfast. I agreed, to let him betray himself if he meant to pressure you in some way. You can tell me if he's said or done something."

She closed her eyes and shook her head.

"He's not threatening you in some way, to keep your silence?"

She sniffed a sad little laugh. "You already have my secret. What else could he threaten?" She opened her eyes and shook her head again. "He meant to be kind."

"Meant to be?"

"He cannot help what he is."

And that was kind, she realized, even beneath the years and layers of obsequious compliance put upon him. That broke her heart a little further, but what was a little more heartbreak today?

Kayvin took her hand again and gently brushed her cheek, wiping her tears more completely and more carefully than her own anxious attempt. "You'll tell me if something changes?"

She stood there, one hand in his, his other hand light upon her face, his concerned expression just above her eyes, and yet again she wanted to cry anew for reasons that were not only sorrow. "There's no reason to worry," she answered with exhausted honesty. "He may be Pasiphae Jade's creature, he may be reporting on us all, but he won't force me." She stopped with a little catch of breath. "If he—if he tells her that I..."

But no, she had told Kayvin alone of the deaths. Dielo knew only of her lurid waking nightmare. He could not report her.

Kayvin must have felt her relief. "You're all right?"

She nodded. She was upset and disoriented, leaking words about her hatred of Dielo and fearing Kayvin would send her away, but she was not in danger, not now.

Kayvin cupped her face with both his hands, looking down to hold her eyes. "I don't have much footing here," he said bluntly. "My power in the court was never what it should have been, and I was too much a fool to see that, and now I'm hardly more than an amusement for Pasiphae Jade's sycophants. But I am still the Amethyst Prince, and I will protect my own people as far as I am able. I have so few I can trust, but you, Yovela, are the nearest. Promise me you'll tell me if I fail to see you need my help."

She felt a small, warm smile blossom in her chest and reflect on her face. "I will serve you ever, my lord."

He released her, but the warm connection remained. "Come with me again when I go back to Sayinia—with me, this time, not following. I would be glad of your help."

"Of course, my lord."

CHAPTER 60

DIELO SAT IN HIS sleeping pit, his arms folded across his knees, his back to the wall. He did not want to sit here in the pit, but he had nowhere else he could think of as his own, and at least the sera qadra men's quarters were still empty.

Yovela was wounded. He had seen similar wounds before. He knew her distress, if not the details, and so he had brought her breakfast despite her disdain for him.

He had not expected the gesture to make them friends. At best, she might be kinder if she did not worry that he meant to use her betraying episode against her. Competition within a sera qadra could be vicious, and he did not know if she expected that of him, but he could demonstrate that it wasn't in him. That was the most he could have expected, if he'd thought to justify his action.

He had not thought the breakfast would make them friends. But he had not expected the burst of honesty, cold and unvarnished.

He had not expected that she would strip the stories from his calling so brutally.

Maybe it's better to hope, even if you hope in vain. But for that, you lie to yourself every morning.

Hope did lead him—as he dressed, as he sang, as he chose furnishings and foods, as he ventured another offer to read to his tired prince.

Was hope so wrong?

They taught you to divide the world and consider others too different to understand, lest you recognize yourself in me. Do you think your decisions were your own?

That indictment sat uncomfortably near to his memories. He had been warned again and again to keep apart from the common courtesans, from the other servants, from the populace, from anyone who was not of their training or not in their lord's household. They had been warned others would try in jealousy to corrupt their purpose and distract them from their tasks.

And they were never to question that purpose, for they had been chosen above the others who could not hope to such achievement or honor.

Your parents are so proud to have you in training. You will be so useful here, so much more worthy. We will teach you how to be wanted. This path leads to prestige, as you are so different from the others, and there may be love, you might find love, you will do what others cannot and you may be loved.

"I help them," Dielo whispered stubbornly. Yovela was so full of judgment and disdain—her words were twisted, born of hate. So many voices, from his father to his selector to his instructors to his fellow students, could not all be wrong. *I help them. They appreciate me, even when they cannot express it. I am costly because I have worth. I am valuable to them.*

In his mind, her face still tear-stained but her expression firm, Yovela snorted. *You are costly because you have a price. You are worth only what you make them feel.*

Even to ask the question was too near rebellion. But the angry sera qadra woman could ask it, if only in his mind, and it would not be wrong to find an answer to refute her, would it?

Prince Kayvin would not have an answer for him. Nor could he ask any courtesan who was not a virilo, whose answer would be tainted by jealousy. He might have asked his tutors, but they would have been angry with him for questioning their emphatic teaching, and anyway he had come to the palace now and was on his own. He could ask another virilo, but he dared not question before Riolo or another who might disdain his weakness.

There was only one in the palace who might answer him, only one who had nothing to conceal, one who had risen to power herself through serving the great. She was not kind, but that meant she would not spare him through gentle dishonesty. She had already spoken bluntly about their roles. And though she was not a virilo, she could hold no jealousy of him, being now the Arch Potentate.

He set a jeweled ear cuff to catch the eye, checked his clothing and his face, and went to the royal quarters.

It was bold to assume he might have an audience, but the Arch Potentate was anxious for word of her prince as she fretted with the delay of his mission. Dielo was admitted to her study after only a short wait.

"Come here, Dielo," she called, gesturing to her side, and her welcome was so unexpected and refreshing that he found himself gratefully sitting beside her chair, leaning close, thinking traitorously of how Prince Kayvin had so rarely placed Dielo beside him. "Tell me what report you bring."

He had to provide some information on the prince; he could not admit he had come only to beg answers about their service to the powerful. "He has sent his servant Nala to her family, so that is another gone from his apartments."

"Nala?"

"The girl who..." At a loss, he indicated his left eye.

"Oh, yes." Pasiphae Jade kept one hand flipping pages on her desk. "So much for protecting his people." She sniffed a delicate laugh. "And is he making better use of his extra time to prepare for Sayinia?"

Dielo's anger burned—how little she thought of destroying the girl, whose name she did not even know—but he swallowed the emotion as he had practiced, presenting the appropriate patient demeanor. "Nala asked to go home. He honored her wish."

Pasiphae Jade nodded once. "And Sayinia?"

"He has been studying history and culture, hoping to blend in more effectively the next time. He reads constantly." He hesitated only a heartbeat before adding, "I have been helping him in his study, so I know his focus."

"How diligent of you. And can you thus give me more specific information?"

He listed a half dozen titles, an honest answer but a boring one.

The tedium irritated her. "Enough! I understand. He's very scholarly." She sniffed. "He has to occupy his time with something, I suppose, if not with you."

It was a crude opening, but it was an opening. "I have done my best," he offered, as if embarrassed. He made his tone hurt and confused, to hide the hurt and confusion in his heart. "He is not like other men."

She laughed.

Dielo looked at Pasiphae Jade, a woman who had risen through pleasure to the throne, and he took his courage in his hands. "You once said we do not serve for pleasure, but for power."

"Or both," she agreed. "Certainly pleasure is there—but power can seem a greater pleasure."

He waited.

"What has you worried, Dielo?"

Yovela had said others had steered him, that his choices were not his own. "What power was there in selecting me to be a virilo?"

She laughed. "Oh, there is so much you don't see," she said. "There is power in naming your own people to be special. A woman afraid of being helpless might gladly believe she has a kind of power in being desired. A man will choose belief that he is part of an elite over belief that he is ordinary. And anyone might justify what they do to others with a story."

He shook his head. "But my parents had no such story to tell."

For a moment, she almost looked sad. "Oh, Dielo. Do you think there was no power in having a child chosen? That there was no sense of achievement in being known beyond other parents, for being called brave?"

He remembered how proud they had been, how eagerly they had announced his selection, how they had shared his new status. They had been paid not only in coin, but in prestige.

He was not special. That was a lie they told—his parents for status and payment, his selector for recognition, his instructors for importance and profit, his fellow virilos for confidence and respect.

Himself, to pretend to worth.

Pasiphae Jade must have seen the recognition of truth flicker in his expression, and for just a moment she looked on him with pity. "Oh, Dielo," she said, and her voice was softer. "It doesn't matter. You can still have the jewels, the warm sleeping pit, the pretense. Don't think about it too much—just enjoy the privileges it has brought you, and make the most of your time."

He nodded obediently. Then he realized what he had done.

She laughed, and the pity was gone. "Now get back and find what hooks will land. You've had the finest training. Use it, or I'll pull your chit and find someone more effective."

CHAPTER 61

KAYVIN HAD NEVER GUESSED how anxious he might be to leave the palace, but after two weeks of chafing, he was almost relieved when Pasiphae Jade sent a brief note: "Magoran is driven off and no longer a threat. Proceed. Remember what is necessary for your people."

He spoke to Yovela, who would not need to sneak after him this time, and determined to leave in the morning.

He wondered, restless in his sleeping pit, why he hadn't thought to ask Dielo to come as well. But immediately his stomach clenched, and he rejected the idea.

There were multiple reasons why Dielo should be left behind. The most obvious was that he was such an artificial creature, a luxury more fit for the palace than the road. Kayvin had struggled in his first weeks alone in the Sayinian towns, and the image of Dielo trying to arrange cushions and scented incense in a greasy tavern was both comical and disastrous.

And then... Kayvin could not forget that Dielo was Pasiphae Jade's virilo, not his. She had chosen him, she held his chit, and she had gone to great lengths to place him in Kayvin's household. If Kayvin did find an amulet, or several, it would be to Pasiphae Jade's advantage to have someone who could quietly knife the inconvenient prince as he slept and carry back the amulets without condition.

No, he would leave Dielo safely behind. Yovela had been not only a commoner but a traveler before she entered the sera qadra, and she would be excellent help as well as a friend.

So in the morning he bade Dielo a kind farewell and left the palace with Yovela. They were escorted through the city and across the initial roads, and the guard left them once they were into the empty eastern foothills.

The land here was better suited for grazing than farming, and there were few villages thriving in modern times, now that the roads were less used. Kayvin thought it was probably a mild insult that the escort turned back before they reached the passage, but he did not mind. It felt good to be out of the palace, and he was anxious for the false freedom he'd feel once alone with Yovela and out of sight of all imperial spies.

They were making good time, heading west and gradually ascending. The breeze came mostly from straight ahead, but the occasional shift brought a scent of rot. Yovela wrinkled her nose. "Dead livestock, I suppose. Something large, anyway."

"Probably left by the magoran," Kayvin agreed. "I'm glad it's moved on, or been driven on. I never thought to hear of one so low in the mountains in these days."

"The paintings are enough for me," Yovela said. "Terrifying beasts. I'd be happy never to see one."

"Well, you're in luck, because Pasiphae Jade was clear she wouldn't let me out while this one was a threat, so it must be long gone by now. Probably moved northwest, if it likes livestock. There's a traditional pasturing range up in the high valleys. But maybe it doesn't prefer livestock." Kayvin paused. "What's that on the hillside, just there?"

Yovela put her hand up to shade her eyes. "I think it's a person. Injured, or dead."

Without speaking further, they left the road and began to pick their way up the hill. Kayvin didn't know what they would do if they found him dead—they couldn't carry him back to the last village for burial, could they?—and he didn't know what they'd do if they found him alive but injured, with neither of them skilled healers, but if necessary he thought they could carry word to a nearby town. It felt wrong to pass by without even looking.

But the man was dead. Decidedly dead, for a few days at least. He was in armor, and sprawled headfirst down the hillside, and his water bag lay in a clump of vegetation twenty paces behind him.

"Where did he come from?" Yovela asked. "So far from..."

The breeze shifted again, and the scent returned, stronger. It did not come only from the dead soldier. With a clench of fear, Kayvin hurried up the remaining climb to the crest of the hill.

The opposite slope descended into a basin littered with bodies. Most had been stripped of armor and weapons. Some had been finished where they lay.

"Empty void," breathed Yovela, her hand to her mouth in horror and to block the foul air. "What happened here?"

A battle, obviously—but who, and why? Kayvin went down a little way, looking right and left. There were maybe four dozen dead, mostly in similar clothing with a rust-brown tunic identifying them as a cohesive organized unit. These weren't bandits or angry farmers.

There was a body near him with one arm still wrapped about a pole—a banner carrier, holding his charge until the end. Kayvin stepped close and gingerly worked the banner from beneath a corpse, drawing it across the dusty ground to spread free.

The banner depicted a four-legged beast with a tasseled tail and a long neck that arched in an improbably dramatic pose. Fangs showed in its open mouth, and one clawed foot stretched forward as if striking an invisible foe.

"Magoran," breathed Kayvin. The significance struck him like a blow, and he stepped backward as if he might sink to the soiled ground.

Yovela hurried to him, catching his arm though he swayed only a little. "What is it?"

He pointed at the magoran banner. "These are Westmarch fighters, in the service of Lord Calsar. The magoran is his emblem. There was no beast here—this was a rebellion. Pasiphae Jade kept me in the palace until it was flattened."

Yovela's fingers tightened on his arm. "Then—there was a rebellion. Some are resisting the new Arch Potentate."

"Or were," he said heavily. He gestured to the garbage dump of dead Rideis. "She would not let me come here unsupervised if I could still be a figurehead."

So many dead. Kayvin's stomach roiled.

He would bring the amulets, for his mother and for Nala and for the others Pasiphae Jade could reach. He would do as she demanded, and he would hate and resent her. But he would not ask others to die for him.

"Should we say something?" Yovela asked quietly.

Kayvin shook his head slowly. "No words of mine can sanctify this ground more than their lives."

Yovela squeezed his arm.

"They didn't know me." He made a savage, curt gesture to encompass the dead. "These soldiers never swore loyalty to me. They had only served a lord who was not favored by Pasiphae Jade and who saw political opportunity in recovering the Bull Throne for the Amethyst Prince."

"Or for himself," Yovela said practically.

Kayvin blew out a breath and wiped weak tears from his eyes. So many dead, and they could not even say whose cause they had died for.

Yovela's cheeks were wet, though she made no sound. She tugged Kayvin's arm. "Let's go."

"But..." It felt wrong to walk away. "We should—"

"The villages know," she said in a low, quick tone. "There was a battle. They saw the survivors and the deserters. They know. If these are here, it is because they are not allowed to collect the dead. That's common with rebellions. If you go into a village and ask them to act, you put them at risk."

Kayvin stared at her.

"Come on." She tugged him back over the hill.

Stability—that was the most crucial thing. His throne did not matter—he was only one person, and he was not well-equipped to make a good prince. Stability mattered, so that no more would die, no more would be pressed into spying or serving, no more would be sent over the mountains, no more would be disfigured or beaten. He would bring the amulets, redeem his mother, and swear to Pasiphae Jade that the Bull Throne was hers, uncontested.

It was terrible to know the exact moment he conceded all to Pasiphae Jade, when she was miles and miles away while he stumbled down a windy hillside, blinking dust and shame from his eyes.

CHAPTER 62

THE ROYAL CHAMBERS, NOW possessed by Pasiphae Jade, were opposite Prince Kayvin's quarters on the far side of the palace. This gave Dielo ample time on the long walk to consider how incredibly stupid his plan was.

There were two possibilities—well, three, but he was certain he didn't have the courage for at least one of them. The first was that he might go to Pasiphae Jade and ask her for his chit, the figurine that represented him and his particular training, and that bound his service.

No, his ownership. For all her vitriol, Yovela was right that he had not made the choices he had been told he made.

But even if she were still here, he could not ask Yovela for help. Her disdain, her disgust, thick enough to color the air as she spoke, meant that she would not aid him with so much as an encouraging word—not unless he admitted his gullibility and gave up what shreds of dignity he had remaining, even more precious now in their scarcity. He was on his own to find a way out.

So, again, his choices. He clenched his fists and set aside Yovela's disdain, screwing down his focus to the task at hand. He could go to Pasiphae Jade and ask her for his chit, which he could then present to Prince Kayvin to make true his service to the Amethyst Prince and not the Arch Potentate. Then she could not take him from the prince, as she had hinted, when she tired of his continued failure.

This plan carried two possible downfalls. If Pasiphae Jade refused him, he would be unable to counter the brutal truth of Yovela's caustic allegations that he was a common slave and a thing rather than a person. That dark chasm yawned too wide and too terrifying to consider leaping into. He dared not give Pasiphae Jade the opportunity to refuse him his chit.

He could go to Pasiphae Jade's royal quarters and simply take the chit. This was a bold plan, though less challenging than it sounded; he was certain he as a virilo could pass into her rooms and out with minimal questioning. Others would of course remember his visit once it was noticed the chit was missing, but by that time he would be wholly Prince Kayvin's, indeed only where Pasiphae Jade had publicly directed him to serve, so she might not wish to publicly quibble. The real challenge lay not in the execution but in the decision, as taking his own chit was an act that seemed contrary to all his purpose.

And if that daunted him, then a final option remained, the simplest and the most difficult. He could, in theory, simply walk away from his chit and follow Prince Kayvin across the mountains, leaving a figurine on Pasiphae Jade's shelf but holding no attachment to it. But this lay in opposition to everything he had been taught, everything he had believed, all he had learned to treasure about himself, and the idea of casting it all away was still too much. Though he could wonder in secret, he was not yet prepared to admit in his deeds that Yovela was right. Even if she had been right, she had given him nothing to rely on as she burned the supports of his world, and he would stay in his prison tower rather than fall.

And so Dielo arrived at the Arch Potentate's apartments with only the knowledge that he had three possible paths to follow Prince Kayvin and the courage to take none of them. He stood in the corridor, confronted with the realization that he should go back to the prince's empty rooms and wait quietly. He did not have the courage to do that, either.

He stood in the corridor, useless.

He was useless to Prince Kayvin, whom he should support and serve. He was useless to Pasiphae Jade, who held his chit but wanted him only for reports that made no difference. He was useless to Yovela, who disliked and distrusted him even in her direst moments. He was useless to himself, unable to earn the regard of master or servant, merely a prop for kitchen maids.

Maybe he could change his clothes, leave his hair unset, discard the jewelry and cosmetics, and maybe he would walk out into the city as an unassuming young man with no particular talents. Maybe he could be someone else, if he were someone else.

But to walk away from everything that he was, everything that defined him, everything that gave him hope for the future...

But was that hope, or wishes?

"Have you come again?" The doorman peered at him through the doorway. "I didn't know you'd been sent for."

Dielo clenched his jaw against the subtle rebuke and made himself smile. "What virilo would wait to be sent for? Her Illustrious Excellency lent me to the Amethyst Prince while he was in residence, but now that he is away on her orders, I've returned to do what I can for her."

The doorman was not convinced, but he didn't mind seeing Dielo make a fool of himself. "Come in, then. She's in her bath."

"I'll wait."

The primary room was unoccupied, and Dielo took a seat on the dais for the Arch Potentate's reclining couch. He looked around—there was no one in the many doorways—and then he shifted over and leaned back against the couch. This was where a favored virilo would sit. This was the ambition of all. He tipped his head back against the couch, imagining someone's fingers trailing through his hair and a caress over the side of his face.

Favored, admired, envied, wanted...

But no. That wasn't to be, and he was a fool to continue wishing instead of recognizing what he had. Prince Kayvin did not want a virilo, but he desperately needed a friend and supporter. Dielo could be true to the spirit of his training by providing what was needed. It was never supposed to be about his wants, anyway.

He sat up and looked around again. No one. He could hear singing and laughing in the distance, probably from the soaking pool. He got to his feet, leaning on the reclining couch, and edged around it to the display cabinet.

A dozen or so small figurines were arranged on a shelf together. Dielo recognized Riolo at the front, but he did not know most of the others. His chit was at the far left, facing outward. The black hair, golden skin, and short kilt were crafted to identify and promote him, and it stung to look at the figure he had not seen in so long. He had not worn a kilt since the day he'd gone to Prince Kayvin.

That did not matter now. None of that mattered now. Yovela said he believed too many lies, and surely this was one. There was no one to care whether his perfect skin was marred—his duty lay in helping Prince Kayvin to find an amulet, and he did not need a kilt for that.

He pulled open the cabinet door.

There were spells on the chits, virilos knew, to help with their service. Dielo did not think any of them were binding. That magic was done with lies, repeated until they were incontrovertible.

He stared into the cabinet, and the lies piled up around him like a wall, and he could not move. Laughter came from the direction of the soaking pool.

Imagine what you could have done for others if you'd chosen yourself to help them.

Dielo reached in and took his chit. The clay was cool and dry in his hand. He closed the cabinet door—how long might it be before anyone thought to count the figures?—and retreated.

He left the apartments and passed through the corridors, trying to keep to a walk as if everything were as usual. He slipped into the prince's garden and sat beneath a trellis of trailing vines, breathing perfumed air in a tiny chamber of green.

He held his own life. For this single moment, he was his own master. Though the chit was only a symbol, the weight of it in his hand tugged at him. He was his own.

But he wasn't, not really. It was a symbol, but it symbolized all that Dielo had learned, and all that he could trust and understand. Even a virilo's prestige, now more dubious in his eyes, was more comfortable than the uncertainty of leaving the palace and knowing himself for the wretched fool that Yovela saw him as.

But he could choose his path, to some degree. He would present this chit to Prince Kayvin. Then Pasiphae Jade could not send him to another, and Dielo could prove himself a better supporter, if not a lover, and prove himself more than what they thought of him.

He would show them he was more. He would be more. As soon as Prince Kayvin returned, he would be more.

TEMPLES AND TRIALS

CHAPTER 63

GENERAL ARTEXTRA WAS A tall woman with muscular arms, and she moved as if she knew how to use the sword that hung at her side. She strode through the antechamber door as if it owed her a favor. "So who is the bright johnny who took on a Selk in single combat and outed him as a prince?"

Galen raised his hand. "That would be me, general."

She grinned. "Well, you've clearly got gonads of solid brass. I could like you. Let's see if you have any sense to go with them."

Lisveth made a tiny sound that might have been a snort. Galen ignored her.

"And who are you?" General Artextra asked, turning to Lisveth.

Lisveth jerked a thumb toward Galen. "It's fallen to me to keep this poor farm rube out of most of the trouble he gets himself into. He and I were the ones to discover the Rideis. I can't let him go on and have all the fun of chasing them back home. And—and this is no small thing—I feel there should be a significant financial reward to so risky an enterprise."

General Artextra laughed. "Your gentleman may have balls the size of summer onions, but you can match him for sheer straightforward foolhardiness."

Lisveth's expression remained neutral. "He's not my gentleman. He's his own gentleman. He can speak for himself and his onions."

"They're no one's onions," Galen retorted, before he realized how stupid that sounded. Both women looked at him, eyes crinkling in suppressed smiles.

"By all conventional wisdom," General Artextra began again, "what you claim is beyond stupid. No one sends their prince alone into enemy territory, and especially not when they've got raiders riling everyone up to look for trouble."

Lisveth nodded. "It doesn't make much sense."

"So if he really is a prince, then there's more to these bandits than the usual banditry."

"And I don't know how the amulets fit in," Galen said.

"What amulets?" the general asked.

Before Galen could answer, Lisveth laughed. "Please excuse my friend," she said with an apologetic smile. "He's actually a bay jellyfish that has lately learned to talk, and sometimes he doesn't make much sense."

Galen stared at her.

"What do you mean?" the general asked.

"He got swindled by a market peddler for an anti-Selk charm, and he hasn't admitted yet that it's a useless con." Lisveth rolled her eyes. "You can take the rube off the farm, but..."

Galen crossed his arms. He wasn't sure what Lisveth was playing at, but she didn't have to humiliate him for it, certainly not in front of the general.

General Artextra only laughed. "You're in good company, then. I'd say we have a complaint a week from an enlisted soldier, mad about a piece of junk they bought for luck in battle or protection or glory or Fortuna knows what. As if they want us to monitor what's sold in the market and check up on their own decisions. Don't worry too much about it, friend, just think twice in the future."

"Right," muttered Galen, realizing his irritation only made his supposed mistake seem more plausible and even more irritated by that.

"Regardless, you're not here for your shopping, but because you're the only people who can describe this alleged prince," Artextra continued. "So come and sit in my meeting, in case we have questions for you."

"What was that?" Galen demanded when they were left alone. "I don't mind the farm boy bit when you're teasing, but why when we have real information? And why in front of the general and her people?"

"I'm sorry," Lisveth said, hands raised in surrender. "I'm really sorry. I just couldn't think of anything else fast enough."

"You couldn't think of anything but to say that I'm gullible?"

"I was desperate for something to say, and the best lies have a bit of truth in them."

He scowled.

"I didn't mean it like that! I mean it was plausible, and even you believed it yourself once upon a time. And as you heard, it's a common mistake, so it was believable. And all that matters now is that we didn't tell her about the amulets."

He crossed his arms. "So I noticed. Is there a reason for that?"

"It came to me all at once, when she said it made no sense for the raiders to go crashing about through the country while the prince is traveling alone."

"I'm not following you."

"It's an old, old trick," she said. "A very clever man wrote about it long ago. Say you have thirty wagons in a caravan, and the only truly valuable thing they carry is a single casket full of jewels hidden in just one of the wagons. Do you take hours to search them all, risking discovery and capture before you find your prize? Or, might you simply set a fire around all the wagons?"

"And wait to see which they run to pull the casket from," Galen finished. "It's like sending a beater ahead of a hunter."

"Exactly."

"And we think Kayvin is looking for the amulets?"

"He said he was looking for something, if you recall, and he became very excited when he was unsuccessful in killing you, and he demanded something like 'Give it to me!' I think it's no far stretch to assume *it* was your amulet."

"So why aren't we telling the general this?"

"You saw that collection of noble dunderclots. If they know the Rideis are searching for the amulets, they'll go right ahead and collect them first."

"Keeping them safe?" suggested Galen.

"Putting them all in one known location," Lisveth corrected. "A far easier target for a thief than having them scattered obscurely across multiple cities."

Galen nodded. "And I suppose you think they'll be safer if they're scattered?"

"I think they'll be safer if we gather them quietly, without alerting anyone else that we're gathering them."

"Fair night." Galen stared at her. "Are you serious?"

"I don't know what those amulets really are, but I know they're powerful and I know the Rideis want them, and probably not for a friendly visit. We can put them back when we know more, but right now, we should get ahead of that invasion."

Galen chewed his lip. "Stealing an amulet to keep people from fighting over it—that sounds somewhat familiar, and look how that turned out."

"I know." Lisveth nodded gravely. "You met me."

"What does..." Galen trailed off, trying to think. "Does that make us thieves? Or heroes?"

"It depends on whom we tell, and whether they agree to pay us for our trouble." She grinned. "Don't you think the legendary amulets should have a nice ransom?"

Galen shook his head and smiled in wonder. "Every time I think you're about to do something for the greater good..."

"My comfort is a very great good," she replied. "Now let's get into that meeting."

Sitting in on the lords' and ladies' discussion was not as exciting or as much of an honor as it sounded. Anela, General Artextra's petite aide, directed Lisveth and Galen to chairs in a corner, directly behind the general and out of the way of the large table where a variety of lords, ladies, and military personnel looked sternly at one another. Lisveth pulled her hood forward over her ears and leaned back in her chair.

Galen watched the bustle of preparation and small, terse disagreements between the various assistants. It was two minutes before he realized Anela cradled her writing board with a wooden hand.

General Artextra served Lady Alberta, who looked as if the Rideis had offended her personally by daring to cross the mountains again. "I don't suppose we have any more sightings of these bandits? Or their supposed leader?"

Galen didn't think Kayvin was the leader of the bandits, given both what he'd said and the bandit's surprise at seeing Kayvin. But he wasn't sure if that would make a difference to the talks, and he was pretty sure Lady Alberta would not appreciate the interruption.

"We've collected a dozen reports of attacks and raids," Lord Bryuki supplied, "that took place both before and after the report brought to me. The path is clear, coming from the Tendertooth Hills area through here and to the northeast."

There was a brief squabble about whose responsibility it should have been to first note the invasion, whether Lord Bryuki had done right to call the local march lords together first instead of sending directly to the Octovirate, and if the Tendertooth Hills should belong to Lord Whelson, who nominally held them now, or Lord Hiske, whose family had held them two generations before but who hadn't noticed the newest invasion either. Lisveth made a noise in her throat and tipped her head back against the wall with an audible thump.

"Are we even sure we're dealing with Selks at all?" suggested a lean, pale young lord. "We have reports, yes, but from peasants and superstitious mercenaries. We're told there was a body, but did the march lord have it properly examined by anyone of authority? No, it was disposed of. And I, for one, am not going to believe the word of dull-witted farmers alone in something so serious."

"I'd be careful about calling a farmer dull-witted, my lord." Lisveth's voice sounded subtly different, and when Galen looked he saw that she wore a different face beneath curly brunette hair. "How many times did you have to sit for your civil service exam?"

The pale young lord jerked around, looking for the speaker. "Who's that? And that doesn't mean anything anyway. All of my friends had to take it at least twice. Some more."

"Mm hmm. And those were your city friends, yes? How often can a farmer fail his work entirely?"

The lord bristled and turned on Lisveth, but Alberta wrestled the topic back to practical action. "Never mind the service exams, unless they were on the handling of bandit invasions. As there's no one here who can recognize a Selk on sight, we're going to assume anyone competent would have made the same judgment from books and pictures. And now we need someone competent to decide what to do about it."

Galen leaned close to Lisveth. "What was that?"

"Easy guess," she answered with a flip of her hand. "His family's always slow on the exams. They only keep taking them to prove they haven't given up on themselves." She tugged her hood forward. "I spent a few months eavesdropping in town."

"This is not typical of their historical invasions," General Artextra was explaining at Lady Alberta's request. "Yes, they've raided before, but as an army, not in a small bandit force like this."

"Indeed, they have not typically penetrated so far into the plains before establishing their stronghold." This was a temple brother, sitting at the far end of the table near Lord Whelson.

Artextra gave him an interested glance. "That's true, as I was saying. I'm sorry, brother, but I don't think you were introduced."

"I'm Brother Lucaw. I asked to be admitted, as I've been copying archives and so had relevant history fresh to mind when news came of this bandit force. May I?"

Artextra gestured.

"Thank you. As I was saying, this is different. There has always been a pattern to their invasion." The temple brother laid his sheaf of papers on the table and began to fan them out. "Excuse me. I had to copy the relevant passages, as the scrolls are too fragile to travel and the newer ones too bulky. But I have brought what I think is necessary."

Anela rose and began to share the pages around the table, balancing them on her wooden hand and distributing with the other. Galen found her freckles incongruous with her workmanlike expression.

"A pattern?" prompted General Artextra. "How so?"

Brother Lucaw found the sheet he wanted and pointed to a particular line. "General Naneton detailed it most clearly in his field notes. The Selks first establish a camp at the base of the mountains. The exact location has varied, but it has always been within twenty leagues of the mountains. They fortify a stronghold, and then they make repeated forays into the surrounding countryside to raid for supplies, to take prisoners, and to patrol for approaching soldiers."

"And why do you think this is significant?"

He shrugged. "Strategy is your expertise, not mine. But so many of the old stories and songs talk about the Selks raiding through the plains and never reaching the capital, thanks to the valiant defense. I don't wish to disparage our valiant defense, but the records don't seem to suggest that they were ever marching upon the capital. Only that they established a camp on this side of the mountains, held it, and then eventually retreated to their homeland."

"Consistently?"

He pointed to the papers. "I have sufficient records of only three incursions, but it was true in each of the three."

General Artextra pursed her lips. "So they were raiding for supplies and prisoners, but they were not trying to take and hold additional ground—or at least they did not seem to be."

"As far as I can tell, that's correct."

"Why would they do that?" Lisveth asked.

The council turned, trying to locate the source of this new voice.

She elbowed Galen, her hood still on. He gave her a curious glance and then cleared his throat. "Uh, yes, we're the mercenaries who fought the bandits and identified the prince. And my question is this: Why would they cross the mountains every hundred years or so, establish a camp to hold at what surely must be a high cost, and then go home after a few months? How does that even make sense?"

They seemed less irritated at the question than Galen feared, perhaps because it was a good one.

Brother Lucaw shook his head. "Who can say? They aren't humans. How could one possibly know why they do what they do?"

Lisveth tipped her head to one side in careless dismissal. "I suppose we could ask them."

A nervous chuckle rose about the table.

"Negotiations aside," General Artextra said, "it seems the next step is to ready the plains for defense. We cannot afford to lose farms and farmers, not if we want to defend the cities, and if they're already coming further west this time, we can't be sure they won't try for the cities. Let's establish a line."

CHAPTER 64

"SO, ESTABLISHING A LINE," Galen said. "That sounds very much like preparing for war."

"It rather does," agreed Lisveth.

Galen felt as much curiosity as dread. He supposed that was a result of only listening to temple histories instead of living them. Or perhaps he had not yet fully understood the threat, not really. "But it's just some bandits. Not even a particularly large group, and not particularly successful. One prince, who ran away."

"Was dragged away," Lisveth reminded him. "But to be honest, I did not get the impression he was eager for war, so why does he want the amulets made for war? None of this makes sense."

"Maybe it will make more sense after noodles." Galen nodded toward a market stall.

"Noodles certainly couldn't make it more confusing." Lisveth started for the stall.

They settled with their steaming bowls near a brightly colored puppet booth. Children had gathered around, and more than a few adults had also stopped to watch the show in progress. A puppet in eye-watering green was slaying demon-shaped puppets with paper lightning bolts.

A boy in the bright colors of the puppet troupe came by, holding up a rack of small items. "Tokens and trinkets! Tokens and trinkets!" He looked at Galen. "Gift for your lady? A charm to charm?"

"We're just having noodles," Galen told him.

The boy, undeterred, turned to Lisveth. "Bracelet of bells? They're from the Vernal House." He jingled a handful of them.

She shook her head sharply, and at last he moved on.

"Do we think Kayvin is really a prince?" Galen wondered aloud. "Couldn't he be a prince of bandits, or something? Like the Fire Brigand had a title?"

Lisveth screwed up her mouth around a bite of noodles. "What did he say, exactly? The bandit he killed?"

The bottler for the puppet show circled, shaking his bottle for coins. Lisveth shook her head at him, and he moved on.

"He called him 'my lord,'" Galen remembered. "That's what started it, and you asked who Kayvin was."

"Pretty sure he said prince." Lisveth eyed Galen's bowl and reached across to spoon out the red peppers on the side.

"I think so, yes. And—heir. I think he said heir. That probably wouldn't be a bandit title, would it?"

The slim hope gone, they sat in silence but for the slurping of their noodles. Galen dipped into Lisveth's bowl for his favorite cardoon stalks which she disliked, a fair trade for the peppers she favored.

The demon puppets suddenly proliferated until they were overwhelming the mage puppet, nearly obscuring him from view.

"And then, with so many enemies, what did the Great Mage Ralston do next?" asked the storyteller.

"Golden Eye!" shouted the children in a rough unison, obviously schooled in the tale.

The half-buried mage puppet threw out his arms, and a third eye on his forehead opened in a yellow oblong. Then the puppet dropped suddenly from view and a gauzy scarf waved in his place.

"Now invisible, the Great Mage Ralston crept to the demon lord's tent." The scarf fluttered its way through the confused demons as they looked up, down, and around.

Lisveth shook her head in mock disappointment, sucking a noodle into her mouth. "Invisibility isn't really possible, but it's a children's story and I suppose anything goes."

"Come on, you make things invisible, don't you?"

"No, I make people see other things. That's different."

"It has the same effect. If you didn't want me to see this bowl of noodles, I wouldn't."

"It's a lot easier to make you think your bowl is empty, or to think you're holding a similarly sized rock, than to make you think you are holding nothing at all while you actually are."

Galen shrugged. "It's all magic to me."

The show's story continued. "And once the Great Mage Ralston was safely beneath the demon lord's bed, he waited until nightfall. When the demon had gone to bed, Mage Ralston came out with the—"

"Golden Eye!" shrieked the children in uneven chorus, too primed for their cue.

Lisveth stiffened slightly. "Golden Eye," she repeated. "Fair night, that's an amulet, isn't it."

"What? It's on his forehead."

"That's because it's a puppet show for children. But he's using it to fight demons—Selks—Rideis. It's a mage using a colored eye for war against the Rideis."

Galen nodded in agreement. "You're probably right. But it makes sense there would be stories. We even had stories in the Heel."

"And an Eye."

The mage plunged a jagged lightning bolt dagger into the demon lord puppet, who thrashed in audience-delighting macabre death throes. The mage lifted his arms in triumph, and the third eye opened and showed yellow. The watching crowd cheered, adults and children alike.

The bottler came by again, and Lisveth beckoned him to pause. Galen began to untie his purse fastening, picking slowly at the knot to give her time to ask, "Everyone seems to know this story. Is it a local history?"

He gestured to the stage. "Who, the Great Mage Ralston? You must have heard of him no matter where you're from. He's one of the great heroes, and a local hero, as you've guessed. He fought the Selks, just as the play says."

Galen drew out a coin. "And he was from this town?"

"Born and raised. Did his greatest deeds defending us. You can still see his Golden Eye on display today." He winked. "In the pawn shop. I suppose he got hard up at the end. Wouldn't be the first! But whether or not you believe in the Eye, the rest of the story's real enough." He pointed across to a side street leading away from the market. "You can't miss his mausoleum, if you want to take a look."

Galen dropped the coin into his bottle and started to fish for another, taking his time. "His mausoleum?"

"It's a bit of a sight itself, if you've an interest in such things. All carved with his deeds and such. They say he was buried with his Golden Eye and other riches—but if that were the case, that would mean the pawnbroker lies, so do with that what you will." He grinned and nodded in thanks as Galen dropped the second coin.

When the man had moved on, Lisveth took a breath. "If there's an amulet in the mausoleum..."

"We're not going to rob a grave," Galen said firmly. "If it's been buried for a couple of centuries, then it's been safe enough all this time."

"And we were able to learn its location in a few minutes at a children's puppet show. Do you think a horde of demon invaders is going to be more particular about grave robbing?"

"I've never heard of the Great Mage Ralston," Galen countered. "He could be entirely made up for the puppet show."

"Well, they probably didn't build a mausoleum to promote a puppet show," Lisveth said practically. "Let's take a look at it. If it's actually for the memory of Goodwife Pinchella, purveyor of eel pies, then that's the end of it."

The cemetery was a pleasant walk from town, warm with the sun and pretty with flowering trees. There were wooden and stone markers of varying sizes and shapes and ages, but the bottler had been right, and it was impossible to miss the great mausoleum in the center of a hillside cemetery.

The mausoleum was shaded by a large chestnut, and moss grew on the shadowed stone. The carvings were stylized but detailed, and they did not suggest a purveyor of eel pies.

"Those have a decidedly martial look," Lisveth said.

Galen nodded in reluctant agreement. "And those are Selks, or at least they resemble the traditional depictions of Selks in my temple lessons. Robes and pointed ears, and marching in groups."

"There's the Eye." Lisveth indicated a figure standing a little above the Rideis, arms extended, with a radiating eye floating just above his head. "And this Eye is not set in his forehead, though I can see why the puppeteers would choose that for effect."

"So you think Mage Ralston had an amulet."

"It seems likely."

"And you think he was buried with it."

"Do you think he hocked it for some quick cash?" She gestured. "This extravagant mausoleum is not the burial site of a pauper. Maybe he pawned the amulet to buy himself a fancy grave?"

"Maybe today's pawnbroker knows how to spin a tale. Might boost the price on an ugly brooch, I suppose. We can walk by and check it out, too." Galen walked around the mausoleum, taking in the carvings. "I don't know much about stonework, but I know this cost a small fortune. I don't feel good about breaking into it. And this door looks pretty solid for its age."

"Stop fussing. We might not need to pull him out." Lisveth held out her hand. "Give me yours, and let me try something."

She nestled Galen's amulet in the grass behind a nearby headstone. "We know it won't give a signature unless magic touches it, but it will react to magic. We just don't know the range. If I can get it to reflect back from an arm's length or two, or through stone..."

Galen crouched where he could see his amulet in the grass as she worked spells, testing if she could sense it even through the headstone. The eye stared blankly up at the sky, as if it had never blinked at them.

"There!" Lisveth gasped at last, opening her own eyes. "It's faint, but I felt a reflection." She measured out the line between her and the amulet. "Right through the stone, too."

"No blinking. Will that be enough? The mausoleum walls may be thicker than a headstone."

Lisveth waggled her head in indecision. "Well... Yes, it will be enough. But there's a sarcophagus inside that mausoleum, too, and that's a lot more stone. We'll have to be inside if I want to try with the other amulet."

"Breaking into the mausoleum?"

"But not the sarcophagus. Probably."

"Fair night," sighed Galen.

"Should be," Lisveth agreed, looking at the sky. "And as picturesque as this place is during the day, we probably don't want to risk any passersby observing our grave robbing, so let's come back then."

If the amulet was on display in the pawnbroker's shop, then they would have no need to break into the mage's grave that night, so it was easy for Galen to recall the extra errand on their way back. "Shall we stop by the pawn shop?"

"It's not going to be in a pawn shop," Lisveth repeated patiently. "But I don't mind stopping in, if it'll make you feel better."

It wasn't much of a detour, and Galen went first through the doorway. He stopped abruptly, so that Lisveth bumped into the small of his back. Though the voices had not carried into the street, the dispute at the counter was unmistakable. A man and woman were facing off, each with a hand on the long box on the counter, while another man behind the counter peered back and forth between them.

"My gran left me that, and it's not yours to sell!"

"It's not selling, it's borrowing against it, and your gran wouldn't want you to lose her field, either!"

Lisveth slid from behind Galen. After a moment she nudged him and nodded at the rear wall. Galen followed her indication.

The Golden Eye was not hard to find, once he took his eyes from the argument. A rear corner was dedicated to it, with a scripted placard and a small wall shelf and a protective inverted glass vase blurred with dust. But the dust was not enough to disguise the falsehood of the object displayed within.

It was not the mage's amulet. Galen did not need to be a sorcerer to see that; even at a distance it was too large, too round and spiky like a sunburst, and nothing at all like the eye under his own shirt.

"Gran would haunt me. You didn't even ask if you could take it!"

"You were never meant to know it was away! I would have had it back in a week or two."

The pawnbroker was looking through the dispute toward them, raising his eyebrows and opening his mouth as if he wanted to invite them in, hoping their presence might defuse the rising argument. Galen shook his head and retreated. "I'll come later," he called, thinking it was probably a lie.

"Gran might haunt them both," Lisveth muttered as they left. "Good for her."

Galen didn't answer, with the last hope for avoiding the mausoleum falling away. He had tried. Now the inevitable remained.

CHAPTER 65

GALEN STILL COULD NOT quite believe they would actually break into a mage's tomb to look for a magical amulet. It sounded so ridiculous, so like a fireside tale, nothing anyone would ever actually consider—and yet his stomach turned over and over with the thought of what they were about to do.

He told himself this was silly. Hadn't he buried corpses himself, or even carried one to Lord Bryuki's house? But that felt different somehow from disturbing one already at formal rest.

"We're not disturbing the body," Lisveth assured him. "Just entering the building it's in. We won't knock, if that helps."

"It does not."

"Then this will." She handed him a short coil of rope. "This is for the lid, if I can't get a clear finding inside."

"The lid?" he echoed incredulously. He studied her. "You're not bothered by this at all, are you?"

She shrugged. "He's been dead a long time. Old bodies don't worry me."

"If he were new?"

"The amulet wouldn't be a question." She set a tool to the door. "Okay, put your farm muscles to leverage here."

The latch snapped, and Lisveth pushed the door back, scraping along the floor. The night was fair, as Galen had unwittingly predicted, but the moonlight did not fall far within the mausoleum.

Lisveth stepped inside, slow despite her previous nonchalance, and raised her hands. "Here goes."

Galen waited, holding his breath as if it might disturb her magic. Long moments passed, and nothing happened.

"I can't sense anything," Lisveth finally said. "We'll have to open the sarcophagus."

"You said we wouldn't need to do that. You said we'd break into the mausoleum, and then you said, 'but not the sarcophagus.'"

"I just need a gap. A small gap."

"Fair night."

"Again, do you think a band of outlaws is going to be more squeamish?"

"More respectful," he corrected, but he brought up the rope she'd given him. She efficiently ran the rope through the lid's side holes using a dry stalk from the cemetery, and Galen closed his eyes—it would not be so wrong if he did not look, maybe?—and lifted the lid slightly, dragging the near end a finger's length to the right with a grind of stone.

He did not know what he'd expected, but it did not happen. There was no gust of infernal wind, no breath of rot, no sense of doom.

"That's all I need." Lisveth squinched her face and cast her magic. Galen kept his eyes on her instead of the sarcophagus. Her expression was tight, and even in the dim light she looked tired. Even for what he suspected was a smaller spell, so many repetitions were taking their toll. It was easy to forget, with her facility for illusions, how challenging other magic could be.

At last she shook her head. "Nothing. I can't get anything."

"Are you sure?"

She rubbed sweat from her face. "Nothing. Put it back; he's got nothing to rob."

Galen replaced the lid and pulled the rope free. He stared at the dark outline of the sarcophagus for a moment, wondering if he should bow or apologize. His temple lessons had never included a prayer for tomb-breaking.

"Let's get back," Lisveth said wearily. "This was a waste of effort."

"I can't believe we robbed a grave for nothing."

"We didn't," Lisveth protested with a glimmer of her usual verve. "We didn't take anything, so we're not grave-robbers."

"Grave-openers? Grave-disturbers?"

Lisveth shook her head. "Surely the Great Mage Ralston, famous for repelling the Selks, would understand that we need to keep his Golden Eye from those same invaders. But it seems it's not here."

Galen nudged the lid back and forth until it aligned more or less precisely, and then he looked at Lisveth, already standing in the moonlight outside. "Hey," he said, "are you all right?"

She nodded. "Just a lot of casting. I'll be fine."

"Let's get back, then."

Lisveth's path wavered as they descended the hill, betraying her fatigue. Galen slowed his pace to match hers.

He didn't think often on Lisveth's past. He had wondered about it more when they'd first met, never quite working up the courage to ask and gradually realizing that if she never offered details, it was probably for a reason. He couldn't think too poorly of that; he wouldn't have deliberately introduced himself with the story of running away to save his family from a fake trinket, either. Lisveth knew only because she'd helped to uncover the deception. Even now, it would be difficult to explain to a new acquaintance why he was living on the road instead of on his farm.

But at times, more widely spaced now, he still wondered. Yes, Lisveth had been a bandit, if one not quite so heartless as her reputation or her later impostor. But even a Fire Brigand might shrink from plundering a grave. Yet for all her unflappable demeanor during the trespass, Lisveth had showed no thrill in it, and she had not looked for the riches the puppet show bottler had mentioned as well. That was remarkable in the woman who always took the lead in negotiations because she had a harder eye for cash.

But he did not ask. Lisveth was generally free with her thoughts; if she did not share something, she did not wish to share it. She did not owe him the story of how she'd become a bandit years before he'd known her.

She was practical, he decided charitably. If someone needed a job done, she would get the most coin for it. If a prince wandered incognito in the foothills, she could pick him out as someone disused to making his own way and open friendly conversation with him. If grave robbing was necessary to keep legendary amulets safe from the raiding Rideis, she would do it. She was ruthlessly practical.

By the time they reached the large house with their shared room, her eyes were drooping. Galen hooked a hand beneath her arm. "No dawdling or midnight kitchen runs, young lady. You go straight on to bed."

"But Uncle," she protested tiredly, "who will test the sweet buns to be sure the nobility will not be poisoned?"

"The only poison will be your lies about where all the sweet buns have gone."

"Then I shall...shall... Fair night, I'm too sleepy to retort." She eyed the stairs accusingly. "Are there more of these than there were this morning?"

Once in their room, she dropped to the bed with a sigh. "Why are my feet so far away?" she moaned.

"Hold still." Galen unlaced her boot and pulled it off, then the other.

When he looked up at her, her eyes were closed, her face soft. He watched her a moment, waiting for her to open her eyes and toss a friendly insult at him, but she only drew a breath through slack lips.

He straightened and pushed her shoulder, tipping her onto the bed. She half-caught herself on an arm but slid to the mattress anyway. "I haven't washed up," she protested blearily.

"Wash twice in the morning."

She sighed. "Sorry. That was too many casts. I just wanted to be sure I didn't miss it."

"Roll over so we can get the blanket out from beneath you."

"Hrfm." But she moved and then wriggled under the thin blanket.

Galen dropped his cloak over her. He wasn't sleepy yet. He could build up a fire and think about whether it was more wrong to break open a mausoleum to preserve an artifact or to let invaders do it to seize one, and what it meant if there was no artifact to be found in the grave.

CHAPTER 66

THE NEXT MORNING, THE kitchen was crowded with servants preparing food, servants wanting food for their noble masters, soldiers and guards and scholars and other coterie hangers-on seeking their own breakfast, and an assortment of dogs and cats taking advantage of the chaos to scavenge. Lisveth and Galen hesitated near the door for a moment, frowning at the rest of the room.

"Seems awfully loud," Lisveth finally observed.

"Want to go to town?"

"Let's."

The noodle booth was not yet open, but the vendor couple was dragging out boxes of ingredients as a great pot simmered. "Go for a walk, come back, we'll be ready," the woman advised them. "It won't be long."

Galen continued to chew on the night's thoughts as he walked. He had robbed a grave—or tried to, which was the same thing. He'd gone to the cemetery a little hesitant, secure in the knowledge that his squeamish reluctance would keep him from erring, and then...

He'd gone along with each of Lisveth's suggestions, and there had never been a clear line—was it breaking the lock on the crypt? Entering it? Removing the sarcophagus lid?—until they had somehow crossed it.

As they came back along the street, the noodle vendor called and held up a bowl. They bought two bowls of noodles and then settled on a nearby bench. It was not the high time for street food, and they had the area to themselves. Lisveth set to work on her bowl, leaving Galen to study his.

At last she noticed his quiet, or at last she determined to ignore it no longer. "What's eating you, then?"

He didn't know how to explain without accusing her—justly, but also of something she apparently found acceptable. "We—we robbed a tomb."

"We didn't take anything," she answered practically.

"We would have, if we could have," he rebutted, "and anyway trying is much the same thing. You'd be angry if someone tried to steal your coin purse and failed, just as if they succeeded."

"No credit for incompetence," Lisveth agreed, pushing another bite into her mouth. "So you didn't like my reasoning for doing it?"

"It wasn't... Your reasoning made sense," Galen said, reluctant but honest. "But also...when did we become grave-robbers? How did I miss that it was happening?"

Lisveth's chewing slowed, and then stopped. She swallowed, and for a moment she only held the bowl.

Galen did not like the sudden stillness.

"I should have done it myself, without you."

Galen did not like this reply, either. "That's not what I mean."

"Then did you want to do it with me? Make up your mind."

Now Galen felt irritation at the idea of being excluded from the grave-robbing, and further irritation at the irrationality of that feeling. "I'm only asking how—"

"How you took one step, and then another, and each step was so short and so easy, and then suddenly you were deep in a chasm and you never remembered stepping off an edge." She spoke quietly, addressing her bowl of noodles.

Galen kept quiet, unnerved by her accuracy.

At last she spoke again, keeping her eyes on the steaming broth. "You knew what I was when you met me."

The statement felt far more stark than its words alone made it. Galen shook his head. "You were the woman who used illusions to rob people instead of real fire. You were the woman who pulled me off the ground when I couldn't see straight and paid my debt to keep me from arrest. You—"

"I was a thief, Galen. It doesn't matter how I did it. You knew I was a highway robber, and you came with me anyway."

"I came because you ruined any chance I had of going back to the caravan guards, who thought I was in league with you."

"That's not making your protest much stronger." Her fingers flexed on the bowl. "You never asked why I was a robber; you just kept pointing out we could take other jobs with our skills, ones that sometimes felt much the same but were less illegal and mostly helpful to someone. That was good of you. And when we ran low on jobs and funds, you volunteered to go into the occasional arena fight for coin, so we wouldn't have to argue over stopping a caravan or traveling party. I never thanked you enough for that."

Galen did not know how they had come here from his question about grave-robbing, but the footing was too unsure to interrupt and ask.

"You'd go in to get hit repeatedly by some sweaty, posturing ox of a man, just so I wouldn't scare a few rich merchants with magic. And it was silly and unfair, because you took more hits than a rich merchant did, but you meant to keep me on the right side of the law and to make me something other than a thief. I knew that, even if I couldn't say it then."

Galen shook his head. "I was in one of those parties you stopped—before we met. I was traveling with a family, or families, and they weren't rich. You took their coin, too."

"As I said, you knew what I was. You still know, even if you don't like to think about it." She set the bowl on her knees, fingers still clenched around it. "Stealing bothers you; you're above thieving. But it's not a reach down for me. It's not even at my eye level." She drew a breath. "And all my reasoning about the amulet and the grave, retrieving it before the raiders could? I meant all of it; it wasn't an excuse. If the Octovirate thought there was a magical weapon in there, they would have gone after it—or ordered someone to do the work for them, which is the same. Would you have been as squeamish if it had been done on the orders of someone with a title? If it saved a village from invaders?"

Galen shifted on the bench. "We don't know yet that it would save a village..."

"But if it did, you wouldn't complain. You wouldn't look at the raiders screaming down the hill and insist we put the amulet back."

Now Galen felt defensive, and that galled him anew. "This isn't about me refusing to save villagers."

She blew out a long breath and sat back on the bench, still facing forward. "Let me put this in terms a farm boy can understand. Let's say you dropped something important, maybe a bag of gold coins, maybe your mother's ring, I don't know, but something that matters, and you knew it had fallen in the manure heap. So some farm boy goes mucking through it to find the bag. It's a messy job, and he's covered in manure before he's done. And then someone else says there's another bag of coins in this other pile of manure. We could call in another farm boy to dig through it. But the first farm boy is already covered in muck, so it makes sense to have him do the second pile, too, doesn't it? No sense in having two boys to wash; that will just foul the stream twice as badly, when it's done. And then that third pile? Well, he's already done two, and this pile has the key to the local temple's coffer that's got the rare medicine, and so why should anyone ask a temple brother or a sick child's mother to dig into the pile, when there's someone available already dirty?"

Galen stared at her. After a moment he said, "I think your example got a bit twisted somewhere along the way. But I understand what you meant."

"I didn't have time to polish it through. I could do better."

"You don't need to do better. It's not a fair example, and even in your scenario, at some point the farm boy gets to clean up and have some supper. There's not always another pile of manure."

"Isn't there?" She looked at him for the first time. "What are these odd jobs that we take, if not other people's piles of manure? They hire us to get the stolen letter back, or to find the hired hand who took a family heirloom, or to do some other task they find difficult or distasteful. We do it for money. Sometimes it's a matter of strength or skill, and that's less mucky. Sometimes it's because they don't want to face it themselves, and that's their manure."

"Can we stop talking in terms of manure?" Galen said irritably. "We've helped a lot of people. If you'd seen Andrea going back to her parents—they were happy, really happy, to be reunited. We did that. And I saw it, even if you didn't."

Her jaw tightened.

"And that job didn't make me dirty. We did a good—"

"We killed a woman," Lisveth snapped. "You killed a woman. Yes, she was trying to kill you, as she'd killed others, but you killed her, all the same."

Galen couldn't answer.

"You don't have to like it, and we don't have to ever talk of it again, but we get hired because they don't want to dig through the piles. That's why they pay us. And yes, you're probably only knee-deep, and that's good, and that's why you balk at grave-robbing, and that's also good. It's *good*. But if there's someone who's already neck-deep, or submerged, then a little hip-wading grave-robbing might even look like an improvement."

Galen blew out his breath. "I don't think killing a murderer who's presently trying to murder you is neck—"

"That's you."

"Fine, then. Then you mean it's highway robbery that's so far—"

"Shut up." The words came fast and low, and they struck him harder than they should have.

Neither of them moved.

Steam no longer rose from the bowls, and Galen set his on the ground. He leaned forward, elbows on his knees, and folded his hands. "I don't like thinking of what we do as digging through manure. But even if it is, the world needs farm boys and stable hands, and I was never ashamed of being a farm boy. I don't like grave-robbing, but you're right, I might have called it something else if the Octovirate had ordered it to protect a village. I don't like it, but I can understand your reasoning, even without picturing you neck-deep in manure." He took a breath, judged his level tone. "Which would require less manure for you than for me, as I'm so much taller."

She snorted, a barely audible puff, and the sound relieved him. If she could snort at him, they would be all right.

"But I want to say one thing, before I take back these bowls. I didn't know you before you paid my bounty in Abbay. I know only who you have been, for some years now. And I think maybe you believe manure lasts longer than it does." He paused and shrugged. "But as a farm boy myself, I know it turns to compost, and compost is a good and useful thing."

She snorted again, louder. "Fair night, farm boy, please stop talking."

"Rich fertilizer for crops, and the smell fades almost entirely, and it gets so dry and crumbly—"

"Stop!" She shook her head, biting her lip against a smile. "You're terrible, and you're not helping."

But he was, he thought, or at least he had scattered the dark shape that had gathered around them as she spoke. He had not vanquished the beast, but he had run it off for another time.

Neither of them were going to finish the noodles now, and he didn't want to insult anyone by returning half-full bowls, so he dumped the remainders for a street dog looking wary and hopeful nearby. Then he tipped the empty bowls into the vendor's bin, and by the time he came back to the bench, Lisveth was sitting up straight and looking at him as if nothing had happened. "Ready to go?" she asked.

CHAPTER 67

THEY STROLLED INTO THE market plaza, already lively, and angled into a shopping street. The tension had passed, but they were not yet back to wholly neutral ground, and without speaking they agreed that they would take their time in working their way back.

They browsed the displays and dodged the late-coming carts, until Galen stopped. "Lisveth." She glanced back at him, and he nodded toward the hanging sign. "The pawn shop?"

"Well." She pursed her lips. "Might as well take a closer look at the fake. What could it hurt? And maybe I'll find some serviceable gloves."

"I'm not sure what you need gloves for, since you make me do all the heavy lifting," Galen grumbled, but it was only to distract them both from the wholly irrational hope that the false amulet might hold some clue to the location of the real one.

Lisveth led the way into the shop. "Good morning!"

The pawnbroker broke into a smile. "Morning! Hello, again! I'm glad you made it back."

"Sorry about yesterday," Galen said. "Did it come out all right?"

"We worked something out," the man assured him. "I'm practiced at working something out. You looking for anything in particular?"

"Just browsing, if that's all right?"

"Well, I hope something will catch your eye." The proprietor grinned. "Go on, look around."

Galen turned his eyes to the false Golden Eye. The fuzzy glass dome over the object on the shelf looked as if it had been collecting dust almost since the Great Mage Ralston's death. Galen approached and gently brushed at it to better see the jewelry within.

"Oh, that's the Painter's Eye," the pawnbroker called. He made his way through the jumble of cabinets and cases toward the rear corner, Lisveth following. "That belonged to Mage Ralston. You know him, of course?"

"I heard the puppet show," Galen said. "Apparently he was from here?"

"Oh, yes. Born here, came back after the wars, died here. Our own hero. We're honored to have his amulet available to display to all, here in the shop."

"Honored," Galen agreed softly, eying the dusty corner shelf.

This pretended amulet was a gaudy piece, holding a perfectly round honey-colored cabochon with a narrow cat's eye effect. Around the cabochon radiated thin spears of bronze or some similarly colored metal, creating a starburst the size of Galen's open hand. It was huge, unwieldy, impossible to wear beneath a shirt or armor.

"My great, great, great and so on grandfather was undertaker then, and family lore says that's how the amulet came down in our family." The pawnbroker grinned and winked.

"So your grandfather robbed the dead?" Galen asked before he could help himself.

"Of course not! He preserved a great treasure for the future. Mage Ralston would have wanted his own descendants protected as well."

Galen nodded in amiable agreement, since it didn't matter anyway. This showy piece had never been used for magical warfare.

"It's only family legend, anyway," the man admitted in a stage whisper. "Good for bringing in travelers, such as yourself. Feel free to browse for anything of interest."

"Could I see these earrings?" Lisveth asked, a case away.

"Of course!" He hurried over to help her.

Galen stared at the false amulet with an odd sense of loss. That something so powerful might be forgotten and replaced with something so gaudy... It felt wrong, somehow.

Lisveth was holding a small pearl earring to the side of her head, measuring how low it dangled against her neck. It did not look like her preference of style, but perhaps she was just trying to be kind to the pawnbroker who had a false amulet. She set it down with a shake of her head. "No, I don't think so. What about those? In the corner, there, the blue."

Galen drifted over to join her, curious about her shopping. She was looking down into a bin of barely sorted jewelry, chains of ordinary metal and semi-precious stones in clumsy settings. It was clearly a pile of low-value pieces that did not merit the more spacious display at the front of the shop.

The pawnbroker drew out an earring of blued glass in a long, thin teardrop and dropped it into Lisveth's outstretched hand. She looked down at it.

She had liked blown glass, Galen remembered. Before...
Before. Was that why this had caught her eye?

The pawnbroker dragged his fingers through the remainder of the pile, back and forth, and at last he shook his head. "Sorry, I don't seem to have the mate to it. Maybe that's why it's here in this discount case."

"Oh, I suppose that's all right," Lisveth said with a tone of regret. "It was pretty. What about that piece, there? You've just uncovered the end. With the twisted wire."

Galen followed her pointed finger and caught the gleam of an iridescent eye.

Fair night.

The amulet was still half-buried in cheap jewelry, and the pawnbroker wriggled it free. "This? My, I'd forgotten all about this."

"It certainly has a look, doesn't it?" Lisveth cocked her head. "It wouldn't pass for much at an Octovirate ball, and yet I almost like it despite the grotesque fashion." She held her hand out. "Do you know anything about it?"

"It was here when I inherited the shop, so I don't know much," he confessed. "Someone must have gone to a lot of trouble to twist all that wire, but I can't remember that style ever being in demand." He rubbed his finger on the amulet in Lisveth's hand. "I'm not sure what kind of wire this is. Might be worth something if melted, might not."

"Then if it's never sold in so long, would you give a good price on it?" Lisveth slipped her hand under Galen's elbow and wrapped his forearm, turning her face up with a bright smile. "Buy it for me?"

Galen's heart quickened, but he kept his expression calm. "What would you do with it? The last brooch I bought you, you wore only two days."

"That's because I lost it. You can't hold that against me. This one has a—oh, look, it has a place for a chain. I could wear it as a necklace instead of a brooch." She leaned her head against Galen's shoulder. "Please?"

Galen looked at the pawnbroker, who grinned and shook his head. "I find my best business is to wait quietly at these times."

"What do you want for it?" Galen asked with what he hoped was a hint of resignation.

"Five taler."

"What? No. Not if we want to have those noodles." Galen began to work Lisveth's hand from his arm.

"Please!" Lisveth turned to the pawnbroker. "Please, it's been here so long. Wouldn't you like to see it sell for a lower price than not at all?"

The man considered, waggling his head.

"We'd need a chain for it," Galen said. "And that blue earring."

"Without a mate?"

"If you look at her from the side, you see only one ear at a time." Galen grinned.

The pawnbroker laughed. "All right, I can do the lot for three and a half—brooch, chain, and one glass earring. How's that?"

"Thank you!" Lisveth squealed. She cradled the amulet in her hand and reached again for the blue teardrop.

"What color chain do you want? I think I can get a close match to the wire."

It was a steep price for pawn shop discards, but they knew the true worth, and that made it easy to play an overeager traveler. Galen paid, and Lisveth beamed at the amulet in her hand, and then she slipped her arm through his again and they left the shop to walk back toward the market plaza.

Once they had rounded the corner, they stopped and stared at one another. "Fair night," Lisveth breathed.

"The pawn shop," Galen said. "But not the one on display."

Lisveth went to a nearby bench and sat with the amulet in her lap. "The Painter's Eye. In a pawn shop." She looked up at Galen with an approving grin. "The last brooch lasted only two days? You're getting pretty good at this."

"I've had a good model to follow."

"I think your stories must be better than you let on. Maybe now you'll tell me one of them."

His neck grew warm. "You were supposed to have forgotten about that." He sat beside her. "How did you find it?"

"I sent a few casts around the shop while you two were looking over the monstrosity on display. I felt something come back from that corner of the case. I figured if I browsed, we'd uncover it eventually." She rubbed perspiration from her face. "It worked out nicely that it was buried. No reason to raise the price on a piece we couldn't even have seen."

"I wonder what it does."

"So do I. I certainly wasn't going to put it on in the shop."

"Oh, that's a good point. Should we go out of town and try it somewhere? Though, I don't have another rabbit."

She shook her head. "I'm trying to remember... I feel as if I've heard the amulets' abilities once, in a lesson somewhere. What did those carvings on the mausoleum show?"

"The puppet threw lightning."

"Yes, but that's excitement for a puppet show, and I'm pretty sure I would have remembered lightning in history. The carvings showed Mage Ralston above the Rideis?"

"It makes you fly?" Galen supposed dubiously.

"No," agreed Lisveth. "But none of the Rideis marching in rows, as you pointed out, looked up—or back. He could have been behind them, if the perspective was a little wonky... Let's just try it."

"Are you—"

But she was already dropping the chain over her head, and the amulet thumped against her chest. Galen looked at it a moment, almost wondering whether it would blink, but nothing happened.

He waited. Nothing happened. He turned back to the market, growing busier every moment. Lisveth knew more about magic; she would work it out. He would only be in the way if he bothered with the amulet while she tried to assess it. He could do more by watching for any trouble.

Or maybe he would go and see if the shirred egg cart was open. He could bring back one. Or he might eat at the cart, so he wouldn't have to walk back too far to return the ramekin when finished.

He had taken three steps from the bench when a hand closed on his arm. He jumped, startled, and turned back as Lisveth tugged the amulet's chain over her head. "Galen!"

"What?" He frowned. "I was just getting breakfast. Er, another breakfast." He frowned. "I was—I'm sorry. I don't know why I thought of leaving you, and with a strange amulet on you."

"It was the amulet." Her eyes gleamed. "It blurs perception, and maybe also thoughts about the wearer."

"Like an illusion? Or invisibility?"

She shook her head. "I don't think so, or you would have noticed immediately when I put it on. You'd see a difference if someone vanished. I think you just...forgot about me."

He thought back. "I started thinking about the amulet, and how I shouldn't bother you while you were testing it, and then I thought about food carts, and then I just... I'm so sorry."

"It wasn't you. It was the amulet." She folded her hands about it, grinning ridiculously. "How has it just been in a pawn shop all this time?"

"I think we can work that out," Galen said thoughtfully. "I think Great-Great-many-more-Greats-Grandfather was indeed an undertaker, and a shady one, and I think he stole the amulet and maybe other things from the burial. But he couldn't sell outright the amulet that was said to have been buried with a local hero, not without raising uncomfortable questions, and maybe he couldn't sell it away from here, either—it's not as if it has a dramatic effect, if you just sort of forget about the person trying to sell it to you. If the undertaker even knew how to use it."

"So it went into a box," Lisveth continued, "maybe with other stolen trinkets. Rather like a bunch of farmers keeping another amulet in a box in the hallway. And family lore says it came from the mage's burial, but after a few generations, that's just lore. They don't open the box much, and they don't think much of the amulet when they see it, and it's easy to confuse with the other pieces."

"So finally our pawnbroker's father or grandfather puts one up in the shop, capitalizing on the family lore and choosing something appropriately outstanding to display, even if it looks a bit garish. Maybe that's another old inherited piece stored in the same old box and looking more plausibly impressive to those who don't know. Meanwhile, the real thing is dumped into a case of cheap pieces, where it's even easier to overlook."

"And now it's ours. We have another of the amulets, and it works." Lisveth slipped it into a pouch, and then she drew out the blue earring. "Was this just to distract from the other purchase?"

Galen felt a bit foolish, now that he had to explain. "I thought—I don't know much about glass, actually. I didn't know if it might be something you'd like."

Lisveth sobered, and for a moment he thought he'd offended her. He really didn't know much about glass. Perhaps he'd guessed entirely wrongly.

But at last she said, "You remembered that?"

"What? Of course. It wasn't that long ago that you said it. And you remembered my stories, even if I'd hoped you'd forget."

Lisveth stared down at the blue teardrop on her palm. "This isn't blown glass. It's lampwork."

"Oh." He felt a little foolish.

She shook her head. "But I do like it." She looked up at him. "Which ear?"

"Which ear do you want it in?" He shrugged. "Either. Does it matter? The left, I guess."

She fixed the earring into her left ear. "Thank you."

Her solemnity was making Galen uncomfortable. "Sorry I couldn't get you a set."

She smiled. "It's more earring than you've ever gotten me before." She stood from the bench. "Let's get some fried dough to celebrate."

CHAPTER 68

LORD BRYUKI'S SUMMONS WAS unanticipated but not wholly a surprise. After all, even a march lord might remember sooner or later that he was lodging a couple of itinerants who had outstayed their usefulness, now that the Octovirate's representatives had been notified of the Rideis incursion.

Galen and Lisveth did not expect to see General Artextra waiting with him, however. "Good afternoon," Lisveth offered. "What can we do for you?"

General Artextra spoke first. "The Selk prince, and the woman who came for him—can you describe them?"

Galen and Lisveth looked at one another. "He was about Galen's height," Lisveth began. "Red hair, good-looking—well, yes, he was, whether or not he's a foreign invader. Well-spoken. About her... It was night, and she grabbed him from behind and dragged him away. She had dark hair, but that's about all I caught."

"She stood about shoulder height to him," Galen added. "Approximately, I mean. Maybe a little taller than that. She was pulling him back, so there wasn't a clear still moment, but that's the impression I have."

General Artextra gave them each a long-suffering look. "Was she pretty? As pretty as he was handsome?"

"With respect, we were engaged in combat, and I didn't know at the time I should have been evaluating her looks," Lisveth answered levelly. "Kayvin we saw repeatedly, in friendly conversation. We have a better sense of him."

"Well, you can put that sense to use." The general turned in her chair. "We have a report of a red-haired man and a woman who just arrived in Pradford."

"That could mean anything," Lord Bryuki admitted. "But red-headed men aren't so common, and one traveling with a woman can be distinctive. So with you here"—he nodded to Galen—"it's worth seeing who he is."

Artextra continued, "The landlord said they seem amiable enough but also not quite right, as if they'd not been out much on their own before."

"Or aren't used to Sayinian society," Galen supplied. "Or possibly not out on their own, if he's indeed a prince."

"Anyway, before we stomp in with a dozen soldiers, go and see if that's the pair. If it's not, no harm done, it's just a couple of folks who speak differently and they'll go their way without us alarming the local populace. If it's our bandit prince, then we'll want to find what he's working on, so don't be seen."

"And you want us to follow him?"

"I don't want him to know we know him. Just pop your head into the public room, give them a quick look, and report back. Think you can do that?"

Galen nodded. "Where do we look?"

"The tavern at the south end of the Pradford stock market. The Selk's Head, ironically enough."

"We'll find it," Lisveth said. "And them, if they're there." Her mouth curved into a small smile. "And for this knowledge and quiet skill, what do you think is a fair price?"

Did you enjoy this book?

If you've enjoyed this story, whether you purchased or borrowed this copy, please leave a review at your favorite retailers or review site. This is really helpful to support a book, and I read every one. Then, please tell a friend who might also like this story!

Next, go to **https://go.lauravab.com/news** to receive free stories immediately as well as sneak peeks, special discounts, advance offers, and more. Enjoy your new books!

The Story Continues

The tale concludes in *The Prince's Song*, book 2 of *The Eyes of Mandoral*.

www.ingramcontent.com/pod-product-compliance
Lightning Source LLC
Chambersburg PA
CBHW020514110726
47899CB00004B/1110